Albert Stratford George Canning

Thoughts on Shakespeare's Historical Plays

Albert Stratford George Canning

Thoughts on Shakespeare's Historical Plays

ISBN/EAN: 9783741186431

Manufactured in Europe, USA, Canada, Australia, Japa

Cover: Foto ©Andreas Hilbeck / pixelio.de

Manufactured and distributed by brebook publishing software
(www.brebook.com)

Albert Stratford George Canning

Thoughts on Shakespeare's Historical Plays

THOUGHTS ON

SHAKESPEARE'S

HISTORICAL PLAYS

BY THE

HON. ALBERT S. G. CANNING

AUTHOR OF "MACAULAY, ESSAYIST AND HISTORIAN," "PHILOSOPHY OF
DICKENS," ETC. ETC.

LONDON:

W. H. ALLEN & CO. 13, WATERLOO PLACE,
PALL MALL, S.W.

1884

CONTENTS.

—o—

CHAPTER I.

JULIUS CÆSAR   PAGE 1

CHAPTER II.

ANTONY AND CLEOPATRA   11

CHAPTER III.

MACBETH   31

CHAPTER IV.

KING JOHN   52

CHAPTER V.

KING RICHARD II.   71

CHAPTER VI.

KING HENRY IV. (First Part)   100

CHAPTER VII.

KING HENRY IV. (Second Part)   129

CHAPTER VIII.

KING HENRY V.   156

CHAPTER IX.

KING HENRY VI. (First Part)   167

CHAPTER X.

KING HENRY VI. (Second Part) . . 179

CHAPTER XI.

KING HENRY VI. (Third Part) . . 196

CHAPTER XII.

KING RICHARD III. 217

CHAPTER XIII.

KING HENRY VIII. . 268

WORKS REFERRED TO.

—o—

Bacon, Lord, Essays and Life of Henry VII.
Boz, Sketches by.
Brewer's English Studies.
Buckle's History of Civilization.
Courtenay's Commentaries on Shakespeare's Historical Plays.
Dowden, Professor, Shakespeare's Mind and Art.
Draper's Intellectual Development of Europe.
Froude, J. A., Reign of Henry VIII.
Furnivall's Introduction to the Royal Shakspere.
Gibbon's Decline and Fall of the Roman Empire.
Green's History of the English People.
Guizot, M., Shakespeare and his Times.
Hallam's Literary History of Europe.
     ,,   Middle Ages.
     ,,   Constitutional History of England.
Hume's History of England.
Jameson, Mrs., Characteristics of Women.
Johnson, Dr. S., Preface and Notes to Shakespeare.
Knight, C., Notes to Shakspere.
Lecky, W. H., History of Rationalism.
Lingard's History of England.
Macaulay, Lord, History of England.
Machiavelli—Essay on "The Prince."
Merivale's Romans under the Empire.
More, Sir Thomas, Life of Richard III.
Napoleon III.'s Life of Julius Cæsar.
Plutarch's Lives.
Staunton, Howard, Notes to the Illustrated Shakespeare.
Scott, Sir Walter, History of Scotland.
    ,,   ,,   Waverley Novels.
Stephens, Sir James, History of the English Criminal Law.
Student's History of Rome.
Suetonius—Lives of the Cæsars.
Stubbs, Professor, Constitutional History of England.
Schlegel's Essays on Shakespeare.
Wordsworth, Bishop, Notes to Shakespeare's Historical Plays.

ERRATUM.

In "Sketch" before "Macbeth" Donalbain should have been described as escaping to Ireland instead of to England, and there is no mention in the play of his return to Scotland.

THOUGHTS

ON

SHAKESPEARE'S HISTORICAL PLAYS.

CHAPTER I.

JULIUS CÆSAR.

Sketch of Play.

THIS play does not describe any of Cæsar's extensive and wonderful foreign conquests. It begins in Rome, whither he returns after his victorious campaigns to be congratulated, applauded, and praised by his fellow-countrymen, many of whom wish to make him sole Ruler. He is offered the imperial crown, amid general acclamation ; but two distinguished Romans, Brutus and Cassius — both sincere republicans—form a conspiracy, and eventually murder him. They are mistaken, however, in expecting general approval ; for the army, together with many Roman citizens, under Octavius Cæsar and Mark Antony, the young nephew and middle-aged lieutenant of Julius Cæsar, declare war against the republicans, headed by Brutus and Cassius, and defeat them at Philippi. The Roman empire then fell nominally under the rule of Triumvirs, Octavius Cæsar (afterwards Augustus the sovereign, and patron of Horace and Virgil), Lepidus, a man of little ability or influence, and the warlike Antony. The latter, an able general, very popular with the army, was probably the most powerful of the three for some time after their joint victory. Brutus and Cassius commit suicide immediately after their defeat. The celebrated orator Cicero, who, though on the side of Brutus, took little part in the war, was executed soon after it by Antony or his followers ; but, though he is introduced, his fate is not recorded by Shakespeare, who ends this play immediately upon the triumph of Octavius and Antony.

B

1

IN his Roman plays Shakespeare chiefly relied on the authority of Plutarch.* This writer, like most who have described Julius Cæsar, represents him as one of the greatest men the world has ever seen.† Both in foreign conquests and in his government of Rome, as well as by his writings, the wonderful power of his mind, the vigour of his intellect, and the variety of his acquirements were proved unmistakably. Even in the present century, his long recorded merits have been praised by able men of totally different characters, positions, and motives from each other. Macaulay compares him favourably to both Cromwell and the first Napoleon, declaring that to their high qualities Cæsar united a learning and refinement which they never possessed,‡ while the Emperor Napoleon the Third calls him the greatest of all kings,§ praising him more in the style of an ardent admirer than impartial biographer.‖ A yet more recent writer declares that Cæsar's occasional cruelty was not owing to his disposition, but to the circumstances and to the age in which he lived.¶ Seldom, indeed, has any one man possessed so many great qualities as Cæsar, combined with an amount of knowledge perfectly amazing, considering his opportunities of acquisition. His Commentaries alone display the taste of the naturalist, botanist, and traveller, as well as the genius of an almost unrivalled general.** Thus, in his career, the spirit of civilization, as far as could be known by a Pagan, seemed to accompany his victories.††

---

* DOWDEN's *Shakespeare: His Mind and Art.*

† "He was as skilful in governing men's passions as in conducting affairs. And as he was well versed in war of all kinds, and as he joined civil and military arts together, nothing could come so suddenly upon him, but he had an expedient ready for it ; nothing so adverse, but he drew some advantage from it."—BACON's *Essay on Julius Cæsar.*

‡ Essay on Hallam.

§ *Life of Cæsar,* vol. i.

‖ In the preface, "written entirely by himself"—B. JERROLD's *Life of Napoleon the Third,* vol. iv.—the Emperor, whose object was to glorify his uncle's memory as well as Cæsar's, writing in exaggerated language, says—"When Providence raises up such men as Cæsar, Charlemagne, and Napoleon, it is to trace out to peoples the paths they ought to follow ; to stamp with the seal of their genius a new era ; and to accomplish in a few years the work of many centuries. Happy the peoples who comprehend and follow them ! Woe to those who misunderstand and combat them ! They do as the Jews did, they crucify their Messiah," &c.

¶ "Suicide was with them—the Romans—the common mode of avoiding otherwise inevitable misfortune, and it was natural that men who made light of their own lives should also make light of the lives of others."—TROLLOPE's *Julius Cæsar: Ancient Classics.* This fact should always be remembered by readers of Shakespeare's Roman plays, as well as by students of classical history.

** This wonderful man was distinguished as "a soldier, statesman, lawgiver, orator, poet, historian, grammarian, mathematician, and architect."—MERIVALE's *Romans under the Empire,* vol. ii.

†† "When he handled the pen he was guided by the self-same principles as when he wielded the sword, directing his attention uninterruptedly to one sole

Yet Shakespeare makes very slight allusion to his many conquests and foreign triumphs.* His sketch of him is only during the last days of his eventful life, when, at Rome, his admiring countrymen wished to make him sole and absolute Ruler. Still, many of the best educated and respected Romans, amid whom Cicero was conspicuous, opposed his power, wishing to retain and strengthen the Republican Government.

To a man of Julius Cæsar's patriotic mind and civilized ideas, it was, doubtless, a grievous disappointment to perceive so many superior men among his foes, and to rely chiefly upon a reckless profligate soldier like Antony as his principal adherent. No men in the Empire desired its welfare more thoroughly than he, his nephew Octavius, the orator Cicero, and the young enthusiast Brutus. But unfortunately, these leaders — so gifted, talented, and noble-minded in their different ways—were completely opposed to each other by their different plans and schemes for their common country's prosperity. The result was that they alike sought assistance, support, and counsel from associates utterly below them in moral worth and sincere patriotism.†

The real hero of this play, according to English, French, and German commentators,‡ is the young Republican Brutus. Yet even Shakespeare cannot make him justify Cæsar's assassination. For Brutus is deceived by his older associate Cassius, and fancies that Cæsar's becoming Emperor is disapproved by most of his fellow-countrymen. Cassius, accordingly, has the art, or rather the baseness, to send anonymous letters to Brutus, inciting him to revolution; though Plutarch, whom Shakespeare chiefly follows, does not attribute these letters solely to Cassius,§ and this deceit is not mentioned by some other Roman historians; but it

object, and to it making all else subservient. As a writer, then, the Roman, when judged by the productions of others under similar circumstances, is still Cæsar the Invincible."—F. SCHLEGEL's *History of Literature.*

* "The Cæsar of the play is not the great conqueror of Britain, but Cæsar old, decaying, failing both in health and mind."—FURNIVALL's *Introduction to the Royal Shakespeare.*

† "The misfortunes of the times obliged the most notable men to have dealings with those whose antecedents seemed to devote them to contempt. . . . . In times of transition, when a choice must be made between a glorious past and an unknown future, the rock is that bold unscrupulous men alone thrust themselves forward. Cæsar had recourse to agents who were but little estimated; but his constant endeavour was to associate to himself the most trustworthy men, and he spared no effort to gain by turns Pompey, Cicero, &c., &c."—NAPOLEON THE THIRD's *Life of Julius Cæsar*, vol. i. chap. ii. "The army and the people generally approved his sole authority."—MERIVALE's *Romans under the Empire*, vol. ii.

‡ C. Knight, Furnivall, Guizot, and Schlegel.

§ *Life of Brutus.*

accords with the cunning, crafty spirit attributed to Cassius in the play. Comparatively the imaginative, generous nature of Brutus appears to great advantage, and he refuses to assassinate Antony, which Cassius urges and even entreats him to attempt.

Having failed to incite Brutus to commit this crime, Cassius tries to bribe Antony by offering him power and influence in the new Republic, while Brutus, with calm dignity, solicits his alliance in manly terms :—

CASSIUS *to* ANTONY. Your voice shall be as strong as any man's
In the disposing of new dignities.—Act. III.

Yet Cassius in this and other instances shows far more knowledge of human nature, as well as Roman politics, than Brutus possesses. Antony's murder was precisely the act most requisite, after Cæsar's death, to confirm the strength of the new Republic. Cicero's brilliant genius would then have been gladly devoted to ardent praise of the new government, and he would have assailed Antony's memory as vehemently and far more safely than when reviling him while the latter was heading a devoted army. Such was the persuasive power of his charming eloquence that, perhaps, only a minority of personally attached soldiers would, in that case, have much regretted the death of Antony. Though Cicero's influence and talents were often, perhaps usually, devoted to upholding right and denouncing wrong, his eloquent enthusiasm was not incapable of making "the worse appear the better reason."* Brutus, however, living in a world of imagination, makes a generous, yet, politically, foolish reply to Cassius, in which he reveals both his ignorance of Antony's character and of his own fellow-countrymen—

BRUTUS. Our course will seem too bloody, Caius Cassius,
To cut the head off and then hack the limbs ;
And for Mark Antony, think not of him,
For he can do no more than Cæsar's arm
When Cæsar's head is off.—Act II. Scene I.

Shakespeare, indeed, makes Brutus anticipate Antony's suicide, or untimely death, with pleasure, which seems inconsistent with his kindly, generous nature. This is apparently the poet's own idea, for it is not attributed to Brutus by Plutarch or by other classic writers.

---

* Plutarch states that Cicero had no share in the conspiracy against Cæsar, though a friend of Brutus ; that he exhorted the Senate to grant an amnesty to all concerned in Cæsar's murder ; and to decree provinces to Brutus and Cassius ; but "none of these things took effect."—*Life of Cicero.* The hatred between him and Antony is mentioned by most historical writers.

> If he love Cæsar, all that he can do
> Is to himself take thought, and die for Cæsar ;
> And 'twere much he should, for he is given
> To sports, to wildness, and much company.
> —Act II. Scene I.

Previous to Cæsar's death, the Roman empire apparently possessed, both in distinguished men as in military power and resources, almost every requisite for worldly grandeur, strength, and prosperity. But when he disappeared from Rome, the talents, feelings, and passions of her greatest men were turned in deadly hatred against each other.*

Brutus, in earnest, dignified, even pathetic words, deplores Cæsar's fate and his share in it to a crowd of his fellow-citizens, few, indeed, of whom shared, or, perhaps, understood, his peculiar character and feelings. Probably had Cicero vindicated Cæsar's murder directly after its occurrence, he would have made a much stronger impression on the Roman mind. He knew his countrymen far better than Brutus did, and for years had watched the effect which his wonderful eloquence usually produced. He was, also, older, far more known, and in every respect better fitted, if not to justify, at least to palliate the deed. Shakespeare makes Brutus reject the advice of Cassius and others, inviting Cicero's co-operation ; but Plutarch does not mention this circumstance. The conspirators truly think that Cicero's judgment, age, and influence would assist their enterprise, and, apparently, make sure of his alliance ; but the young revolutionist makes an impetuous, almost insolent reply, considering Cicero's position and character at Rome.

> CASSIUS.   But what of Cicero?   Shall we sound him ?
> I think he will stand very strong with us.
> CASCA.   Let us not leave him out.
> CINNA.   No, by no means.
> METELLUS CIMBER.   O, let us have him ; for his silver hairs
> Will purchase us a good opinion,
> And buy men's voices to commend our deeds.
> It shall be said his judgment ruled our hands ;
> Our youths, our wildness shall no whit appear,
> But all be buried in his gravity.

---

* "The death of Julius Cæsar was soon followed by the final termination of the contest between the Republican and Monarchical principle. Shakespeare saw the grandeur of the crisis, and he seized upon it for one of his lofty expositions of political philosophy. He has treated it as no other poet could have treated it, because he saw the exact relations of the contending principles to the future great history of mankind."—CHARLES KNIGHT's *Edition of Shakspere.*

> BRUTUS.   O, name him not, let us not break with him,
> For he will never follow anything
> That other men begin.—Act II. Scene I.

Brutus himself, however, makes a speech, which, though eloquent, rather resembles a soliloquy ; expressing, doubtless, his own feelings accurately, but little fitted to influence the majority of his hearers.

> BRUTUS.   If there be any in this assembly—any dear friend of Cæsar's—to him I say, that Brutus' love to Cæsar was no less than his.   If, then, that friend demand why Brutus rose against Cæsar, this is my answer—not that I loved Cæsar less ; but that I loved Rome more.   Had you rather Cæsar were living and die all slaves, than that Cæsar were dead to live all freemen ?   As Cæsar loved me, I weep for him ; as he was fortunate, I rejoice at it ; as he was valiant, I honour him ; but, as he was ambitious, I slew him.   There is tears for his love, joy for his fortune, honour for his valour, and death for his ambition.*—Act III. Scene II.

Accordingly, Antony's splendid speech, combining real feeling with thorough knowledge of the Romans, destroys whatever impression Brutus' former speech may have made.

> ANTONY.   The noble Brutus
> Hath told you Cæsar was ambitious.
> If it was so, it was a grievous fault ;
> And grievously hath Cæsar answered it.
>
> .   .   .   .   .
>
> He hath brought many captives home to Rome,
> Whose ransoms did the general coffers fill.
> Did this, in Cæsar seem ambitious ?
> When that the poor have cried, Cæsar hath wept.
> Ambition should be made of sterner stuff.
> Yet Brutus says he was ambitious ;
> And Brutus is an honourable man.

He also showed Cæsar's will to the people, leaving money and granting public gardens to them.

> ANTONY.   Here is the will, and under Cæsar's seal.
> To every Roman citizen he gives,
> To every single man he gives, seventy-five drachmas.
> CITIZENS.   Most noble Cæsar !—we'll revenge his death.

But when Antony declares that Cæsar has left all his

---

* "The speech of Brutus is unable to raise any enthusiasm among his hearers for liberty or an ideal of justice. The people require a Cæsar. The political idealist—Brutus—adds another to his series of fatal miscalculations."—DOWDEN'S *Shakespeare: His Mind and Art.*

" walks, private arbours, and new planted orchards " for public enjoyment, the delighted, grateful Romans declare they will burn the traitors' houses ; and the successful orator exclaims in secret triumph—

> Now let it work !—Mischief, thou art afoot ;
> Take thou what course thou wilt.—Act III. Scene II.

At this news the people are as overjoyed as grateful children justly rewarded for good conduct. Cicero, remembering the former glories of Roman Republicanism, would likely have protested against any gratitude towards a general whose testamentary gifts to a free people could never atone for previous usurpation of rights which should have been inalienable. But Antony's skilful, affecting, yet thoroughly practical speech, succeeded as completely as he could have wished ; and Shakespeare's poetical version is apparently confirmed by both Plutarch and Suetonius. Yet Shakespeare passes, almost immediately after Cæsar's death, to the war between his slayers and avengers ; though history* says that Octavius, nephew and heir of Julius Cæsar, at first opposed Antony, and was allied with Cicero, who vehemently denounced the latter to the Roman people. This alliance between young Octavius and Cicero did not last long, and was, perhaps, never thoroughly sincere. The strong attachment of Antony to the Cæsar family apparently effected a complete reconciliation between the loyal general of the great Julius and his acknowledged heir, who, though only eighteen, at this time, already showed signs of that great sagacity, self-control, and resolution which finally made him one of the ablest of the Roman Emperors. The majority of the people, who had almost deified Julius, rallied round Antony and Octavius, who were soon allied ; and the Republicans, under Brutus and Cassius, were utterly routed by them at Philippi.

Previous to this decisive battle, Shakespeare describes the celebrated quarrel and reconciliation between Brutus and Cassius, one of the most favourite passages for modern declamation. Brutus reproaches Cassius for withholding money which should have been devoted to the Republican cause. This accusation Cassius vehemently repels, and at last, after a violent scene, Brutus believes him, and they are reconciled. A common danger now threatens both, and forces these men, though of such different characters, into a bond of close union. Cicero, their most illustrious ally, had been executed previously by Antony or his followers ; but

---

* Tacitus, Suetonius, and Student's History of Rome.

these Republican leaders never mention his death. The Roman army was naturally disposed to follow Antony, not merely from love to Cæsar's memory, but from personal attachment. He was, in every sense, a popular general resembling Scott's spirited description of a soldier's favourite leader.*

Cicero's execution, which so disgraced Antony's triumph, is not mentioned in this play, which ends with the suicide of Brutus and that of Cassius, after their defeat at Philippi. The apparition of Cæsar's ghost to Brutus, and the latter's complete fearlessness, so powerfully described by Shakespeare, are recorded by Plutarch, who, however, states that the ghost twice appeared to Brutus—the last time without speaking. But Antony's noble words at seeing the dead body of Brutus seem to be Shakespeare's invention, as the spirit they show is quite inconsistent with Antony's fierce, vindictive temper.

> ANTONY.   This was the noblest Roman of them all.
> All the conspirators, save only he,
> Did that they did in envy of great Cæsar.
> He only in a general honest thought,
> And common good to all made one of them.—Act V.

Throughout this play Brutus is made the most interesting character. Modern readers may surely regret that Cæsar was not made more prominent.† He might in Shakespeare's hands have made most interesting and instructive allusions to his foreign conquests and campaigns, especially in Britain ; but in the play he is exclusively occupied with the conflicting passions and feelings of his fellow-Romans. Brutus himself seems to be alone, in his peculiar ideas, unselfishness, and bravery, mingled with rare gentleness of spirit. He is unlike both friends and foes, and, considering the period, was probably not well understood by either. His last noble words before suicide show that he believed himself

---

*   " Yet, trained in camps, he knew the art
>   To win the soldier's hardy heart ;
>   They love a captain to obey—
>   Boisterous as March, yet fresh as May ; —
>   With open hand, and brow as free ;
>   Lover of wine and minstrelsy ;
>   Ever the first to scale a tower ;
>   As venturous in a lady's bower.
>   Such buxom chief shall lead his host,
>   . From India's fires to Zembla's frost."
>   —*Marmion*, Canto III.

Plutarch terms Antony "the darling of the Roman army."

† "The spirit of Plutarch's Brutus is well seized, the predominance of Cæsar is judiciously restrained."· · HALLAM's *Literary History*, vol. iii. chap. 6.

a martyr, but his conduct throughout was more like an enthusiast than a patriot :—

> I shall have glory by this losing day,
> More than Octavius and Mark Antony
> By this vile conquest shall attain unto.
> So, fare you well at once ; for Brutus' tongue
> Hath almost ended his life's history.—Act V.

He firmly believes in the glorious happiness of a Roman Republic without, apparently, studying whether his fellow-countrymen, at that time, desired such a form of government, or what the views of the majority were upon the subject.

History differs from Shakespeare about his state of mind after the Philippi defeat. The poet makes him gratefully declare that he found everybody true to him, while, according to Merivale,* he became almost heart-broken, and declared he found virtue only a name. His last words contemptuously class Antony and young Octavius together as allied foes to their country, ignoring the plain truth that they, unaided by foreign power, represented the majority of his fellow-countrymen. It being Shakespeare's wish to make Brutus the hero of this tragedy, he easily portrays him as the most interesting person in it. An able modern writer on Shakespeare† declares that he would rather fail with Brutus than triumph with Octavius. If their lives had ended at the same time, such might be the feelings of most modern readers. But history proves that the triumph of Octavius was destined to be that of a wise, just, and discerning ruler, over an amiable, impetuous idealist, who, as Mr. Dowden says, " lived among his books, nourished himself with philosophies, and was secluded from the impression of facts." Such a character was, indeed, unfit to rule or even influence the turbulent, yet thoroughly practical Romans. The extreme gentleness of Brutus towards his young wife Portia—who fully shares his political principles, though with less energy—and also towards his servant lad Lucius, is worthy of a more civilized age. He was, in fact, a man unsuited to his times, his bravery and sincerity making him respected alike by ardent friends and generous foes, without either of them really understanding his character. In patriotism and love for his country, this gentle, yet devoted enthusiast resembled Octavius more than his chief ally or chief foe, Cassius and Antony. These two are, indeed, men of much coarser mould, far more selfish and worldly than their noble

---

* *Romans under the Empire*, vol. ii.
† DOWDEN'S *Shakespeare: His Mind and Art.*

and comparatively civilized associates. Cassius and Antony
understand one another, the former hating Julius Cæsar,
partly, if not chiefly, through personal envy ; the latter
following his fortunes, thereby promoting his own, and gratifying his worldly passions. This play leaves the Roman
Empire under the rule of Antony, though Octavius, not yet
twenty years old, nominally shared supreme authority with
his late uncle's victorious general and successful avenger.*

---

* Gibbon states of Octavius that "both his virtues and vices were artificial :
according to his interest he was at first the enemy and then the father of the
Roman world."   Also that when young he had "a cool head, an unfeeling heart,
and a cowardly disposition."—*Decline and Fall of the Roman Empire*, vol. i.
Yet it is evident, even from Gibbon's account, that the more powerful Octavius
became the more were his virtues displayed : for both as a sovereign and a man he
was certainly beloved and respected by all classes of his subjects.—*See* SUETONIUS'
Lives of the Cæsars ; also MERIVALE'S *Romans under the Empire.*

CHAPTER II.

ANTONY AND CLEOPATRA.

Sketch of Play.

AFTER the battle of Philippi, Antony went to Egypt, while Octavius, with his colleague Lepidus, remained chiefly at Rome, or in the eastern provinces of the Empire. When in Egypt Antony is completely fascinated by its queen, Cleopatra, and she weans his affection from his wife Fulvia, who remained in Rome, but devoted to her husband's interests. At her death he returns there, and, after a short time, marries Octavia, sister of Octavius Cæsar. He again goes to Egypt, and, as before, falls under the influence of Cleopatra. Octavius and the Romans generally are much irritated against him ; but Antony, relying on his popularity with his soldiers, and ruled by Cleopatra, defies Cæsar, who declares war against him, and invades Egypt. Antony is defeated at the battle of Actium, and accuses Cleopatra of treachery ; she, however, regains a short-lived influence over him, but the triumphant advance of Octavius Cæsar alarms her, and she tries to make peace with him unknown to Antony. He discovers her talking with Cæsar's messenger, and is furious. Cleopatra, afraid to offend either of the Roman leaders, pretends to commit suicide. Her death is announced to Antony, who mortally wounds himself at the news ; but when she hears this she again sees him, and he expires in her presence. She then has an interview with Octavius, trying to appease and fascinate him ; but she finds her artifices fail, and that he is resolved to lead her captive through Rome in a triumphal procession. Of this Cleopatra has not only been secretly informed, but she also guesses Cæsar's intention from his manner. She perceives that her powers of alluring, previously so successful with Pompey, Julius Cæsar, and Antony, have no effect on Octavius, whose love for his injured sister Octavia hardens him against her rival. Cleopatra then resolves on suicide, to escape the public disgrace of the Roman procession. Octavius admits his intention in the last scene, when

Antony and Cleopatra being both dead, he returns in triumph to Rome. " The action in this play comprehends the events of ten years."—HOWARD STAUNTON'S *Notes to the Illustrated Shakespeare.*

ANTONY'S great popularity with the Roman army, and the cautious deference of young Octavius towards him, after their joint victory at Philippi, inclined him to indolence and self-indulgence.* (Shakespeare, accordingly, begins this play by describing the angry regret of two of Antony's officers at the complete abandonment of their commander to a sensual life.) These men—Demetrius and Philo—are evidently accustomed to his licentious habits ; but never before was he so completely enslaved, though " the measure " they mention doubtless exceeded the usual limits even of Roman profligacy.

> PHILO.   Nay, but this dotage of our general's
> O'erflows the measure : those his goodly eyes,
> That o'er the files and musters of the war
> Have glowed like plated Mars, now bend, now turn,
> The office and devotion of their view
> Upon a tawny front.—Act I.,—

meaning Cleopatra's dark complexion compared to that of Roman ladies. Antony, though a libertine, had probably never known, among his numerous acquaintance, such a character as Cleopatra. This beautiful woman was alike bold, crafty, energetic, and cruel. Shakespeare, doubtless, knew Plutarch's account, confirmed by other writers, of her savage experiments on slaves and criminals, by having them bitten or stung to death, in her presence, by different kinds of snakes, to discover the most painful and the most easy deaths inflicted. This practice, though not mentioned in the play, well explains her angry threats of torture against the unwelcome announcer of Antony's second marriage. She had successively fascinated the illustrious rivals, Pompey and Julius Cæsar, and was, therefore, well acquainted with the Roman character in its grandest specimens.† Thus, after

---

* " He talked with the soldiers in their own swaggering and ribald strain : ate and drank with them in public ; he was pleasant on the subject of his amours ; ready in assisting the intrigues of others ; and easy under the raillery to which he was subjected by his own."—PLUTARCH'S *Life of Antony.*

† A recent writer of an interesting learned work on Egypt believes that Cleopatra was living near Rome, with her son, Cæsarion, at the time of Julius Cæsar's murder ; but Shakespeare makes no allusion to it. This writer confirms Shakespeare's account of the luxurious life of Antony and Cleopatra, and also of the latter's death by the bite of an asp.—EBERS's *Egypt,* vol. i.

her successful artifices with these illustrious men — statesmen as well as warriors—her subsequent conquest of the comparatively uneducated, reckless Antony was an easy triumph.*

Egypt, over which she nominally ruled, was completely subject to Rome, and had been so for many years. So thoroughly had it become a Roman province, that little mention is made in history, and none in the play, of any neighbouring country or ruler having much influence or intercourse with it, except King Herod "of Jewry," whose head Cleopatra hoped to "have" through Antony's means. Shakespeare never mentions Abyssinia, Syria, or Tripoli, nor does he allude to the Bedouin Arab inhabitants of the Desert. The whole play is engrossed with Roman characters and politics, while Cleopatra's evident policy is to please her Roman sovereigns, and to study and imitate what she herself calls "the high Roman fashion" in everything.†

During the first part of this play Cleopatra is fully occupied in providing amusements and arranging festive entertainments for Antony, whom she believes, and who believes himself, now supreme in the Roman Empire. The enamoured Antony, when beside his enchantress, utters the following high-sounding words, which, though Shakespeare's invention, clearly reveal the Roman general's state of mind :

> Let Rome in Tiber melt ! and the wide arch
> Of the rang'd empire fall !   Here is my space.—Act I.

Such words would surely arouse indignation in every Roman mind, considering Antony's position of trust at the head of the Imperial army. But in the midst of his enjoyments, news comes from Rome of his wife Fulvia's death. This woman, a person of high spirit and haughty temper, had steadily supported her absent, faithless husband's interests against the increasing power of Octavius.‡ At news of her death, Antony, knowing her earnest affection for him, and devotion to his political interests, despite his conduct, is shocked and saddened. He resolves to return to Rome, yet finds it difficult to leave Cleopatra. Thus, during the first

---

* "Antony had little of the literary polish so widely diffused among his equals in station."—MERIVALE'S *Romans under the Empire*, vol. iii.

† MERIVALE confirms Shakespeare's account of Cleopatra's schemes to please the Roman voluptuary, Antony, adding that "she had secured, as she hoped, by alliance with him, the stability of her ancestral throne." He accepts Shakespeare's version of her character, saying that "the Roman point of view makes her only vain and selfish ; but she really had a love for Antony." This last assertion, considering both her conduct and position in Egypt, seems rather doubtful.

‡ Plutarch.

shock caused by Fulvia's death—whom he had always trusted more as a friend, apparently, than loved as a wife—he reveals to his follower, Enobarbus, his real feeling towards Cleopatra. It is neither affection nor confidence, but a distrust, almost amounting to dread, which, in her presence, changes to an admiring, jealous infatuation. He longs and resolves to return home, yet has hardly moral courage to say so before this extraordinary woman, who, combining such love as that of which she was capable, with steady devotion to her own worldly interests, he knows would oppose his leaving Egypt, where he, nominally her sovereign, is really her subject. Enobarbus, who evidently knows Cleopatra better than Antony does, declares that she will pretend to die when she hears of his departure, and congratulates Antony on Fulvia's death, while the widower neither thanks nor checks him.

ANTONY.   I must be gone.
ENOBARBUS.   Cleopatra catching but the least news of this, dies instantly; I have seen her die twenty times upon far poorer moment; I do think there is mettle in death, which commits some loving act upon her, she hath such a celerity in dying.
ANTONY.   She is cunning past man's thought.
Would I had never seen her.—Act I.

Antony evidently believes what his follower says of Cleopatra's deceit, and thus is aware what a thorough actress she is. He never reproves Enobarbus for being, certainly, very outspoken about her; but, dreading his loss of influence at Rome after his wife's death, he hastens to apprise Cleopatra of his immediate return there.

At this crisis Cleopatra's real feelings, so often concealed by false pretences, are, for a short time, revealed. She is rejoiced at Fulvia's death, yet mortified to find Antony depressed and resolved to leave her, though only for a short time. Her interest, as well as her passion for him, induce her to oppose his departure; for, while he remains in Egypt, under her influence, her almost absolute power is secure, though nominally she is a vassal of Rome. Her artful, fierce spirit indulges in raillery, sorrow, and reproach, mingled with occasional signs of affection for him, real or pretended. Her jealousy as well as her fears are aroused, knowing that Antony, now a widower, will soon be amid the most attractive ladies of his nation, who, viewing her as a semi-barbarian, despite her beauty, wealth, and accomplishments, may supplant her in his inconstant affections. In this remarkable scene Cleopatra sarcastically asks her female attendant Charmian to watch Antony's agitated expression, who, doubtless, obeys her mistress, while prudently saying nothing.

> ANTONY.   My precious queen, forbear ;
> And give true evidence to his love, which stands
> An honourable trial.
> CLEOPATRA.   So Fulvia told me.
> I prithee, turn aside, and weep for her ;
> Then bid adieu to me, and say the tears
> Belong to Egypt : good now, play one scene
> Of excellent dissembling ; and let it look
> Like perfect honour.
> ANTONY.   You'll heat my blood . no more.
> CLEOPATRA.   You can do better yet ; but this is meetly.
> ANTONY.   Now, by my sword,—
> CLEOPATRA.   And target,—still he mends ;
> But this is not the best.   Look, prithee, Charmian,
> How this Herculean Roman does become
> The carriage of his chafe.
> ANTONY.   I'll leave you, lady.
> CLEOPATRA.   Courteous lord, one word.
> Sir, you and I must part,—but that's not it.
> Sir, you and I have loved,—but that's not it ;
> That you know well : something it is I would,—
> O, my oblivion is a very Antony,
> And I am all forgotten.
>   But, sir, forgive me ;
> Since my becomings kill me, when they do not
> Eye well to you : your honour calls you hence ;
> Therefore be deaf to my unpitied folly,
> And all the gods go with you ! upon your sword
> Sit laurel victory, and smooth success
> Be strew'd before your feet !—Act I.*

Cleopatra, having thus provoked Antony as far as she dared, and finding him resolved to return home, changes her manner, speaks affectionately, and, wishing him every success, they separate, though only for a short time.   Antony leaves immediately for Rome, and Cleopatra remains in Egypt, anxious, jealous, and apprehensive, lest her influence over her powerful dupe may be superseded.   Before reaching Rome

---

* MRS. JAMESON : *Characteristics of Women*, vol. ii., agrees with Merivale that Shakespeare's Cleopatra is the real historical character, and mentions her "artful mockery, triumphant petulance, and imperious coquetry ; " she calls her "a compound of contradictions of all that we most hate with what we most admire." Yet, in Shakespeare's description, there seems little, indeed, to admire throughout, except in personal appearance and ready wit. For her deceit, pride, and jealousy rule her conduct alternately, and she neither utters nor acts upon a single generous sentiment.

Antony sent a loving message to Cleopatra, who, during his absence, is often in a state of extraordinary excitement.* Her fierce, crafty, jealous spirit incessantly dreads losing its hold over Antony, on which her own power depends, as she knows nothing of young Octavius or Lepidus, and is yet a Roman subject. She recalls both Pompey and Julius Cæsar—her former lovers—whom she had so completely captivated in her younger and happier days. Yet she mentions neither of them with the least tenderness, but only as gratifying proofs of her powers of fascination.

> CLEOPATRA.   Now I feed myself
> With most delicious poison :—Think on me,
> That am with Phœbus' amorous pinches black,
> And wrinkled deep in time?   Broad-fronted Cæsar,
> When thou wast here above the ground, I was
> A morsel for a monarch : and great Pompey
> Would stand, and make his eyes grow in my brow ;
> There would he anchor his aspect, and die
> With looking on his life.—Act I. Scene V.

Their noble lives and untimely deaths have, apparently, made no impression on her selfish nature. Her wild anxiety about Antony at first seems like real, though fantastic, affection ; although when her former life and language are recalled, which her sly, yet faithful, attendant Charmian remembers, it is evident that her worldly interests, now so involved with Antony, actuate her more than any love for him.

> CLEOPATRA.   Did, I, Charmian,
> Ever love Cæsar so ?
>   CHARMIAN.   O, that brave Cæsar !
>   CLEOPATRA.   Be chok'd with such another emphasis !
> Say the brave Antony.
>   CHARMIAN.   The valiant Cæsar !
>   CLEOPATRA.   By Isis, I will give thee bloody teeth,
> If thou with Cæsar paragon again
> My man of men !
>   CHARMIAN.   By your most gracious pardon,
> I sing but after you.

* The poet Coleridge and Mr. Furnivall, one of the latest commentators on Shakespeare, agree that Cleopatra is one of the most wonderful women he ever described. The former says, "No other historical play is so thoroughly founded on history ;" the latter, "Shakespeare borrows his main lines from Plutarch in describing Cleopatra." It is evident, therefore, that Shakespeare relied less on his imagination in this play than in many others. For the real history of Antony and Cleopatra was so eventful that it required less of Shakespeare's unassisted genius, upon which King Lear and even Macbeth, to some extent, are comparatively dependent.

> CLEOPATRA.   My salad days !
> When I was green in judgment,—cold in blood,
> To say as I said then !—Act I. Scene V.*

When Antony reaches Rome, he finds Octavius displeased at his wasting so much time in voluptuous indulgence at Alexandria, while Sextus Pompeius—son of Julius Cæsar's great rival—is waging civil war, or rebellion, against the Triumvirs. Antony hears the just rebukes of Octavius with surprising meekness, considering his age and character. It is probable that this young prince's manner reminds him of his late revered master, the immortal Julius, for, surely, from no other living man would Antony have endured the same reproach with patience. A reconciliation, however, takes place between Octavius and Antony, and a marriage is arranged between the latter and Cæsar's sister Octavia. This woman, though always mentioned favourably in the play, Shakespeare does not make nearly so interesting as he might have done, considering her amiable, virtuous, and for-giving character, as recorded by history.† She, indeed, rather resembled his own delightful creation, Cordelia, in King Lear ; and her whole conduct during an eventful, most trying life, was worthy of a better age than the semi-barbarous period in which she lived. In the play, the Roman officer Mecænas praises her in terms which are confirmed rather than lessened by historical record.

> "If beauty, wisdom, modesty, can settle
> The heart of Antony, Octavia is
> A blessed lottery for him."—Act II.

The deep, constant affection between her and her brother presents a noble moral contrast to the wild passions of the profligate Antony, and the mingled deceit and violence of the artful Cleopatra. Yet this unscrupulous pair are con-sidered the hero and heroine of this fine tragedy, though Octavius and his sister are infinitely more worthy alike of interest and admiration.‡ Shakespeare, however, apparently

---

* Cleopatra's threat to strike Charmian, which the latter apparently fears by ceasing to mention provoking recollections, was, perhaps, in Dr. Johnson's mind when pronouncing Shakespeare's Cleopatra " too low."

† It was the general hope that a woman of Octavia's beauty and distinguished virtues would acquire such an influence over Antony as might, in the end, be salutary to the State. "The eyes of all," she said, "are necessarily turned on me, who am the wife of Antony, and the sister of Cæsar, and should these chiefs of the empire, misled by hasty counsels, involve the whole in war, whatever may be the event, it will be unhappy for me."—PLUTARCH'S *Life of Antony.* Plutarch adds that Octavius had a great affection for his sister, "a woman of extraordinary merit."—*Life of Antony.*

‡ "Antony, indeed, was given him by history, and Shakespeare has but em-bodied, in his own vivid colours, the irregular mind of the Triumvir, ambitious

takes little interest in Octavia, being resolved to make his description of her rival Cleopatra as powerful as his matchless pen could render it. Accordingly, he gives a magnificent description, through Enobarbus—when Antony and he return to Rome—of the first meeting of his master and Cleopatra.

ENOBARBUS.   When she first met Mark Antony, she pursed up his heart, upon the river of Cydnus.

> The barge she was in, like a burnish'd throne,
> Burnt on the water : the poop was beaten gold ;
> Purple the sails, and so perfumèd that
> The winds were love-sick with them : the oars were silver ;
> Which to the tune of flutes kept stroke, and made
> The water, which they beat, to follow faster,
> As amorous of their strokes.   For her own person,
> It beggar'd all description : she did lie
> In her pavilion (cloth of gold, of tissue),
> O'er-picturing that Venus, where we see
> The fancy outwork Nature : on each side her
> Stood pretty dimpled boys, like smiling Cupids,
> With divers-colour'd fans, whose wind did seem
> To glow the delicate cheeks which they did cool,
> And what they undid, did.
> Her gentlewomen, like the Nereides,
> So many mermaids, tended her i' the eyes,
> And made their bends adornings : at the helm
> A seeming mermaid steers ; the silken tackle
> Swell with the touches of those flower-soft hands,
> That yarely frame the office.   From the barge
> A strange invisible perfume hits the sense
> Of the adjacent wharfs.   The city cast
> Her people out upon her ; and Antony,
> Enthron'd in the market-place, did sit alone,
> Whistling to the air ; which, but for vacancy,
> Had gone to gaze on Cleopatra too,
> And made a gap in Nature.
> Upon her landing, Antony sent to her,
> Invited her to supper : she replied,
> It should be better he became her guest ;
> Which she entreated : our courteous Antony,
> Whom ne'er the word of ' No ' woman heard speak,
> Being barber'd ten times o'er, goes to the feast ;
> And for his ordinary, pays his heart,
> For what his eyes eat only.—Act II. Scene II.

On this occasion her beauty and attractions are praised to

and daring against all enemies but himself. In Cleopatra he had less to guide him.   This character not being one that can please; its strong and spirited delineation has not been sufficiently observed."—HALLAM'S *Literary History*, vol. iii.

the utmost by Enobarbus, without a single virtue being ascribed to her. Thus from her introduction, Shakespeare seems resolved to make Cleopatra as attractive as any person can be, without the aid of a single noble or generous quality. Enobarbus, an intelligent, ready-witted man, evidently admires her beauty and talents, and almost fears them, without having the least respect or attachment towards her. He predicts that Antony will never tire of one whom "age cannot wither," and whose amazing influence over the licentious general he himself has witnessed.

Antony's marriage with Octavia gave general satisfaction at Rome; but Antony, apparently, only married her for political reasons, and is secretly resolved to return to Cleopatra, the only woman who, throughout his licentious life, had gained complete ascendency over him.

> ANTONY.   I will to Egypt,
> And though I make this marriage for my peace,
> I' the East my pleasure lies.—Act II.

Shakespeare introduces an Egyptian soothsayer at Rome, perhaps an agent or spy of Cleopatra's, who, soon after Antony's marriage to Octavia, irritates him against her brother, as a formidable rival to his political power. This incident Plutarch does not mention; but, in the play, it hastens Antony's return to Egypt. Meantime Cleopatra, when told of Antony's marriage, bursts into a violent, even frantic passion, which, though consistent with her character, and vividly described, is not recorded by Plutarch, whom the poet usually follows. Her attempt to stab the messenger of this unwelcome news, and her malignant curiosity about Octavia's appearance, are alike consistent with her real character, and natural in her position; but the detailed scene seems derived from Shakespeare's own brilliant imagination.

> MESSENGER.   Madam, he's married to Octavia.
> CLEOPATRA.   The most infectious pestilence upon thee!
> > [*Strikes him down.*
> MESSENGER.   Gracious Madam,
> I, that do bring the news, made not the match.
> CLEOPATRA.   Say, 'tis not so, a province I will give thee.
> MESSENGER.   He's married, madam.
> CLEOPATRA.   Rogue! thou hast lived too long.
> > [*Draws a dagger.*

At this violence the messenger naturally retires with all speed, but is recalled, and, after bitter reproaches, Cleopatra petulantly exclaims—

> The merchandise which thou hast brought from Rome
> Are all too dear for me; lie they upon thy hand,
> And be undone by them.

Having thus dismissed him, the furious queen exclaims to her female attendants, Charmian and Iras, and the eunuch Alexas,—

> In praising Antony, I have dispraised Cæsar.
>   CHARMIAN.   Many times, madam.
>   CLEOPATRA.   I am paid for 't now.
> Lead me from hence;
> I faint; O, Iras, Charmian!—'Tis no matter.
> Go to the fellow, good Alexas; bid him
> Report the feature of Octavia, her years,
> Her inclination; let him not leave out
> The colour of her hair:—bring me word quickly.
>   [*Exit* ALEXAS.
> Let him for ever go:—Let him not—Charmian,
> Though he be painted one way like a Gorgon,
> The other way he's a Mars:—Bid you Alexas
> Bring me word how tall she is.—Pity me, Charmian,
> But do not speak to me.—Lead me to my chamber.—Act II.

She thus revives, for a moment, her recollection of Julius, whom she regrets having previously disparaged before Charmian; but no tenderness ever appears in any of her allusions to former lovers. She has evidently treated and viewed Pompey. Cæsar, and Antony as temporary dupes to be coaxed, amused, and gratified in turn, while her reward was the secure preservation of her almost regal authority in Egypt.* She may, indeed, feel more anxiety about Antony than she ever did about the others, for she is now middle-aged, and, though still wonderfully beautiful and attractive, probably begins to feel more jea'ous than ever of younger rivals.

After describing her terrible, almost frantic excitement, Shakespeare changes the scene to Rome, where he mentions a remarkable banquet, at which Octavius, Antony, and Lepidus, the three Triumvirs, meet their former foe, Sextus Pompeius, on terms of friendship. At this joyous feast Antony describes the Egyptian crocodiles to his drunken colleague Lepidus, while Octavius, ever careful, sober, and watchful, observes this strange scene with close attention. Antony's reckless nature, ready to drink and jest with Pompeius, or any one, does not yet arouse Cæsar's suspicions, who still thinks and hopes that his beloved sister has made

---

* " She was the public slave of any man's passion whose political interest she required."—MERIVALE'S *Romans under the Empire*, vol. iii.

a happy marriage for herself, as well as for her country.
His parting from her is, perhaps, one of the most beautiful
passages in this play, yet it has been comparatively little
noticed.

CÆSAR *to* ANTONY.   You take from me a great part of myself;
Use me well in it.—Sister, prove such a wife
As my thoughts make thee, and as my farthest bond
Shall pass on thy approof.—Most noble Antony,
Let not the piece of virtue which is set
Betwixt us, as the cement of our love,
To keep it builded, be the ram to batter
The fortress of it : for better might we
Have loved without this mean, if on both parts
This be not cherished.
    ANTONY.   Make me not offended
In your distrust.
    CÆSAR.   Farewell, my dearest sister, fare thee well,
The elements be kind to thee, and make
Thy spirits all of comfort ! fare thee well.
    OCTAVIA.   My noble brother !
    ANTONY.   The April's in her eyes : it is love's spring,
And these the showers to bring it on.   Be cheerful.
                              —Act III. Scene II.

Most of Octavius's and his sister's actions and sentiments
are worthy of civilized, enlightened times, though they are
placed, while both young, amid violent, unscrupulous friends
and foes.   Though Shakespeare follows history in all the
sentiments he attributes to them, he yet keeps both in the
background, preferring to devote the reader's special attention to Antony and Cleopatra.

After the parting of Cæsar from Octavia, who accompanies her husband to Greece, Shakespeare again describes
Cleopatra's eager curiosity about her rival's appearance.
This scene is almost comic in the trifling details which
interest her ; but she is quite in earnest, her fierce, worldly
passions being now excited to the utmost through fear of
losing influence over Antony.   Through him she rules Egypt,
not, apparently, feeling much interest in her subjects or in
her country, as she never evinces any patriotism, nor the
least idea of royal duties.   She rarely mentions Egypt at
all, only once alludes to its famous pyramids, when declaring,
in frenzy, she would rather be hung in chains upon them
than be led captive in Cæsar's triumph.   Her thoughts, fears,
and hopes are alike centred in Rome, and in Romans.   She
makes scarcely any allusion to anything connected with
Egypt ; neither its ancient history, its mummies, pyramids,

&c., which have always made that country so remarkable, and interesting to the mediæval and modern world. The scene of this play is, indeed, chiefly in Alexandria, but Roman events, characters, and intrigues are alone recorded and studied. Cleopatra's whole object is, apparently, to live in voluptuous enjoyment ; amusing or being amused ; recalling, with vain, selfish exultation, her former conquests of Pompey and Julius Cæsar. Upon hearing an unflattering account of Octavia's appearance and manners, her jealous vanity is rather gratified. She never asks about her rival's character, education, mind, or temper.

CLEOPATRA.   Didst thou behold Octavia ?
MESSENGER.   Ay, dread queen.
CLEOPATRA.   Is she as tall as me ?
MESSENGER.   She is not, madam.
CLEOPATRA.   Didst hear her speak ? Is she shrill-tongued, or low ?
MESSENGER.   Madam, I heard her speak ; she is low-voiced.
CLEOPATRA.   That's not so good :—he cannot like her long.
CHARMIAN.   Like her?   O Isis ! 'tis impossible.
CLEOPATRA.   Guess at her years, I prithee.
MESSENGER.   Madam,
She was a widow.
CLEOPATRA.   Widow?   Charmian, hark.
MESSENGER.   And I do think she's thirty.
CLEOPATRA.   Bear'st thou her face in mind? Is't long or round ?
MESSENGER.   Round even to faultiness.
CLEOPATRA.   For the most part, too, they are foolish that are so.
Her hair, what colour?
MESSENGER.   Brown, madam : and her forehead
As low as she would wish it.
CLEOPATRA.   There's gold for thee.
Thou must not take my former sharpness ill.—Act III. Scene III.

Cleopatra has no more esteem for virtue in the one sex than the other, and, once satisfied that Octavia is plain and awkward compared to herself, she asks no more about her, and prepares, with renewed energy, to tempt Antony back again, caring for nothing but her own power and gratification.*

Shakespeare then describes the last interview betwee Antony and Octavia, at Athens, where he reveals his enmit to her brother, which she had almost anticipated. He com. plains that Octavius has suddenly renewed war agains Sextus Pompeius, and has spoken contemptuously of himse f

* "Cleopatra, as a woman, deserves neither love nor admiration ; but, as a queen, her ambition was bold and her bearing magnanimous."—MERIVALE s *Romans under the Empire*, vol. iii.   Yet neither history nor Shakespeare recor much, if any, proof of her magnanimity.

since they left Rome. Octavia pathetically deplores this quarrel between husband and brother, and Antony sends her back to Rome, nominally to make peace between him and Octavius, while he again goes to Egypt unknown to his wife. Here Shakespeare rather deviates from history, which states that Antony fought against the Parthians—those bravest enemies of the Romans—before he rejoined Cleopatra ; but in the play, when Antony is again introduced after leaving Octavia, he is once more in Egypt. Previous to describing his arrival there, Shakespeare introduces a beautiful scene between Octavius and his sister, who, not suspecting Antony's desertion of her, or his devotion to Cleopatra, implores her brother to make peace, if possible, with her husband. Octavius, who now knows Antony's character and conduct better than his sister does, exposes them to her with suppressed indignation, mingled with tender love and pity for Octavia.

> OCTAVIA. My Lord, Mark Antony,
> Hearing that you prepar'd for war, acquainted
> My grieved ear withal : whereon, I begg'd
> His pardon for return.
> CÆSAR. Which soon he granted,
> Being an obstruct 'twixt his lust and him.
> OCTAVIA. Do not say so, my lord.
> CÆSAR. I have eyes upon him,
> And his affairs come to me on the wind.
> Where is he now ?
> OCTAVIA. My lord, in Athens.
> CÆSAR. No, my most wronged sister ; Cleopatra
> Hath nodded him to her.—-Act III. Scene VI.

He treats her with the utmost kindness, but prepares for war against Antony with calm and resolute determination.

Meanwhile, Antony, again with Cleopatra, is as much under her influence as ever, and prepares to resist Cæsar's forces. When, at the battle of Actium, Cleopatra's vessels, or those which obey her orders, take to flight suddenly, Antony is completely defeated, and Cæsar's victory easy and decisive. Neither history nor the play state very clearly if the Egyptian fleet fled from panic or treachery.* Antony, however, suspects the latter, and, in despairing confusion, blames and reproaches Cleopatra, who, by merely expressing sorrow, immediately pacifies him. This first breach between them—his sad reproaches, and her submission, which quite melts him—well displays the artful queen's complete ascendency over the passionate and sensual Roman general.

* Compare PLUTARCH'S *Life of Antony* and *Student's History of Rome.*

ANTONY.   You did know
How much you were my conqueror ; and that
My sword, made weak by my affection, would
Obey it on all cause.
      CLEOPATRA.   Pardon, pardon.
      ANTONY.   Fall not a tear, I say ; one of them rates
All that is won or lost : give me a kiss ;
Even this repays me.—Act III.

It would appear that, at this time, Cleopatra is undeter-
mined how to act : she apparently hopes to make a conquest
of Octavius, whose success she probably anticipates, yet is
unwilling to desert Antony, knowing her power over him, and
that her success with his young foe is very doubtful, considering his relationship to her rival Octavia, together with
his self-control and firmness of character. Yet she gladly
receives Thyreus, Cæsar's messenger, unknown to Antony.
In reply to his persuasions to abandon Antony, she sends
a most submissive reply to Octavius, without mentioning
Antony, and assures Thyreus of her complete obedience to
young Cæsar's will, whom she acknowledges as ruler of
Egypt.

      THYREUS.   He [Cæsar] knows that you embrace not Antony
As you did love, but as you fear'd him.
      CLEOPATRA.   O !
      THYREUS.   The scars upon your honour, therefore, he
Does pity, as constrained blemishes,
Not as deserved.
      CLEOPATRA.   He is a god, and knows
What is most right : mine honour was not yielded,
But conquer'd merely.
Say to great Cæsar this, in disputation
I kiss his conqu'ring hand : tell him I am prompt
To lay my crown at 's feet, and there to kneel.
                              —Act III. Scene XI.

Antony, however, bursts in upon this singular conference,
and in a violent passion orders Thyrcus to be soundly
whipped, though aware of his coming from Cæsar, while he
assails Cleopatra with reproaches.* She hears him with the
meekness of an accomplished actress, convincing him of her
love and fidelity. Antony again believes her, and prepares
for a desperate resistance to Cæsar.
When Octavius receives Antony's personal challenge, he
scorns and rejects it, calling him an old ruffian, and replie

---

* It is on this occasion that the observant, sly Enobarbus well compares
Octavius to "a lion's whelp," and Antony to "an old one dying."

that he has many other ways to die.   Antony is disappointed,
being probably a redoubted swordsman, which, perhaps,
Octavius was not; but the latter is steadily becoming more
popular with the Roman army, now beginning to despise
and desert Antony.   Cleopatra and he both knew, therefore,
that in single combat Antony would probably be victor, but
that in a pitched battle, heading their respective forces, Cæsar
had more chance of success.   The old general now addresses
his followers in a state of nervous excitement unusual with
him, evidently anticipating defeat and death, though his
natural bravery renders him incapable of fear.

> ANTONV.   Tend me to-night;
> May be it is the period of your duty :
> Haply, you shall not see me more ; or if,
> A mangled shadow : perchance, to-morrow
> You'll serve another master.   I look on you
> As one who takes his leave.

But when Enobarbus says this language dispirits his friends,
and makes them weep, Antony, with a faint sparkle of his
former spirit, rejoins—

> You take me in too dolorous a sense ;
> .   .   .   .   Know, my hearts,
> I hope well of to-morrow ; and will lead you
> Where rather I'll expect victorious life,
> Than death and honour.   Let's to supper ; come,
> And drown consideration.—Act IV. Scene I.

Yet he evidently feels no more a soldier's pleasure in the
present war.   Except when in Cleopatra's enchanting presence, who completely fascinates him, Antony deeply feels
his present degraded position—viewed as a selfish, weak
profligate by most of his countrymen, who are now rapidly
transferring their confidence from him to his noble opponent,
Octavius.   He again seeks Cleopatra, who assists in buckling
on his armour with peculiar skill, for which her brave, in-
fatuated dupe praises her while preparing for battle.   Cæsar
wishes Antony captured alive, feeling sure of victory, and
anticipates the happy future when the vast Roman Empire,
under his rule, shall again enjoy peace and happiness.

> OCTAVIUS.   The time of universal peace is near :
> Prove this a prosperous day, the three-nook'd world
> Shall bear the olive freely.—Act IV. Scene VI.*

* This sublime anticipation which Shakespeare attributes to the future Emperor
was fully verified, according to history :—" Mildew corroded blade and spear-head,

In a brief land engagement, a mere skirmish, Antony gains
some success, which, though slight, raises his excitable spirits ;
yet he apparently thinks that his rival has many advantages
over him, which he had not foreseen, and that his own age
" will not be defied."*   On the day after his trifling success over
Cæsar's land forces his fleet surrenders to the enemy, and he,
for the second or third time, believes and declares that Cleopatra, " this foul Egyptian," has betrayed him.   In the midst
of his indignation Cleopatra appears, and he reproaches and
threatens her with such fury, that, despairing of any artifice
save one, she leaves his presence, and declares to her confidant, Charmian, that he is madly furious against her.   For
the first time Antony is now thoroughly enraged against
Cleopatra, even mentioning his deserted wife, " patient
Octavia," with tenderness.   This allusion, considering Cleopatra's jealous nature, was, perhaps, " the unkindest cut of
all," for she attempts neither justification nor reply, though so
well skilled in all the arts of deception.   Her wily attendant suggests resorting to her old trick of pretended death,
that she should lock herself up in a monument, and have
Antony apprised of her sudden decease.   Cleopatra follows
this advice, sending another of her people, the eunuch Mar-
dian, with the news to Antony.   The latter is now in a state
of mingled despair and rage—despair about his own fate,
and rage against her whom he believes to have been the
cause of it.   But the news of her sudden death, from alleged
grief at his anger with her, takes away his rage while it completes his despair.   If she is really dead through love for
him, all his former suspicions of her treachery must be
groundless, and, his fury having hastened her death whom he
again believes faithful to him, destroys all hope of happiness, and all wish for life.

The idea of suicide—that terrible remedy among the
Romans for all human misery and thought so blameless by
them—now tempts him with irresistible power.   Like Brutus,
he forthwith asks his attendant Eros to slay him, but upon
his follower's committing suicide at the fatal request, Antony
inflicts a mortal wound upon himself.   He has just done
this when told that Cleopatra, locked in the monument,
is not dead, and begs him to visit her.   Antony's anger is

but spared the growing crops ; the sword was turned into a pruning-hook ; the
corselet into a ploughshare ; the altar of Peace was erected solemnly in the
Roman Curia.   On such occasions the praises of Augustus, as the author of so
much happiness, held always the foremost place.   The poets urged their countri-
men to remember in every prayer and thanksgiving the restorer of order, the
creator of universal felicity."—MERIVALE's *Romans under the Empire*, ch. xxxii.
  * BACON's *Essays.*

now over ; he knows his end is come, and longs again to see
the fatal enchantress for whom he has lost the world. He
is conveyed to the monument, where Cleopatra receives him
with many signs of love and sorrow ; for she recognizes in
the dying warrior her latest conquest, now following the
shadows of Pompey and Julius' Cæsar. Excited to the
utmost by the peril of her situation, and surrounded by
dangers, Cleopatra is naturally grieved and terrified, as her
brave old general dies before her eyes without another word of
reproach, with his last breath charging her to trust only one
of Octavius Cæsar's followers, a certain Proculeius. It is
then that Cleopatra declares she will commit suicide, and
again says so to her women after Antony's death. When
he is gone for ever she finds herself alone, and confronted
with " the young Roman boy," as Antony called him, who,
like the destroying angel, has advanced irresistibly upon
them. Yet she has not really abandoned all hope of life, and
of appeasing, if not fascinating, the young conqueror, whom
she now sees in the monument. During this extraordinary
interview, Octavius is said to have kept his eyes steadily
fixed on the ground,* and spoke to her with calm but cold
courtesy. Cleopatra is all submission ; but, before this scene,
she had asked Proculeius if his master was really determined
to lead her in a public triumph through the streets of Rome.
Upon the answer of this one trusty man her fate virtually
depends, and his reply, brief, explicit, and hopeless, leaves
no doubt on the question : " Madam, he will ; I know it."
From that moment Cleopatra's proud spirit knows no remedy,
perceives no escape, save by what she terms elsewhere the
" high Roman fashion " of suicide. Yet in her interview
with Octavius, she apparently nourishes a faint hope that
her grace, beauty, and address may, at least to some extent,
subdue her conqueror.† But she has now to deal with a totally
different person from any she had previously known. It
was, doubtless, a terrible disappointment to her, when middle-
aged, yet still beautiful, to find all her arts and attractions
prove ineffectual. She evidently finds herself at a disadvan-
tage never known before. For Octavius is not only much
younger than herself, but the loving, trusted brother of the
virtuous woman she had wronged. Accordingly, his calm
composure, founded partly on contempt natural to such a man

---

* PLUTARCH'S *Lives* and MERIVALE'S *Romans under the Empire.*

† Mrs. Jameson calls Cleopatra "a coquette to the last" (*Characteristics of
Women*, vol. ii.), "luxurious in her despair ; " but in her spirited and able account
of her Mrs. Jameson surely evinces undeserved admiration. Except her beauty
and talent, which she employs for selfish, worldly purposes only, there seems
little, if anything, to admire or respect in her character and conduct.

for such a woman, baffles and confounds her. His cold, watchful manner, utterly different from her recollections of Pompey, Cæsar, and Antony, she probably never experienced before.

She surrenders some of her plate, jewels, and treasure, but is betrayed by her steward Seleucus revealing that she yet retains enough to re-purchase all she has offered to Octavius. At this statement Cleopatra's temper is roused for the last time, while she bitterly reproaches Seleucus. During this singular scene, Octavius preserves his usual calmness, speaks politely, and leaves her with the same cold courtesy, yet she perceives from his manner that all her efforts to cajole, charm, or influence him are hopeless, and, remembering the warning words of Proculeius, feels no doubt that he is resolved to lead her a captive through Rome. When convinced of his intention, as well as her utter inability to influence him, she desperately resolves on suicide, and, addressing her devoted attendants, Charmian and Iras, describes in revolting language the public disgrace which surely awaits them in the projected Roman triumph. Both history and Shakespeare state that she then, arrayed in royal robes, perished with her two attendants ; but whether from the bite of an asp or not seems uncertain.* Shakespeare, however, describes a curious conversation between her and an Egyptian peasant, who brings an asp in a basket of fruit, and talks, perhaps, more like an English peasant or labourer than an Oriental. Cleopatra dismisses the man, and, applying two asps to her breast, dies quickly, and almost painlessly, from their poison.†

Octavius, when informed of the event, hastens to the monument, and beholds the remains of the beautiful Egyptian queen. He now owns his late intention of leading her in triumph through Rome, and, ordering her interment beside Antony, which is, perhaps, singular, considering his sister's position, he announces a speedy return to Italy. His words end both this play and that of Julius Cæsar ; but his character is not yet fully developed, and it is scarcely given sufficient prominence, considering his noble position, and equally noble conduct.‡ There seems no doubt that, the older and more powerful he became, the more excellent was

* Merivale, though doubtful about the asp story, says it was generally believed. and that, in the triumphant return of Octavius to Rome, Cleopatra's figure was represented on a couch with the asp clinging to her arm. —*Romans under the Empire.*

† "She from dread of vulgar taunts died—theatrically vain and ease-seeking to the last—the gentlest death she could secure."—FURNIVALL's *Introduction to the Royal Shakespeare.*

‡ Merivale states that when he was emperor, and took the name of Augustus, he "then wiped his blood-stained sword, and became a mild, clement, and noble

his rule, and the more exemplary his conduct.* He returns to Rome after this extraordinary Egyptian campaign, and there, assuming the name of Augustus, ruled gloriously both for himself and his grateful countrymen, who literally worshipped his memory, and deified his name. He consoled and cherished Octavia, who, in the true spirit of Christianity— a religion she was never fated to know—educated and brought up the children of Antony and Cleopatra, and proved herself an example to all the Pagan world.† Her "noble brother," as she terms him, while raising the Roman empire to the highest point of martial strength and glory, encouraged men of genius with the discerning, appreciative liberality of a truly patriotic sovereign. Horace and Virgil both owned and experienced his well-deserved generosity. Worldly power and prosperity seemed only to develop and display, rather than corrupt or enervate, the character of this great ruler, who, practically as wise as the wisest of kings in Scripture, possessed the blessings of this world only to make the best use of them.‡ After a long, happy, and beneficent reign, the inevitable end approached. Then, in a spirit more worthy of that faith which he and his sister never

ruler."—*Romans under the Empire.* " It was reserved for Augustus to relinquish the ambitious design of subduing the whole earth, and to introduce a spirit of moderation into the public councils. Happily for the repose of mankind, the moderate system recommended by the wisdom of Augustus was adopted by the fears and vices of his immediate successors."—GIBBON's *Decline and Fall*, vol. i. The account given by Suetonius (*Lives of the Cæsars*), though dry and unimpassioned, would surely impress any thoughtful reader with the highest admiration for the character and conduct of Augustus.

* Schlegel's opinions of the personages in this play seem strangely at variance both with itself and the Roman history on which it is founded. He says, "As Antony and Cleopatra die for each other, we forgive them for having lived for each other." Antony may have died for Cleopatra, though indirectly ; but surely Cleopatra cannot be said to have died for him. On the contrary, had Octavius admired her as Pompey, Julius Cæsar, and Antony had done, there is every reason to believe he would have been her fourth favourite, and any one repeating her former praises of Antony would, probably, have been again threatened with "bloody teeth" for comparing a dead paramour with her new "man of men." Schlegel also mentions the heartless littleness of Octavius, whom Shakespeare seems to have completely seen through without allowing himself to be led astray by the position and power of Augustus. But what proof does history, Shakespeare, or Schlegel give of "heartless littleness?" Sincere and constant affection for his virtuous sister ; a clemency and moderation which astonished the Roman world, according to Suetonius, Merivale, and Gibbon ; and a long life of pre-eminent wisdom, justice, and glory, surely repudiate this assertion.

† Mrs. Jameson's account of Octavia : *Characteristics of Women*, vol. ii. ; also PLUTARCH's *Life of Antony*.

‡ "He filled the world with wonder, at a moderation which it could not comprehend. With the world at his feet, he began to conceive the real grandeur of his position. He rose to a sense of the awful mission imposed upon him. He became the greatest of Stoic philosophers, inspired with the strongest enthusiasm, and impressed the most deeply with a consciousness of divinity within him. He acknowledged, not less than a Cato or a Brutus, that the man-God must suffer as well as act divinely."—MERIVALE's *Romans under the Empire*, vol. iii.

knew, than of Paganism, he asked his attendants to give him their applause at the last, if they thought he deserved it. How the strange religion of Jupiter could have influenced such characters as Augustus, Octavia, and so many other virtuous Pagans, has often surprised classical students; but that Shakespeare did not make this illustrious brother and sister more prominent in his magnificent play seems very remarkable.*　.For, while self-control, wisdom, and charity are considered the greatest of human qualities, and no writer valued them more highly than did Shakespeare, the unspeakable superiority of this noble pair to the reckless, profligate Antony, and the deceitful woman who caused his ruin, is proved by all impartial history.

* "If ever mortal had a great, serene, well-regulated mind, it was Augustus Cæsar. Mindful of his mortality, he seemed to have thoroughly weighed his ends, and laid them down in admirable order. First, he desired to have the sovereign rule; next, he endeavoured to appear worthy of it; then thought it but reasonable, as a man, to enjoy his exalted fortunes; and lastly, he turned his thoughts to such actions as might perpetuate his name. Hence, in his youth he affected power; in his middle age, dignity; in his decline of life, pleasure; and in his old age, fame and the good of posterity."— BACON'S *Essay on Augustus Cæsar.*

CHAPTER III.

MACBETH.

Sketch of Play.

KING DUNCAN of Scotland, an aged and mild ruler, has two sons, Malcolm and Donaldbain. Macbeth, one of his generals, is heir to the crown after the two princes. He bravely and loyally commands the king's forces against the rebellious Macdonald. Macbeth, with his fellow-general, Banquo, on returning from their victorious campaign, meet three witches on a lonely heath, who inform Macbeth that he will become king of Scotland, and tell Banquo that not he, but his descendants, shall succeed to the Scottish throne. Macbeth is deeply impressed by this disclosure, and writes about it to his wife, while Banquo is less credulous. When these generals meet their gratified old sovereign, he praises and rewards them, and soon after visits Macbeth and his wife at their Castle of Dunsinane. Here Macbeth is induced, partly by her and partly by his own ambition, to murder their royal guest, while they lay the blame alike on Malcolm and Donaldbain, who, horrified at the crime and accusation, escape to England, followed by Macduff, a loyal general of the late king. Banquo is soon after murdered by assassins hired by Macbeth, who now assumes the title of king. The three witches standing round their cauldron, have an interview with the usurper, who visits them when engaged in their mysterious rites, and they invoke apparitions, who assure him he will never be conquered till a certain wood that he knows shall come to his castle, and that no man born of woman shall ever harm him. They refuse, however, to answer more questions, but hint that Banquo's descendants shall hereafter rule not only Scotland, but England and Ireland also. The witches and the apparitions vanish, leaving Macbeth angry and astounded, both excited and alarmed, by these strange intimations. Meanwhile the princes, Malcolm and Donaldbain, obtain English assistance, and invade Scotland with Macduff, whose wife and children were slain by Macbeth, or his followers, during his absence. Lady Macbeth, though incapable of repentance, suffers terribly in mind for all the atrocities which she and her husband have committed. After vaguely intimating, while walking in her sleep, her share in King Duncan's murder, she dies either from suicide or despair, without making any absolute confession; while Macbeth strives, despite his accusing conscience and failing spirits, to resist the princes who, supported by English allies, now attack him. He is slain in single fight by Macduff, who, bearing his head to Prince Malcolm, proclaims him king of Scotland amid general acclamation.

THIS play differs considerably from its historical derivation. Shakespeare closely follows the account of Holinshed; but Sir Walter Scott, who probably knew more of Scottish history, gives a different version of the real events on which the tragedy is founded. King Duncan, his son and successor Malcolm the Third, Macbeth, his wife, and Macduff, were real personages; while Banquo and his son, Fleance, never existed. Yet so many characters and events in this play are real, that it may surely be considered among the historical plays. The scene is almost entirely in Scotland—the land "of purple heather and grey rock"—but none of the personages, except a few in name, have any Scottish characteristic. It has, indeed, been remarked* that Banquo rather resembles a "canny Scot," but neither he nor any of the subordinate persons speak with a Scottish accent, though Shakespeare was acquainted with it.† The ancient Gaelic language is not mentioned, the words Highland and Lowland are only used once, the plaid dress of the country, and its old weapons—dirks and claymores—are never introduced. Were it not for the historical incidents and a few names, the characters and events of this play might be imagined in any European country.

The first act introduces the three witches who take such an important part in the tragedy. In reality Macbeth either saw them in a dream, or may have met three cunning old impostors,‡ who, knowing the prevailing Scottish belief in the power of witchcraft, made money by telling fortunes, and were everywhere believed and dreaded.§ They vanish,

* MR. FURNIVALL's *Introduction to the Royal Shakespeare.*

† *See* King Henry the Fifth, where a Captain Jamy represents Scotland, both in accent and character.

‡ *See* Sir WALTER SCOTT's *History of Scotland,* vol. i.

§ "It has been observed that, while according to the old English creed the witch was a miserable, decrepit hag, the slave rather than the mistress of the demons which haunted her, she in Scotland rose to the dignity of a potent

after a few words announcing their coming interview with Macbeth, and the next scene introduces King Duncan, with his sons and officers, who hear from a wounded captain, and also from Lord Rosse, about the bravery of his two generals, Macbeth and Banquo, in quelling the revolt of the Macdonalds, allied with Norwegian invaders, aided by the Lord of Cawdor, who in another part of Scotland rebelled against Duncan, but was captured and executed.

The king now declares that his loyal general, Macbeth, shall obtain all the titles and property belonging to the treacherous Lord of Cawdor, and the next scene re-introduces the witches on a heath during a thunderstorm.* These beings, in the dream or excited fancy of the real Macbeth, were of lofty stature, and great beauty,† but the vague legends which Shakespeare follows describe them as " withered and weird " in appearance, with beards, said to be the sure sign of a witch‡—otherwise they resembled women, probably, in voice and dress. These three, in their first conversation together, reveal malignant hatred to the human race, as well as their great, yet strangely limited power, and also their complete union in design and thought. One of the witches relates having been refused some chestnuts by a sailor's wife, and vindictively discloses her plan of revenge on the husband, regretfully admitting her limited powers of mischief, which enable her to torment the luckless sailor for a certain time, but not to destroy his vessel :—

> Her husband's to Aleppo gone, master o' the Tiger :
> But in a sieve I'll thither sail,
> And like a rat without a tail,
> I'll do, I'll do, and I'll do.
>   2ND WITCH.   I'll give thee a wind.
>   1ST WITCH.   Thou art kind.
>   3RD WITCH.   And I another.
>   1ST WITCH.   I myself have all the other,
> And the very ports they blow,
> All the quarters that they know.

sorceress who mastered the evil spirit, and, forcing it to do her will, spread among the people a far deeper and more lasting terror."—BUCKLE's *Civilization*, vol. iii.

* Buckle thinks that the Scottish climate and scenery greatly strengthened belief in witchcraft, mentioning "the storms and the mists ; the darkened sky flashed by frequent lightning ; the peals of thunder reverberating from mountain to mountain, and echoing on every side," &c., as marked contrasts to the milder climate and less romantic scenery of England.—*History of Civilization*, vol. iii. Shakespeare, certainly, associates thunder and storms, mists and heath-covered mountains, with these witches, as if such were their natural surroundings.

† SCOTT's *History of Scotland*, vol. i.

‡ STAUNTON's *Notes to Macbeth*.

> I' the shipman's card,
> I will drain him dry as hay :
> Sleep shall neither night nor day
> Hang upon his penthouse lid ;
> He shall live a man forbid :
> Weary sev'n nights, nine times nine ;
> Shall he dwindle, peak, and pine :
> Though his bark cannot be lost,
> Yet it shall be tempest-toss'd.
> Look what I have.
>   2ND WITCH.   Show me, show me.
>   1ST WITCH.   Here I have a pilot's thumb,
> Wreck'd, as homeward he did come.—Act I. Scene III.

Macbeth and Banquo then appear on the heath, perceive and wonder at the three witches, who, disregarding the latter, never speak till their future dupe, Macbeth, addresses them, when they severally greet him as Lord of Glamis, Lord of Cawdor, and future King of Scotland.* Macbeth starts, and shows fear at these words, while Banquo boldly asks about his own fortunes. They mysteriously answer that his descendants, not he, shall reign in Scotland, and seem moving away, for Macbeth entreats them to stay and tell more ; but they vanish, leaving the astonished generals to discuss and ponder over their vague intimations.† Upon Macbeth they make immediate impression, but little, if any, upon Banquo, who is throughout a calm, practical, brave officer, without either the ambition or imagination of Macbeth. The latter is soon after saluted by Duncan's messengers, proclaiming him Lord of Cawdor, thus confirming in his anxious mind a part of the witches' prophecy. The two generals then meet their

* "It is probable that Shakespeare—it is certain that the immense majority even of his most highly-educated and gifted contemporaries—believed with an unfaltering faith in the reality of witchcraft. Shakespeare was, therefore, perfectly justified in introducing into his plays personages who were of all others most fitted to enhance the grandeur and the solemnity of tragedy, when they faithfully reflected the belief of the audience."—LECKY's *Rationalism*, vol. i.

† "For many centuries after Macbeth's period, the power and influence of pretended witches prevailed in Scotland, even among people of comparative education. Witchcraft and demonology, even during the reign of George the Second, were believed in by almost all ranks."—SCOTT's *Heart of Midlothian*, ch. 9. In the *Bride of Lammermoor*, Scott introduces a malevolent hag, called Ailsie Gourlay, stating that she was a historical character, and was charged with having, "by the aids and delusions of Satan, shown to a young person of quality, in a mirror-glass, a gentleman, then abroad, to whom the said person was betrothed, and who appeared in the mirror to be bestowing his hand upon another lady."—ch. 31. This unfortunate impostor was tried and executed by the Scottish Privy Council for alleged witchcraft. Scott adds—"Notwithstanding the dreadful punishments inflicted upon the supposed crime of witchcraft, there wanted not those who, steeled by want and bitterness of spirit, were willing to adopt the hateful and dangerous character for the sake of the influence which its terrors enabled them to exercise in the vicinity, and the wretched emolument which they could extract, by the practice of their supposed art."

old sovereign, who, welcoming them as loyal, valiant subjects, greets them with thanks and compliments, while announcing his approaching visit to Macbeth's castle.

Before they arrive, Lady Macbeth, at her husband's home, hears both of the coming royal visit, and also of the appearance and words of the three witches. Although a bold, ambitious, worldly woman, she from the first believes them, implicit faith in witchcraft and magic being evidently general, if not universal, in Scotland at this period.* She has all her husband's ambition, without a particle of his loyalty to the king, which prevents his following her counsels as speedily and eagerly as she wishes. Directly she hears of the king's visit, she resolves in her own mind that he shall never never leave Macbeth's castle alive. For she thoroughly believes the witches' prediction about her husband's becoming king, and, though they never suggested crime as necessary to accomplish their prophecy, she resolves to persuade Macbeth to remove every obstacle to its fulfilment, by murder or otherwise. It is, perhaps, strange that the idea never occurs to her superstitious mind that probably Duncan and his sons were alike fated to die before Macbeth, which would ensure his lawful as well as predicted accession to the Scottish throne. This hope apparently occurred to Macbeth himself, on first hearing the prophecy, when he exclaimed,

> If chance will have me king, why, chance may crown me,
> Without my stir.—Act I.

But Lady Macbeth, more relentless as well as more ambitious than her husband, immediately conceives the horrible idea of murdering her royal guest, which she urges upon Macbeth, against his will, with the most ruthless determination. Such a crime, involving deliberate regicide, with the most fearful violation of the duties of hospitality, the real Lady Macbeth never contemplated, though a resolute woman, and personally hostile to King Duncan.† Indeed, a crime of this kind, which would horrify Mahometan Arabs of the desert, was wholly inconsistent with the ideas and feelings even of the most savage and ignorant Scottish chieftains.

On Macbeth's arrival home, soon after his wife hears of the royal visit, she congratulates him on his new dignity and promised royalty, immediately suggesting to his agitated, unwilling mind the murder of their guest and sovereign.‡

---

* "The high pretensions of Scotch witchcraft never degenerated, as in other countries, into a mere attempt at deception, but always remained a sturdy and deep-rooted belief."—BUCKLE's *Civilization*, vol. iii.

† SCOTT's *History of Scotland*.

‡ Mrs. Jameson truly says that Lady Macbeth bears less resemblance to her

She is a thoroughly hardened, ambitious woman, resolute and utterly unscrupulous. Her love for Macbeth, upon which so much stress has been laid, seems, when considered in reference to her worldly position and interests, worthy of little, if any, commendation. She knows her fortunes are now linked with his, and that with his increasing power her own will rise proportionately, owing to her influence over him. Shakespeare's noble language alone gives an apparent dignity to a base, shameless character, whose ambition is selfish and worldly. The language with which this hateful woman persuades her brave yet weak husband to slay the king is in Shakespeare's grandest style. The same ideas, methods, and designs expressed in common parlance would surely excite only horror and disgust, with a laudable desire to punish both the temptress and tempted. For there is really nothing redeeming in their thoughts ; nothing palliating in their circumstances ; nothing, in short, to arouse the least sympathy for their conduct in any way. Were they suffering from any sense of real or supposed injustice, or had they any object whatever beyond their ambition and the worldly pleasures expected from its gratification, there would be some reason, even if morally insufficient, for the deep interest, resembling compassion, if not sympathy, with which the Macbeths have been often regarded. But if their expressed thoughts are carefully examined, apart from Shakespeare's splendid language, they are merely a cruel, ungrateful, selfish couple, " choked with ambition of the meaner sort,"* who commit crime after crime without the least provocation, and only for the mean object of obtaining power and wealth, with their attendant pleasures. Yet Lady Macbeth has been represented both on the stage and in essays with a dignity and grandeur almost worthy of Catherine of Aragon, Joan of Arc, or Margaret of Anjou. In truth, she ought to be ranked with Goneril and Regan, the wicked daughters of King Lear ; as, except in her love for Macbeth, with whom her worldly interests are completely involved, she never evinces an unselfish feeling, never utters a single noble sentiment, and seems never inspired by a single generous motive.

Perhaps the most morally affecting scene in the whole play is where Macbeth, while still innocent and not ungrateful to his kind sovereign, almost begs his wife to let him abandon

---

historical prototype than Cleopatra and Octavia to theirs, and is, therefore, more of Shakespeare's own creation. " She revels, she luxuriates in her dream of power."—*Characteristics of Women.* Mrs. Jameson thinks that her ambition is more for her husband's sake than her own ; but surely neither her words nor conduct warrant this assumption.

* *Henry IV.*

the assassination scheme. But she is thoroughly determined, using her influence over him with far more fiendish purpose and success than the witches had attempted to do. For, even after his interview with them, he retains some touch of right feeling, of which she never shows the least sign; and he gradually yields completely to her wishes and persuasion.

MACBETH. We will proceed no further in this business:
He hath honour'd me of late; and I have bought
Golden opinions from all sorts of people,
Which would be worn now in their newest gloss,
Not cast aside so soon.
LADY MACBETH. Was the hope drunk,
Wherein you dress'd yourself? hath it slept since?
And wakes it now, to look so green and pale
At what it did so freely? From this time,
Such I account thy love. Art thou afeard
To be the same in thine own act and valour,
As thou art in desire? Wouldst thou have that
Which thou esteem'st the ornament of life,
And live a coward in thine own esteem?

These and many other such high-sounding words, when spoken by Mrs. Siddons and other great actresses, have apparently invested Lady Macbeth with a grandeur and interest of which her character and conduct are quite undeserving. They might well become a heroine inspiring some craven ally with courage to attempt a daring exploit. In this case, a cruel, hardened woman is urging a brave, ambitious, but not yet thoroughly unscrupulous husband to murder an old, helpless man—their benefactor—while asleep in their house, for the purpose of obtaining his kingdom and possessions.

Lady Macbeth's courage is often mentioned; but, considering the many artful precautions she and her husband take while committing murder in their own castle, surrounded by adherents, and without giving their helpless victims the least chance either of defence or flight, it is not easy to see where they display any courage, except in braving possible consequences. Had not Macbeth's troubled conscience beset him, which his wife always dreaded, but could not entirely foresee, his usurpation of the Scottish throne might have been a permanent success. The young princes had fled the country. Macbeth was both powerful and popular with the army, and all Scotland acknowledged his rule. When tormented not only by his conscience, but by the ghosts of his victims, he was, of course, confounded, amazed, and unable to refute the suspicions which his own nervous fears aroused. Had he been as hardened as his wife, and not troubled by ghosts, his enterprise promised as good a chance of success as any bold usurper would have wished, or at least expected. But neither in the successive murders of King Duncan, his two servants, Banquo, Lady Macduff and her children, is the least sign of courage shown by either Macbeth or his wife. In each case, their safety is nearly as well secured as they could have desired. The old king is slain asleep, while his two attendants, having been drugged into heavy slumber, are also killed, when all three are helpless and unconscious. The gallant Banquo is murdered by two hired armed ruffians, who, had they failed, would never have been believed, if Macbeth disavowed employing them. Lastly, Lady Macduff, a helpless woman, in her husband's absence, with her children, are also slain by hired assassins. Throughout these cowardly atrocities, Macbeth and his wife are exposed to no risk, and yet they exhort, praise, and animate each other, in grand language worthy of a true hero and heroine, which is entirely owing to Shakespeare's genius and fancy, their acts and designs being alike incompatible with true courage or heroic sentiment of any kind. When planning the king's murder, and after its commission, this wicked pair never say a word about the state of Scotland, or express any idea of advancing its prosperity.*

Many assassinations and other crimes have been committed with a vague idea of doing evil that good might ensue. In Macbeth's position, had he or his wife possessed redeeming qualities, they might have believed, or tried to believe, that King Duncan, though their benefactor, yet oppressed or misgoverned their country, and that they would rule the kingdom better. No such idea is ever mentioned : they have no object whatever but to seize the government of Scotland, with its accompanying advantages and anticipated pleasures. For this purpose, Macbeth, though at first reluctant, is induced by his wife to slay the king. He also kills two servants, when asleep ; after which Lady Macbeth stains them with blood, she and her husband pretending that these attendants were induced by Prince Malcolm to kill his father, and that Macbeth slew them, when he discovered they had murdered the king. Shakespeare vividly describes Macbeth as conscience-stricken and horrified before and after the murder. This account is imaginary, as history represents him quite a different man ; while Holinshed's legends, which

---

* " The real Macbeth killed his sovereign Duncan in battle, and not in his own castle, and was a just and equitable ruler."—SCOTT'S *History of Scotland*, vol. i.

are chiefly followed in the play, scarcely mention his state of
mind. Before the king's murder Macbeth's excited fancy
makes him believe himself tempted to commit the crime by
an invisible evil spirit, and he apprehensively exclaims :—

> Is this a dagger which I see before me,
> The handle toward my hand ? Come, let me clutch thee :—
> I have thee not, and yet I see thee still.
> Art thou not, fatal vision, sensible
> To feeling as to sight ? or art thou but
> A dagger of the mind, a false creation,
> Proceeding from the heat-oppressèd brain ?
> . . . . . There's no such thing.—Act II.

Macbeth's reluctance and his wife's desire to commit this
murder are described in Shakespeare's most powerful language. He feebly protests against the crime, but his wife,
after scornfully ridiculing his reluctance, which she thinks a
sort of cowardice, arranges the assassination in her own way,
and thus reveals her plan :—

> When Duncan is asleep
> (Whereto the rather shall his hard day's journey
> Soundly invite him), his two chamberlains
> Will I with wine and wassail so convince,
> That memory, the warder of the brain,
> Shall be a fume, and the receipt of reason
> A limbeck only ; when in swinish sleep
> Their drenched natures lie, as in a death,
> What cannot you and I perform upon
> The unguarded Duncan ? what not put upon
> His spongy officers ; who shall bear the guilt
> Of our great quell ?

Shakespeare's Macbeth is surely not a natural character, and we know he was quite different from the real one.
For he is a brave, loyal officer, who a short time before this
scene had risked his life in King Duncan's service, and been
richly rewarded for his merits. Yet now, on hearing this not
only cruel, but thoroughly base and treacherous plot proposed, he apparently thinks it a proof of his wife's courage,
for he rejoins, in a sort of admiring ecstasy,—

> Bring forth men-children only,
> For thy undaunted mettle should compose
> Nothing but males,

and completely yields to her guidance. But there is surely
nothing "undaunted" in her designs ; for she takes every
precaution against the least possible risk both to herself and

him.   She is evidently meant to be a person of great spirit and daring, but her plot against the king is worthy of the most cowardly assassin who was ever deservedly executed. Shakespeare makes Lady Macbeth confess that, had not Duncan resembled her own father when asleep, she would have slain him herself.   This very slight touch of human feeling has been much commented on, as if it were rather redeeming, yet, if examined, it is surely of very little consequence.   She was about to commit a cruel murder, but fancied the intended victim resembled one of her own family, so preferred to have him killed by another.   Had he resembled any one else, she would have murdered him without scruple.   Immediately after Duncan's murder, Macbeth's nervousness and his wife's utter callousness of spirit are contrasted in Shakespeare's most expressive language :—

> MACBETH.   Methought I heard a voice cry, "*Sleep no more!*
> *Macbeth does murder sleep*,"—the innocent sleep,
> Sleep that knits up the ravell'd sleeve of care,
> The death of each day's life, sore labour's bath,
> Balm of hurt minds, great nature's second course,
> Chief nourisher in life's feast,—
> LADY MACBETH.   What do you mean ?
> MACBETH.   Still it cried, "*Sleep no more!*"—Act. II.

She then scornfully bids him return to the apartment of the slain king, and to stain the attendant grooms with blood. Macbeth, like a terrified child, replies :—

> I'll go no more ;
> I am afraid to think what I have done ;
> Look on't again I dare not.
> LADY MACBETH.   Infirm of purpose !
> Give me the daggers ; the sleeping and the dead
> Are but as pictures : 'tis the eye of childhood
> That fears a painted devil.   If he do bleed,
> I'll gild the faces of the grooms withal ;
> For it must seem their guilt. [*Exit.*]—Act II.

While she is thus employed Macbeth exclaims, in bewildered horror at his crimes :—

> Will all great Nepture's ocean wash this blood
> Clean from my hand ?   No ; this my hand will rather
> The multitudinous seas incardine,
> Making the green one red.—Act II.

After the king's assassination, the Princes Malcolm and Donalbain escape to England and Ireland, Macduff returning to Fife, while Banquo, once intimate with Macbeth, remains in his castle, though no longer in his confidence. On the flight of the princes, Macbeth is proclaimed king, or assumes the title, though it is not clearly shown in the play why the prior rights of Malcolm and Donalbain are not immediately advocated by some of the Scottish chieftains.

Macbeth and Banquo now distrust each other, the latter suspecting the truth ; and the newly-crowned king and queen, guessing his thoughts, resolve to destroy him also. Macbeth, however, accomplishes Banquo's murder without his wife's assistance, by bribing two murderers to slay both him and his son Fleance. These ruffians kill Banquo, but Fleance escapes to England, and there rejoins Prince Malcolm. Macbeth, in full power and unopposed, takes more trouble to effect Banquo's murder than many chiefs equally powerful and unscrupulous woul l have done. Instead of employing devoted adherents to himself—Highland bravos, bullies, or "boys of the belt," as Scott calls them—he summons, addresses, and bribes two strangers, personally hostile to Banquo, who are very poor, unfortunate, and desperate, but not particularly attached to him, and whom he has appaently seen only once before.

> 2ND MURDERER.   I am one, my liege,
> Whom the vile blows and buffets of the world
> Have so incens'd, that I am reckless what
> I do, to spite the world.
> 1ST MURDERER.   And I another,
> So weary with disasters, tugg'd with fortune,
> That I would set my life on any chance,
> To mend it, or be rid on 't.
> KING MACBETH.   Both of you
> Know Banquo was your enemy.
> 2ND MURDERER.   True, my lord.—Act III.

After Banquo's death, Macbeth gives an entertainment to his adherents and followers. At this feast Banquo's ghost appears, visible to him only. He is so terrified that his wife, though herself quite composed, has to send away the guests, wondering at Macbeth's frightened looks and words. Hitherto Lady Macbeth has never shown the least remorse for any of the murders of which she has been either the chief instigator or fully cognizant. But from the first she has been apprehensive about her husband's remorseful terrors, and now becomes utterly confounded at being unable to inspire him with her own consistent hardihood. He recovers spirit, however, when alone with her, and they both remark Macduff's absence from the feast, Macbeth avowing that he has spies employed about the house of every important person. He declares that he will see the witches next day, and apparently guesses where to find them ; but his wife expresses no desire to accompany him, and they retire to rest.

The next scene is again on the witches' heath, where Hecate, their queen, reproves her three subordinates for " trafficking with Macbeth in riddles and affairs of death " during her absence. She then departs, ordering them to meet her next morning at the pit of Acheron, and to have all their spells and charms ready, for Macbeth will certainly visit them then and there, to know his destiny.* She then flies off in a cloud, and the witches, having heard her rebuke in silence, hasten to obey, in evident fear of her superior powers. Why Hecate should rebuke them, and why they are not quite agreed, is unexplained ; but the three have apparently first met Macbeth of their own accord, without asking the terrible "mistress of their charms, the close contriver of all harms, to bear her part, and show the glory of their art." Yet the influence they obtained over Macbeth without Hecate's assistance was apparently complete.

The next scene introduces two Scottish lords, evidently perplexed and alarmed at all the recent horrors in their country, and hardly daring to utter suspicions of the successful usurper, which they intimate rather than avow. They state that Macduff, rejecting Macbeth's late invitation to the palace, where he would probably have met the fate of Banquo, has fled to England, where, with Prince Malcolm, at King Edward's Court, he intends seeking the active assistance of Lord Northumberland—"warlike Siward," a powerful nobleman—for the invasion, or rather liberation, of Scotland.†

After this short but important allusion to real history, the fourth Act opens with the grandest imaginative scene of the whole play. The three witches, now in accord with Hecate, are in a dark cave, around their boiling cauldron, while thunder is heard. They fill it with poisonous herbs, limbs of snakes, toads, and lizards ; also with the liver, nose, and lips of Jews, Tartars, and Turks, while repeating thrice in unison the words,

* Gibbon states that firm belief in magic and witchcraft "reigned in every climate of the globe, and adhered to every system of religious opinion," even since Christianity, and that the nations of the Roman world "dreaded the mysterious power of spells and incantations, of potent herbs and execrable rites, which could extinguish or recall life, inflame the passions of the soul, blast the works of Creation, and extort from the reluctant demons the secret of futurity." —*Decline and Fall*, ch. 29.

† Hume states that old Siward's daughter had been married to the murdered King Duncan. By order of his sovereign, Edward the Confessor, "he marched an army into Scotland, defeated and killed Macbeth in battle, and restored Malcolm to the throne of his ancestors."—*History of England*, ch. 3.

> " Double, double, toil and trouble ;
>   Fire burn, and cauldron bubble."

Although so utterly malignant—even fiendish—in mind and conduct, these hags evince a nominal Christianity, by terming Jews blasphemers, and it seems uncertain if they call them so in mere mockery, or in accordance with the Christian ideas of the period, for of these three unchristian nations the Jews were, even in Shakespeare's time, viewed with peculiar, bitter, and prejudiced dislike. The witches, after boiling their cauldron, pronounce their charm " firm and good," when Hecate appears. She now praises their diligence, telling them to sing round the cauldron, and, promising some indefinite reward, vanishes ; and Macbeth alone enters the cavern, again confronting the three temptresses for the second and last time in his doomed life.*

Macbeth, in this last scene with the witches, likewise acknowledges their malignant power over winds, corn crops, trees and castles, but not over human life. They are now more communicative and triumphant than when they had first met him on the blasted heath of Forres, as their prediction about his being king is so unexpectedly and rapidly fulfilled. For he is now King of Scotland, and, though threatened with English invasion and domestic revolution, his present rule within Scotland is undisputed. His faith in the witches being thoroughly confirmed, he entreats them in desperate language to reveal more of his future fortunes.

> MACBETH.   I conjure you, by that which you profess
> (Howe'er you come to know it), answer me :
> Though you untie the winds, and let them fight
> Against the churches : though the yesty waves
> Confound and swallow navigation up :
> Though bladed corn be lodg'd, and trees blown down :
> Though castles topple on their warders' heads :
> Though palaces, and pyramids, do slope
> Their heads to their foundation : though the treasure
> Of nature's germins tumble altogether,
> Even till destruction sicken, answer me
> To what I ask you.—Act IV.

They ask him, perhaps in mockery, if he had rather be informed by them or by their masters. He chooses the latter, and immediately three apparitions—-of an armed man's head,

* For many centuries after Macbeth's period, belief in witches and witchcraft existed even among the most learned and pious Europeans. In 1484, Pope Innocent VIII. declared that these beings " destroy the births of women and the increase of cattle ; they blast the corn on the ground, the grapes in the vineyards, the fruits of the trees, and the grass and herbs of the field."—DRAPER'S *Intellectual Development of Europe*, ch. 4.

and then two children—the first stained with blood, the second wearing a crown, and with a tree in its hand—address him by name. The first warns him against Macduff, who, since Banquo's death, has often been in Macbeth's mind as his greatest foe. The others console him by declaring severally that none " born of woman " shall harm him, and that he shall never be vanquished till Birnam wood comes to Dunsinane Hill. He knows both places well, and, reassured by these promises, fully believes he will die a peaceful death, and probably after a long and prosperous reign. Still, his jealous fear of the murdered Banquo, increased by the terror inspired by the victim's ghost, disturbs his mind, and he asks if Banquo's descendants will ever rule Scotland. His anxiety upon this point appears strange, for Malcolm and Donalbain are young ; they have a right to the crown before both himself and Banquo, so there is every chance of themselves or their descendants claiming, if not obtaining, their ancestral rights before Banquo's family. The real Macbeth had one son,* but he is never mentioned in the play, nor do the Macbeths ever say who is the person they wish to be their heir. The witches, in reply to Macbeth's question about Banquo's posterity, for the first time seem hostile to his wishes. They tell him to ask no more, while the cauldron sinks into the ground. Macbeth angrily persists, and the witches, then speaking together, summon the figures of eight kings, who silently pass in order before them.

> WITCHES.   Show his eyes, and grieve his heart ;
> Come like shadows, so depart.

After the last figure enters Banquo, who smiles triumphantly at his murderer, while the eighth king carries a glass, in which Macbeth sees many following kings, and some bearing treble sceptres, indicative of the future union of the three kingdoms under one monarch. Macbeth is in bewilderment, while the mocking witches dance round him, vanish, and never appear again. They have, indeed, done their work, and, with a power somewhat like that of Mephistopheles over Faust, have turned a brave, loyal general into a murderous usurper, or, rather, have first inclined him to become such, for his final and more wicked temptress is his wife.† To her the witches never appear ; yet she is practically under their influence far more than her husband. From the moment she hears of their prophecy on Forres heath, she believes it,

---

* SCOTT's *History of Scotland.*

† " Macbeth is excitably imaginative, and his imagination alternately stimulates and enfeebles him. With Lady Macbeth to perceive is forthwith to decide ; to decide is to act."—DOWDEN's *Shakespeare: His Mind and Art.*

urging Macbeth with all the ardour of her resolute spirit to commit a succession of crimes which she thinks necessary for its thorough fulfilment. The witches, though odious and malevolent, hating the whole human race, never suggested murder, or, indeed, any actual crime, to Macbeth's mind ; but he has now become so reckless, hardened, and unscrupulous that each subsequent atrocity seems easier than the last. Accordingly, when the witches vanish, and he hears of Macduff's flight to England, he resolves to slay Lady Macduff and her children. This horrid massacre is thus committed by his direct orders. The hapless lady is only once introduced with her eldest son, a bold, spirited lad, the first of the doomed family, who is slain by hired assassins. For committing this wholesale atrocity there seems little inducement, even to such a villain as Macbeth has now become ; and there is no historical foundation for it in Holinshed's legends. It seems entirely Shakespeare's invention, who thus "on horror's head horrors accumulates." Macduff's children are young—some, probably, girls—yet neither they nor their mother are spared.

After this dreadful event, Shakespeare changes the scene to England, describing a long conversation between Prince Malcolm and Macduff, the latter just arrived. This scene is taken almost literally from Holinshed's account, and, therefore, can hardly be considered Shakespeare's composition.* Malcolm, for some reason which he does not explain, describes himself to Macduff as the most profligate, evil character possible, and then asks if such a person would be fit to rule. Macduff, evidently a brave, straightforward man, not particularly shrewd, believes Malcolm, and passionately bewails the fate of Scotland, thus claimed by a murderous usurper and the vicious young prince beside him. In horrified indignation, Macduff then renounces allegiance to the son of his late sovereign, and contemplates abandoning Scotland, when Malcolm retracts his words, declaring he never meant what he said, and assures his faithful but shocked general that he will follow his guidance, adding that "devilish Macbeth" had often tried in former years to corrupt him. This statement is made by Holinshed, and is once mentioned by Shakespeare, but there is no allusion in the beginning of the play to any such conduct on Macbeth's part. It seems, indeed, inconsistent with his previous character—which was that of a brave and trusted officer of Duncan—to be all the time trying secretly to corrupt the mind of his young heir ; and there seems no foundation for it in history.

* HOWARD STAUNTON'S *Notes to the Illustrated Shakespeare.*

While Macduff is perplexed at Malcolm's sudden retracta-
tion of his self-description, a physician, belonging, probably,
to King Edward's Court, tells Malcolm that many sick people
are waiting to be cured by the touch of the excellent English
monarch called Edward the Saint and Confessor.*   The
beautiful description which Malcolm gives of this virtuous
sovereign to the astonished Macduff is, indeed, a pleasing
change from the guilt and mental misery which this terrible
tragedy contains.

> MALCOLM.   A most miraculous work in this good king :
> Which often, since my here-remain in England,
> I have seen him do.   How he solicits heaven,
> Himself best knows : but strangely-visited people,
> All swoln and ulcerous, pitiful to the eye,
> The mere despair of surgery, he cures ;
> Hanging a golden stamp about their necks,
> Put on with holy prayers : and 'tis spoken,
> To the succeeding royalty he leaves
> The healing benediction.   With this strange virtue,
> He hath a heavenly gift of prophecy ;
> And sundry blessings hang about his throne,
> That speak him full of grace.—Act IV.

Macduff has just heard it, when the dreadful massacre of his
family is announced to him by his cousin, Lord Rosse.   He
is, of course, horrified and infuriated.   Malcolm tries to console him, and, now thoroughly agreeing, the prince and his
two generals repair to King Edward, who, both in the play
and in history, gave them practical assistance in liberating
Scotland from the usurper.

The next act reverts in Scotland, to Dunsinane Castle,
where the guilty Macbeths are preparing to resist the combined invading forces of Malcolm and Siward—the former
commanding Scottish troops with Macduff, the latter heading the English.   Lady Macbeth's resolute mind has now
given way, owing to bodily illness, caused by mental anxiety,
and intense disappointment.   Had Macbeth been from the
first as determined and remorseless as herself, she would
probably have retained her naturally firm, hardened spirit to
the last.   But he is her only weak point, and she knew it.

> Yet I do fear thy nature ;
> It is too full o' the milk of human kindness,

she had exclaimed, after her joy at hearing the witches' pro-

* "Edward, to whom the monks gave the title of Saint and Confessor, was
the first that touched for the king's evil ; the opinion of his sanctity procured
belief to this cure among the people."—HUME'S *History*, ch. 3.

phecy. Ever since the first murder—even just before it—Macbeth had suffered from fits of horror and remorse, of which, while health remained, she appeared incapable. She had vainly tried, after Duncan's murder, which she herself instigated, and also after that of Banquo, to inspire Macbeth with her own callousness of feeling. He obeyed her directions, followed her guidance, and promoted her views with almost frantic energy; but his nature, as she had herself apprehended, he could not make like hers. He was haunted by terrors, anxieties, and fancies, which, while in bodily health, she altogether defied. The result was that his agitated mind soon became unfit to maintain his dangerous position as a successful usurper. Even in his brief time of peaceful triumph, his mind was tormented by the remembrance of Duncan's murder, and by the fearful apparition of Banquo. Now, when really threatened by armed foes, led by his mortal enemies, Malcolm and Macduff, his bold spirit, though roused by new danger, no longer animates a firm, resolute mind. He has become an altered man—moody, violent, and fearful, yet still relying on the vague assurances of the witches about his own personal safety. To see his hopeless dejection, and the utter failure of all hopes of happiness, in the midst of apparent triumph, is, perhaps, the worst punishment which his hardened wife is capable of feeling. She has apparently neither male nor female confidant; her disappointment cannot be safely told to any one; all her energy she has vainly devoted to rouse and animate him, and, failing in these reiterated attempts, her health and mind give way at last. Even then her hard heart prevents her either repenting or seeking consolation from religion or faithful adherents. She does not consult or trust anybody, and her distracted state of mind is finally revealed in sleep, when, walking through her castle with a lighted taper, watched but not understood by either her nurse or physician, she utters a confused soliloquy, and with sighs and groans retires to rest. Her words, even when unconscious, reveal what has really broken her stern spirit more than any crime could have done. It is evidently Macbeth's weakness, as she considers it—his fear and remorse—which, ruining their enterprise, have affected her reason. Her last words appeal to him, though she is still asleep, while her physician and servant vainly try to guess their real meaning.

LADY MACBETH. Fie, my lord, fie! a soldier, and afeard! What need we fear who knows it, when none can call our power to account?—Yet who would have thought the old man to have had so much blood in him! The Thane of Fife had a wife; where is she now?

What, will these hands ne'er be clean ?—No more o' that, my lord,
no more o' that : you mar all with this starting.   Wash your hands,
put on your night-gown ; look not so pale :—I tell you yet again,
Banquo's buried ; he cannot come out of his grave.   To bed, to bed ;
there's knocking at the gate.   Come, come, come, come, give me
your hand.   What's done cannot be undone ; to bed, to bed, to bed.
                                                              [*Exit.*

> PHYSICIAN.   Foul whisperings are abroad : unnatural deeds
> Do breed unnatural troubles : infected minds
> To their deaf pillows will discharge their secrets.
> More needs she the divine than the physician.
> God, God forgive us all !   Look after her ;
> Remove from her the means of all annoyance,
> And still keep eyes upon her.—Act IV.

Not a word of pity for her and her husband's victims
escapes her ; no sign of contrition or of tenderness towards
any one, or the least token of religious feeling.   Her words
convey merely a vague terror at being unable to efface blood-
stains from her hands, while dreamily reiterating her previous entreaties to her absent husband to show neither fear,
remorse, nor agitation.   Her despair at Macbeth's incurable
terrors, and at the consequent failure of her ambitious hopes
and plans, have finally destroyed her strength of mind, and,
with it, her bodily health.   She is thenceforth " troubled with
thick-coming fancies, that keep her from her rest," so her
doctor states to Macbeth.   The latter briefly urges him to
quiet her, if possible ; while he fears that he himself is likewise threatened with a similar state of mental despair, which
he has hitherto somewhat resisted, owing to excitement from
the coming war.

> MACBETH.   Cure her of that ;
> Canst thou not minister to a mind diseas'd :
> Pluck from the memory a rooted sorrow ;
> Raze out the written troubles of the brain ;
> And, with some sweet oblivious antidote,
> Cleanse the stuff'd bosom of that perilous stuff,
> Which weighs upon the heart ?—Act V.

To this passionate appeal—which would have been more suit-
ably addressed to a clergyman, or trusted friend, than to a
medical man—the doctor, who does not pretend to understand the workings of a guilty conscience, calmly replies :

> Therein the patient
> Must minister to himself.

Macbeth's bold spirit, roused and perhaps relieved by the thoughts of coming battle, fiercely rejoins :

> Throw physic to the dogs, I'll none of it.—
> Come, put mine armour on ; give me my staff.

Lady Macbeth soon after either commits suicide—as the doctor had before apprehended, and which is vaguely intimated—or dies from the effects of despair. Meanwhile, Macbeth is distracted between his ever-tormenting conscience and his exertions to inspirit his army against the advancing foe. He is terribly excited, not trusting his followers— many of whom secretly incline to Prince Malcolm—and often repeats the encouraging assurances he heard from the apparitions in the witches' cavern. He is told of his wife's death, while preparing to defend his castle against Malcolm. The fatal news has a strange effect on his troubled mind, now perplexed and excited to the last degree, though not yet in despair. He first exclaims, " She should have died hereafter " —when the coming enemy should have been defeated, which he still expects, and his power confirmed. The fact that her strong spirit is gone, that her voice will never more animate his courage, or rouse his ambition, plunges his mind into a brief yet wise reflection on the shortness and uncertainty of human life.

> MACBETH.   To-morrow, and to-morrow, and to-morrow,
> Creeps in this petty pace from day to day,
> To the last syllable of recorded time :
> And all our yesterdays have lighted fools
> The way to dusty death.   Out, out, brief candle !
> Life's but a walking shadow ; a poor player,
> That struts and frets his hour upon the stage,
> And then is heard no more : it is a tale
> Told by an idiot, full of sound and fury,
> Signifying nothing.—Act V.

Yet neither his character nor position permit him to indulge long in such reflections. He is now startled by the strange news that his enemies have cut down Birnam Wood, and are advancing, with its branches in their hands, upon the castle. He storms at the messenger of this unwelcome news, and begins for the first time to distrust the witches. Still he clings resolutely to his last hope—that none of woman born should vanquish him—and prepares for a desperate defence. In the midst of his military preparation and bold defiances, he owns both to his follower, Lord Seyton, and to himself that he is now weary of life, while exerting all his remaining energies of mind and body to defend it.

> MACBETH.   I have liv'd long enough : my way of life
> Is fallen into the sere and yellow leaf :
> And that which should accompany old age,
> As honour, love, obedience, troops of friends,
> I must not look to have ; but, in their stead,
> Curses, not loud but deep, mouth-honour, breath,
> Which the poor heart would fain deny, and dare not.—Act V.

When attacked by his united English and Scotch foes, he kills Siward, the brave son of Northumberland, in single fight, thereby strengthening his fond belief that no man shall slay him. Macduff vainly seeks him for some time, longing for vengeance on the murderer of his family. Just before they meet, Macbeth for the first time mentions suicide contemptuously, his passions being now thoroughly roused by the conflict. He scornfully alludes to the " Roman fools " who have thus ended their lives, and furiously declares that while he sees living foes " the gashes do better upon them." When uttering these words, Macduff meets and defies him. The furious tyrant at first rather shrinks from the encounter, telling his injured enemy that he bears a charmed life, which none born of woman can destroy. Macduff undauntedly bids him to distrust his charm, for that he who now challenges him to mortal combat was from his mother's womb " untimely ripp'd." This news for the moment quells Macbeth's spirit as much, though from a different cause, as when he trembled and grieved after Duncan's murder. He has now no longer his determined wife beside him to animate his courage. His brave foe, however, seeing his despair, and unwilling apparently to take unfair advantage of it, scornfully threatens him with being publicly paraded as a cruel monster, if he yields. This bitter taunt immediately rouses his passions, and Macbeth, in a last access of fury, defies his foe, with a desperate curse on whichever of them should yield. He is slain by his destined conqueror, who bears his head—according to the savage custom of the times, and even of more recent ones—to the nominal victor, Prince Malcolm, whom, in the presence of Northumberland and many Scottish noblemen, Macduff proclaims King of Scotland.

It is remarkable that even to the end of this play no one save Macbeth, his wife, and Banquo seem personally to know about the appearance of the witches. The fact of Macbeth's being literally " bewitched " and utterly changed from his former self is seldom mentioned. At the beginning of the play, he is termed "valiant cousin," "worthy gentleman," " noble Macbeth," &c., by Duncan, who rewards his loyal bravery with titles and honours : while his son and Macduff soon after have ample reason to term him, "This fiend of Scotland," "Hellhound," "Worse than any name," "This dead butcher and his fiend-like queen," &c. Yet little surprise is shown by Malcolm or any of the Scottish chiefs at the almost miraculous change in Macbeth's conduct and character.

King Malcolm's words end this play, inviting all present to his approaching coronation at Scone, and mentioning the rumour, which he apparently believes, of Lady Macbeth's suicide. Throughout this tragedy Malcolm is seldom introduced, but all he says and does proclaim him a sensible and virtuous prince, which his subsequent conduct as king fully proved.* His friendship with the excellent King of England, Edward the Confessor, and his liking for English ways, manners, and customs—then, probably, more civilized than those of Scotland—raised him far above the fierce, turbulent thanes and chiefs of that country, whom he appears to have ruled with justice, wisdom, and success.

* Scott's *History of Scotland*, ch. 3.

CHAPTER IV.

KING JOHN.

Sketch of Play.

ALTHOUGH King John began his reign in England unopposed, King Philip of France immediately espouses the cause of Prince Arthur, son of John's elder brother, Geoffrey. The first scene opens with Philip's imperious demand, by the voice of his ambassador, Count Chatillon, that John should yield up not only England, but Ireland also, with some French provinces then held by the English, to Arthur. This demand John refuses, and war is therefore declared. After some fighting, a peace is arranged between England and France, which is, however, prevented by the arrival of Cardinal Pandulf from Pope Innocent III., insisting that John should acknowledge Stephen Langton, Archbishop of Canterbury.   This also John refuses, and, Pandulf forbidding the French king to make peace with him, war is resumed. During this contest, Arthur is captured by John, who intends putting him secretly to death ; but the prince is killed while attempting to escape from prison.   Nothing, however, being known for certain about Arthur's fate, many English nobles demand his liberation, and the whole country revolts against John.   The Pope lays England under an interdict, and the French Dauphin, son of King Philip, invades it.   He is joined by a number of English, who detest the king, while Pope Innocent absolves his subjects from their allegiance.   John, beset with enemies and dangers, submits completely to the Pope, and soon after falls ill, having been, as some suppose, poisoned by a monk, as he had insulted, plundered, and irritated the clergy to such a degree as to make this idea generally believed.   He dies while hearing from his illegitimate nephew, Falconbridge, about the loss of many of his troops by sudden floods ; and his son, Prince Henry, is proclaimed king.   During this play, John's mother, Queen Elinor, and his sister-in-law, Constance, Arthur's mother, evince bitter hostility to each other.   Their characters, as well as conflicting interests, may be derived from history—Elinor's especially—though this tragedy seems rather more founded on a former play of the same name than on historical records.* It yet represents many of the chief characters and incidents, in accordance with what was generally known and believed respecting them. Prince Arthur, however, was in reality much older and more bold than the modest, even timid, boy in the play.

SHAKESPEARE'S earliest allusion to English history is in Macbeth, when mentioning Edward the Confessor, and rather more than a hundred and fifty years of his country's history had elapsed before the great poet again describes it. During this interval, the Norman rule over England and part of Ireland had been commenced and was thoroughly confirmed. Six French or Norman kings had reigned and disappeared, and the seventh, King John, was now ruling over England—his mother, Elinor, assisting him with her counsel, favour, and experience. She was, from all accounts, a woman of uncommon spirit and resolution, and her fierce temper instantly resents the haughty language of the French envoy when terming her favourite son's regal power " borrowed majesty." John, who, amid all his evil qualities, always loved her as much as he was capable of loving any one, begs her to be silent, while he returns a defiant answer to the equally defiant words of the French king. After Chatillon departs, Elinor lays all the blame of Philip's hostility on the ambition of her hated daughter-in-law, Constance, now with her son Arthur at the Court of France.

> QUEEN ELINOR. What now, my son ? have I not ever said,
> How that ambitious Constance would not cease,
> Till she had kindled France, and all the world,
> Upon the right and party of her son ?
> KING JOHN. Our strong possession, and our right, for us.
> ELINOR. Your strong possession much more than your right ;
> Or else it must go wrong with you and me :
> So much my conscience whispers in your ear ;
> Which none but Heaven, and you, and I, shall hear.—Act I.

John, while contemplating an attack on France, reveals his plan for plundering the monasteries and abbey lands of England, to " pay this expedition's charge." This scheme, despite great opposition, he strove to accomplish, with the fatal obstinacy of his strange character.

* " The Troublesome Reign of King John."—*See* H. STAUNTON's remarks in his edition of Shakespeare ; also, Mr. FURNIVALL's *Notes to the Royal Shakspere.*

In the next scene there occurs a curious dispute between two half-brothers, which is brought before King John and his mother, who, somewhat like modern judges, hear and decide the case. The disputants bear the name of Falconbridge. The elder was disinherited by his supposed father, who declared his belief to the younger that his brother was a son of the late King Richard Cœur-de-Lion. This case greatly interests Elinor and John, for they recognize in the gallant bearing, noble figure, and frank manner of Philip Falconbridge their late son and brother, whom Elinor always loved, and to whom John had every reason to be grateful for unmerited generosity. They well know that no danger to their power could arise from a bastard relative ; that the bar sinister prevents the least chance of rivalry more than perhaps anything else could do; and yet Richard I. in many ways again stands before them—young, respectful, and completely devoted to their interests. Such a valuable friend and adherent is, indeed, precious at this time, when they are threatened by the chivalrous French king espousing the rightful cause of the injured Prince Arthur. Accordingly, John knights Philip Falconbridge by the name of Sir Richard Plantagenet, while Elinor, greeting him yet more eagerly, calls herself his grandmother, and asks him to call her so.

> QUEEN ELINOR. I am thy grandame, Richard ; call me so.
> BASTARD. Madam, by chance, but not by truth : what though ?
> Something about, a little from the right,
> In at the window, or else o'er the hatch.—Act I.

The young knight respectfully demurs, with the singular modesty and frankness which mark his peculiarly interesting character, and prepares to accompany the king and queen-mother to France, while cheerfully congratulating his younger brother on obtaining his father's lands, which was the cause of their dispute ; for the bastard is now a "landless knight," while his brother is a "landed squire." He then announces this change to his mother, Lady Falconbridge, who, on hearing it, admits that he is her son by the late king.

Act II. changes to France, where King Philip, allied with the Archduke of Austria, and accompanied by his son, the Dauphin Lewis, are assembled, together with the Princess Constance and her son Arthur. These three foreign princes now unite in hatred to King John, and in the wish to obtain for Arthur his royal rights.* It is certain, however, that

---

* Bishop Wordsworth, in his notes to *Shakespeare's Historical Plays*, says that King John was not considered a usurper of his nephew's rights at this period ; and adds, "John was bad enough, without having to bear the blame of faults which were not his."

Philip's own interests chiefly incline him to this policy ; for then John ruled several French provinces, some—perhaps all —of which the former would probably claim and receive from Arthur, in return for his assistance in case of success. Philip is throughout a chivalrous, yet very politic prince, and was, indeed, one of the wisest kings who ever occupied the French throne.* His envoy, Chatillon, announces the landing of John, with the undaunted queen-mother, her niece the Princess Blanche, and also the newly-knighted Richard Plantagenet, with other English noblemen and officers, whom he calls "rash, inconsiderate, fiery volunteers." The two kings, with their respective allies, relations, and adherents, then meet, exchanging angry defiances, during which Philip again charges John with usurping Arthur's rights. The rival queen and princess, Elinor and Constance—both proud, ambitious, and devoted to their respective son's conflicting interests— reproach each other bitterly, the bastard Richard rather diverting himself by ridiculing and taunting the proud, dull Austrian Archduke, whose base treatment of his father, Cœur-de-Lion, he now resents, and finally avenges.† In this scene, Queen Elinor mentions having a will, which she declares would bar Arthur's right of succession, and this Constance scornfully denies.

    Queen Elinor.   Come to thy grandame, child.
    Constance.   Do, child ; go to it grandame, child ;
Give grandame kingdom, and it grandame will
Give it a plum, a cherry, and a fig :
There's a good grandame.
    Prince Arthur.   Good my mother, peace !
I would that I were low laid in my grave ;
I am not worth this coil that's made for me.
    Elinor.   His mother shames him so, poor boy, he weeps.
    Constance.   Now shame upon you, whe'r she does, or no !
His grandame's wrongs, and not his mother's shames,
Draw those heaven-moving pearls from his poor eyes,
Which heaven shall take in nature of a fee ;
Ay, with these crystal beads heaven shall be brib'd
To do him justice, and revenge on you.
    Elinor.   Thou monstrous slanderer of heaven and earth !
    Constance.   Thou monstrous injurer of heaven and earth !
Call not me slanderer ; thou, and thine, usurp

---

* " No prince comparable to him in systematic ambition and military enterprise had reigned in France since Charlemagne. From his reign the French monarchy dates the recovery of its lustre."—Hallam's *Middle Ages*, vol. i.

† Bishop Wordsworth states that the Austrian Archduke who imprisoned Richard I. died before this time, and his introduction, therefore, was a mistake, and borrowed by Shakespeare from the old play, *The Troublesome Reign of King John.*

The dominations, royalties, and rights
Of this oppressed boy.
   ELINOR.   Thou unadvised scold, I can produce
A will, that bars the title of thy son.
   CONSTANCE.   Ay, who doubts that? a will! a wicked will;
A woman's will; a cankered grandame's will!
   KING PHILIP.   Peace, lady; pause, or be more temperate.—
Act II.

This document, however, was the late King Richard's second will, who appears to have desired John's succession in preference to his nephew, though surely he had no more right than any other English monarch to name a successor contrary to law.*

The angry language which Elinor and Constance use, though coarse and abusive, seems consistent enough with the fierce, violent temper of the old queen; while history says little about Constance, whose injurious reproaches Elinor seems to have somewhat deserved, though peculiarly irritating to hear from her own daughter-in-law.† Philip silences them, in words rather too abrupt and rude for a polished French monarch—" Women and fools, break off your conference "—and a battle begins between the French and English armies, when John's devoted Norman follower, Hubert de Burgh, proposes a peace, by marrying the Dauphin Louis to the Princess Blanche, John agreeing to create Arthur Duke of Bretagne, and to give him French territory now held by England. This plan, which, perhaps, might, under the circumstances, have been a happy one, is warmly denounced by Constance (Act II.), who will be satisfied with nothing less than the restitution of her son's rights, and the consequent deposition of the reigning English king. In vain, Philip of France tries to reconcile her to the project. She wildly appeals to his sense of honour, while scornfully reproaching

* Hume states that Richard I. made two wills—the first declaring Arthur his heir, the second naming John instead, which change he considers was probably caused by Queen Elinor, who really hated Constance as vehemently as represented in this play. Hume adds—" The authority of a testament was great in that age, even where the succession to a kingdom was concerned."—*History of England*, vol. i. ch. I.

† According to Hume, Queen Elinor's antecedents were little fitted to bear severe handling. She was married when very young to Lewis VII. of France, and went on a crusade with him to Syria, where, being suspected of "gallantry with a handsome Saracen," Lewis divorced her, and she then, about six weeks after, married Prince Henry of England, afterwards Henry II., though much older than he. She " who had disgusted her first husband by her gallantries was no less offensive to her second by her jealousy, and after this manner carried to extremity, in the different periods of her life, every circumstance of female weakness."—*History of England*, vol. i. Shakespeare's account of her rather agrees with history. Her strong affection for her son John, however, was constant, and sincerely returned by him, during his troubled reign, while living together in perpetual danger and insecure power.

the Austrian Archduke for, as she thinks, abandoning her son's cause.

In the midst of this violent scene, a new personage appears, destined to take a very decided part both in history and in the play. This is Cardinal Pandulf, sent by Pope Innocent III. to insist upon King John's allowing Stephen Langton to be installed Archbishop of Canterbury.* Pandulf, evidently a resolute and conscientious man, occupies, amid these fierce kings and their warlike followers, a singularly grand position.† Yet his imperious demand irritates John more than all the passionate reproaches of Constance, and he replies by angrily denouncing not only the Pope's right to appoint bishops in England, but also his spiritual supremacy generally. This language John probably neither used nor wished to use, and in his position, unassisted by theologians and unsupported by public opinion, it would have been to no purpose ; for at this time few, if any, in England would have approved his words, except the Jews, to whom he certainly never thought of appealing, save to obtain money, occasionally by force or torture. The French king, shrewd and politic, is shocked at the words of his royal brother ; while Pandulf, without condescending to argument, threatens John with excommunication. In this menace he is eagerly joined by the vehement Constance, who passionately declares that unless her wrongs are considered, "no tongue hath power to curse him right." The cardinal, rather embarrassed, if not scandalized, at the vehemence of this eager ally, gravely assures her that "there is law and warrant" for *his* curse, thus drawing a marked, important distinction between the Papal malediction he pronounces in due form and the violent wrath of this enraged princess. It is evident that the Pope had no idea of denying John's right to the English Crown, or of acknowledging Prince Arthur, which, perhaps, was a great disappointment to Constance, and a surprise to the French king. However, John's obstinacy in resisting the Pope's

---

* Both Mr. Stubbs and Mr. Green, in their recent English histories, agree with Hume in praising this excellent prelate, whose high character and attainments were evidently appreciated by Pope Innocent, but were no recommendations to King John's favour.

† Macaulay's remarks, though probably intended for previous reigns to that of King John, seem still applicable to his period :—"The childhood of the European nations was passed under the tutelage of the clergy. The ascendency of the sacerdotal order was long the ascendency which naturally and properly belongs to intellectual superiority. The priests, with all their faults, were by far the wisest portion of society. It was, therefore, on the whole, good that they should be respected and obeyed."—MACAULAY'S *History of England*, vol. i. Mr. Green makes similar remarks respecting English public feeling during King John's reign, which he says decidedly supported Pandulf in his conduct to John. —*History of the English People*, vol. i.

authority immediately renews war between France and England, Pandulf all the time denouncing John, while carefully abstaining from favouring Arthur's claims.   During this war, Arthur is captured by John, who commits him to the charge of Hubert de Burgh.   This man—brave, trusty, and quite devoted to him—John resolves shall be the instrument for destroying his nephew, and, accordingly, has a private interview with this adherent, in which he states his fears of the Prince, and suggests his murder with nervous eagerness.

> KING JOHN.   Good Hubert, Hubert, Hubert, throw thine eye
> On yon young boy : I'll tell thee what, my friend,
> He is a very serpent in my way ;
> And wheresoe'er this foot of mind doth tread
> He lies before me : dost thou understand me ?
> Thou art his keeper.
> HUBERT.   And I'll keep him so,
> That he shall not offend your majesty.
> KING JOHN.   Death.
> HUBERT.   My lord ?
> KING JOHN.   A grave.
> HUBERT.   He shall not live.
> KING JOHN.   Enough.
> I could be merry now : Hubert, I love thee.
> Well, I'll not say what I intend for thee :
> Remember.—Act III. Scene III.

His language to Hubert greatly differs from Macbeth's words to the hired assassins, though each murderous king speaks with a like design.   John evidently longs for Arthur's death, yet hesitates as to how he could be safely disposed of, he himself being most unpopular in England ; for nobles, clergy, and people dislike him, and he knows it.* If, therefore, it were known that Arthur was murdered by him, the result might be as dangerous to him as the prince's escape.   History and Shakespeare apparently agree in this, for though Arthur was supposed to be slain by John's own hand,† yet his fate was never known for certain ; while Shakespeare makes the unscrupulous king tempt Hubert to slay him with eager, nervous, yet artful entreaties, appealing alike to his love, gratitude, and self-interest.‡   Hubert, gratified by John's confidence, listens

---

* "King John trusted no man, and no man trusted him."—STUBBS's *Constitutional History*, vol. i.   Yet Shakespeare makes him place great confidence in his illegitimate nephew, Richard Plantagenet ; but for this there appears no historical foundation.

† HUME's *History*, vol. i.

‡ "He trembles lest he should have said too much ; he trembles lest he should not have said enough ; at last the nearer fear prevails, and the words, 'Death,' 'A grave,' form themselves upon his lips.   Having touched a spring which will produce assassination, he furtively withdraws himself from the mechanism of crime."—DOWDEN's *Shakespeare's Mind and Art*, ch. iv.

respectfully, and satisfies the anxious king that his young rival shall "not live," without actually naming assassination.

The next scene introduces the unfortunate Constance, grieving for her captured child before King Philip and Cardinal Pandulf. She evidently expects the worst, for she never solicits the French monarch's power nor the cardinal's influence in behalf of her son, but considers him already dead, and despairingly declares she shall never see him again. Though Constance, in utter despair, wishes herself dead, she never hints at suicide, which some people have committed from less mental misery than she wildly expresses. The cardinal, who has doubtless beheld deep sorrow in many forms during his ecclesiastical life, and often known it to lead to religious seclusion, is evidently surprised at her frantic language, and exclaims,—

> Lady, you utter madness, and not sorrow.
> CONSTANCE.   Thou art not holy to belie me so ;
> I am not mad : this hair I tear is mine ;
> My name is Constance ; I was Geoffrey's wife ;
> Young Arthur is my son, and he is lost ;
> I am not mad ;—I would to heaven I were !
> For then 'tis like I should forget myself :
> O, if I could, what grief should I forget !—
> .   .   .   .   .
> I am not mad ; too well, too well I feel
> The different plague of each calamity.

Then, when Pandulf calmly observes—

> You hold too heinous a respect of grief,

the bereaved mother almost proudly replies—

> He talks to me that never had a son.

Neither Philip nor Pandulf can offer much consolation, though the former attempts it ; while the cardinal soon after has a remarkable interview with the Dauphin Louis, who loves the Princess Blanche, and is beloved by her.

The observant cardinal foresees Arthur's death by the order of John, with whom all the clergy are more displeased than ever, as he has empowered his reckless nephew, Richard, to plunder the English abbeys and monasteries. This strange commission Richard was executing with the eager impetuosity of his fiery nature ; but it was in every way a most impolitic act, as it irritated the clergy, without apparently conciliating or pleasing any section of the king's subjects. Pandulf, knowing the popular discontent, urges Louis to invade England with a French force, believing he would soon be joined by numbers of John's disaffected subjects. In this belief he was right, for at present the Normans, now paramount in England, considered themselves almost Frenchmen, despising the subjected Saxons, who, in their turn, hated John's Norman origin as well as his character.* Louis agrees to this proposal, and they then consult King Philip, who was, indeed, well qualified both in character and position to direct any such enterprise.

The next act (IV.) opens, perhaps, with the most pathetic scene in the whole play. It has, however, no historical foundation, though Arthur's mysterious disappearance might well cause, if not justify, any sad story about him. Hubert de Burgh, with two attendants, tells the little captive that he has orders to blind him, while Arthur, represented as a quiet, melancholy child, entreats him to forbear. Hubert shows him a warrant, apparently for this horrid object, but it was never mentioned by John in his interview with the former, though the king, indeed, clearly intimated that nothing short of the prince's death would serve his purpose, or make his throne secure. Arthur, however, pleads so eloquently that Hubert relents, and does him no injury, despite his grateful attachment to the king.

The following scene introduces John being crowned a second time before several dissatisfied, murmuring English noblemen, who, uneasy at Arthur's imprisonment, now demand his liberation. John is forced to answer them more mildly than he wishes, owing to the general discontent, which, with a threatened French invasion, make his rule very insecure. He promises to release Arthur, when Hubert, entering secretly, informs him of the prince's death, which John then announces to the indignant noblemen, some of whom vaguely hint at insurrection, and leave his presence. John, not having the courage of his brave family, and knowing his unpopularity with clergy, nobility, and commons,

* " It is certain that when John became king, the distinction between Saxon and Norman was strongly marked, and that before the end of the reign of his grandson it had almost disappeared. In the time of Richard I., the ordinary imprecation of a Norman gentleman was, 'May I become an Englishman !' His ordinary form of indignant denial was, ' Do you take me for an Englishman ? ' The descendant of such a gentleman, a hundred years later, was proud of the English name."—MACAULAY'S *History of England*, vol. i. ch. i. This passage well explains the different position of the French in this play from what they occupy in Shakespeare's other historical plays, describing a later period, as more than the century which Macaulay mentions elapsed between King John's death and Richard II.'s accession, whose reign is the next that Shakespeare presents in historical course.

suddenly regrets authorizing Arthur's death, not from humanity, but from fears for his own life, which he now thinks would be safer had the prince been kept in close captivity, or well guarded. While he is in great agitation, news is brought of the coming invasion, headed by the Dauphin Louis. He eagerly asks after his mother, Elinor, who had remained in France, representing his power and devoted to his interests, but hears of her unexpected death.

> KING JOHN. Where is my mother's care,
> That such an army could be drawn in France,
> And she not hear of it?
> MESSENGER. My liege, her ear
> Is stopped with dust; the first of April, died
> Your noble mother.
> KING JOHN. Withhold thy speed, dreadful occasion!
> O, make a league with me, till I have pleas'd
> My discontented peers!—What! mother dead?
> How wildly, then, walks my estate in France!—Act IV.

His dismay is at its height, for Elinor seemed to combine in herself the courage of his elder brother, Cœur-de-Lion, with a shrewdness which neither Richard nor he possessed, and these qualities she, even in old age, devoted to his cause.[*]

He suffers at this moment from as much sorrow and regret as his hardened nature is capable of, but these emotions never soften his heart, for, while still grieving at the fatal news, his nephew, Richard brings him, as a prisoner, a certain eccentric hermit, called Peter of Pomfret, who, perhaps, reckoning on John's unpopularity, as well as upon his quarrel with the Pope, had rashly foretold that on next Ascension Day John should yield up his crown. The king, in vicious anger, apparently unchecked by law or remonstrance, orders his faithful officer, Hubert, to have Peter executed on the very day he had named, and to keep him imprisoned till these cruel orders were carried out.[†] Richard then tells John of the secret suspicions now rife among the nobility about Arthur's death by his order, and the perplexed king instantly sends him with soothing messages to them, being dismayed at the double dangers impending—of domestic revolt and foreign invasion. Hubert has a private interview with his distracted, guilty sovereign, in which he describes the increasing anger of the people, and their indignation at the suspected murder of Arthur. Shakespeare, in-

---

[*] "King John had in his mother, Queen Elinor, though near eighty, a counsellor of much experience in continental politics, of great energy, and devoted faithfulness."—STUBBS'S *Constitutional History*, vol. i.

[†] HUME'S *History*, vol. i.

stead of introducing a scene among the lower classes—which
he could have done so admirably, and would have been an
interesting change—makes Hubert describe them with a
graphic power that effectually terrifies the nervous king.

> HUBERT.   Young Arthur's death is common in their mouths :
> And when they talk of him, they shake their heads,
> And whisper one another in the ear ;
> And he that speaks doth gripe the hearer's wrist ;
> Whilst he that hears makes fearful action,
> With wrinkled brows, with nods, with rolling eyes.
> I saw a smith stand with a hammer, thus,
> The whilst his iron did on the anvil cool,
> With open mouth swallowing a tailor's news,
> Who, with his shears and measure in his hand,
> Standing in slippers (which his nimble haste
> Had falsely thrust upon contrary feet),
> Told of a many thousand warlike French,
> That were embattled and rank'd in Kent :
> Another lean unwashed artificer
> Cuts off his tale, and talks of Arthur's death.
>   KING JOHN.   Why seek'st thou to possess me with these fears?
> Why urgest thou so oft young Arthur's death ?—Act IV.

John's stern yet sensitive nature is curiously revealed in
this scene. He believes that Hubert has already slain
Arthur by his orders, and, completely overcome by grief
and terror—the former caused by his mother's death, the
latter by his own perils—he tries, in nervous, petulant anger,
more like that of a fretful child than a man, to lay the
blame of Arthur's supposed murder on Hubert's too eager
obedience to his vague intimations.*

Hubert's personal appearance was what is commonly
called "against him," or, as Charles Dickens wittily remarks of an imaginary personage, " he might have brought
an action against his face for defamation of character, and
recovered heavy damages." John, knowing that Hubert is
wholly in his power, owing to his devotion to himself, and

* Macaulay terms John "a trifler and a coward."—*History of England*, ch. 1.
In this scene he certainly merits both appellations, yet during his eventful life he
displayed considerable energy. Shakespeare's account of him in age—moody,
suspicious, fearful, and violent by turns—resembles Scott's description in *Ivanhoe*,
when a petulant young prince, " flushing with the pride of a spoilt child," tempting, flattering, and irritating his best friends, and thus often losing all influence
over them.   Hume's account (vol. i.) is, if possible, more odious and contemptible
than those of the poet or the novelist. A more recent historian, however,
declares that, " with all his vices, he yet possessed all the quickness, vivacity,
cleverness, good humour, and social charm which distinguished his House," and
that he was the ablest prince of his family.—GREEN'S *History of the English
People*, ch. 1.

to his having doubtless made many enemies in consequence, has the final meanness to reproach him with it,
having previously tried to lay all the blame of Arthur's suspected assassination upon him.

> KING JOHN.   Thy hand hath murder'd him : I had a mighty
>   cause
> To wish him dead, but thou hadst none to kill him.
>   HUBERT.   No had, my lord ! why, did you not provoke me ?
>   KING JOHN.   It is the curse of kings, to be attended
> By slaves that take their humours for a warrant
> To break within the bloody house of life ;
> And, on the winking of authority,
> To understand a law.—Act IV.

Then Hubert, with steady calmness, shows the guilty monarch
his "hand and seal."   The sight of this apparently forgotten
document completes, for the moment, John's mental pros-
tration.

> KING JOHN.   O, when the last account 'twixt Heaven and earth
> Is to be made, then shall this hand and seal
> Witness against us to damnation !
> How oft the sight of means to do ill deeds
> Makes ill deeds done !   Hadst thou not been by,
> A fellow by the hand of nature mark'd,
> Quoted, and sign'd, to do a deed of shame,
> This murder had not come into my mind :
> But, taking note of thy abhorr'd aspect,
> Finding thee fit for bloody villainy,
> Apt, liable, to be employ'd in danger,
> I faintly broke with thee of Arthur's death ;
> And thou, to be endeared to a king,
> Made it no conscience to destroy a prince.—Act IV.

Yet even then the fiery spirit of his family soon rouses him
from depression to rage, and he orders Hubert away at once,
which touches with compassion, instead of irritating, his
faithful adherent, who is, indeed, worthy of a better master.
Hubert hears John's vehement—even foolish—reproaches
with the steady self-control of one devotedly loyal to the noble
Plantagenet family, and personally grateful to its present
unworthy representative. For in the conscience-struck prince
before him, Hubert still sees the incarnate majesty of England, though surrounded by dangers menacing the whole
kingdom with himself.   Hubert, with calm dignity, and
having, as it were, justly punished his wicked tempter by
letting him believe his cruel orders were executed, now declares that Arthur is alive.   John, who before had so eagerly

desired his nephew's death, hears the news with relief, hastily apologises for his words to Hubert, and sends him to announce Arthur's safety to the "discontented peers."

The next scene describes the unfortunate prince escaping from his prison, and killed by a fall from the walls. This account is Shakespeare's invention, nor does he say if Hubert, in whose charge he is, has furnished the "ship-boy's dress" in which he tries to escape; but he has evidently had assistance. His body is found by some English noblemen, and also by Richard Plantagenet, who, with Lord Salisbury, fiercely charges his keeper with having slain Arthur. Hubert eagerly defends himself, and is at last believed, after having being sternly reproached by Sir Richard, who at first suspects him "grievously." Richard's conduct about Arthur is not very intelligible; for Shakespeare makes him nearly as devoted as Hubert to King John, and yet to have the sincerest respect, as well as pity, for his victim. Both he and Hubert are, indeed, brave, patriotic, honest Englishmen, yet strangely obedient to a mean-spirited, yet in some respects energetic sovereign, whose character and motives, were he not their king, they would surely abhor and despise to the last degree.

Act V. introduces, in Shakespeare's brilliant style, the historical episode of John's humilation before cardinal Pandulf, the able, resolute representative of Pope Innocent III.* The part which Pandulf plays at this time is very remarkable, both in history and in this tragedy. He mingles with quarrelling kings, fierce nobles, and their armed retainers, as if bearing a charmed life—fearless, observant, determined, and exacting, or unwillingly obtaining, the respect of all. Yet he is always labouring for the interests of the Church he represents, and never for private purposes. He compels John to yield up the English Crown, which he returns to him, observing that he now holds it by the Pope's authority. John, no longer defiant, entreats him to use his potent influence to stop the French invasion; for, being now recognized as king by the Pope, John naturally reckons upon the Church's assistance to maintain his power.

> KING JOHN. Now keep your holy word : go meet the French ;
> And from his holiness use all your power

* "John came into the legate's presence, who was seated on a throne; he flung himself on his knees before him; he lifted up his joined hands, and put them within those of Pandulf; he swore fealty to the Pope; and he paid part of the tribute which he owed for his kingdom as the patrimony of St. Peter. The legate, elated by this supreme triumph of sacerdotal power, could not forbear discovering extravagant symptoms of joy and exultation. He trampled on the money which was laid at his feet as an earnest of the subjection of the kingdom." —HUME's *History*, vol. i.

To stop their marches, 'fore we are inflam'd.
Our discontented counties do revolt;
Our people quarrel with obedience;
Swearing allegiance, and the love of soul,
To stranger blood, to foreign royalty.
This inundation of mistemper'd humour
Rests by you only to be qualified.
    PANDULF.   It was my breath that blew this tempest up,
Upon your stubborn usage of the Pope:
But, since you are a gentle convertite,
My tongue shall hush again this storm of war,
And make fair weather in your blustering land.
On this Ascension Day, remember well,
Upon your oath of service to the Pope,
Go I to make the French lay down their arms.—Act V.

Pandulf agrees, telling John to remember this Ascension Day, when he had publicly submitted to the Pope's authority. The king now recollects and believes the prophecy of the luckless Peter of Pomfret, but that unfortunate hermit was nevertheless executed, without either priest or layman apparently making any effort to save him.* During this important scene, Pandulf probably calls to mind the former contests between the Plantagenet kings and the clergy, and the murder of Thomas a'Becket by the instigation, if not orders, of John's father. But having now brought the obstinate, yet nervous king completely under the Pope's rule, the zealous cardinal has no wish to see him dethroned by the invading French Dauphin. On the contrary, he resolves to do all he can to preserve John's power, now that it is restrained by the Pope's supreme authority.† He thus leaves the king, promising to make peace between France and England, or, rather, between the French, allied with many of the English, against those who still adhere to John; and after he has gone, Sir Richard enters. This warlike gentleman has perhaps less respect for Pandulf than the other personages manifest; but they never dispute, or a

* "Though the man pleaded that his prophecy was fulfilled, the defence was supposed to aggravate his guilt."—HUME'S *History*, vol. i.

† "In after times men believed that England thrilled at the news with a sense of national shame, such as she had never felt before. 'He has become the Pope's man,' the whole country was said to have murmured; 'he has forfeited the very name of king; from a free man he has degraded himself into a serf.' But this was the belief of a time still to come, when the rapid growth of national feeling, which this step and its issues did more than anything to foster, made men look back on the scene between John and Pandulf as a national dishonour. We see little trace of such a feeling in the contemporary accounts of the time. All seem rather to have regarded it as a complete settlement of the difficulties in which king and kingdom were involved. As a political measure, its success was immediate and complete. The French army at once broke up in impotent rage." GREEN'S *History of the English People*, book iii.

F

stormy scene would doubtless ensue. Richard, now excited by war and irritated at the French invasion, earnestly counsels John in almost peremptory language to have no treaty with the enemy, and to resist them to the last. The king, whose secret wishes are perhaps with him, hears his energetic language, without, however, sharing any of its animation. He seems, indeed, so completely overwhelmed by the dangers around him, and by the recent agitation caused by his mother's death, that he hears his reckless young adviser with a sort of feeble admiration. In him he doubtless perceives and remembers the dauntless character of his heroic brother of the "lion heart," so different from his own nervous, if not craven spirit. That very same fearless heroism, which in the late king had been the obstacle to John's ambition and check to his hopes, was now in the bastard nephew devoted heart and soul to his service. He merely answers, "Have thou the ordering of this present time," but those few words reveal both his own dejection and his admiring confidence in young Richard, in whom he recognizes, perhaps with feelings of personal shame, the high spirit of their gallant race.

The next scenes describe important conferences between the ambitious Dauphin Louis and his English ally, Lord Salisbury, and also with Pandulf, who insists on the war being abandoned and John's authority being undisputed, owing to his peace with the Pope. Louis, disappointed and vexed at being thus suddenly stopped in what promises to be a successful war, for some time resists and almost defies the cardinal.

PANDULF.   King John hath reconcil'd
Himself to Rome ; his spirit is come in,
That so stood out against the holy Church,
The great metropolis and see of Rome :
Therefore thy threat'ning colours now wind up,
And tame the savage spirit of wild war ;
That, like a lion foster'd up at hand,
It may lie gently at the foot of peace,
And be no further harmful than in show.
Louis.   Your breath first kindled the dead coal of wars
Between this chastis'd kingdom and myself,
And brought in matter that should feed this fire ;
And now 'tis far too huge to be blown out
With that same weak wind which enkindled it.
You taught me how to know the face of right,
Acquainted me with interest to this land,
Yea, thrust this enterprise into my heart ;

> And come you now to tell me John hath made
> His peace with Rome?   What is that peace to me?—Act V.

Pandulf hears the angry youth with the same calm, steady resolution he evinces with everybody—with the obstinate, unruly John, the eager, passionate Constance, and the politic, astute Philip.   The Church, her interests, authority, and dignity alone rule his mind, and, firmly adhering to what he believes his sacred duty, he never yields to any one, nor deviates from the most invincible consistency.   While Louis warmly, almost boyishly, opposes him—declaring that his invasion of England was at first encouraged by the Pope, that it is in a fair way of success, and that after Prince Arthur he claims the English crown, through his marriage with the Princess Blanche, ignoring, however, the rights of John's son, Prince Henry—Pandulf listens without the least emotion, and calmly replies, "You look but on the outside of this work." This brief remark well expresses the spirit ·of the zealous Churchman of the period.   What signified French or English triumphs, or any earthly success and disappointment to him, when compared to the Church's interests!   Those interests being now secured by John's submission to Pope Innocent, the Dauphin Louis immediately changes, in Pandulf's estimation, from a useful champion into a petulant obstacle.*

Yet the future French king is not to be rebuked very severely, for he is heir to the eldest son of the Church, and hitherto has acted in conformity with her wishes.   In the midst of Louis's vexation, Sir Richard enters, coming from King John, and asks if peace is yet made.   His warlike mind is delighted at finding it is not, and Pandulf, thus placed between these fiery spirits, for the present is unable to obtain a hearing.   A battle seems now inevitable between armed forces, headed by such impetuous leaders, when news comes of John's sudden illness, for he is reported to be poisoned by a monk.

Many of the English under Richard Plantagenet were at this time drowned by unexpected floods.   Hubert de Burgh and Richard exchange their disastrous news of John's illness and the loss of the flower of the English army in the

---

* "It must be acknowledged that the influence of the prelates and the clergy was often of great service to the public.   It seemed to unite together a body of men who had great sway over the people, and who kept the community from falling to pieces by the factious and independent power of the nobles ; and, what was of great importance, it threw a mighty authority into the hands of men who, by their professions, were averse to arms and violence, who tempered by their mediation the general disposition towards military enterprise, and who still maintained, even amidst the shock of arms, those secret links without which it is impossible for human society to subsist."—HUME's *History*, ch. 12.

Lincolnshire "washes," and apprehend the certain triumph of the French in consequence.   Hubert and Richard, in their manly devotion to England—their bravery and straightforwardness—have much in common ; but, under such an odious sovereign as John, neither their characters nor abilities can much benefit their distracted country.   Their loyal devotion to the unworthy king, whose evil qualities they never discuss or even mention, is a remarkable proof of the strength of loyal principles at this historical period.   Such a character as John—nervous, obstinate, and ungrateful—both these men would have despised in a comrade, opposed in a relation, and distrusted in a follower ; yet being their sovereign he is only met by respectful remonstrance.*

The next scene ends the play.   King John, attended by his son, Prince Henry, and several noblemen, is brought into the orchard of Swinstead Abbey, in a chair, dying.   He declares to his son he believes himself poisoned, longing for cold winds and waters to cool his burning frame.   Prince Henry, who already evinces the amiable character he afterwards displayed as king, shows an affection for his wretched father which that sovereign never felt towards his own father, nor perhaps for any one.

> PRINCE HENRY.   How fares your majesty ?
> KING JOHN.   Poison'd—ill-fare ;—dead, forsook, cast off :
> And none of you will bid the winter come,
> To thrust his icy fingers in my maw ;
> Nor let my kingdom's rivers take their course
> Through my burn'd bosom ; nor entreat the north
> To make his bleak winds kiss my parched lips,
> And comfort me with cold :—I do not ask you much,
> I beg cold comfort ; and you are so strait,
> And so ingrateful, you deny me that.
> PRINCE HENRY.   O, that there were some virtue in my tears,
> That might relieve you.
> KING JOHN.   The salt in them is hot.
> Within me is a hell ; and there the poison
> Is, as a fiend, confin'd to tyrannize
> On unreprievable condemned blood.—Act V.

It is only in this last scene that the future king is introduced, but his few words denote almost as amiable a disposition

* " The character of King John is nothing but a complication of vices equally mean and odious, and alike ruinous to himself and destructive to his people. Cowardice, inactivity, folly, levity, licentiousness, ingratitude, treachery, tyranny, and cruelty—all these qualities appear too evidently in the several incidents of his life to give us room to suspect that the disagreeable picture has been anywise overcharged by the prejudices of the ancient historians."—HUME'S *History*, vol. i.

as the sketch of Prince Arthur.* Yet the unfortunate John apparently derives no comfort from him, nor does he show any paternal affection or interest in the prince. His conscience and illness now alike beset him, and, while bitterly complaining that none around afford him any relief, the impetuous Richard rushes to his presence, hastily announcing the loss of the greater part of his army. In this fiery young man—so like John's warlike brother—Shakespeare makes the king repose a trust and confidence which he places in no one else. Richard's frank manner, high spirit, and unflinching courage remind John of his gallant family ; while the bastard's own position prevents all feelings of jealousy. He is, in fact, just the man who, by character and situation, seems fitted to cheer a prince of John's moody, sensitive, and suspicious nature. But, though a brave soldier, true friend, and loyal subject, Richard has neither prudence nor sound judgment. His rash counsels have prolonged the war with France up to this moment, despite the exertions of Pandulf and the expressed wishes of the invalid king. Yet, in his latest moments, John apparently feels some relief at seeing him, though Richard has only disasters to announce. John foresees his own death from the despairing excitement which the fatal news is sure to cause in his weak state, and he expires while hearing from his brave but reckless nephew of his army's destruction by the Lincolnshire floods.

> KING JOHN.   O cousin, thou art come to set mine eye :
> The tackle of my heart is crack'd and burnt ;
> And all the shrouds, wherewith my life should sail,
> Are turnèd to one thread, one little hair :
> My heart hath one poor string to stay it by,
> Which holds but till thy news be utterèd ;
> And then all this thou seest is but a clod,
> And module of confounded royalty.
> BASTARD.   The Dauphin is preparing hitherward :
> Where, heaven he knows how we shall answer him :
> For, in a night, the best part of my power,
> As I upon advantage did remove,
> Were in the washes, all unwarily,
> Devour'd by the unexpected flood.   [*The King dies.*

The bold Richard, grieved yet undismayed by the king's death, which appals Prince Henry, Lord Salisbury, and others, demands more aid against the advancing French, when Salisbury declares he has even later news than Richard has

---

* Hume says of Prince Henry :—"Gentle, humane, and merciful even to a fault. Of all men, Nature seemed to have least fitted him for a tyrant."—*History of England*, vol. i.

announced, which he never told to the late king. For
Cardinal Pandulf, Salisbury says, has just brought terms of
honourable peace from the Dauphin, obtained, indeed,
through that energetic prelate's influence. Thus with King
John's life disappears all present danger to England, which
now acknowledges Henry as lawful king. The young
monarch, in a few touching words, expresses his grateful love
and confidence in Richard, Salisbury, and the other ministers
around him ; and thus ends this tragedy, which, though
chiefly founded on an older play of the same name, and
departing from facts in some particulars, yet represents
John, Elinor, Philip, Prince Henry, Cardinal Pandulf, and
Hubert de Burgh in accordance with history ; while the
characters of Constance, Arthur, and Richard, though all
consistent and natural, seem more derived from the poet's
fancy than from historical record. The few words which
Shakespeare ascribes to Prince Henry manifest that pleasing
promise which his amiable disposition and long reign of
fifty-six years fully justified. Henry III. was indeed different
from his wicked father in every respect ; and the last page of
this noble yet gloomy play is brightened by the excellent
spirit this prince shows while very young, and which history
states that he really possessed.

CHAPTER V.

KING RICHARD II.

Sketch of Play.

KING RICHARD II. hears his cousin, Bolingbroke, bring charges against the Duke of Norfolk, both of having been concerned in the murder of the Duke of Gloster, their uncle, and also of having misapplied public money. The disputants are about to engage in mortal combat in the king's presence, when they are stopped by Richard, who banishes them from England—Bolingbroke for six years, and Norfolk for life. Soon after this sentence, John of Gaunt (Duke of Lancaster and Bolingbroke's father) dies, in his son's absence, bitterly reproaching his nephew Richard for misgoverning England. Richard, directly after Gaunt's death, confiscates his property, and goes to Ireland. Meanwhile, Bolingbroke—now Duke of Lancaster—returns to England, claiming his rights, is joined by all the army, and finally by his uncle, the Duke of York, whom Richard had left to rule England in his absence. The king returns from Ireland, and finds England already in the virtual power of his cousin, to whom he has to surrender, and is led captive through London. He then publicly resigns his crown to Bolingbroke—now styled Henry IV.—and is sent a prisoner to Pomfret Castle. In this stronghold he is slain by Sir Pierce of Exton, who hopes to please the new king by destroying his vanquished foe. Henry IV., however, though troubled by numerous revolts in behalf of the deposed Richard, professes to disapprove his murder, and banishes Exton. The new king's power is thoroughly established when the play ends.

ABOUT a hundred and sixty years elapsed between King John's death and Richard the Second's accession, and during that time four kings had reigned in England. It seems uncertain if Shakespeare wrote about any of these four, for, though the play of *Edward III.* is attributed to him by some, it is not always reckoned among his works. But *Richard II.* is undoubtedly his own composition, comprising, however, only the last two years of this luckless sovereign's reign, and seems chiefly founded on Holinshed's Chronicles.* It is observed by an able French statesman that Shakespeare's later historical plays adhere more and more strictly to history as they approach nearer the poet's own time ;† and even *Richard II.* seems, on the whole, more founded on fact, and less on vague tradition, than *King John.* The first scene introduces at once the two chief characters in the drama—the weak, excitable, imprudent king, occasionally displaying high spirit, but usually indolent, nervous, and often fanciful; while the brave, shrewd, resolute Bolingbroke appears in many respects a fine specimen of English character—daring, fearless, and enterprising when young ; cautious, wise, and reflecting when in middle age.‡ They are now both young men, in the full vigour of early manhood. But Richard has already begun to waste time and money among mean, worthless favourites, apparently disregarding the many perils which encompass his throne.§ He, indeel, occupied a dangerous position—not so much from its own importance as from the numerous ambitious kinsmen, old and young, who surrounded him.‖ His uncles, John of Gaunt and the Duke of York, are both vexed at his reckless conduct, and probably suspect his having had some share in the mysterious death of their brother, the Duke of Gloster.¶ Richard's strange position amid so many hostile kinsmen was probably caused by Gloster's death, and partly explains why this prince, distrusting most of his relatives, placed his confidence in favourites of comparatively low rank—Sir John Bushy, Sir Henry Green, &c.—who,

---

* STAUNTON's *Preface to Richard II.*

† GUIZOT's *Criticism on Shakespeare's Historical Plays.*

‡ "The new Duke of Lancaster had acquired, by his conduct and abilities, the esteem of the public ; he had joined to his other praises those of piety and valour. The people, who found nothing in the king's person which they could love or revere, and were even disgusted with many parts of his conduct, easily transferred to Henry that attachment which the death of the Duke of Gloster had left without any fixed direction."—HUME's *History,* vol. ii.

§ "Indolent, profuse, addicted to low pleasures, he spent his whole time in feasting and jollity, and dissipated, in idle show or in bounties to favourites of no reputation, that revenue which the people expected so see him employ in enterprises directed to public honour and advantage. He forgot his rank by admitting all men to his familiarity."—HUME's *History,* vol. ii.

‖ "Richard II. was a peaceful monarch, thwarted at every turn by ambitious kinsmen."—STUBBS's *Constitutional History,* vol. ii.

¶ Hume inclines to believe, though not positive on the subject, that Richard had been privy to Gloster's murder, who was, however, generally suspected of treasonable designs against the young king.—Vol. ii.

like most of their class, having "no friends," were all the more obedient to their royal patron.

In the first scene, Richard, after vainly trying to make peace between Bolingbroke and Norfolk, appoints a day for their mortal combat in his presence, at Coventry.*   Between John of Gaunt and his brave son there is evidently a strong affection, and probably a thorough confidence.   Norfolk, while trying to repel Bolingbroke's charges, appeals to Gaunt as "the honourable father of my foe;" but that powerful nobleman, who, though called "time-honoured Lancaster," was hardly sixty years old, never answers, but, in obedience to King Richard, he also vainly tries to make peace between his son and Norfolk.   It is evident, from the next scene between the widowed Duchess of Gloster and Gaunt, her brother-in-law, what deep indignation Gloster's supposed murder has caused among the royal family.

> DUCHESS.   But Thomas, my dear lord, my life, my Gloster—
> One phial full of Edward's sacred blood,
> One flourishing branch of Edward's royal root,
> Is crack'd, and all the precious liquor spilt ;
> Is hack'd down, and his summer leaves all faded,
> By envy's hand, and murder's bloody axe.
> Ah, Gaunt ! his blood was thine.—Act I.

The duchess vaguely urges Gaunt to avenge Gloster's death, without positively accusing the king ; but it is clear that she and all her husband's kinsfolk dislike and distrust him, viewing Bolingbroke as their champion.   Gaunt tries to soothe his sister-in-law, telling her to seek religious consolation, and intimating that even if Richard had instigated Gloster's murder, he would never rebel against him.

> DUCHESS.   In suffering thus thy brother to be slaughter'd,
> Thou show'st the naked pathway to thy life,
> Teaching stern murder how to butcher thee.
> What shall I say ? to safeguard thine own life,
> The best way is to 'venge my Gloster's death."
> GAUNT.   God's is the quarrel ; for God's substitute,
> His deputy anointed in His sight,
> Hath caus'd his death : the which if wrongfully,
> Let Heaven revenge ; for I may never lift
> An angry arm against His minister ?
> DUCHESS.   Where, then, alas ! may I complain myself ?
> GAUNT.   To God, the widow's champion and defence.
> DUCHESS.   Why, then, I will.—Act I.

* Sir James Stephens says that "trial by combat was introduced by William the Conqueror ;" adding, that it was "only private war under regulations."— *English Criminal Law*, ch. iii.

But he dearly loves his spirited son, Bolingbroke, whose talents and popularity are gradually making him more formidable to Richard and his adherents. In loyalty to the king, the brothers Gaunt and York, though men of such different characters, resemble each other. They refuse to aid any revolt, yet both blame Richard's conduct, and detest his favourites ; while their respective sons, the gallant Bolingbroke and the mean, treacherous Aumerle, contemplate a future rebellion long before it commenced. The Duchess of Gloster, while hating Norfolk, and wishing success to Bolingbroke in the coming fight, speaks kindly of her other brother-in-law, York, who, throughout this play, as in history, seems a strange, flighty, peculiar man, placed in a highly-important position. His son, Aumerle, the duchess does not name, though he was suspected of having had some share in Gloster's death, and was very differently disposed from his father. The widowed duchess, in deep dejection, parts from Gaunt, after a touching interview, and never appears again.

The next scene is at Coventry, where the combatants appear, armed and eager for their encounter, before the king and court. John of Gaunt wishes all good fortune to his son in the coming duel ; while Richard speaks kindly to both parties, apparently sympathizing most with Norfolk, though his subsequent conduct towards him does not bear out his words. He says to Bolingbroke—

> Cousin of Hereford, as thy cause is right,
> So be thy fortune in this royal fight !

And to Norfolk—

> Farewell, my lord : securely I espy
> Virtue with valour couchèd in thine eye.—Act I.

Yet he immediately afterwards forbids the combat, banishing Norfolk for life and Bolingbroke for six years. Both combatants warmly complain of this sentence, which Richard seems to pronounce without the advice of any one, unless, indeed, it was secretly suggested by some of his many favorites. Norfolk, in leaving England, utters prophetic words about Bolingbroke, which no one notices at this time, but were probably remembered by all who heard them. Bolingbroke haughtily asks him to confess the truth of the charges against him before he leaves the king for ever, and Norfolk boldly replies,

> No, Bolingbroke ; if ever I were traitor,
> My name be blotted from the Book of Life,

And I from heaven banished, as from thence !
But what thou art, God, thou, and I do know ;
And all too soon, I fear, the king shall rue.
Farewell, my liege.—Act I.

Richard at this moment seems in a most singular position.
He banishes for life one whom he believes loyal, and, as if wishing to appease hostile kinsmen, shortens Bolingbroke's banishment from ten to six years, for the sake of Gaunt, who, with
cold thanks, however, observes that this change will make no
difference to him, as his old age will never permit him to see
his son again.   This language Gaunt never used, but it seems
historically true that Bolingbroke's banishment greatly
offended the king's relatives, among whom, indeed, the
latter does not seem to have had any real friend.   Richard is
irritated at finding Gaunt so grieved at his son's comparatively
short banishment, and, his suspicions of both being apparently
excited or increased, he insists on the sentence being en-
forced, and leaves the father and son together with their
nephew and cousin, Aumerle, and their friend, the Lord
Marshal.   Bolingbroke warmly expresses his grief at being
banished ; his father vainly tries to console him, while the
others show strong sympathy, for young Bolingbroke is
already very popular at court and in England. ·

    GAUNT.   All places that the eye of Heaven visits,
Are to a wise man ports and happy havens.

Look, what thy soul holds dear, imagine it
To lie that way thou go'st, not whence thou com'st.

For gnarling sorrow hath less power to bite
The man that mocks at it, and sets it light.
    BOLINGBROKE.   O, who can hold a fire in his hand,
By thinking on the frosty Caucasus ?
Or cloy the hungry edge of appetite,
By bare imagination of a feast ?
Or wallow naked in December snow,
By thinking on fantastic Summer's heat ?
O, no ! the apprehension of the good
Gives but the greater feeling to the worse.
    GAUNT.   Come, come, my son, I'll bring thee on thy way :
Had I thy youth and cause, I would not stay.
    BOLINGBROKE.   Then, England's ground, farewell ; sweet
        soil, adieu ;
My mother, and my nurse, that bears me yet !
Where'er I wander, boast of this I can,
Though banish'd, yet a true-born Englishman.—Act I.*

* "As Henry Bolingbroke left London, the streets were crowded with people
weeping for his fate ; some followed him even to the coast.   His withdrawal

The next scene is the first that mentions Aumerle's deceit, who, after condoling with Bolingbroke while in his presence, and in that of his father, Gaunt, now assures Richard that he has no affection for him. The king openly expresses distrust of his banished cousin, even owning to Aumerle that both he and his three followers—Bushy, Green, and Bagot—have observed "his courtship to the common people," and already suspect his having designs against the throne. The three favorites thoroughly share Richard's views, who announces his intention of going to Ireland, when he is summoned to the death-bed of his uncle, Gaunt. Richard, with heartless levity, scarcely consistent with his not unamiable character, avowedly wishes Gaunt dead, that he may seize his money, and spend it on the Irish war. It is evident that Richard, who, in the beginning of his reign, had shown both energy and good feeling, became more and more frivolous, reckless, and unjust, perhaps owing partly to the influence of Bushy, Green, &c., whom he trusted and consulted more than any other advisers.* These obsequious courtiers, with Aumerle, accompany the king to John of Gaunt's house. Previous to their arrival, the dying Duke of Lancaster has a remarkable conference with his brother, York. These two princes, though firm allies, are great contrasts in character. Gaunt is brave, resolute, patriotic, and has a high sense of duty to the sovereign whom he cannot help despising, and a strong affection for his banished son, whose secret ambition he does not apparently encourage. York is weak, excitable, and hesitating; he has no confidence in Richard, and abhors the favorites; yet has no idea of raising a rebellion against him.† The dying Gaunt, in a noble speech to his sympathizing brother, deplores the present misgovernment of England, and foresees additional disasters from the reckless conduct of the young king. He pathetically exclaims,—

removed the last check on Richard's despotism. He forced on every tenant. of the Crown an oath to recognize the acts of his committee as valid, and to oppose any attempts to alter or revoke them."—GREEN's *History of the English People,* book iv.

* "Richard II. was a man of considerable talents; but his ordinary conduct belied the abilities which on rare occasions shone forth. Extreme pride and violence, with an inordinate partiality for the most worthless favourites, were his predominant characteristics."—HALLAM's *Middle Ages,* ch. viii.

† "In a single year, the whole colour of Richard's government had changed. He had revenged himself on the men who had once held him down, and his revenge was hardly taken before he disclosed a plan of absolute government. . . . Forced loans, the outlawry of seven counties at once, on the plea that they had supported his enemies, and must purchase pardon—a reckless interference with the course of justice—roused into new life the existing discontents."—GREEN's *History of the English People,* vol. i.

This royal throne of kings, this scepter'd isle,
This fortress, built by Nature for herself,
Against infection and the hand of war ;
This happy breed of men, this little world ;
This precious stone set in the silver sea,
Which serves it in the office of a wall ;
This blessed plot, this earth, this realm, this England,
Dear for her reputation through the world,
Is now leas'd out (I die pronouncing it)
Like to a tenement, or pelting* farm :
England, bound in with the triumphant sea,
Whose rocky shore beats back the envious siege
Of watery Neptune, is now bound in with shame,
With inky blots, and rotten parchment bonds ;
That England, that was wont to conquer others,
Hath made a shameful conquest of itself :
O, would the scandal vanish with my life,
How happy then were my ensuing death !—Act I.†

He finishes speaking as Richard enters with the queen,
Aumerle, and the three favorites. Gaunt, indignant at the
king's conduct, and knowing he has only a short time to live,
no longer speaks respectfully, but earnestly reproaches him ;
declaring he is surrounded by flatterers, and that he is ruining both his kingdom and his relatives. This grand scene
never occurred,‡ yet it apparently displays the real feelings
of the royal family, represented by Gaunt, about the king's
conduct and policy. Richard, instead of being softened
by his dying uncle's warning, is roused to fury, and declares
that were he not a near relative, he would have had him
beheaded before he had spoken so far. This violent language
rouses the high-spirited Gaunt to reproach Richard with his
suspected share in his late uncle Gloster's murder, with which
no one had yet openly charged him.

KING RICHARD. Now by my seat's right royal majesty,
Wert thou not brother to great Edward's son,
This tongue, that runs so roundly in thy head,
Should run thy head from thy unreverend shoulders.

* Paltry.
† Hume is surprised that Shakespeare did not make Gaunt mention English
civil laws and liberty in this grand speech.—*History of England*, vol. i., Appendix iii. But Shakespeare probably thought that, although English princes
might bravely defend and sincerely love their country, yet in those times the
privileges or liberty of subjects from royal control were to them rather causes for
jealous apprehension than pride or satisfaction. Hume admits that in " Shakespeare's historical plays, the manners, characters, and even the transactions of the
several reigns are exactly copied." This is valuable praise from the learned
historian, who yet surely underrates Shakespeare's genius in writing for the stage.
—*Appendix to Reign of James I.*
‡ *See* Mr. FURNIVALL's *Preface to Richard II.*

> GAUNT.   O, spare me not, my brother Edward's son,
> For that I was his father Edward's son.
>
> My brother Gloster, plain, well-meaning soul,
> May be a precedent and witness good,
> That thou respect'st not spilling Edward's blood:
> Join with the present sickness that I have:
> And thy unkindness be like crooked age,
> To crop at once a too-long wither'd flower.
> Live in thy shame, but die not shame with thee!—
> These words hereafter thy tormentors be!—Act II.

On this occasion, the Duke of York strongly displays the utter want of judgment which marks his flighty, strange character throughout. He must know that the banished Henry Bolingbroke (Lord Hereford) cannot be friendly to Richard, even if he does not openly rival him; while Gaunt, though indignant with the king, has never been suspected of disloyalty by Richard's most faithful adherents. Yet, in an awkward attempt to soothe the king, York foolishly declares that Gaunt is as loyal to Richard as his ambitious son is. To this unlucky exclamation Richard makes a sarcastic reply—one of the few occasions that his passionate, giddy temper resorts to irony of any sort—and evidently the talkative frivolous York feels confounded, for he attempts no rejoinder.

> YORK.   I do beseech your majesty, impute his words
> To wayward sickliness and age in him:
> He loves you, on my life, and holds you dear
> As Harry, Duke of Hereford, were he here.
>   KING RICHARD.   Right; you say true: as Hereford's love, so
>   his;
> As theirs, so mine; and all be as it is.—Act II.

Lancaster is then borne out of the room, and dies; his brother York and Northumberland announcing the news to Richard, who immediately declares that he will confiscate Gaunt's property. York indignantly remonstrates against this wild injustice, reminding his royal nephew of the cruel injury this act would inflict on Bolingbroke, now Duke of Lancaster. Richard hears his uncle with utter contempt, yet feels sure of his loyalty, for he intends leaving him to govern England during his own approaching absence in Ireland. Whether Richard was induced by the cunning Aumerle to so trust his father, or why he had so much more confidence in York's loyalty than in his judgment, does not appear; but the thoughtless king goes to Ireland, while several English nobles, with the crafty Earl Northumberland, express deep indignation at Richard's conduct, and their warmest sympathy for the illegally-disinherited Duke of Lancaster. Northumberland, seeing his companions sufficiently angry with the king, informs them that Bolingbroke is already on his way home from France, attended by several English gentlemen, who are as disgusted as they are with Richard's government.* This prelate is only once mentioned, and not introduced in this play.

Evidently, an insurrection is now preparing, and so the young queen fears in the next scene, where she owns to Bushy and Bagot her uneasiness about the king's affairs. Her apprehensions are then confirmed by Green's entrance, announcing that the revolution has actually broken out, headed by Bolingbroke, and supported by the Northumberland family. The queen, who was very much attached to Richard, entreats York, who enters soon after Green, to comfort her. But this the Duke cannot do ; he himself is now old, and his nervous mind is agitated by conflicting emotions. He pities the king and queen ; knows he is left in a responsible position by Richard, whom he represents, and to whom, according to the strict monarchical ideas of the time, he is conscientiously loyal ; yet every other feeling, wish, and sentiment urge him to side with the advancing Lancaster.† He is therefore quite perplexed, and, though he tried to rally the royal forces, he was unable to do so. While pitying the queen, he evidently sympathizes more with his wronged nephew, Lancaster, than his own loyal instincts approve.

YORK. If I know how, or which way, to order these affairs,
Thus disorderly thrust into my hands,
Never believe me. Both are my kinsmen ;—
The one is my sovereign, whom both my oath
And duty bids defend ; the other again
Is my kinsman, whom the king hath wrong'd,
Whom conscience and my kindred bids to right.

.   .   .   .   .   .

All is uneven,
And everything is left at six and seven.—Act II.

* " Richard seized the Lancastrian estates. Archbishop Arundel hastened to Paris, and pressed the Duke of Lancaster to return to England, telling him how all men there looked for it, especially the Londoners, who loved him a hundred times more than they loved the king. For a while, Henry Bolingbroke remained buried in thought, ' leaning on a window overlooking a garden.' but Arundel's pressure at last prevailed."—GREEN's *History of the English People*.

† " The Duke of York was left guardian of the realm—a place to which his birth entitled him, but which both his slender abilities and his natural connections with the Duke of Lancaster rendered him utterly incapable of filling in such a dangerous emergency."—HUME's *History*, vol. ii.

After the queen and he leave the room, the three favorites—Bushy, Bagot, and Green—have an anxious conference together. These unlucky men foresee the end of their power, and, in their position, they know that loss of life is its probable accompaniment. They apparently have no military talent or influence ; are hated by both nobles and people, their only friend being the absent king, whose dangers are rapidly increasing. Bagot goes to Ireland to rejoin the king, while the others remain in England ; but they evidently believe themselves doomed, as they never mention escape to the continent, which alone might have saved their lives.

> BUSHY.   For us to levy power,
> Proportionable to the enemy,
> Is impossible.
>   GREEN.   Besides, our nearness to the king in love,
> Is near the hate of those love not the king.
>   BUSHY.   For little office
> Will the hateful commons perform for us :
> Except, like curs, to tear us all to pieces.
>   BAGOT.   Farewell, if heart's presages be not vain,
> We three here part, that ne'er shall meet again.
>   BUSHY.   That's as York thrives to beat back Bolingbroke.
>   GREEN.   Alas, poor duke ! the task he undertakes
> Is numb'ring sands, and drinking oceans dry :
> Where one on his side fights, thousands will fly.
>   BUSHY.   Farewell at once ; for once, for all, and ever.
>   GREEN.   Well, we may meet again.
>   BAGOT.   I fear me, never.—Act II.

The next scene changes to Gloucestershire, where Bolingbroke, joined by Northumberland, is at the head of an increasing force, advancing steadily on London. These two leaders are just the men likely to conduct a successful insurrection, being alike brave, cautious, and determined. Northumberland is much older—perhaps more of a statesman than a warrior ; while Bolingbroke, even when a young man, was distinguished in both capacities. In the present enterprise, however, their great qualities are little needed, for nearly all England declares for them, and revolts from Richard at first as unanimously as, nearly three centuries later, the whole country abandoned James II., in favour of the invading Prince of Orange, without a single battle.* In this scene,

---

* " Richard's government for nearly two years [the period comprised in this play] was altogether tyrannical, and, upon the same principles that cost James II. his throne, it was unquestionably far more necessary, unless our fathers would have abandoned all thoughts of liberty, to expel Richard II."—HALLAM's *Middle Ages*, ch. viii.

Northumberland's brave son, Harry Percy—surnamed Hot-spur—makes his first appearance, now quite a youth. He at first hardly recognizes Bolingbroke, or waits for his father to introduce him, who presents him to his future sovereign.

> NORTHUMBERLAND. Have you forgot the Duke of Hereford,
>   boy?
> PERCY. No, my good lord; for that is not forgot
> Which ne'er I did remember; to my knowledge,
> I never in my life did look on him.
> NORTHUMBERLAND. Then learn to know him now; this is the
>   duke.
> PERCY. My gracious lord, I tender you my service,
> Such as it is, being tender, raw, and young;
> Which elder days shall ripen, and confirm
> To more approved service and desert.
> BOLINGBROKE. I thank thee, gentle Percy; and be sure,
> I count myself in nothing else so happy
> As in a soul rememb'ring my good friends;
> And, as my fortune ripens with thy love,
> It shall be still thy true love's recompense:
> My heart this covenant makes, my hand thus seals it.—Act II.

This first meeting between the calm Bolingbroke and the dashing, fiery youth, Harry Percy, was long remembered, when, in after years, they were destined to become mortal foes. At this time Bolingbroke—now styled Duke of Lancaster—is already far more shrewd and cautious than when fiercely challenging Norfolk, about two years before, with an impetuous courage like that of young Percy himself. The bold daring of his youth is being now gradually suc-ceeded by the firm energy of early manhood; while Harry Percy resembles what he was in dauntless courage, but has none of that steady sense and coolness which Bolingbroke always possessed. Between these two brave spirits the crafty Northumberland acts as introducer, presenting his fiery son to the ambitious prince, whom he now considers king, and supports with all his power, yet who was fated, in a few years, to destroy both him and his family. Bolingbroke is evidently pleased at the ready, frank loyalty of the bold youth before him, who, sharing his father's views, or obey-ing his wishes, is yet rather a contrast to him, being as eager and impetuous as Northumberland is cautious and designing. At this time of their lives, Bolingbroke seems to unite in himself much of Northumberland's calm prudence with Hotspur's daring bravery; and this distinguished trio are now in complete alliance. They are soon joined by more

G

nobles, with their adherents, and at last the Duke of York, nominal governor of England, meets the successful and unopposed insurgents. He at first, with the loyal spirit of the times, sharply reproaches his ambitious nephew for even returning to England while under legal sentence of banishment. To this reproach Bolingbroke makes a dignified, touching reply, which is specially calculated to impress his uncle, who hears it with assumed indifference.

> BOLINGBROKE. As I was banish'd, I was banish'd Hereford:
> But as I come, I come for Lancaster,
> And, noble uncle, I beseech your grace,
> Look on my wrongs with an indifferent eye:
> You are my father, for methinks in you
> I see old Gaunt alive; O, then, my father!
> Will you permit that I shall stand condemn'd
> A wand'ring vagabond; my rights and royalties
> Pluck'd from my arms perforce, and given away
> To upstart unthrifts? Wherefore was I born?
> If that my cousin king be king of England,
> It must be granted I am Duke of Lancaster.
> You have a son, Aumerle, my noble kinsman;
> Had you first died, and he been thus trod down,
> He should have found his uncle Gaunt a father,
> To rouse his wrongs, and chase them to the bay.
> My father's goods are all distrain'd, and sold;
> And these, and all, are all amiss employ'd.
> What would you have me do? I am a subject,
> And I challenge law: attorneys are denied me;
> And therefore personally I lay claim
> To my inheritance of free descent.—Act II.

York sees, however, that resistance on his part is hopeless, and coldly invites his formidable nephew to Berkeley Castle —perhaps not sorry that he has no alternative. Bolingbroke, who, all his life, showed great knowledge of human nature, then succeeds in rousing York's anger against the king, by skilfully alluding to the detested trio, " the upstart unthrifts " —Bushy, Bagot, and Green—whom he terms " the caterpillars of the commonwealth, whom " he has " sworn to weed and pluck away." Immediately York's excitable temper is aroused, and he declares he will join Bolingbroke; then partly recalls his words.

> YORK. It may be I will go with you:—but yet I'll pause;
> For I am loath to break our country's laws.
> Nor friends, nor foes, to me welcome you are:
> Things past redress are now with me past care.

This almost childish hesitation between his feelings and his
duty doubtless amused and gratified the crafty Northumberland and many of Bolingbroke's followers. For though
York was a prince of little ability, he was yet the nominal
ruler in Richard's absence, eldest member of the royal
family, and the only surviving brother of the late king. His
alliance, or even neutrality, was therefore very valuable, and
Bolingbroke's success from this time was rapid and complete.
Still, some noblemen—Lord Salisbury, Lord Wiltshire, Sir
Stephen Scroop, the Bishop of Carlisle, &c.—adhered to
Richard, but could not delay the triumphant advance of
Bolingbroke, who soon captured and executed two of the
unhappy favorites—Bushy and Green—apparently without
any trial. He sentences them in presence of York, who never
intercedes for them ; while Northumberland and his son,
Percy, are also beside him, and see his orders executed.

> BOLINGBROKE. Bushy and Green, I will not vex your souls
> (Since presently your souls must part your bodies)
> With too much urging your pernicious lives,
> For 'twere no charity : yet, to wash your blood
> From off my hands, here, in the view of men,
> I will unfold 'some causes of your deaths.
> You have misled a prince, a royal king,
> A happy gentleman in blood and lineaments,
> By you unhappied and disfigur'd clean.*
> Myself—a prince, by fortune of my birth ;
> Near to the king in blood ; and near in love,
> Till you did make him misinterpret me,—
> Have stoop'd my neck under your injuries,
> And sigh'd my English breath in foreign clouds,
> Eating the bitter bread of banishment ;
> While you have fed upon my seignories,
> Dispark'd my parks, and fell'd my forest woods ;
> From mine own windows torn my household coat,
> Raz'd out my impress, leaving me no sign—
> Save men's opinions, and my living blood—
> To show the world I am a gentleman.
> This, and much more, much more than twice all this,
> Condemns you to the death.
> My Lord Northumberland, see them despatch'd.—Act III.

To which request that zealous, unscrupulous nobleman makes
no objection, though most of their offences were committed
by the will of Richard II. Bolingbroke then sends a cautious
message to the captured queen, who is at the Duke of York's
house, assuring her of respectful treatment, and prepares to

* Completely.

encounter the Welsh chief, Owen Glendower, who had shown some signs of resistance in behalf of the king.

The next scene describes Richard's return to England, attended by his faithful adherent, the Bishop of Carlisle, and by his cousin, the deceitful Aumerle. Richard, in this important scene, reveals more of his peculiar character than has yet appeared. He is at first delighted at returning to England, and confident that directly his arrival is known, all rebellion will cease. He speaks, therefore, in high-flown, exaggerated language, but his excitable spirit is soon depressed by Salisbury's arrival, telling him that a large part of his army has already joined Bolingbroke.* Sir Stephen Scroop follows, with yet more disastrous news of Bolingbroke's complete success throughout England. Richard, amazed, asks about Lord Wiltshire, Bushy, Green, &c., and now losing confidence in every one, suspects they have also "made peace" with his enemy. Scroop gravely replies that they have, indeed, "made their peace" with him, which Richard mistakes for their treachery. He utters furious reproaches against his late favorites, for whom he had always, perhaps, more liking than esteem; but his rage turns to despair at hearing of their executions by Bolingbroke's order. Bagot, however, was not executed, and Scroop does not name him. Richard's despair is now complete; he sees nothing but treason, desertion, and ruin before him.

> KING RICHARD. Of comfort no man speak :
> Let's talk of graves, of worms, and epitaphs;
> Make dust our paper, and with rainy eyes
> Write sorrow on the bosom of the earth.
> Let's choose executors, and talk of wills :
> And yet not so—for what can we bequeath,
> Save our deposed bodies to the ground?
> Our lands, our lives, and all, are Bolingbroke's,
> And nothing can we call our own but death.
>
> . . . . . .
>
> For God's sake, let us sit upon the ground,
> And tell sad stories of the death of kings :—
> How some have been depos'd, some slain in war,
> Some haunted by the ghosts they have depos'd :
> Some poison'd by their wives, some sleeping kill'd ;
> All murder'd :—for within the hollow crown
> That rounds the mortal temples of a king

* "Richard alternates between abject despondency and an airy, unreal confidence. There is in Richard, as Coleridge has finely observed, 'a constant overflow of emotions, from a total incapability of controlling them, and thence a waste of that energy which should have been reserved for actions, in the passion and effort of mere resolves and menaces.'"—DOWDEN's *Shakespeare's Mind and Art.*

> Keeps Death his court ; and there the antic sits,
> Scoffing his state, and grinning at his pomp—
> Allowing him a breath, a little scene,
> To monarchize, be fear'd, and kill with looks ;
> Infusing him with self and vain conceit—
> As if this flesh, which walls about our life,
> Were brass impregnable—and, humour'd thus,
> Comes at the last, and with a little pin
> Bores through his castle wall, and—farewell king !—Act III.

The Bishop of Carlisle tries to console and rouse him, and is apparently succeeding, when the final news of his uncle York's defection arrives. This intelligence probably depresses Richard's advisers as much as himself, for no word of hope or encouragement is uttered after its announcement. The king dismisses his remaining followers, repairing to Flint Castle, there to await his triumphant foe, whose prisoner he already considers himself, and against whom he abandons all idea of resistance.*

The next scene brings Bolingbroke, with York, Northumberland, young Hotspur, &c., before the walls of Flint Castle, where Richard, with the Bishop of Carlisle, Aumerle, Lord Salisbury, and Sir Stephen Scroop, are helplessly awaiting their fate. Aumerle, however, is in little danger, owing to his father's influence, who is treated with the highest respect by Bolingbroke. York's present position as an elderly, whimsical prince, surrounded by ambitious, fiery young men, and crafty old ones, is embarrassing, yet almost ludicrous. He pettishly reproves Northumberland, even at this crisis, for naming Richard without his kingly title, for which omission the ambitious earl, probably laughing to himself, offers a slight apology. York even comforts his own vexed spirit and uneasy conscience by slightly reprimanding his triumphant nephew, who hears him with politic calmness, but, doubtless, secret impatience.

> YORK.   It would become the Lord Northumberland
> To say *King* Richard.
> NORTHUMBERLAND.   Your grace mistakes ; only to be brief,
> Left I his title out.
> YORK.   The time hath been,
> Would you have been so brief with him, he would
> Have been so brief with you, to shorten you,
> For taking so the head, your whole head's length.

* "The sincere concurrence which most of the prelates and nobility, with the mass of the people, gave to changes, which would not otherwise have been effected by one so unprovided with foreign support as Henry Bolingbroke, proves this revolution (1399) to have been, if not an indispensable, yet a national act."—HALLAM's *Middle Ages*, ch. viii.

> BOLINGBROKE.   Mistake not, uncle, farther than you should.
> YORK.   Take not, good cousin, farther than you should,
> Lest you mistake : the heavens are o'er our heads.
> BOLINGBROKE.   I know it, uncle, and oppose not myself
> Against their will.—Act III.

For he now summons the unfortunate king, through North-umberland, to surrender. Richard reproaches the latter, then bewails his misfortunes, and finally surrenders to Bolingbroke.

> KING RICHARD.   What must the king do now ?   Must
>   he submit ?
> The king shall do it.   Must he be depos'd ?
> The king shall be contented : Must he lose
> The name of king? o' God's name let it go :
> I'll give my jewels, for a set of beads ;
> My gorgeous palace, for a hermitage ;
> My gay apparel, for an almsman's gown ;
> My sceptre, for a palmer's walking staff ;
> My subjects, for a pair of carved saints ;
> And my large kingdom, for a little grave,
> A little, little grave, an obscure grave :—
> Or I'll be buried in the king's highway,
> Some way of common trade, where subjects' feet
> May hourly trample on their sovereign's head :
> For on my heart they tread, now whilst I live ;
> And, buried once, why not upon my head?—Act III.

Bolingbroke preserves a respectful manner to his royal prisoner, which never comforts Richard, who, without either defying him or showing personal fear, apparently finds a morbid relief in describing and exaggerating his own humiliation. Although his grand language is Shakespeare's invention, the feelings it expresses agree with historical records of both his disposition and state of mind.* Aumerle, however, is represented more steadily faithful to Richard than he really was, and, indeed, Shakespeare's sketch of him is not very clear or satisfactory. For he is trusted by Richard in his extremity, and yet accuses the king's unhappy favorite, Bagot, when a prisoner in the presence of Bolingbroke.

Previous to this scene, Shakespeare introduces one entirely of his own invention, where the young Queen Isabella is staying at her uncle the Duke of York's country residence. In his garden, she, with her attendant, overhear the gardeners talking over public affairs, and professionally comparing her husband's executed favourites to " weeds plucked up by the

* HUME'S *History* ; also, HALLAM'S.

roots." Also, they hear that Bolingbroke has actually captured the king, of which the queen was not hitherto aware. In angry impatience, she asks the gardeners if their news is true, and, when convinced of it, rather petulantly hopes that their plants may never grow, and then hastens to London, to meet, if possible, her captive husband.

The next scene describes, amid a large assemblage of influential men, the unfortunate Bagot—now a prisoner before Bolingbroke—accusing Aumerle of a share in the Duke of Gloster's murder, many years before. Bagot's subsequent fate is not mentioned, but he probably escaped that of his luckless friends, Bushy and Green.* Aumerle, however, boldly denies this charge, and is then challenged by several noblemen, who believe him guilty, to single combat. Even Hotspur, though only a youth, eagerly offers to fight him, already showing that fiery spirit which made him so remarkable even in that fierce age.

AUMERLE.   Princes and noble lords,
What answer shall I make to this base man?

    .   .   .   .   .   .

There is my gage, the manual seal of death,
That marks thee out for hell : I say, thou liest,
And will maintain what thou hast said is false,
In thy heart-blood, though being all too base
To stain the temper of my knightly sword.
    BOLINGBROKE.   Bagot, forbear ; thou shalt not take it up.
    FITZWATER.   If that thy valour stand on sympathies,
There is my gage, Aumerle, in gage to thine :
I heard thee say, and vauntingly thou spak'st it,
That thou wert cause of noble Gloster's death.
If thou deny'st it twenty times, thou liest ;
And I will turn thy falsehood to thy heart,
Where it was forged, with my rapier's point.
    AUMERLE.   Thou dar'st not, coward, live to see the day.
    PERCY.   Aumerle, thou liest ; his honour is as true,
In this appeal, as thou art all unjust :
And, that thou art so, there I'll throw my gage,
To prove it on thee to the extremest point
Of mortal breathing : seize it, if thou dar'st.
    AUMERLE.   And if I do not, may my hands rot off,
And never brandish more revengeful steel
Over the glittering helmet of my foe!—Act IV.

---

* "It appears from a petition of 1400 that one Bagot had been impeached by the Commons of 'many horrible acts and misprisions.' He was put to answer before the Lords, and produced 'a charter of general pardon,' on which the Lords considered 'that the said Monsieur William ought not to be prevented making a reply through the law.'"—STEPHENS's *English Criminal Law*, ch. v. Perhaps, therefore, Bagot was more fortunate than Bushy and Green.

Bolingbroke, as brave as any of them, but with more sagacity, well fitted to be their chief, listens to their eager defiances with calm interest, perhaps remembering the time when he, young like them, was equally impetuous in defying the Duke of Norfolk.* He resolves, however, on having Aumerle tried, and on recalling his old enemy, Norfolk, from banishment, and restoring him his property, when he regretfully hears of his death from the Bishop of Carlisle, the steady adherent of Richard, and who evidently believes in Norfolk's innocence of the many mysterious charges against him.

Bolingbroke having postponed Aumerle's trial, now hears from York that Richard consents to name him his heir, and to yield up the crown. With unwonted eagerness, he exclaims, "In God's name, I'll ascend the regal throne," when the Bishop of Carlisle interposes, remonstrating with courageous eloquence, though in exaggerated terms, against such a proceeding. Northumberland, furious at this interruption, wants to arrest him for treason, although against an unacknowledged king ; but Bolingbroke, with his usual calmness, refuses to sanction this proposal, and orders the captive monarch to be brought before them all. York then conducts the unfortunate Richard to the presence of his successful foe, now surrounded by powerful adherents, and really King of England already, by the submission, if not will of the nation.† Richard again, as when he landed in England, and when surrendering to Bolingbroke, for the third time, indulges—perhaps relieves—his saddened mind by dwelling on and exaggerating every circumstance of his humiliation. He is apparently broken-hearted, neither defending his past conduct nor accusing his enemies, but making long speeches, addressed more to his own agitated mind than to any one present ; yet heard by all, and, of course, with much interest. As if acting a scene on the stage, he asks Bolingbroke to hold the crown upon one side, while he supports it on

---

* "Bolingbroke utters a few words in *Richard II.*, yet we feel that from the first the chief force centres in him. He is dauntless, but his courage is under the control of his judgment. All his faculties are well organized, and help one another."—DOWDEN'S *Shakespeare's Mind and Art.*

† "In this revolution of 1399 there was as remarkable an attention shown to the formalities of the constitution—allowance made for the men and the times —as in that of 1688 [the accession of William and Mary in place of James II.]. Upon the cession of the king, as upon his death, the parliament was no more. Yet Henry Bolingbroke was too well pleased with his friends to part with them so readily, and he had much to effect before the fervour of their spirits should abate. Hence an expedient was devised of issuing writs for a new parliament, returnable in six days. These neither were, nor could be, complied with, but the same members as had deposed Richard sat in the new parliament, which was regularly opened by Henry's commissioners, as if they had been duly elected." —HALLAM'S *Middle Ages,* ch. viii.

the other, and, while in this strange attitude, resigns it to his victorious cousin.*

> KING RICHARD.   Now is this golden crown like a deep well,
> That owes two buckets filling one another ;
> The emptier ever dancing in the air,
> The other down, unseen, and full of water :
> That bucket down, and full of tears, am I,
> Drinking my griefs, whilst you mount up on high.
>   BOLINGBROKE.   Are you contented to resign the crown ?
>   KING RICHARD.   Ay, no ;—no, ay ;—for I must nothing be :
> Therefore no, no, for I resign to thee.
> Now mark me how I will undo myself :—
> I give this heavy weight from off my head,
> And this unwieldy sceptre from my hand,
> The pride of kingly sway from out my heart ;
> With mine own tears I wash away my balm,
> With mine own hands I give away my crown.

He again expatiates upon all he surrenders—crown, sceptre, rents, revenues, manors, &c., &c.—annuls in word all his acts, decrees, and laws ; wishes himself dead, and Bolingbroke long life as king, &c.   But all this extraordinary language he utters in mingled grief and confusion, perhaps with some lingering hope that detailing his misfortunes and losses will yet arouse sympathy, and in this idea he was not altogether mistaken, as the sequel proved ; but no feeling for him is openly shown by any one in this scene.   Bolingbroke is quite master of the situation, and his eager adherent, Northumberland, not satisfied with Richard's humiliating resignation, insists on his reading a list of charges against both himself and his followers, and acknowledging their truth.†   This list of accusations against the captive king is in the play shown to him.   In reality he apparently never saw it, though it was publicly presented to the Parliament. This last insult rouses the unfortunate king from utter despondency to violent, though despairing rage.   Perhaps being addressed by his former subject, Northumberland, in

---

* "Without any of true kingly strength or dignity, Richard has a fine feeling for the royal situation.   Instead of comprehending things as they are, and achieving heroic deeds, he satiates his heart with the grace, the tenderness, or the pathos of situations   .   .   .   Richard is, as it were, fading out of existence. Bolingbroke seems not only to have robbed him of his authority, but to have encroached upon his very personality, and to have usurped his understanding and his will."—DOWDEN's *Shakespeare's Mind and Art.*

† "Bolingbroke purposed to have Richard solemnly deposed in Parliament for his pretended tyranny and misconduct.   A charge of thirty-three articles was accordingly drawn up against him, and presented to that assembly. . . . . . The greater part of these grievances imputed to Richard seems to be the exertion of arbitrary prerogatives."—HUME's *History,* vol. ii.

more insolent words than he has yet heard, or recollecting his dead favorites—Bushy, &c.—whose offences, probably exaggerated, are now thrust before his eyes, arouse some of the spirit of his race, even at this moment of public shame.

KING RICHARD.   What more remains?
NORTHUMBERLAND.   No more, but that you read [*offering a paper*]
These accusations, and these grievous crimes,
Committed by your person, and your followers,
Against the state and profit of this land ;
That, by confessing them, the souls of men
May deem that you are worthily depos'd.
   KING RICHARD.   Must I do so? and must I ravel out
My weav'd-up follies ! Gentle Northumberland,
If thy offences were upon record,
Would it not shame thee, in so fair a troop,
To read a lecture of them?   If thou wouldst,
There shouldst thou find one heinous article,
Containing the deposing of a king,
And cracking the strong warrant of an oath,
Mark'd with a blot, damn'd in the Book of Heaven.—Act IV.

After vehemently reproaching Northumberland and others for treason, he blames himself for having resigned the crown. He asks for a looking-glass, and, gazing at it, sees his own agitated features.

KING RICHARD.   No deeper wrinkles yet?   Hath sorrow struck
So many blows upon this face of mine,
And made no deeper wounds?—O, flattering glass,
Like to my followers in prosperity,
Thou dost beguile me !   Was this face the face
That every day under his household roof
Did keep ten thousand men?
Was this the face that fac'd so many follies,
And was at last out-fac'd by Bolingbroke?
A brittle glory shineth in this face :
As brittle as the glory is the face.*

[*Dashes the glass to the ground.*

He again pathetically deplores his downfall, and asks permission to leave this trying scene. Bolingbroke calmly orders his conveyance to the Tower of London, still preserving, in language and manner, the same studied deference

* Shakespeare follows history here, for Hume writes :—"Richard's household consisted of ten thousand persons ; he had three hundred in his kitchen. . . . . Such prodigality was probably one chief reason of the public discontents."—*History of England*, vol. ii.

to the captive monarch which he has done throughout, yet which never propitiates or in any way consoles Richard.* When he is gone, Bolingbroke announces his approaching coronation, and also retires with his courtiers, leaving three malcontents—the Abbot of Westminster, the Bishop of Carlisle, and Lord Aumerle—together. They are shocked at the late sad, humiliating scene, and the abbot hints at some coming opposition to the new king, without giving particulars; but several noblemen—Lords Salisbury and Spencer among them—though they were unable or unwilling to resist Bolingbroke's invasion of England, are indignant at his rapid elevation to the throne. To these men the abbot probably alludes, and they withdraw to consult and determine on what course to follow.

Act V. opens with a scene of Shakespeare's pure invention—the meeting and parting of Richard and the queen. The king, with the same morbid melancholy which he has shown ever since his misfortunes, partly relieves and partly indulges grief by dwelling with pathetic minuteness upon their sorrow. He tells her, instead of suggesting either consolation or dignified resignation, to spend the long winter evenings in future in describing his dethronement, and to try to elicit the tearful sympathy of her listeners.

> KING RICHARD. In winter's tedious nights, sit by the fire
> With good old folks : and let them tell thee tales
> Of woful ages, long ago betid :
> And, ere thou bid good-night, to quit their grief,
> Tell thou the lamentable fall of me,
> And send the hearers weeping to their beds.—Act V.

This meeting is not recorded in history, though, had the queen been older, much of the conversation attributed to them might naturally have occurred.† Northumberland, the new king's most zealous subject, separates them, announcing that his master's mind is changed—he orders Richard to Pomfret Castle, and the queen to return immediately to

---

* Hume differs from Hallam in thinking that this revolution resembled that against James II. in 1688. He says that the latter movement "deliberately vindicated established privileges," but that the deposing of Richard II. "was the act of a turbulent and barbarous aristocracy, plunging headlong from the extremes of one faction into those of another."—*History of England*, vol. ii. Shakespeare seems to favour Hume's view, but Hallam, having great literary advantages, considering his enlightened times, is perhaps the best authority.

† "The young queen, daughter of the French king, returned to France soon after the revolution, and was not allowed, even had she wished, to share her deposed husband's imprisonment."—HUME's *History*, vol. ii. She seems to have been amiable and popular, from Mr. Staunton's account in his notes to the *Illustrated Shakespeare ;* but no detail of her parting from Richard is apparently recorded.

France. Richard then bitterly reproaches Northumberland
—who, of all his subjects, has been the most insolent— and
foretells a dangerous quarrel between him and the new king
—a prediction which was fatally verified.

> KING RICHARD.   Northumberland, thou ladder wherewithal
> The mounting Bolingbroke ascends my throne,
> The time shall not be many hours of age
> More than it is, ere foul sin, gathering head,
> Shall break into corruption : thou shalt think,
> Though he divide the realm, and give thee half,
> It is too little, helping him to all :
> He shall think that thou, which knowest the way
> To plant unrightful kings, wilt know again,
> Being ne'er so little urg'd another way,
> To pluck him headlong from the usurped throne.—Act V.

Northumberland, however, listens incredulously, and hurries
off the king and queen in different directions. This scene,
though Shakespeare's invention, probably well describes the
real feelings of the unfortunate Richard and of his rebellious
subject, Northumberland, whose whole object now is to fulfil
the new king's wishes, and to confirm his power. The next
scene is in the Duke of York's palace, where he describes
to his wife, with mixed feelings of regret and pleasure, the
public triumph and disgrace of his rival nephews, in their
late procession through London.

> YORK.   The duke, great Bolingbroke,
> Mounted upon a hot and fiery steed,
> Which his aspiring rider seemed to know,
> With slow, but stately pace, kept on his course,
> While all tongues cried, " God save thee, Bolingbroke ! "
>
> Whilst he, from one side to the other turning,
> Bare-headed, lower than his proud steed's neck,
> Bespake them thus : " I thank you, countrymen : "
> And thus still doing, thus he pass'd along.
> DUCHESS.   Alas, poor Richard ! where rode he the whilst ?
> YORK.   As in a theatre, the eyes of men,
> After a well-graced actor leaves the stage,
> Are idly bent on him that enters next,
> Thinking his prattle to be tedious :
> Even so, or with much more contempt, men's eyes
> Did scowl on Richard ; no man cried, " God save him ! "
> No joyful tongue gave him his welcome home :
> But dust was thrown upon his sacred head ;
> Which with such gentle sorrow he shook off,
> His face still combating with tears and smiles,

> The badges of his grief and patience,
> That had not God, for some strong purpose, steel'd
> The hearts of men, they must perforce have melted,
> And barbarism itself have pitied him.
> But Heaven hath a hand in these events;
> To whose high will we bound our calm contents.
> To Bolingbroke we are sworn subjects now,
> Whose state and honour I for aye allow.
>   DUCHESS.   Here comes my son Aumerle.
>   YORK.   Aumerle that was;
> But that is lost, for being Richard's friend,
> And, madam, you must call him Rutland now:
> I am in parliament pledge for his truth,
> And lasting fealty to the new-made king.—Act V.

York—an excitable, rather frivolous man—deeply pities Richard, yet greatly admires Bolingbroke ; the duchess sympathises entirely with the deposed king, and shows no admiration for the new monarch, when their son Aumerle enters. This young man, created Duke of Albemarle, or Aumerle, as Shakespeare prefers to call him, by Richard, was deprived of this title by the new government, and styled Earl of Rutland. His conduct during this civil war is somewhat differently described by Shakespeare and Hume—the former representing him faithful to Richard ; the latter, with probably more truth, as being treacherous to both his contending cousins. He is now, however, plotting in Richard's behalf, which his father suspects ; and, finding a treasonable letter on him, York, despite his wife's entreaties and his son's terror, declares he will reveal all to the new sovereign, whom he has formally acknowledged. York probably feels that it is now hopeless to attempt any revolution in Richard's favour, the new king having the strength of England on his side ; and that an insurrection now would only ruin the insurgents and injure the country. He resolves, therefore, to tell all to Bolingbroke, and to trust in his mercy ; for he well knows that the new sovereign has no desire to punish him or any of the royal family, but may be induced to do so, and perhaps execute his rebellious cousin, if pressed by Northumberland, and other zealous adherents, to crush all rebellion in the blood of its leaders. Aumerle, whose previous adherence to Richard has apparently been excused by Bolingbroke, also hastens to him, arriving at the palace shortly before his father. Previous to his entrance, the new king (Henry IV.) had revealed his first disappointment during his present complete triumph. He had asked about his " unthrifty son," Prince Henry—his heir, the hope, and yet the vexation of his troubled life. The inquiry had been provokingly answered by young Hotspur—a youth rather older than Prince Henry, but who, unlike him, assists his father, Northumberland, with all the spirited eagerness of his ardent character.

> BOLINGBROKE.   Can no man tell of my unthrifty son?
> 'Tis full three months since I did see him last :
> If any plague hang over us, 'tis he.
> I would to God, my lords, he might be found :
> Inquire at London, 'mongst the taverns there,
> For there, they say, he daily doth frequent,
> With unrestrained, loose companions.—Act V.

It seems strange that Bolingbroke should so openly censure his son before a youth like Percy and the other lords ; but he has now little time to lament his son's misconduct.   He deplores it for a moment, yet foresees his future amendment, when Aumerle hastily enters his presence.   Bolingbroke, having no idea of his treachery, receives him, with some surprise at his hurried manner, admitting him to a private conference with closed doors.

York now arrives, and, with perhaps assumed or exaggerated indignation, confesses to Bolingbroke his son Aumerle's treason, showing him the letter, which reveals some secret plot.   Bolingbroke is perplexed at this discovery, and at his strange position between his eager, accusing uncle and his guilty, terrified, supplicating cousin.   York warmly requests him not to pardon his son, when the duchess arrives, eagerly pleading for Aumerle, while York apparently opposes them both.*   Bolingbroke hears them all three attentively—perhaps with derision.   He doubtless knows that, despite York's apparent eagerness to have Aumerle punished, his hitherto reluctant loyalty will be greatly strengthened by extending unasked clemency to his son and heir.   While speaking affectionately to his aunt, the duchess, he freely pardons Aumerle ; but resolves to punish the rest of the conspirators.

> BOLINGBROKE.   With all my heart
> I pardon him.
> DUCHESS.   A god on earth thou art.

* "The scene is ill-conceived, and worse executed throughout, but one line is both atrocious and contemptible. The duchess having dwelt on the word pardon, and urged the king to let her hear it from his lips, York takes her up with this stupid quibble : 'Speak it in French, king : say, *Pardonnez moi.*' "—HALLAM'S *Literary History*, vol. iii. ch vi.   Mr. Hallam, usually so cool and judicious, is perhaps hardly fair to Shakespeare here.   The quibble, indeed, may be, as he says, stupid and contemptible, yet consistnt enough with the character of the eccentric, flighty, trifling York, "the madcap duke" (*Henry IV.*) whom Shakespeare had to represent.   It possibly, if not probably, amused the king, who had shown signs of relenting before it was uttered.

> BOLINGBROKE.   Good uncle, help to order several powers
> To Oxford, or where'er these traitors are :
> They shall not live within this world, I swear,
> But I shall have them, if I once know where.
> Uncle, farewell—and cousin too, adieu :
> Your mother well hath prayed, and prove you true.—Act V.

Throughout this trying scene, Bolingbroke maintains the same shrewdness and self-control he always displayed, and which, indeed, made him well worthy of the throne he had acquired. All through this play, wherever he appears, he is evidently the wisest man among either friends or foes. He possesses a daring courage, fully equal to all the fiery, warlike spirits around him, uniting with that splendid gift a firmness of which none can boast in the same degree. He is, perhaps, as a warrior, statesman, and ruler, as grand a specimen of the English character of his unsettled period as could be conceived. When Bolingbroke and his relatives leave the apartment, a certain Sir Pierce of Exton enters it, with an attendant, who agree together that they have heard the new king exclaim, perhaps since discovering the last plot,

> Have I no friend will rid me of this living fear ?

Exton imagines the "living fear" meant the imprisoned Richard, and also fancies that the king looked expressively at him when saying the words. He secretly declares that he will obey his sovereign's supposed wishes, and starts for Pomfret with avowedly murderous intent, for which even this unscrupulous man cannot say he has sufficient warrant.

The next scene is in Pomfret Castle, where the imprisoned king bewails to himself all his griefs, in the same strange manner he had previously done before his own followers, his triumphant foe, and lastly before his queen. He is now alone, and, without showing either manly resignation or any religious feeling, indulges gloomy thoughts by expressing them in a vague style, revealing a state of mind which might probably have led to insanity, had his prison life been much prolonged.

> KING RICHARD.   I have been studying how I may compare
> This prison, where I live, unto the world :
> And, for because the world is populous,
> And here is not a creature but myself,
> I cannot do it ;—yet I'll hammer it out.
> .   .   .   .   .   Sometimes am I king ;
> Then treason makes me wish myself a beggar,

> And so I am : then crushing penury
> Persuades me I was better when a king ;
> Then am I king'd again : and, by-and-by,
> Think that I am unking'd by Bolingbroke,
> And straight am nothing.—Act V.

His sad reflections, however, are interrupted by a groom's entrance. This man was formerly in Richard's service, and he greatly pities his luckless master, to whom he has somehow obtained access. He tells the deposed king that on Bolingbroke's coronation-day, the new sovereign had ridden one of Richard's horses, which he, as groom in the royal stable, had often harnessed and "dress'd" for his use.

> KING RICHARD.　Rode he on Barbary?　Tell me, gentle friend,
> How went he under him ?
> 　GROOM.　So proudly, as if he disdain'd the ground.
> 　KING RICHARD.　So proud that Bolingbroke was on his back !
> That jade hath eat bread from my royal hand ;
> This hand hath made him proud with clapping him.
> Would he not stumble ?　Would he not fall down
> (Since pride must have a fall), and break the neck
> Of that proud man that did usurp his back ?
> Forgiveness, horse ! why do I rail on thee,
> Since thou, created to be aw'd by man,
> Wast born to bear?—Act V.

This news interests and irritates Richard, when a jailor enters, bringing his food, and orders the groom away, who departs in suspicious terror. This jailor refuses to taste the food first as he had done previously, saying that orders from the new king have forbade him doing so. Richard, probably suspecting poison, strikes the jailor, who calls for help, and Exton, with armed followers, enter. Richard kills or wounds two of them, when Exton and the others strike him down, mortally wounded. He dies uttering a few noble words, worthy, indeed, of a greater man.

> KING RICHARD.　That hand shall burn in never-quenching fire,
> That staggers thus my person.—Exton, thy fierce hand
> Hath with the king's blood stain'd the king's own land.
> Mount, mount, my soul ! thy seat is up on high ;
> Whilst my gross flesh sinks downward, here to die. [*Dies.*]—Act V.

Exton, gazing at the dead king, feels momentary remorse, but resolves to bear the body to the new monarch, hoping for and expecting approval of his dreadful deed. This account of Richard's fate, though believed by many, is doubted by Hume and some other historians, for what caused Richard's death was never known.*   He certainly died in Pomfret Castle, and, his death being a political advantage as well as a mental relief to the new monarch, it was suspected that Richard's end was hastened by his direct orders or secret intimations. Yet Bolingbroke was by no means cruel or unscrupulous during the most trying period of his life, and it seems inconsistent with his character to have sullied his triumph by so base a crime as the murder of a prisoner. If Richard were actually assassinated, he might have been poisoned by some zealous adherent of the new king, without any warrant from that monarch himself.† Evidently, there was a report of his murder, which the new king tried to refute by the only means in his power ; but it does not seem unlikely that Richard died of a broken heart, considering his position and state of mind ; and in this case the fatal workings of "the tortured soul," to use his own words (Act IV.), would not be visible to mortal eye.

The last scene is at Windsor Castle. Bolingbroke—now styled Henry IV.—with his uncle York, is surrounded by ministers and adherents.   He is in full triumph, hearing from different messengers the welcome news of the speedy, complete suppression of the revolt raised in behalf of the captive Richard. Northumberland enters, announcing, with his usual zeal, that he has sent to London the heads of Lords Salisbury, Spencer, Blunt, and Kent, giving in a paper particulars of their capture ; for they were not slain in battle, but deliberately executed.   King Henry thanks Northumberland, and then hears from another eager adherent, Lord Fitzwater, of the execution of two more "traitors," Brocas and Sir Bennet Seely. These men never really engaged the king's forces, but were betrayed by Aumerle—now called Earl of Rutland—who, anxious to show gratitude for his late pardon, eagerly delivered up his unlucky confederates.‡ The king having also thanked Fitzwater, and promised him reward, next receives the gallant Percy, who, instead of presenting the head, or announcing the execution of some prisoner, brings as a captive the Bishop of Carlisle —the most faithful of Richard's adherents. Shakespeare

---

* STAUNTON'S *Notes to the Illustrated Shakespeare.*

† "It is more probable that he was starved to death in prison. . . This account is more consistent with the story that his body was exposed in public, and that no marks of violence were found upon it."—HUME'S *History*, vol. ii.   Yet, had he been starved, his emaciated body would surely have aroused suspicions of murder as well as "marks of violence" could have done.

‡ "Rutland appeared carrying on a pole the head of Lord Spencer, his brother-in-law, which he presented in triumph to Henry IV., as a testimony of his loyalty."—HUME'S *History*, vol. ii.   Hume calls Rutland an "infamous man— treacherous to all parties, yet keeping himself on the safe side."

makes Henry generously pardon and praise his venerable foe, in words worthy of his position ; yet Hume states that he was imprisoned.   Probably, however, he was soon after liberated and pardoned, as there is no record of his trial or punishment for certain hostility to the new monarch.   Lastly Sir Pierce of Exton enters, with attendants bearing Richard's body under a covering.   Exton announces having brought Henry his " buried fear," for that

> Herein all breathless lies
> The mightiest of thy greatest enemies.

At this sight, the king is apparently grieved, and blames Exton for the deed, who, like Hubert to King John, declares he had his implied warrant.   Henry, however, banishes him for ever from his sight, and announces his intention of going on a pilgrimage to the Holy Land,

> To wash this blood from off my guilty hand.

This whole scene, so well adapted to stage effect, is Shakespeare's own imagining, as there is no record of Richard's body being brought from Pomfret to Windsor, neither did Henry nor his adherents ever admit their guilt in the late king's death.   Yet historians seem doubtful about Henry's innocence in the matter.   Even those most friendly to him cannot deny that the circumstances were suspicious ; while his life was certainly in danger, from the murderous plots of his imprisoned rival's adherents.   Nevertheless, the king himself was evidently more merciful, just, and moderate than either his friends or foes were, for in many ways he was worthy of a better age.*

The triumph of the house of Lancaster was now complete. On the English throne sat the illustrious son of the noble John of Gaunt—a prince worthy, indeed, of his high position, though, from policy or necessity, often forced to reward men and applaud acts which in better times he would probably have

---

* " Henry had shown little taste for bloodshed in his conduct of the revolution.   Though a deputation of lords, with Archbishop Arundel at their head, pressed him to take Richard's life, he steadily refused, and kept him a prisoner at Pomfret.   The judgments against Gloster, Warwick, and Arundel were reversed, but the lords who had appealed to the duke were only punished by the loss of the dignities which they had received as a reward.   In spite of a stormy scene among the lords in parliament, Henry refused to exact further punishment ; and his real temper was shown in a statute which forbade all such appeals, and left treason to be dealt with by ordinary process of law.   But the times were too rough for mercy such as this.   Clouds no sooner gathered round the new king than the degraded lords leagued with Salisbury and the deposed Bishop of Carlisle to release Richard and to murder Henry."—GREEN'S *History of the English People*, vol. i. ch. v.

gladly disavowed.*   Thus Richard's many follies, errors, and weaknesses had ended in dethronement and untimely death. From the first, surrounded by ambitious, fierce, and often hostile kinsmen, this sovereign was in a very difficult position, though, had he shown firmness and prudence, his uncles Gaunt and York might never have been alienated. But his own pride being equal to theirs, he scorned their opinions, distrusted their motives, and placed entire confidence in favourites, who, however faithful from interest or duty, were utterly unable to oppose the offended royal family, when allied with the nobles, by influencing the nation at large. In fact, princes, lords, commons, and people alike resented Richard's partiality to these men, whose destruction was thus an inevitable consequence ; and in their downfall was involved that of their imprudent and ultimately friendless patron.†

* "A great council, held after the suppression of the revolt, prayed 'that if Richard, the late king, be alive, as some suppose he is, it be ordained that he be well and securely guarded ; but if he be dead, that he be openly showed to the people.' The ominous words were soon followed by news of Richard's death in prison. His body was brought to St. Paul's, Henry himself, with the princes of the blood royal, bearing the pall."—GREEN's *History of the English People*, vol. i.

† "At the end of this king's reign it was enacted 'that every one should be guilty of treason which compasseth the death of the king or to depose him, or to render up his homage or liege, or he that riseth against the king to make war within his realm.' Nothing is said of any overt act. The trial was to be in Parliament. It is difficult to understand the object of this statute, unless it was to convert into treason mere words, or indeed anything whatever which could be considered to indicate in any way hostility to the king. The Act was passed in 1397, when Richard was, no doubt, fully aware of the dangers which were gathering round him, and which in 1399 led to his deposition. It was repealed ten years afterwards by Henry IV."—STEPHENS's *English Criminal Law*, ch. xxiii.

CHAPTER VI.

FIRST PART OF KING HENRY IV.

Sketch of Play.

OWEN GLENDOWER, a Welsh chief, allied with the Scottish Earl of Douglas, continues to resist Henry IV., even after Richard's death.   Glendower has previously captured a distinguished and valuable prisoner, Sir Edmund Mortimer, Hotspur's brother-in-law, and uncle to the young Earl of March, whom Richard had considered his heir, and who was kept in custody by King Henry.   Hotspur wishes to ransom his captured brother-in law, which the king refuses to do, dreading both him and his nephew March, owing to their regal pretensions.   Upon this refusal, Hotspur not only refuses to deliver up some prisoners to Henry, but forms an alliance with Glendower.   Mortimer, who has married his captor Glendower's daughter, cordially joins his father-in-law and brother-in-law.   Hotspur's father and uncle, Northumberland and Worcester, also revolt against the king, though they had been his first and chief adherents.   The insurgents, however, are all defeated, Hotspur is killed in battle, and his uncle Worcester captured and executed.   The Scottish Earl Douglas is also captured, but liberated, and the king's triumph is complete ; while Glendower retires to the Welsh mountains.   In this play Prince Henry—afterwards Henry V.—is introduced, associating with Sir John Falstaff, Poins, Peto, and other dissolute companions, in the taverns of London.   He, however, bravely assists in quelling the rebellion, and slays Hotspur, after which he relapses into his former habits, to the great vexation of his father and his ministers.

THE first scene describes King Henry gladly hearing of Hotspur's victories over Glendower and his Scottish ally, Earl Douglas.   This war, as described by Hume and Shakespeare, caused not only much bloodshed, but occasioned singular alliances between opposing parties.   Hotspur, the brave son of Northumberland, the most zealous adherent of Henry IV., after defeating the king's enemies, thought, as did his uncle Worcester and his father, that owing to their great services to Henry, they should have more power than that sagacious prince was willing to grant to them. The discontent of the older men is fully shared by the younger one, and rouses him into fury. He not only refuses to deliver up his prisoners to Henry, which, by his allegiance, he was bound to do,* but quarrels with the king because the latter would not "ransom home" his captured brother-in-law, Edmund Mortimer.† This man —Glendower's captive, and afterwards son-in-law— Henry IV. dreads and distrusts, keeping Mortimer's nephew, Lord March, in prison, knowing their claims to the throne, both by legitimate descent and by the express wish of the late king. Amid so much excitement and warfare, Henry's observant mind perceives the high qualities of his brave young officer and future foe, Hotspur, who first perilled his life in his cause, and soon after was ready to risk it against him. Henry sadly compares this youthful hero to his own dissolute son, whom neither his firm will, example, nor regal power can influence in the least, cordially wishing he could exchange his incorrigible heir for his brave young subject. He evidently feels how thankful he should be could he reckon upon Hotspur's courage, intelligence, and devotion in a dutiful child, instead of in the son of the ambitious dis- contented Northumberland, who, as Richard had foreseen, now expected, together with his brother Worcester, an amount of power and influence in return for their services which probably a monarch could not safely grant. Hearing from Westmoreland of Hotspur's victories in his cause, Henry exclaims,—

> Yea, there thou mak'st me sad, and mak'st me sin
> In envy that my Lord Northumberland
> Should be the father of so blest a son :
> A son, who is the theme of honour's tongue ;
> Amongst a grove, the very straightest plant ;
> Who is sweet fortune's minion, and her pride :
> Whilst I, by looking on the praise of him,
> See riot and dishonour stain the brow
> Of my young Harry. O, that it could be prov'd
> That some night-tripping fairy had exchang'd
> In cradle-clothes our children where they lay,

---

* HUME's *History*.

† Mr. Staunton (*Notes to the Illustrated Shakespeare*) states that Hotspur was justified by the law of arms in retaining the prisoners, but this was probably a disputed point.

> And call'd mine Percy, his Plantagenet !
> Then would I have his Harry, and he mine.—Act **I**.

The formidable discontents of his former adherents forced
Henry to seek new friends in Lord Westmoreland, Sir H.
Blunt, and others—and to postpone his journey to the
Holy Land, which, indeed, he never made, being menaced
with fresh revolts, now headed by his old adherents, the
Percy family, instead of by hereditary opponents. He has
scarcely ceased admiring Hotspur's bravery, however, when
he complains of his unruly conduct to Westmoreland, his
cousin, foreseeing the troubles that may yet arise from the
powerful house of Percy, hitherto his ardent supporter.

> KING HENRY.   What think you, coz',
> Of this young Percy's pride? the prisoners
> Which he in this adventure hath surpris'd,
> To his own use he keeps ; and sends me word,
> I shall have none but Mordake Earl of Fife.
> WESTMORELAND.   This is his uncle's teaching, this is Worcester,
> Malevolent to you in all respects ;
> Which makes him prune himself, and bristle up
> The crest of youth against your dignity.
> KING HENRY. But I have sent for him to answer this :
> And for this cause, awhile we must neglect
> Our holy purpose to Jerusalem.
> Cousin, on Wednesday next our council we
> Will hold at Windsor ; and so inform the lords ;
> But come yourself with speed to us again ;
> For more is to be said, and to be done,
> Than out of anger can be uttered.—Act **I**.

The second scene introduces Prince Henry, with his
favourite associate, Sir John Falstaff, in a London tavern.
This witty, unscrupulous debauchee not only amuses and
influences the Prince of Wales, but maintains a sort of
ascendancy over his yet more desperate companions—Poins,
Peto, and Bardolph. Although these fellows often ridicule
his constant boasting and alleged cowardice, he not only
participates in all their pranks and robberies, but contrives
to obtain more profit and run less risk than any of them.*
He is both their jester and chief instigator, Prince Henry
deriving an amusement from his wit, joking, and effrontery
not to be found in the rest of the gang. Of his early history

* "Falstaff's effrontery is inimitable. He is neither a coward nor courageous.
He only asks which will pay best—fighting or running away—and acts accordingly. He evidently had a reputation as a soldier, and was a professed one ;
was sought out, and got a commission."—FURNIVALL'S *Introduction to the Royal
Shakspere.*

nothing is said by himself or his associates. He appears in the play as an old, very fat, white-bearded man; when hurried or fatigued, almost helpless, from his unwieldy corpulence. Yet his constant wit, fun, and coarse gaiety make him as light-hearted as the prince himself, and infinitely more merry and diverting than any of his roguish companions. He occupies a sort of middle position between the prince and his comrades, for, though they all laugh at him, he is more familiar with Prince Henry than they are. He is also supposed to have the most influence over the heir-apparent, while he is far less venturous, if not less courageous, than any of his companions. He never shows a really good quality from first to last, being a compound of self-indulgence, falsehood, licentiousness, and shameless roguery. He has neither a friend nor a bitter enemy, nor apparently does he wish to be either to any one. He knows how to please the prince, without either flattering or coaxing; while Poins, Peto, &c., satisfied to see how their comrade amuses the Prince of Wales, doubtless believe themselves all the more secure from either justice or poverty. Falstaff, however, often mentions the much-desired future, when his "sweet wag, Hal," shall be king, and, in half-jest, half-earnest, wishes to know how he and his friends will then be considered and treated under the new *régime*, when their young patron must be, of course, at the head not only of the military and naval forces, but also of the judicial power in the realm.

FLASTAFF. Marry, then, sweet wag, when thou art king, let not us that are squires of the night's body be called thieves of the day's beauty; let us be—Diana's foresters, gentlemen of the shade, minions of the moon: and let men say, we be men of good government: being governed as the sea is, by our noble and chaste mistress the moon, under whose countenance we—steal.

PRINCE HENRY. Thou say'st well; and it holds well too: for the fortune of us, that are the moon's men, doth ebb and flow like the sea; being governed as the sea is by the moon. As for proof, now, a purse of gold most resolutely snatched on Monday night, and most dissolutely spent on Tuesday morning: got with swearing—lay by; and spent with crying—bring in: now, in as low an ebb as the foot of the ladder; and, by and by, in as high a flow as the ridge of the gallows.—Act I. Scene II.

There is great cunning in these hints of Falstaff, but Prince Henry, with a shrewdness not unworthy of his cautious father, always evades the subject, usually talking of present times with as much wild recklessness as his knavish associates can wish, but preserving a determined silence about his and their own future positions. Thus, throughout all their gay conversations from first to last, the prince never makes Falstaff or his friends the least promise of future favour, or even protection, while diverting himself with their wit, and profligacy to the fullest extent. In this first scene he asks Falstaff when they shall attempt their next robbery ; calls him and Poins, " Jack " and " Ned," and is called by the former " Hal," and " sweet wag," in return.   Poins, the boldest of the party, proposes, chiefly to amuse the prince, to incite Falstaff and his comrades to way-lay and rob some peaceful travellers, who, he knows, will be on the high road near Rochester early next morning ; and that after this the prince and he should despoil their associates, though not apparently to repay the plundered people. Henry eagerly agrees, and they first resolve to amuse themselves at the expense both of the travellers and of their own comrades.

When the prince is alone, after Poins leaves him, he utters a remarkable soliloquy, which Shakespeare introduces to explain the wonderful change which really came over the wild young man in after life.

> PRINCE HENRY.   I know you all, and will awhile uphold
> The unyok'd humour of your idleness;
> Yet herein will I imitate the sun,
> Who doth permit the base, contagious clouds
> To smother up his beauty from the world,
> That, when he please again to be himself,
> Being wanted, he may be more wonder'd at,
> By breaking through the foul and ugly mists
> Of vapours that did seem to strangle him.
>
> So, when this loose behaviour I throw off,
> And pay the debt I never promised,
> By how much better than my word I am,
> By so much shall I falsify men's hopes ;
> And like bright metal on a sullen ground,
> My reformation, glittering o'er my fault,
> Shall show more goodly, and attract more eyes,
> Than that which hath no foil to set it off.—Act I.

From historical record, the change in him seems to have been chiefly caused by the last words of his father as well as by his altered position, when monarch, immediately on hearing them.*   Yet, though constantly associating with Falstaff and

---

* According to Hume, Henry IV., through jealousy, excluded his heir from all share in public business, and " was even displeased to see him at the head of armies, where his martial talents might prove dangerous to his own authority. The active spirit of young Henry, restrained from its proper exercise, broke out into extravagancies of every kind . . . There even remains a tradition that, when

his set, he never shows the least shame or disgust either at their licentious talk, profligacy, or dishonesty, all of which he indeed encourages, by free participation or by jeering applause. Although his speech to himself sounds grand—even noble—in Shakespeare's splendid words, yet, when considered in relation both to his conduct and position, it surely deserves neither praise nor indulgence. Satisfying his too easy conscience by purposing reformation, he never considers the vile example every hour of his life sets even to his younger brothers—none of whom, happily, follow it—nor the grief and shame, if not danger, which it causes to his toil-worn father, to whose sense and energy he owes alike his present position and high expectations. He flatters himself that the more dissolute he now is the more noble will his altered conduct make him appear in future, forgetting that he might die at any moment, leaving a reputation disgraceful and even dangerous to his family and the nation.

Probably, however, at this wild time of his life, Prince Henry never felt the emotions ascribed to him. All his conduct as recorded both in history and the play proves that while Prince of Wales, without real power, yet the certain heir to the crown, he indulged his spirits and exuberant energies, which were checked by his cautious father, in wild excess and with dissolute companions. He fortunately, however, never seemed to wish either his brothers or any of the young nobility—his proper companions—to join him in his wild way of life. He somehow found out or was introduced to Falstaff, Poins, &c., and, taking them as they were, threw himself headlong into their society, talked like them, acted with them, and lived chiefly among them, thus avoiding both his father's friends and enemies. Doubtless had he, like some heirs-apparent, complained of his father's harshness or jealousy, he would soon have found many dissatisfied, cunning statesmen ready and willing to encourage his discontent and flatter his pride, for the sake of possible future favour. Prince Henry does nothing of the sort. He leaves his father's court and council-chamber, entirely devoting his time and company to a set of companions far too contemptible and despised to endanger the king's authority in any way.

Yet both in history and in the play he showed, even when a youth, great military talents, which the formidable rebellions against his father soon called into action ; for the

heated with liquor and jollity, he scrupled not to accompany his riotous associates in attacking the passengers on the streets and highways, and despoiling them of their goods, and he found an amusement in the incidents which the terror and regret of these defenceless people produced on such occasions."—*History of England*, ch. xix.

next scene introduces the memorable and predicted quarrel
between Henry IV. and the Percy family—the " ladders," as
Richard II. called them, by which he had ascended the throne.
The Earls of Worcester and Northumberland come before
him with their son and nephew, Hotspur. The king sternly
declares that henceforth he will make them fear him, to
which Worcester bitterly replies that owing to their assistance he is now on the throne. The irritated king makes
no reply, save by dismissing Worcester instantly from his
presence.

> WORCESTER.   Our house, my sovereign liege, little deserves
> The scourge of greatness to be used on it ;
> And that same greatness too which our own hands
> Have holp to make so portly.
>   KING HENRY.   Worcester, get thee gone, for I do see
> Danger and disobedience in thine eye.
>
> You have good leave to leave us ; when we need
> Your use and counsel we shall send for you.—Act I.

Northumberland says little, being evidently confounded at
this breach between his family and the king, for whom they
had done so much. Hotspur, with the rash boldness of his
nature, now vindicates himself for withholding the prisoners.
He sharply ridicules the royal messenger who had demanded
their surrender, and Henry, who hears his spirited speech,
perceives no sign of submission in it.

> HOTSPUR.   My liege, I did deny no prisoners.
> But, I remember, when the fight was done,
> When I was dry with rage and extreme toil,
> Breathless and faint, leaning upon my sword,
> Came there a certain lord, neat, and trimly dress'd.
> He was perfumèd like a milliner ;
> And as the soldiers bore dead bodies by,
> He call'd them untaught knaves, unmannerly.
>   *   *   *   *   *   *
> With many holiday and lady terms
> He questioned me ; among the rest, demanded
> My prisoners, in your Majesty's behalf.
> I then, all smarting, with my wounds being cold,
> To be so pester'd with a popinjay,
> Out of my grief and my impatience,
> Answer'd neglectingly, I know not what ;
> He should, or should not ;—for he made me mad,
> To see him shine so brisk, and smell so sweet,
> And talk so like a waiting gentlewoman
> Of guns, and drums, and wounds (God save the mark !) ;

> . . . .   And, but for these vile guns
> He would himself have been a soldier.
> This bald unjointed chat of his, my lord,
> I answered indirectly, as I said ;
> And, I beseech you, let not his report
> Come current for an accusation,
> Betwixt my love and your high Majesty.—Act I.

Henry, irritated at his boldness, sternly refuses Hotspur's previous request that his brother-in-law, Mortimer, now Glendower's captive, should be "ransomed home," in return for obtaining Hotspur's prisoners. Henry even accuses Mortimer of treason against him, knowing the claims of his family to the throne, although Mortimer was captured while fighting in his service against Glendower. Hotspur instantly and vehemently repudiates this charge of treason against Mortimer, praising him highly, when the incensed King forbids him ever to mention Mortimer again, thus revealing his secret fear of that personage, and angrily leaves the apartment with his courtiers.

> KING HENRY.   I shall never hold that man my friend
> Whose tongue shall ask me for one penny cost
> To ransom home revolted Mortimer.
> HOTSPUR.   Revolted Mortimer !
> He never did fall off, my sovereign liege,
> But by the chance of war ;—To prove that true
> Needs no more but one tongue for all those wounds,
> Those mouthed wounds, which valiantly he took.
> When on the gentle Severn's sedgy bank,
> In single opposition, hand to hand,
> He did confound the best part of an hour
> In changing hardiment with great Glendower.
>
>   .   .   .   .   .   .
> Never did base and rotten policy
> Colour her working with such deadly wounds ;
> Nor never could the noble Mortimer
> Receive so many, and all willingly :
> Then let him not be slander'd with revolt.
>   KING HENRY.   Thou dost belie him, Percy, though dost
>   belie him,
> He never did encounter with Glendower.
>
>   .   .   .   .
> Art thou not asham'd ?   But, sirrah, henceforth
> Let me not hear you speak of Mortimer :
> Send me your prisoners with the speediest means,
> Or you shall hear in such a kind from me
> As will displease you.—My Lord Northumberland,

> We license your departure with your son :—
> Send us your prisoners or you'll hear of it.
>   [*Exeunt* KING HENRY *and train.*
> HOTSPUR.   And if the devil come and roar for them,
> I will not send them.—Act I.

Northumberland and his son are now joined by Worcester. These chiefs of the Percy family own how different is the reigning Henry IV. from the disinherited invader Bolingbroke whom they had so zealously supported up to the present moment.   On the other hand, it might be said that no English king could endure the dictation, or satisfy the demands, of such ambitious subjects, with honour to himself or safety to the realm.   In this·remarkable scene the older men are calm, thoughtful, and sad—Northumberland especially ; while Hotspur denounces the king with a vehemence which neither father nor uncle can restrain, though they both attempt it.

> HOTSPUR.   But shall it be that you, that set the crown
> Upon the head of this forgetful man,
> And, for his sake, wear the detested blot
> Of murd'rous subornation—shall it be,
> That you a world of curses undergo ?
>
>   .   .   .   .   .   .
>
> Shall it, for shame, be spoken in these days,
> Or fill up chronicles in time to come,
> That men of your nobility and power
> Did 'gage them both in an unjust behalf—
> As both of you, God.pardon it ! have done—
> To put down Richard, that sweet lovely rose,
> And plant this thorn, this canker, Bolingbroke ?
> And shall it, in more shame, be further spoken,
> That you are fool'd, discarded, and shook off
> By him for whom these shames ye underwent ?—Act I. Sc. III.

After blaming each of them for having deposed Richard and supported Bolingbroke—to which reproach his saddened relatives listen for some time in repentant silence—the fiery young man continues to abuse the king so eagerly that he cannot even listen to a new plot against him, which the crafty Worcester already devises.   Northumberland urges him to be patient, and hear his uncle, when his impatient son exclaims,—

> Why, look you, I am whipp'd and scourg'd with rods,
> Nettled, and stung with pismires, when I hear
> Of this vile politician, Bolingbroke.

In Richard's time—what do you call the place?—
A plague upon't!—it is in Gloucestershire;—
'Twas where the madcap duke his uncle kept;
His uncle York; where I first bowed my knee
Unto this king of smiles, this Bolingbroke—'s blood!—
When you and he came back from Ravenspurg.
    NORTHUMBERLAND.   At Berkley Castle.
    HOTSPUR.   You say true :—
Why, what a candy deal of courtesy
This fawning greyhound then did proffer me !
Look—*when his infant fortune came to age,*
And—*gentle Harry Percy*—and, *kind cousin*—
O, the devil take such cozeners !—God forgive me !—
Good uncle, tell your tale, for I have done.—Act I. Scene III.

Worcester is now the most crafty, if not the most eager plotter, Hotspur being too angry to talk about anything coolly; while Northumberland, once so zealous and vehement, says little, and perhaps can hardly yet fully realize the fact of this complete breach between them and the prince whom they have raised to the throne. For their past conduct they are reproached warmly, yet respectfully, by Hotspur, in ardent language, which they cannot refute, and which evidently produces its silent, yet powerful effect ; as Worcester interrupts him with his plot against the king, which his nephew is too excited to hear. When he cools, he highly praises Worcester's plan of a future insurrection ; while Northumberland agrees with them only in a few words, being evidently overcome by disappointment and regret.

The Percies then part company, resolved upon declaring war against Henry, and allying themselves with Glendower, Mortimer, Earl Douglas, and the Archbishop of York, whose brother, Sir Stephen Scroop, having been lately executed for treason, joins the more eagerly in the plot against the king. The fiery spirit of Hotspur, the craft of Worcester, and the sad decision of the once active, zealous Northumberland, are strikingly contrasted in this important scene, clearly indicating a coming storm.

    WORCESTER.   And 'tis no little reason bids us speed,
To save our heads by raising of a head ;
For, bear ourselves as even as we can,
The king will always think him in our debt ;
And think we think ourselves unsatisfied,
Till he hath found a time to pay us home.
And see already how he doth begin
To make us strangers to his looks of love.
    HOTSPUR.   He does, he does ; we'll be revenged on him.
    WORCESTER.   Cousin, farewell ;—no further go in this

Than I by letters shall direct your course.
When time is ripe (which will be suddenly),
I'll steal to Glendower and Lord Mortimer ;
Where you and Douglas and our powers at once,
As I will fashion it, shall happily meet,
To bear our fortunes in our strong arms,
Which now we hold at much uncertainty.
  NORTHUMBERLAND. Farewell, good brother : we shall thrive,
    I trust.
  HOTSPUR. Uncle, adieu :—O, let the hours be short,
Till fields and blows and groans applaud our sport !—Act I.

Richard II.'s prediction is now fully verified, and henceforth the king and his earliest adherents, the Percies, are
implacable and, indeed, mortal foes.

Act II. changes to Rochester, where Prince Henry, Falstaff,
Poins, Gadshill, Peto and Bardolph meet together. The
prince and Poins, by pre-arrangement, conceal and disguise
themselves, while Falstaff, and the others rob some luckless
travellers, who make no resistance, being apparently unarmed,
and the thieves hope to divide the booty among themselves.

  FALSTAFF. Come, my masters, let us share, and then to horse
before day. An the prince and Poins be not two arrant cowards,
there's no equity stirring : there's no more valour in that Poins
than in a wild-duck.
  PRINCE HENRY *and* POINS (*rushing out upon them*)—Your
money !
  POINS. Villains ! [*They all run away, and* FALSTAFF, *after a blow
or two, runs away too, leaving the booty behind them.*]
  PRINCE HENRY. Got with much ease. Now merrily to horse :
The thieves are scatter'd, and possess'd with fear
So strongly, that they dare not meet each other ;
Each takes his fellow for an officer.
Away, good Ned. Falstaff sweats to death,
And lards the lean earth as he walks along ;
Were't not for laughing, I should pity him.
  POINS. How the rogue roar'd !—Act II.

Thus while Falstaff and the others were about to share
their booty, the prince and Poins, having far more courage
than the rest, attack them, and seize it. Falstaff and the
others, not knowing them, run off as fast as the fat knight
can, leaving the prince and Poins to enjoy the success of
their trick.

The next scene is in Hotspur's castle, whence he is
actively corresponding with the other leaders of the coming
revolt. He hints that York secretly favours his enterprise

against the king, but this does not seem to be historically true. The leaders are his uncle Worcester, Glendower, and Mortimer—the latter's captive, but now his friend and son-in-law—aided by Earl Douglas with some Scottish troops ; while Northumberland, though favouring the revolt, does not take the field. Hotspur's wife, Lady Percy, vainly tries to discover her warlike husband's designs, but he gently, yet firmly, refuses to disclose them, being evidently uneasy about his chance of success, though his intrepid nature is incapable of fear.

> LADY PERCY.   I' faith,
> I'll know your business, Harry, that I will.
> I fear, my brother Mortimer doth stir
> About his title ; and hath sent for you.

Hotspur persists in concealing his plans, at length exclaiming,—

> But hark you, Kate ;
> I must not have you henceforth question me
> Whither I go, nor reason whereabout ;
> Whither I must, I must ; and, to conclude,
> This evening I must leave you, gentle Kate.
> I know you wise ; but yet no further wise
> Than Harry Percy's wife : constant you are,
> But yet a woman : and for secrecy,
> No lady closer : for I well believe
> Thou wilt not utter what thou dost not know.—Act II.

He sets off to Wales immediately, his wife agreeing to follow him next day, his high spirit and ardent mind being now devoted to the cause of the "down-trod Mortimer," his brother-in-law, whose nephew, Lord March, is a prisoner in the king's power. This prince had been named by Richard II. as his heir, yet the Percies apparently never thought of his claims till their own quarrel with the king, whose usurpation they had so zealously supported.

After this slight glance at the stirring history of the times, Shakespeare describes fresh scenes in the London tavern at Eastcheap, where are assembled the prince and his dissolute companions. The former and Poins now expect much amusement from Falstaff at being deserted, as he thinks, by them, and thereby losing his booty, which he believes has been stolen by some bolder thieves than those who compose his gang. He accordingly enters the tavern where they usually assemble, sulky and fretful, accusing the prince and Poins of deserting him and the others just as they had secured a rich prize.

FALSTAFF.   A plague of all cowards, I say, and a vengeance too !
marry, and amen !—Give me a cup of sack, boy. . . . . A plague
of all cowards, I say, still.

PRINCE HENRY.   Why, you round man, what's the matter ?

FALSTAFF.   Are not you a coward? answer me to that; and
Poins there ?

POINS.   'Zounds, ye fat paunch, an ye call me coward, by the
Lord, I'll stab thee.

FALSTAFF.   I call thee coward !   I'll see thee damned ere I call
thee coward : but I would give a thousand pound I could run as
fast as thou canst.   You are straight enough in the shoulders, you
care not who sees your back : Call you that backing of your friends?
A plague upon such backing ! give me them that will face me.
Give me a cup of sack :—I am a rogue if I drunk to-day.

PRINCE HENRY.   O, villain ! thy lips are scarce wiped since thou
drunk'st last.

FALSTAFF.   All's one for that.   A plague of all cowards, still
say I.—Act II.

In assumed ignorance, Prince Henry asks how he lost the
booty, and Falstaff invents a story, first of two robbers
attacking him, and, increasing the number, as he apparently
thinks himself believed, ends by declaring that not less than
eleven men, in buckram suits, seized the plunder he had just
secured, and that he had no chance against so many, though
he slew several before he ran for his life.   These absurd lies
highly amuse the listeners, and even Falstaff is evidently
gratified, despite his disappointment, at seeing the prince and
his comrades so diverted at such wonderful effrontery.   The
prince, however, after hearing his version, tells the truth, confirmed by Poins, about his running away, jeeringly asking
what excuse he can now make for undeniable cowardice.   At
this question, Falstaff, never taken aback by any one, immediately declares he knew the prince was one of his despoilers,
and, of course, never thought of resisting him, but loyally
ran away.

PRINCE HENRY.   Mark now, how a plain tale shall put you down.
—Then did we two set on you four : and with a word, out-faced
you from your prize, and have it ; yea, and can show it you here in
the house :—and, Falstaff, you carried yourself away as nimbly, and
with as quick dexterity, and roared for mercy, and still ran and
roared, as ever I heard bull-calf.   What a slave art thou to hack thy
sword as thou hast done ; and then say, it was in fight !   What
trick, what device, what starting-hole, canst thou now find out, to
hide thee from this open and apparent shame ?

POINS.   Come, let's hear, Jack : What trick hast thou now ?

FALSTAFF.   By the Lord, I knew ye as well as He that made ye.
Why, hear ye, my masters : Was it for me to kill the heir apparent ?

Should I turn upon the true prince?   Why, thou knowest I am as valiant as Hercules : but beware instinct ; the lion will not touch the true prince.   Instinct is a great matter ; I was a coward on instinct. I shall think the better of myself, and thee, during my life ; I for a valiant lion, and thou for a true prince.   But, lads, I am glad you have the money.—Hostess, clap to the doors ; watch to-night, pray to-morrow.—Gallants, lads, boys, hearts of gold, all the titles of good fellowship come to you !   What, shall we be merry ? shall we have a play extempore ?

PRINCE HENRY.   Content ; and the argument shall be, thy running away.

FALSTAFF.   Ah ! no more o' that, Hal, an thou lovest me.— Act II.

In the midst of all this merriment, a messenger comes from the court, asking to see the prince, who sends Falstaff to speak to him, while he jests and laughs with his companions about Sir John's boasting and cowardice, he being their constant subject for merriment, and occasional practical jokes.   Falstaff soon re-enters with political news about the sudden rebellion of Worcester and Northumberland, who, with Hotspur, are now allied with Douglas and Glendower, against the king.   Prince Henry, who is brave as a lion, hears all this news, and also the likelihood of his soon having to head the royal troops, with perfect coolness, still amusing himself with Falstaff, who now pretends to speak like the king, and reproves the prince, advising him to leave all his wild companions except himself.   The other thieves say little, but probably watch this strange scene with more interest than amusement.   Prince Henry then pretends to be his father, and censures Falstaff—who, in turn, personates the prince—for associating with such an old sinner, on which the old knight comically defends himself at the expense of his less witty comrades, who hear all this performance without speaking.

PRINCE HENRY.   Now, Harry? whence come ye?

FALSTAFF.   My noble lord, from Eastcheap.

PRINCE HENRY.   The complaints I hear of thee are grievous.

FALSTAFF.   'Sblood, my lord, they are false :—nay, I'll tickle ye for a young prince, faith.

PRINCE HENRY.   Swearest thou, ungracious boy ? henceforth ne'er look on me.   Thou art violently carried away from grace : there is a devil haunts thee, in the likeness of a fat old man . . . . Wherein is he good, but to taste sack and drink it ? wherein cunning, but in craft ? wherein crafty, but in villainy ? wherein villainous, but in all things ? wherein worthy, but in nothing ?

FALSTAFF.   I would your grace would take me with you.   Whom mean your grace ?

PRINCE HENRY. That villainous abominable misleader of youth, Falstaff, that old white-bearded Satan.

FALSTAFF. My lord, the man I know.

PRINCE HENRY. I know thou dost.

FALSTAFF. But to say I know more harm in him than in myself, were to say more than I know. . . . . No, my good lord ; banish Peto, banish Bardolph, banish Poins ; but for sweet Jack Falstaff, kind Jack Falstaff, true Jack Falstaff, valiant Jack Falstaff, and therefore more valiant, being as he is, old Jack Falstaff, banish not him thy Harry's company ; banish plump Jack, and banish all the world.—Act II.

Suddenly, however, they are all startled by the entrance of Mrs. Quickly, their hostess, announcing that the sheriff and his men are at the door, meaning to search the house, at which news Falstaff and the others hide themselves, leaving the prince and Peto to receive the unwelcome official. The prince hears that he seeks a man of Falstaff's description, on account of the late robbery near Rochester. Henry equivocates by declaring that Falstaff is not there, and thus prevents the house being searched. He promises the sheriff, however, that he will send Sir John to him next day, and meantime asks him to depart, which he does, leaving the prince and Peto together, while Falstaff has fallen "fast asleep behind the arras." They rifle his pockets, and laugh over the bills which they find there ; after which the prince, thinking of graver matters, declares he will go to the court next day, for all must take part in the coming civil war ; that he will procure an infantry command for Falstaff ; and that the stolen money must be returned to the claiming travellers. Thus ends this extraordinary scene, in which the heir to the English Crown jests, laughs, and enjoys himself with reckless, dissolute companions, encouraging all their revelry by his presence and participation, but without making to any of them the least promise of future favour or even safety. Yet they must all know that their liberties, if not their lives, are in constant danger, even from the irregular and ill-administered laws of the period. The prince diverts his active mind and restless spirit with these unworthy associates, as if resolved not to trouble his jealous father by interfering in public affairs, who, though often regretting his wildness, never really allowed him to assist in the government.*

The next scene introduces the insurgent leaders—Hotspur, Worcester, Mortimer, and Glendower. These four, though in league against Henry IV., are none of them his equals in

* HUME'S *History*, vol. ii.

combined valour and politic wisdom. In personal courage Hotspur is unsurpassed, but is too impetuous to be as formidable as he would otherwise have been. Worcester is more of a wily politician than a soldier. Edmund Mortimer was more known as a warrior than as a statesman. Owen Glendower, though brave, energetic, and persevering, was unfitted for power over Englishmen, of whom Hotspur was in many respects a fine specimen. The Welsh chief somewhat resembled the Celtic princes in Ossian's poems—fanciful and superstitious, with absurd notions of his own supernatural powers, derived from faithful adherents, and imbibed from songs and local traditions. His ideas, therefore, are keenly ridiculed by the practical Hotspur, as they would have been doubtless by all the youth of England, though perhaps not generally with such blunt, even insolent impatience.

GLENDOWER.   At my nativity,
The front of heaven was full of fiery cressets : and, at my birth,
The frame and huge foundation of the earth
Shak'd like a coward.
    HOTSPUR. Why, so it would have done at the same season,
if your mother's cat had but kitten'd, though yourself had never
been born.
    GLENDOWER. I say, the earth did shake when I was born.
    HOTSPUR. And I say, the earth was not of my mind,
If you suppose, as fearing you it shook.
    GLENDOWER. The heavens were all on fire, the earth did tremble.
    HOTSPUR. O, then the earth shook to see the heavens on fire,
And not in fear of your nativity.
    GLENDOWER.   Cousin, of many men
I do not bear these crossings. Give me leave
To tell you once again—that at my birth,
The front of heaven was full of fiery shapes ;
The goats ran from the mountains, and the herds
Were strangely clamorous to the frighted fields.
These signs have mark'd me extraordinary ;
And all the courses of my life do show
I am not in the roll of common men.
    HOTSPUR. I think there is no man speaks better Welsh : I will
to dinner.
    MORTIMER. Peace, cousin Percy : you will make him mad.
    GLENDOWER. I can call spirits from the vasty deep.
    HOTSPUR. Why, so can I ; or so can any man :
But will they come when you do call for them ?
    GLENDOWER. Why, I can teach thee, cousin, to command
The devil.
    HOTSPUR. And I can teach thee, coz, to shame the devil,
By telling truth ; *Tell truth, and shame the devil.*—
If thou have power to raise him, bring him hither,

> And I'll be sworn I have power to shame him hence.
> O, while you live, *tell truth, and shame the devil.*—Act III.

These singular allies soon quarrel about the practical subject of territorial divisions in England and Wales between themselves, should they overcome the existing government. Glendower, evidently used to great respect, if not adulation, from his Welsh followers, is irritated at Hotspur's contempt for him; while the latter despises the chieftain with all the fiery scorn of his impetuous temper. The Welsh chief proudly boasts, in answer to Hotspur's taunt, that he cannot speak good English; of having been "trained up" at Richard II.'s court, which was historically true,* and he was ever after devoted to the deposed monarch. For, unlike the Percies, he had never acknowledged Henry IV.'s usurpation, being his consistent foe, but now finds himself strangely allied with the new king's former adherents.

> GLENDOWER.   For I was train'd up in the English court:
> Where, being but young, I framed to the harp
> Many an English ditty, lovely well,
> And gave the tongue a helpful ornament;
> A virtue that was never seen in you.
>   HOTSPUR.   Marry,
> And I'm glad of it with all my heart:
> I had rather be a kitten and cry *mew*,
> Than one of these same metre ballad-mongers.—Act III.

Worcester and Mortimer, both less vehement than the others, make peace between them; while Glendower's daughter, Lady Mortimer, and Hotspur's wife, Lady Percy, Mortimer's sister, soothe and entertain their anxious relatives with music, for which the blunt, eager Hotspur has neither taste nor talent.

The next scene describes an interview between Henry IV. and the Prince of Wales, in London, founded on fact, though expressed in Shakespeare's noble language. Henry reproaches his son, more in sorrow than in anger, about his habits, tastes, and society; tells him that his younger brothers have to take his place in the council, and forcibly reveals how he himself, when a young man about the prince's age, had acquired popularity throughout the nation. Prince Henry, to calm his agitated father, promises reformation, which, however, he does not intend at present, Falstaff's society still having a charm for him, and he never alters during his father's life. The king, whose observant mind keenly examines friends and foes, then tells his son that his

---

* STAUNTON'S *Notes to the Illustrated Shakespeare.*

conduct reminds him of his reckless predecessor, Richard II.
It must have been peculiarly galling to this wise sovereign
to perceive, when in middle age, and oppressed with endless
cares, similar faults and follies in his own son, of which his
superior mind had taken such advantage when triumphing
over his former rival. He seems, indeed, to apprehend in
this resemblance a sort of retributive justice.

> KING HENRY.   For all the world,
> As thou art to this hour, was Richard then,
> When I from France set foot at Ravenspurg ;
> And even as I was then is Percy now.
> Now, by my sceptre, and my soul to boot,
> He hath more worthy interest to the state,
> Than thou the shadow of succession.
>
>   .   .   .   .   .
>
> And what say you to this ? Percy, Northumberland,
> The Archbishop's Grace of York, Douglas, Mortimer,
> Capitulate against us, and are up.
> But wherefore do I tell these news to thee ?
> Why, Harry, do I tell thee of my foes,
> Which art my near'st and dearest enemy ?
>
>   .   .   .   .   .   .
>
> Thou dost, in thy passages of life,
> Make me believe, that thou art only mark'd
> For the hot vengeance and the rod of heaven
> To punish my mistreadings.—Act III.

While blaming and exhorting his son with all his energy, he
reveals no idea of attempting to effect his disinheritance. Yet
for this course he has many inducements, his three other
sons being all dutiful contrasts to the eldest, never joining
in his wild life, but devoted to their father's interests and
their own. King Henry acknowledges the prince's rights
firmly, though with anxiety, grief, and apprehension, as his
heir's faults are peculiarly difficult and painful for him to
deal with.* For the prince never shows a mutinous spirit
against his father ; never encourages, by word or deed, any
disaffection—a course only too common for heirs apparent to
follow, as the troubled king well knows. Henry, therefore,
cannot reasonably suspect him of treason or active enmity.
It is the future disgrace and misery of England which his
son's conduct and character hitherto cause all men to apprehend, and which the courageous king dreads more than any
of his numerous and powerful foes. This constant fear,

* "The king saw in his son's behaviour the same neglect of decency, the same
attachment to low company, which had degraded the personal character of
Richard II., and of which, more than all his errors in government, had tended
to overturn his throne."—HUME'S *History*, ch. xix.

indeed, both in history and the play, is a greater affliction to the vigorous mind of Henry IV. than any other grief, trial, or danger could have been to a spirit so firm and self-reliant. During this conversation, however, Prince Henry, roused by the exciting perils of the time, and really inheriting all the martial spirit of his family, satisfies and even gratifies his father more than he had ever done. The idea of warfare, indeed, both in his youth and prime, surpassed all other attractions for Henry. In times of peace, his reckless love of dissipation resembled that of his remote successor, Charles II., though, whereas the latter revelled and jested among profligate courtiers and ladies of ennobled rank, Prince Henry preferred the society of a witty rogue like Falstaff, and coarse, boasting desperadoes like Poins, Peto, &c. War, however, diverted him from all such company, for a short time, even while Prince of Wales, but permanently when King of England. On this occasion, he again promises his father not only reformation, but active assistance, the king believing what he says, and trusting that the promised change may be permanent. The father and son, now quite agreed, decide upon the plan of the campaign, and are for a time sincerely reconciled, owing chiefly to the danger which besets them.

The next scene reverts to Mrs. Quickly's Boar's Head Tavern, where Falstaff declares he has lost his purse, upon which the hostess reproaches him for not only slandering her house, but owing her money.

HOSTESS. The tithe of a hair was never lost in my house before.

FALSTAFF. You lie, hostess; Bardolph was shaved, and lost many a hair: and I'll be sworn my pocket was picked: go to, you are a woman, go.

HOSTESS. Who, I? I defy thee: I was never called so in mine own house before.

FALSTAFF. Go to, I know you well enough.

HOSTESS. No, Sir John; you do not know me, Sir John: I know you, Sir John: you owe me money, Sir John, and now you pick a quarrel to beguile me of it: I bought a dozen shirts to your back.

FALSTAFF. Dowlas, filthy dowlas: I have given them away to bakers' wives, and they have made bolters of them.

HOSTESS. Now, as I am a true woman, holland of eight shillings an ell. You owe money here besides, Sir John, for your diet and by-drinkings, and money lent you, four and twenty pounds.

FALSTAFF. He [Bardolph] had his part of it, let him pay.

HOSTESS. He? alas, he is poor! he hath nothing.

FALSTAFF. How! poor? look upon his face; what call you

rich? let him coin his nose, let him coin his cheeks; I'll not pay a denier.—Act III.

This woman constantly quarrels with Falstaff, who usually gets the best of the argument. Their language, like that of Poins, Peto, &c., is alike coarse and odious, when not relieved by Falstaff's extraordinary wit, cunning, and quaint remarks. It is he whose influence over, or rather attraction for the prince, maintains this respectable party in the tavern; for Mrs. Quickly, though distrusting them all, and equally scorned by them in return, is naturally proud of the prince's patronising presence, and, while often disputing with Falstaff, has no wish to lose him or any of the party as customers in her premises. The prince hears all their quarrelling and joking with evident amusement, his presence always preventing any actual violence among them, which would otherwise have probably occurred.

PRINCE HENRY. What didst thou lose, Jack?

FALSTAFF. Wilt thou believe me, Hal? three or four bonds of forty pounds apiece, and a seal of my grandfather's.

PRINCE HENRY. A trifle, some eightpenny matter.

HOSTESS. So I told him, my lord; and I said I heard your grace say so: and, my lord, he speaks most vilely of you, like a foul-mouthed man as he is; and said he would cudgel you.

PRINCE HENRY. What! he did not?

HOSTESS. There's neither faith, truth, nor womanhood in me else.

FALSTAFF. There's no more faith in thee than in a stewed prune; nor no more truth in thee than in a drawn fox.—Act III.

The prince never brings either a courtier or servant with him to this tavern, but mingles with these coarse, disreputable rogues, male and female, on strange terms of contemptuous familiarity. They probably deem themselves safe, at least during his life, from any severe ,legal penalty; while he prefers their coarse jests and habits to all the gaiety, pleasure, or dissipation of the court. He tells Falstaff, before Mrs. Quickly, that he himself had searched his pockets, and found nothing but tavern reckonings, and having pacified and sent off the hostess, informs Sir John he has got a military command for him in the ensuing campaign. Falstaff, though an idle voluptuary, has been, and still is, a soldier. He enjoys ease in time of peace, yet jests and cheers both himself and others in the present time of impending danger.

FALSTAFF. Now, Hal, to the news at court: for the robbery, lad—how is that answered?

PRINCE HENRY.   O, my sweet beef, I must still be good angel to thee :—the money is paid back again.

FALSTAFF.   I do not like that paying back, 'tis a double labour.

PRINCE HENRY.   I am good friends with my father, and may do anything.

FALSTAFF.   Rob me the exchequer, the first thing thou dost, and do it with unwashed hands too.

BARDOLPH.   Do, my lord.

PRINCE HENRY.   I have procured thee, Jack, a charge of foot.

FALSTAFF.   I would it had been of horse. Where shall I find one that can steal well ?   O, for a fine thief, of two and twenty, or thereabouts !—Act III.

Prince Henry also presses Poins, Bardolph, and all his associates to enter the royal army, and they prepare to leave London for a campaign against the insurgents.

Act IV. introduces Hotspur, Worcester, and their Scottish ally, Douglas, in their camp near Shrewsbury. Letters are brought to Hotspur from his father, the crafty Northumberland, who is now ill, or feigns to be so, while fully approving his son's enterprise, and wishing all success to the rebellion. They do not, however, at present proclaim another king, but inveigh bitterly against Henry IV.'s ingratitude and hostility to those who had " helped him to the throne."   Shakespeare seems to follow history closely in these particulars, ascribing to king, royalists, and insurgents the ideas which their conduct revealed, though expressed in his own grand language.* Hotspur, though loving his father, hears of his illness with impatience if not incredulity, exclaiming, " Hath he leisure to be sick now ? " while the plotting Worcester much regrets his brother's absence ; but the fiery Douglas agrees with Hotspur in wishing to engage the foe at once.

Sir Richard Vernon, an ally and cousin of Hotspur's, now announces that part of the royal army approaches, commanded by Henry IV.'s younger son, Prince John of Lancaster, and the remainder, headed by the king and Prince of Wales, are following. He gives a fine martial description of the wild prince, whom Hotspur mentions with natural

* " The obligations which Henry IV. had owed to Northumberland were of a kind the most likely to produce ingratitude on the one side and discontent on the other.   The sovereign naturally became jealous of that power which had advanced him to the throne, and the subject was not easily satisfied in the returns which he thought so great a favour merited.   The impatient spirit of Henry Percy, and the factious disposition of Worcester, younger brother of Northumberland, inflamed the discontents of that nobleman.   He entered into a correspondence with Glendower.   He made an alliance with the Earl of Douglas.   He roused up all his partisans to arms, and such unlimited authority at that time belonged to the great families that the same men whom, a few years before, he had conducted against Richard II. now followed his standard against Henry."—HUME'S *History*, vol. ii.

ntempt, but whom he now longs to engage in single
mbat.

> VERNON.   I saw young Harry, with his beaver on,
> His cuisses on his thighs, gallantly arm'd,
> Rise from the ground like feather'd Mercury,
> And vaulted with such ease into his seat
> As if an angel dropp'd down from the clouds,
> To turn and wind a fiery Pegasus,
> And witch the world with noble horsemanship.
>   HOTSPUR.   No more, no more; worse than the sun in
>   March,
> This praise doth nourish agues.   Let them come.
> . . . . I am on fire,
> To hear this rich reprisal is so nigh,
> And yet not ours :—Come, let me take my horse,
> Who is to bear me, like a thunderbolt,
> Against the bosom of the Prince of Wales :
> Harry to Harry shall, hot horse to horse,
> Meet, and ne'er part, till one drop down a corse.—Act IV.

either Glendower, with his Welshmen, nor Northumber-
ad have yet joined Hotspur, Worcester, and Douglas ; but
ese three leaders—one cautious and reluctant, the others
ld and impetuous—resolve to risk a battle without their
ies.

The next scene introduces Falstaff and Bardolph, the
·mer styled a captain, now in marching order, with the
yal army, Sir John having enlisted some miserable recruits,
iom he describes and ridicules, first to himself, and then to
ince Henry, who, with Westmoreland, are surprised to see
:h followers.

FALSTAFF.   There's but a shirt and a half in all my company ;
1 the half shirt is two napkins tied together, and thrown over the
)ulders like a herald's coat without sleeves ; and the shirt, to say
: truth, stolen from my host at St. Alban's, or the red-nosed inn-
:per at Daventry : but that's all one ; they'll find linen enough on
:ry hedge.
  [*Enter* PRINCE HENRY *and* WESTMORELAND.]
PRINCE HENRY.   Tell me, Jack ; what fellows are these that
ne after?
FALSTAFF.   Mine, Hal, mine.
PRINCE HENRY.   I did never see such pitiful rascals.
FALSTAFF.   Tut, tut ; good enough to toss : food for powder,
d for powder ; they'll fill a pit as well as better ; tush, man,
rtal men, mortal men.—Act IV.

id any other officer enlisted them, he might have been
/erely reprimanded ; but Falstaff is evidently a standing

joke with the prince, and no one censures him, though Westmoreland expresses some discontent. Falstaff hears him with
saucy contempt, while Prince Henry, after jesting with his
old favourite, announces that Hotspur is already in the field,
which Falstaff hears without any dismay, though certainly
preferring his former times of peace in the Boar's Head
Tavern.

After this fanciful comic scene, Shakespeare reverts to
history, again describing Hotspur, Worcester, and Douglas
in the camp at Shrewsbury, resolved to fight the royal forces
immediately, when Sir Walter Blunt arrives as a messenger
from the king, to ask the cause of this sudden rebellion of
the Percies, while acknowledging their previous services to
his cause. Hotspur replies, with angry complaints of Henry
IV.'s ingratitude, in words which doubtless express his
father's and uncle's feelings, as well as his own.

> HOTSPUR.   The king is kind; and, well we know, the king
> Knows at what time to promise, when to pay.
> My father, and my uncle, and myself,
> Did give him that same royalty he wears :
> And, when he was not six and twenty strong,
> Sick in the world's regard, wretched and low,
> A poor unminded outlaw sneaking home,
> My father gave him welcome to the shore.
>
> .   .   .   .   .   .
> In short time after, he depos'd the king ;
> Soon after that, depriv'd him of his life ;
> And, in the neck of that, task'd* the whole state :
> To make that worse, suffer'd his kinsman March
> (Who is, if every owner were well plac'd,
> Indeed, his king) to be engag'd in Wales,
> There without ransom to be forfeited :
> Disgrac'd me in my happy victories ;
> Rated my uncle from the council-board ;
> In rage dismiss'd my father from the court ;
> Broke oath on oath, committed wrong on wrong :
> And, in conclusion, drove us to seek out
> This head of safety ; and, withal, to pry
> Into his title, the which we find
> Too indirect for long continuance.

Sir Walter Blunt returns to the royal camp, having heard
this answer ; but Hotspur has not yet decided upon actual
battle, and suggests an interview between the king and his
uncle Worcester before an engagement. With this proposal
Blunt returns to the king, and the next scene is in York, at

* Taxed.

Archbishop Scroop's palace.   This prelate—brother to Lord Wiltshire, Richard II.'s adherent, who was executed, like Bushy and Green, by the new Government—was the determined foe of Henry IV.   Evidently a man of great resolution and energy, though, of course, no warrior, he actively co-operates with Northumberland and the other malcontents. How far his political conduct was approved by the Pope or the English clergy does not appear in history.   He seems, however, to have been the only prelate who actually took the field against the reigning king, though others, like the Bishop of Carlisle, who had opposed Henry's usurpation in Richard's lifetime, probably wished him dethroned, and the House of Mortimer in his place.   At present the Archbishop is merely corresponding with the other insurgent leaders, using all his influence on their behalf, though later he himself took the field, and was among the most resolute and determined of the king's foes.

Act V. describes the king, with the Princes Henry and John of Lancaster, and their officers, including Falstaff, at the royal camp, near Shrewsbury.   It is here that Henry IV. receives Lord Worcester and Sir Richard Vernon, who come to discuss terms, and sternly reproaches Worcester for heading this rebellion against him.

KING HENRY.   How now, my Lord of Worcester? 'tis not well,
That you and I should meet upon such terms
As now we meet : You have deceiv'd our trust ;
And made us doff our easy robes of peace,
To crush our old limbs in ungentle steel :
This is not well, my lord, this is not well.
What say you to it? will you again unknit
This churlish knot of all-abhorrèd war?
And move in that obedient orb again,
Where you did give a fair and natural light?
WORCESTER.   It pleas'd your majesty, to turn your looks
Of favour from myself, and all our house ;
And yet I must remember you, my lord,
We were the first and dearest of your friends.
For you, my staff of office did I break
In Richard's time ; and posted day and night,
To meet you in the way, and kiss your hand.

.   .   .   .   .   .

It was myself, my brother, and his son
That brought you home, and boldly did outdare
The danger of the time.—Act V.

Worcester, who was among the first to desert Richard, and join Henry's standard, while his brother Northumberland headed the English nobility in placing him on the throne, is now before him, an avowed enemy, in armed rebellion against his authority.   He therefore makes bitter complaints in reply to the king's reproach, though less vehement than those of his nephew Hotspur, about Henry's ingratitude to the Percies, and his arbitrary conduct generally.   The offended king and the equally offended subject upbraid each other, when Prince Henry, addressing Worcester, sends his personal challenge to Hotspur, whom he longs to encounter in single fight.   After this defiant message, the king dismisses Worcester, promising, however, free pardon, and even hope of favour, to all in arms, without exception, if they return to their allegiance.

Worcester and Vernon then return, and in the next scene the former declares that he will not tell his nephew Hotspur of the king's offer of peace, which he himself admits to be "liberal and kind."   Vernon regrets his resolution, but Worcester, ever suspicious and crafty, fancies that Henry will never really pardon his family, and that no peace with him is therefore desirable.   He resolves to conceal the king's offer of terms from Hotspur, which, as Shakespeare represents, was a dishonourable act ; but it seems rather doubtful what Worcester's real conduct was on this important occasion.*   He therefore invents a proud, insulting reply from the king, while Vernon reports the prince's challenge to Hotspur, who, with the warlike Douglas, now long for a battle.   They then prepare for a resolute encounter ; the royal forces attack them, and the contest rages for some time with desperate fury.†   In reality, the brave Hotspur was slain "by an unknown hand," but Shakespeare invents a personal encounter between him and Prince Henry, who slays him in presence of Falstaff.

He then describes a succession of single combats, in one of which the prince puts Earl Douglas to flight, who had attacked the king.   This seems a strange idea, for Douglas's bravery was owned by all, even by Shakespeare,

* Mr. Staunton says that Henry IV. and Hotspur might have made peace, and avoided the battle, but that Worcester, who had an interview with the king at his nephew's request, "so misinterpreted the conversation between them " that war was inevitable.—*Notes to the Illustrated Shakespeare.*   Worcester's duplicity in this case is not recorded by Hume, though it is not unlikely, under the circumstances, considering the mutual distrust between him and the king.

† "We shall scarcely find any battle in those ages where the shock was more terrible and more constant.   Henry exposed his person in the thickest of the fight.   His gallant son, Prince Henry, whose military achievements were afterwards so renowned, and who here performed his noviciate in arms, signalized himself on his father's footsteps.   Percy [Hotspur] supported that fame which he had acquired in many a bloody combat.   Earl Douglas performed feats of valour which are almost incredible.   He seemed determined that the King of England should fall by his arm ; he sought him all over the field of battle."—HUME'S *History*, vol. ii. ch. xviii.

who yet makes him fly from a youth like the Prince of Wales. The Scottish earl, however, soon reappears. He longs to slay the king, and has already killed some brave warriors who personate Henry IV. in the field, to ensure that monarch's safety, when he encounters Falstaff, who, falling down, feigns to be dead, thereby not only deceiving his foe, who immediately leaves him, but also Prince Henry, who expresses real sorrow at seeing, as he thinks, the dead body of his amusing old companion.

> PRINCE HENRY.   What! old acquaintance! could not all this flesh
> Keep in a little life?   Poor Jack, farewell!
> I could have better spared a better man.
> Death hath not struck so fat a deer to-day,
> Though many dearer, in this bloody fray :—
> Embowell'd will I see thee by and by :
> Till then, in blood by noble Percy lie.   [*Exit.*
> FALSTAFF (*rising slowly*).   Embowell'd! if thou embowel me to-day, I'll give you leave to powder me and eat me too to-morrow. 'Sblood, 'twas time to counterfeit, or that hot termagant Scot had paid me scot and lot too.   Counterfeit?   I lie, I am no counterfeit : for he is but the counterfeit of a man who hath not the life of a man : but to counterfeit dying, when a man thereby liveth, is to be no counterfeit, but the true and perfect image of life indeed.   The better part of valour is discretion ; in the which better part I have saved my life.—Act V.

Falstaff's comic wit on this occasion, and, indeed, all he says and does throughout, present a most effective, amusing contrast to the tremendous events, as well as to the many heroic characters, amid which this witty old profligate is so strangely involved.   No one resembles him at all ; he has apparently no relative, intimate friend, or connection of any kind. He is thus a puzzle to every one, patronized by Prince Henry, and wondered at by his own companions, but evidently not acquainted with the other young princes.   When the prince leaves him, Falstaff takes up the body of the gallant Hotspur, after stabbing it, to make sure that his noble burthen is really lifeless, and intends declaring himself his slayer, when the Princes Henry and John of Lancaster meet him.   Falstaff, alone before these young men, thinks he can say what he likes, and boldly declares that he has slain Hotspur, while Prince Henry steadily maintains that he himself has killed him.

> FALSTAFF.   There is Percy : if your father will do me any honour, so ; if not, let him kill the next Percy himself.   I look to be either earl or duke, I can assure you.

PRINCE HENRY.   Why, Percy I killed myself, and saw thee dead.

FALSTAFF.   Didst thou ?—Lord, Lord, how the world is given to lying !—I grant you I was down, and out of breath : and so was he : but we rose both at an instant, and fought a long hour by Shrewsbury clock.—Act V.

His grave, practical younger brother never laughs at Falstaff or his jokes.   He resembles his politic father in caution, but, though equally brave, is his inferior both in shrewdness and knowledge of character.   Prince Henry, never angry with Falstaff, hears his falsehoods with the utmost good humour, and departs with his brother, bidding Falstaff follow with Hotspur's body.

The last scene describes Henry IV., with his sons Henry and John, surrounded by ministers and generals, while his captured foes, Worcester and Vernon, are brought before him. Earl Douglas was also captured and liberated, not being an English subject ; but the king has somehow discovered Worcester's deceit in not conveying his offers of peace, and, after reproaching him for his conduct, sentences him and Vernon to execution.   Except these, no prisoners were executed, though Henry had many captives ; and, considering the harsh laws and fierce spirit of the time, it is evident that the king was thought to have made a merciful use of his triumph.*

The battle of Shrewsbury ends the first part of this play, but the rebellion or civil war is not yet over, though this crushing defeat has destroyed all hope of its success.   The harassed king, who, alike before and after his accession to the throne, was beset with enemies and dangers, prepares resolutely to continue the struggle till all opposition is over. The Welsh chief Glendower, the Archbishop of York, Northumberland, and some other noblemen still defy his authority, though Glendower is the only man among them of much military genius or experience.   Yet the wealth, high position, and craft of Northumberland, and the archbishop's influence, rendered them rather formidable ; while Glendower, in the Welsh mountains, though more inaccessible, was perhaps less likely to rouse other English subjects against the Government.   The king has now his sons to depend on, having lived to see his most zealous adherents become his mortal foes.   Prince Henry, when once amid the excitement of warfare, assists his father to the utmost, and for a time seems a different man from the dissipated "sweet wag, Hal," in the Boar's Head Tavern ; while Prince John, whose re-

* HUME'S *History*.

markable character is more developed in the second part of this divided play, firmly supports his family's interests with the steady consistency of his resolute spirit.

In this play Hotspur is the chief hero. He appears in *Richard II.* as a spirited, promising youth. He is here, in early manhood, the pride of the English nation, as even the king admits, and the hope and glory of his distinguished family. Unfortunately for them, however, his impetuous spirit and eager appeals incline both his admiring father and uncle to follow his guidance in open rebellion, whereas those shrewd old statesmen, though angry with the king, might never have declared open war but for their fiery young relative, whose high courage and great popularity doubtless inspired them with reasonable hopes of success. It appears from both history and the play, however, that peace might have been made, and the Shrewsbury battle avoided, had not Worcester's duplicity, or, rather, deep distrust of the king, made him doubtful, if not of pardon, at least of any future favour or benefit to himself and his family.* For Henry IV., despite his many great qualities, seems not to have possessed much power of conciliation. It was his fate, during an eventful career, to make mortal enemies of nearly all his most distinguished subjects. The end of *Richard II.* left Henry rewarding the Percies and others for defeating or executing Lords Salisbury, Spencer, &c., in his behalf ; and the end of this play leaves him ordering the execution of his former adherents, Worcester and Vernon, after slaying their relative Hotspur, and also preparing for a final campaign against Northumberland, the head of the Percies, and the Archbishop of York, now his implacable foes. In these proceedings, the dramatic description is supported in all chief events by historical record.† It does not seem, however, very clear, either in the play or in history, what new government these distinguished insurgents really wished to establish, though their desire to dethrone the king is sufficiently evident. The imprisoned young Earl of March and his uncle, Sir Edmund Mortimer, who remained with the chief Glendower, had prior claims to the crown, but neither seem to have been proclaimed king by the insurgents, nor

---

* "No house had played a greater part in the overthrow of Richard II., or had been more richly rewarded by the new king. But old grudges existed between the House of Percy and the House of Lancaster. Northumberland had been at bitter variance with John of Gaunt, and, though a common dread of Richard's enmity had thrown the Percies and Henry together, the new king and his powerful subjects were soon parted again."—GREEN's *History of the English People*, ch. v.

† HUME's *History*.

was the formal deposition of Henry IV. publicly advocated or proposed.*

This civil war or rebellion apparently first arose chiefly from the great irritation and disappointment of the new king's former adherents, who allied themselves with Glendower and Sir Edmund Mortimer, and, had they succeeded, would doubtless have deposed Henry, and crowned Mortimer or his nephew March, for which, indeed, they had the sanction of the late King Richard, who had named the latter his heir.† King Henry was now in middle age, supported by brave and loyal sons. He was far less dependent than before on either ambitious statesmen or warriors to secure the stability of his throne. The end of this play, therefore, leaves the sagacious king and his warlike sons in complete triumph—more united, indeed, during warfare than in peace, and though still opposed by some influential subjects, yet with every prospect of success.

* " Henry Percy [Hotspur] became the centre of a great conspiracy to place the Earl of March upon the throne. His father Northumberland and his uncle Worcester joined in the plot. Sir Edmund Mortimer negotiated for aid from Glendower. Earl Douglas threw in his fortunes with the confederates."—GREEN'S *History of the English People*, ch. v. Still there seems to have been no actual proclamation of young March as king by the rebel leaders, though they probably intended to make him so.

† " Henry IV. detained Lord March in honourable custody at Windsor Castle, but he had reason to dread that, in proportion as that nobleman grew to man's estate, he would draw to him the attachment of the people, and make them reflect on the fraud, violence, and injustice by which he had been excluded from the throne."—HUME'S *History*, ch. xviii.

CHAPTER VII.

SECOND PART OF KING HENRY IV.

Sketch of Play.

NORTHUMBERLAND and the Archbishop of York, with Lords Mowbray, Hastings, and others, continue to oppose the king, without risking a battle. Prince John of Lancaster heads the royal forces, and at length the insurgents surrender to him. Some of the leaders, including the archbishop, are executed. Northumberland, however, escaping to Scotland, returns, and is slain in a subsequent engagement. His overthrow is merely announced to the king, who dies soon after. During this play, Prince Henry's conduct becomes more and more reckless, and is a constant grief to his troubled father, who much prefers his younger son John. Falstaff continues to be the Prince's favourite associate, and with him and other more desperate companions the heir apparent is represented as spending his time, during peace, in drinking, debauchery, and occasionally robbing travellers. The dying king sadly reproaches him, and his solemn words produce a permanent effect ; for directly he dies, the prince seems to change his character with his position. He dismisses Falstaff and others from his society, surrounds himself with the late king's ministers and judges, and prepares to show that he is worthy of the great inheritance left him by his energetic and illustrious father. This play ends with the thankful surprise of all at the young monarch's sudden and complete transformation ; and the whole of England acknowledges his authority without either opposition or apparent discontent.

AT this exciting period in England, when there were no newspapers, it was, indeed, a time for rumours of all sorts to spread uncontradicted. Shakespeare therefore makes the spirit of Rumour appear before Northumberland's castle at Warkworth, revealing that he is not really ill, as pretended, but, being more of a statesman than a soldier, thus excuses himself from taking the field, while carefully watching events. Contradictory news is brought him by his adherents, Morton and Travers, first of his son's victory, then of his defeat and

death.   The old earl is at first incredulous, but, when convinced of the fatal news, he utters almost frantic language of
defiance against the king.

> MORTON.   Douglas is living, and your brother, yet :
> But, for my lord your son———
> NORTHUMBERLAND.   Why, he is dead.
> See what a ready tongue suspicion hath !
> He that but fears the thing he would not know,
> Hath, by instinct, knowledge from others' eyes,
> That what he fear'd is chanced.   Yet speak, Morton ;
> Tell thou thy earl his divination lies.
> MORTON.   You are too great to be by me gainsaid :
> Your spirit is too true, your fears too certain.
> NORTHUMBERLAND.   For this I shall have time enough to mourn,
> In poison there is physic ; and these news,
> Having been well, that would have made me sick,
> Being sick, have in some measure made me well.
> . . . . Hence, therefore, thou nice crutch ;
> A scaly gauntlet now, with joints of steel,
> Must glove this hand : and hence thou sickly coif !
> Thou art a guard too wanton for the head
> Which princes, flesh'd with conquest, aim to hit.
> Now bind my brows with iron : and approach
> The ragged'st hour that time and spite dare bring,
> To frown upon the enrag'd Northumberland !—Act I.

For he is now placed in an extraordinary position.   He,
once Henry IV.'s chief adherent, has become his chief
enemy.   His son and brother are slain and captured by that
monarch—the former killed in battle, the latter soon to
perish on the scaffold, and he himself is almost sure to be
exposed to either the one fate or the other.   His personal
hatred to the king, therefore, probably exceeds that of any
other foe.   But Northumberland is both old and careworn.
His brave son was evidently the hope, as well as the pride of
his advanced age.*   He at this moment alone represents
the Percy family, now menaced with ruin and extirpation.
He soon hears from Morton and Travers that his son's
ally, the archbishop, is in the field, striving to give the
checked, yet not quelled, rebellion the character of a holy
war.†   Yet Henry, when known as Bolingbroke, was most

---

* Hume states that Northumberland submitted to the king, and was pardoned,
after Hotspur's death—which Shakespeare does not state—but that he again rose
in rebellion, and joined the Archbishop of York and Lord Nottingham, who,
" though they had remained quiet while Henry Percy was in the field, still hated
the king, and determined, with Northumberland, to seek revenge against him."
—Ch. xviii.

† Hume states that when the English people calmly reflected on the many
illegal acts which attended Henry IV.'s accession, the deposition and suspected

popular, and apparently encouraged by the nation generally in his aspiration to the throne. His celebrated triumphal procession through London, leading Richard captive amid enthusiastic applause, together with his first unopposed triumph over the king's forces, proved that his accession was generally expected and desired. But Archbishop Scroop was evidently a man of high courage, and his hatred to Henry, owing to his brother Lord Wiltshire's execution, was more consistent, if less vehement, than the sudden animosity of Northumberland against that monarch. Shakespeare mentions, probably from some tradition, that this prelate had even shown Richard II.'s blood to the people to excite them all the more against his reigning foe. For Morton tells Northumberland,

> The gentle Archbishop of York is up
> With well-appointed powers; he is a man
> Who with a double surety binds his followers.
>
> .   .   .   .
>
> Turns insurrection to religion :
> Suppos'd sincere and holy in his thoughts,
> He is follow'd both with body and with mind ;
> And doth enlarge his rising with the blood
> Of fair King Richard, scrap'd from Pomfret stones.—Act I.

Northumberland, whose energy, pride, and anger, now all of them thoroughly aroused, struggle against the depressing effects of age and grief, resolves to join the archbishop in a last desperate attempt against the new king, whom he was the first to make such, yet to whom he attributes the ruin of his family.

The next scene is in London, where Sir John Falstaff has returned, in evident high spirits, after his campaign, in which, if not very distinguished, he certainly suffered from no bodily injury or mental sorrow. He returns to town all the prouder, if not the richer, for he speaks of new satin for his cloak, though the tailor naturally tells his servant-lad that he must have better security than that of his roguish comrade Bardolph. While Falstaff is walking through the streets of London, and railing at this disobliging tailor, he is addressed by Chief Justice Gascoigne, who knows him well, and grieves at his influence over the Prince of Wales. This man was the celebrated judge who, on a former occasion, had sent the

murder of Richard II., and the imprisonment of Lord March, the heir to the crown, "These enormities sanctified all the rebellions against him, and made the executions, though not remarkably severe, which he found necessary for the maintenance of his authority, appear cruel as well as iniquitous to the people."— Ch. xviii.

wild prince to prison for assaulting or threatening him when trying one of his riotous companions. This very short imprisonment of the heir apparent caused immense sensation at the time, and has been much noticed in subsequent history ; yet, considering the prince's lawless and even outrageous conduct, in robbing, or encouraging others to rob, his father's subjects, which was generally believed, and which had been continued so long with impunity, this penalty was, indeed, but very slight.   Falstaff, though his wit and effrontery are invincible, is yet rather uneasy before the judge, who has both the right and the will, but not the power, to punish him, and who certainly does not appreciate his jokes.   Sir John, therefore, tries to avoid him, but Gascoigne persists in reproving him — vainly as he might have well known, except to gratify his own vexed spirit, by telling him the truth.   He rightly accuses him of misleading the prince—perhaps, in his mind, the most heinous of Falstaff's offences, as being the most dangerous to the future welfare of England ; for doubtless he and all the chief lawyers, with other loyal subjects, viewed the heir-apparent's present and probable future conduct with the utmost disgust and apprehension.

CHIEF JUSTICE.   Sir John, you live in great infamy.
FALSTAFF.   He that buckles him in my belt cannot live in less.
CHIEF JUSTICE.   Your means are very slender, and your waste is great.
FALSTAFF.   I would it were otherwise : I would my means were greater and my waist slenderer.
CHIEF JUSTICE. You have misled the youthful prince.
FALSTAFF.   The youthful prince hath misled me.
CHIEF JUSTICE.   You follow the young prince up and down, like his ill angel.
FALSTAFF.   Not so, my lord ; your ill angel is light ; but, I hope, he that looks upon me will take me without weighing. . . . . For the box o' the ear that the young prince gave you, he gave it like a rude prince, and you took it like a sensible lord.   I have checked him for it ; and the young lion repents : marry, not in ashes and sackcloth, but in new silk and old sack.
CHIEF JUSTICE.   Well, God send the prince a better companion.
FALSTAFF.   God send the companion a better prince !   I cannot rid my hands of him. —Act I.

The witty jests of Falstaff and his friends afford, indeed, no amusement to them, but only display the bold, insolent mockery of mischievous, unpunished rogues, who were becoming more and more dangerous to the peace of the community.   Falstaff's wit, however, has amused generations of delighted Englishmen ; even the moral Dr. Johnson is enthusiastic in admiration, yet, had he known Falstaff, or witnessed this scene between him and Gascoigne, besides many others in which Sir John distinguished himself, he would probably have viewed the dishonest, shameless old profligate with unmitigated aversion.* Falstaff's ready wit and constant effrontery, so amusing to hear in Shakespeare's language, would, in a living corruptor of youth and associate of rogues, have been most provoking. The Chief Justice dislikes, distrusts, and probably longs to punish him, but keeps his temper, which is sorely tried by the insolent banter of the shrewd old sinner. He tells Falstaff, however, that the king has "severed" him from the prince for a time, ordering him to march against the insurgen⸱s with Prince John ; while the king and his eldest son are to attack Glendower in Wales. This arrangement does not please Sir John, who would much prefer to be with Prince Henry than with his stern, grave younger brother ; but he has no choice in the matter.   .

The next scene is at York, where Archbishop Scroop, with Lords Hastings and Mowbray, and other insurgent leaders, are discussing their plans. Since Hotspur's death, this prelate was the most resolute of all Henry IV.'s enemies, except Northumberland, whose age and misfortunes render his great energy less formidable. Scroop never forgot either his brother Lord Wiltshire's execution, nor the death of the late king, to whom his family were devotedly attached. He again recalls the triumphal procession of Henry IV. through London, the humiliation of the unfortunate Richard on that day, which, perhaps, he witnessed, and imagines that the English are as dissatisfied with the new king as they were with his predecessor.   .

ARCHBISHOP.   Let us on ;
And publish the occasion of our arms.
The commonwealth is sick of their own choice.

They that when Richard liv'd, would have him die,
Are now become enamoured of his grave :
They that threw dust upon his goodly head,
When through proud London he came sighing on

---

* " Falstaff, unimitated, inimitable Falstaff ! how shall I describe thee ? Thou compound of sense and vice—of sense which may be admired, but not esteemed ; of vice which may be despised, but hardly detested. . . . . He is stained with no enormous or sanguinary crimes, so that his licentiousness is not so offensive but that it may be borne with for his mirth."—JOHNSON'S *Notes to Henry IV.* Yet, had Johnson really known Falstaff, his " licentiousness," shown in a life of dishonest profligacy, would have probably shocked the strict moralist far more than such "mirth" as his would have amused him.

> After the admir'd heels of Bolingbroke,
> Cry now, " O earth, yield up that king again,
> And take thou this !"—Act I.

But in this idea he and the other insurgents were mistaken, for, though the new king had indeed made many enemies among his more influential subjects, and lost much of his popularity, the public seem generally to have favoured and supported him during his whole career.*

Act II. is again in London, where Falstaff's hostess, Mrs. Quickly, wants him arrested for his debt to her, before he leaves town for another campaign. She employs two con-stables—Fang and Snare—to seize him, but Falstaff, with Bardolph, draw their swords, and a scuffle is beginning, when Gascoigne appears, orders all to keep the peace, and inquires about the dispute. Mrs. Quickly eagerly assures him that Falstaff has not only " eat her out of house and home," and owes her money, but has also promised to marry her.

> CHIEF JUSTICE.   Are you not ashamed to enforce a poor widow to so rough a course to come by her own ?
> FALSTAFF.   What is the gross sum that I owe thee ?
> HOSTESS.   Marry, if thou wert an honest man, thyself and the money too.   Thou didst swear to me upon a parcel-gilt goblet, sitting in my Dolphin-chamber, at the round table, by a sea-coal fire, upon Wednesday in Whitsun-week, when the prince broke thy head for liking his father to a singing-man at Windsor ; thou didst swear to me then, as I was washing thy wound, to marry me, and make me my lady thy wife.   Canst thou deny it ?   Did not goodwife Keech, the butcher's wife, come in then, and call me gossip Quickly ? . . . . And didst thou not, when she was gone downstairs, desire me to be no more so familiar with such poor people ; saying that ere long they should call me madam ?   And didst thou not kiss me, and bid me fetch thee thirty shillings ?   I put thee now to thy book-oath : deny it, if thou canst.
> FALSTAFF.   My lord, this is a poor mad soul : and she says, up and down the town, that her eldest son is like you : she hath been in good case, and, the truth is, poverty hath distracted her.—Act II.

Gascoigne, who abhors Falstaff, befriends this woman, perhaps more than she deserves, as Sir John perceives, and calls her aside, while a messenger from the court to the judge diverts his thoughts from the worthy couple for a short time.   Falstaff succeeds in coaxing and pacifying Mrs.

---

* " After a few years, the Government of Henry IV. became extremely un-popular.   Perhaps his dissension with the great Percy family, which had placed him on the throne, and was regarded with partiality by the people, chiefly con-tributed to this alteration of their attachment."—HALLAM'S *Middle Ages*, ch. viii.

Quickly ; sending his comrade Bardolph away with her, promising to sup at her tavern, and there meet a certain Dolly
Tearsheet.   This woman is a young ally of the hostess, and
Falstaff's favourite ; for, while he is intimate with the prince,
and induces him to visit her house, Mrs. Quickly tries to
make it as pleasant as she can for the old profligate, though
often quarrelling with him, through fear of losing money by
his wasteful extravagance.

The next scene is in one of the London streets, where
Prince Henry and Poins, his most constant associate, except
Falstaff, are together.   They discuss the news of the king's
illness, which evidently gratifies Poins, but not the prince, who,
while allowing this worthless fellow to be familiar, in reality
neither trusts him nor any of his comrades.

PRINCE HENRY.   But I tell thee, my heart bleeds inwardly, that
my father is so sick : and keeping such vile company as thou art,
hath in reason taken from me all ostentation of sorrow.

POINS.   The reason ?

PRINCE HENRY.   What wouldst thou think of me if I should
weep ?

POINS.   I would think thee a most princely hypocrite.

PRINCE HENRY.   It would be every man's thought.—Act II.

Falstaff's servant-lad, a sharp-witted little fellow, not im-
proved by his new master, now brings the prince a note from
him, which the latter, after reading, shows to Poins.   In this
epistle, Falstaff, perhaps half in joke, declares that Poins
wishes the prince to marry his sister, and warns him against
that worthy.   Poins is enraged, while the prince is amused.
They both ask if Falstaff sups that night in Eastcheap, and
hearing that he will do so, also that Mrs. Quickly and Doll
Tearsheet will be with him, they resolve to go in disguise to
the same place, and have another wild, dissipated revel there.

PRINCE HENRY.   Where sups he? doth the old boar feed at the
old frank ?

BARDOLPH.   At the old place, my lord; in Eastcheap.

PRINCE HENRY.   Sup any women with him ?

PAGE.   None, my lord, but Mistress Quickly and Mistress Doll
Tearsheet.

PRINCE HENRY.   What pagan may that be ?

PAGE.   A proper gentlewoman, sir, and a kinswoman of my
master's.

PPINCE HENRY.   Shall we steal upon them, Ned, at supper ?

POINS.   I am your shadow, my lord : I'll follow you.

PRINCE HENRY.   Sirrah, you boy—and Bardolph ;—no word to
your master that I am yet come to town : There's for your silence.

BARDOLPH.   I have no tongue, sir.

PAGE.   And for mine, sir—I will govern it.

PRINCE HENRY.   Fare ye well: go. [*Exeunt* BARDOLPH *and* PAGE.]   How might we see Falstaff bestow himself to-night in his true colours, and not ourselves be seen?

POINS.   Put on two leather jerkins and aprons, and wait upon him at his table as drawers.

PRINCE HENRY.   From a prince to a prentice? a low transformation! that shall be mine: for, in everything, the purpose must weigh with the folly.   Follow me, Ned.—Act II.

The next scene reverts to Warkworth Castle, where the heart-broken Northumberland, with his wife and daughter-in-law, Hotspur's widow, are lamenting over their own condition as well as that of England.   At this time, perhaps Northumberland, of all his fellow-countrymen, has most reason to be in profound grief and dejection.   During the last years of the late reign, and for a short time after Henry's accession, this restless, energetic nobleman's ambition had not only irritated but actually hastened the ruin of the king he had helped to depose, while it had offended and alienated the new monarch whom he was the first to acknowledge.   Richard II.'s adherents well remembered his vehement hostility to that unfortunate sovereign on behalf of the prince, who, having slain his son and brother, now contemplates his own death or exile.   The old earl's high spirit and family pride still animate him, despite alike his age and his grief, for he longs to join the Archbishop and the remaining insurgents, but is persuaded by his wife and Lady Percy—who dread losing their remaining male relative—to "fly to Scotland" for the present, and there await events.   They doubtless know that a statesman of his advanced age would be of no service on the battlefield, while his mental distress would, for the present at least, render him of little use in counsel.   He at last follows their advice, and escapes from England as a fugitive from the wrath of that king for aiding whose accession so zealously he had incurred a " world of curses," as his brave son Hotspur truly told him.   Hume and Shakespeare in their accounts of Northumberland's career agree on the whole ; but the historian (Chap. XVIII.) states that he was pardoned after the battle of Shrewsbury, and fled to Scotland on the capture of Archbishop Scroop, but subsequently heading another rebellion, was slain in battle.   His sudden yet implacable hatred to Henry IV. is thus historically proved, confirming Richard II.'s prediction that these his two chief enemies would turn against each other that fierce energy they both possessed, and which, in rebellious alliance, had easily effected his own destruction.*

This remarkable man, though again mentioned, never re-appears in the play. His triumph in the last days of the late king had been apparently as complete as the most ambitious English rebel could desire. The last act of *Richard II.*, which in this instance strictly follows history, leaves him praised, rewarded, and exultant by the throne of the new king, alike his first adherent and most honoured subject. The play of *Henry IV.*, equally true to history, describes him moody, disappointed, and finally incited by his bold son to open rebellion. And now, in the Second Part of *Henry IV.*, Shakespeare, still relying on history, describes him escaping for his life to Scotland, mourning for his son and brother, both slain, the one in battle, the other on the scaffold, by his enraged sovereign. Yet the king's anger was not more deep or implacable than his own against Henry, and thus their mutual hatred and disappointment—as the king's triumph never made him a happy man—fully verified the prophecy of their luckless victim, Richard II.†

The next scene is in the Boar's Head, where Mrs. Quickly and Dolly receive Falstaff, and spend what they think a pleasant evening. The hostess apparently knows that her own charms, whatever they once were, have lost their attractions ; for, though formerly wooed by Falstaff, as she declares, she now much prefers his money to his love, and is content to see her young friend Dolly inherit all the endearments of which she was once the alleged recipient. Dolly, however, has another admirer in a certain swaggering bravo called Pistol, who follows her to the tavern, where he is alike unwelcome to the hostess, Falstaff, and Dolly. Bardolph and the page, who both obey Falstaff, probably owing to his supposed influence with the prince, enter the tavern with Pistol, but the latter soon finds himself terribly out of favour with Dol'y, who angrily scolds him for following her, and a violent quarrel ensues among this excellent company. Pistol is now quite confounded, Dolly utterly scorning him, and fondling old Falstaff, to the delight of Mrs. Quickly, Bardolph, and the page.

---

* Hallam states (*Middle Ages*, ch. viii.) that the House of Commons thanked the king for pardoning Northumberland ; but, on the other hand, it is evident that this ambitious old adherent never forgave his offended, but, as he thought, most un-grateful sovereign.

† "Although Henry IV. was a great king, and the founder of a dynasty, the labour and sorrow of his task was ever more present to his mind than the solid success which his son was to inherit.'—STUBBS's *Constitutional History of England.*

Doll.   For God's sake, thrust him downstairs ; I cannot endure such a fustian rascal.

Falstaff.   Quoit him down, Bardolph, like a shovel-groat shilling : nay, an he do nothing but speak nothing, he shall be nothing here.

Bardolph.   Come, get you downstairs.

Pistol.   What ! shall we have incision ? shall we imbrue. [*Snatching up his sword.*]

Hostess.   Here's goodly stuff indeed !

Falstaff.   Give me my rapier, boy.

Doll.   I prithee, Jack, I prithee, do not draw.

Falstaff.   Get you downstairs.   [*Drawing.*]

Hostess.   Here's a goodly tumult ! I'll forswear keeping house, afore I'll be in these tirrits and frights.   So ; murder, I warrant now. Alas, alas ! put up your naked weapons, put up your naked weapons.

[*Exeunt* Pistol, Bardolph, *and* Page.

Doll.   I prithee, Jack, be quiet ; the rascal is gone.

Hostess.   Are you not hurt i' the groin ? methought he made a shrewd thrust at your belly.

Re-enter Bardolph.

Falstaff.   Have you turned him out of doors ?

Bardolph.   Yes, sir.   The rascal's drunk : you have hurt him sir, in the shoulder.

Falstaff.   A rascal ! to brave me !

Doll.   Ah, you sweet little rogue, you !—Act II.   Scene IV.

Pistol is thus expelled the premises by general consent, while the rest of the party enjoy themselves as usual, drinking and jesting, when Prince Henry and Poins enter, disguised as drawers or waiters.   They hear Falstaff describe them both to the inquisitive Dolly with tolerable accuracy.

Doll.   Sirrah, what humour is the prince of ?

Falstaff.   A good shallow young fellow : he would have made a good pantler, he would have chipped bread well.

Doll.   They say Poins hath a good wit.

Falstaff.   He a good wit ? hang him, baboon ! his wit is as thick as Tewksbury mustard ; there is no more conceit in him than in a mallet.

Doll.   Why doth the prince love him so, then ?

Falstaff.   Because their legs are both of a bigness : and he plays at quoits well ; and eats conger and fennel ; and jumps upon joint-stools ; and swears with a good grace ; and wears his boots very smooth, like unto the skin of the leg ; and breeds no bate with telling of discreet stories ; and such other gambol faculties he hath, that show a weak mind and an able body, for the which the prince

admits him : for the prince himself is such another ; the weight of
a hair will turn the scales between their avoirdupois.

PRINCE HENRV.   Would not this nave of a wheel have his ears
cut off?

POINS.   Let's beat him.—Act II.

When Henry reveals himself, to the general surprise, Dolly,
perhaps with a vague hope of pleasing the prince, or fearing
he is offended, turns sharply on Falstaff, exclaiming, " You
fat fool, I scorn you," while Henry and Poins question, scold,
and ridicule Falstaff, who ably defends himself with his
usual ready wit.

PRINCE HENRY.   How vilely did you speak of me even now,
before this honest, virtuous, civil gentlewoman !

HOSTESS.   God's blessing of your good heart ! and so she is, by
my troth.

FALSTAFF.   Didst thou hear me?

PRINCE HENRY.   Yes ; and you knew me, as you did when you
ran away by Gadshill : you knew I was at your back ; and spoke it
on purpose, to try my patience.

FALSTAFF.   No, no, no, not so ; I did not think thou wast within
hearing.

PRINCE HENRY.   I shall drive you then to confess the wilful
abuse ; and then I know how to handle you.

FALSTAFF.   No abuse, Hal, on mine honour ; no abuse.

PRINCE HENRY.   Not ! to dispraise me ; and call me " pantler,"
and " bread-chipper," and I know not what ?

FALSTAFF.   No abuse, Hal.

POINS.   No abuse !

FALSTAFF.   No abuse, Ned, in the world ; honest Ned, none.   I
dispraised him before the wicked, that the wicked might not fall in
love with him :—in which doing I have done the part of a careful
friend, and a true subject, and thy father is to give me thanks for it.
No abuse, Hal ;—none, Ned, none ;—no, boys, none.—Act II.
Scene IV.

He has pacified the prince, who, perhaps, was never really
angry with him, when Peto arrives, with news from the court.
Prince Henry and Falstaff are required to march against the
remaining insurgents, and the former leaves the tavern
immediately.   Dolly then reluctantly parts from Falstaff,
who promises to see her again, to the delight of Mrs. Quickly,
who wishes to increase this intimacy, hoping that they, with
the prince, may be frequent guests at her house.   Apparently
Prince Henry's presence and patronage chiefly maintain this
strange establishment, for his previous short imprisonment
by Judge Gascoigne has hitherto produced no permanent
effect on the royal scapegrace, who, never considering the

mischievous example he sets to all the youth of England, frequents the Boar's Head Tavern with Falstaff whenever he can spare time from his military duties, in which, however, he always delighted. No courtier, friend, or relative accompanies him to this place from first to last. He associates alone with these low, profligate companions, male and female, utterly despising his anxious father's remonstrances, who, having overcome all his most dangerous foes, now finds himself practically and constantly disobeyed by his eldest son and lawful successor.

Act III. represents the invalid king, sleepless and care-worn, perhaps, in his weak state, exaggerating the diminished dangers which still threaten him. He summons his new counsellors, Lords Surrey and Warwick, to read some despatches, and, before they come, utters a thoughtful, sad soliloquy about his own agitated mind, and the comparative happiness and peace of his subjects.

> KING HENRY.   How many of my poorest subjects
> Are at this hour asleep!   O sleep, O gentle sleep,
> Nature's soft nurse, how have I frighted thee,
> That thou no more wilt weigh my eyelids down,
> And steep my senses in forgetfulness?
> Why rather sleep, liest thou in smoky cribs,
> Upon uneasy pallets stretching thee,
> And hush'd with buzzing night-flies to thy slumber,
> Than in the perfum'd chambers of the great,
> Under the canopies of costly state,
> And lull'd with sounds of sweetest melody?
> O, thou dull god! why liest thou with the vile
> In loathsome beds, and leav'st the kingly couch
> A watch-case, or a common 'larum bell?
> Wilt thou upon the high and giddy mast
> Seal up the ship-boy's eyes, and rock his brains
> In cradle of the rude imperious surge,
> And in the visitation of the winds,
> Who take the ruffian billows by the top.
> Curling their monstrous heads, and hanging them
> With deaf'ning clamours in the slippery clouds,
> That, with the hurly, death itself awakes?
> Canst thou, O partial sleep! give thy repose
> To the wet sea-boy in an hour so rude,
> And in the calmest and most stillest night,
> With all appliances and means to boot
> Deny it to a king?   Then happy low, lie down!
> Uneasy lies the head that wears a crown!—Act III.

Henry, though quite the reverse of a timid or nervous man, always shewed a very thoughtful disposition, often recalling the past ; and his serious mind, when not engaged in matters of war or politics, inclines more to melancholy reflection than to pleasure, triumph, or self-congratulation.*

When his ministers come, they rather cheer him about the news, for they know that, since the Shrewsbury defeat, the insurgents have lost all chance of success, and that Northumberland, as Warwick sarcastically observes, "will soon be cooled." This expression about his former most zealous adherent affects the weak king deeply. He instantly recalls the memorable day when Richard II., "checked and rated by Northumberland," had prophesied that his insulting, powerful subject would become an equally dangerous rebel to his triumphant foe.

> KING HENRY. O God! that one might read the book of fate,
> And see the revolution of the times.
>
> The happiest youth, viewing his progress through,
> What perils past, what crosses to ensue,
> Would shut the book, and sit him down and die.
> 'Tis not ten years gone,
> Since Richard and Northumberland, great friends,
> Did feast together, and, in two years after,
> Were they at wars : it is but eight years since
> This Percy was the man nearest my soul ;
> Who like a brother toil'd at my affairs,
> And laid his love and life under my foot ;
> Yea, for my sake, even to the eyes of Richard,
> Gave him defiance. But which of you was by,
>
> When Richard,—with his eye brimfull of tears
> Then check'd and rated by Northumberland,— '
> Did speak these words, now prov'd a prophecy ?
> " *Northumberland, thou ladder, by the which*
> *My cousin Bolingbroke ascends my throne ;*"
>
> *The time shall come,* thus did he follow it,
> " *The time will come, that foul sin, gathering head,*
> *Shall break into corruption ;* "—so went on
> Foretelling this same time's condition,
> And the division of our amity.—Act III.

Had Henry been in his usual health, he might, when mentioning Northumberland, have severely blamed him before his ministers, and justified his own conduct towards him. But now he names him without the least anger, his oppressed

* " The inquietude with which Henry IV. possessed his envied greatness, and the remorses with which it was said he was continually haunted, render him an object of our pity, even when seated upon the throne."—HUME'S *History*, ch. xviii.

mind recalling the past with more interest and animation than he apparently feels about the present.   He mentions, however, though evidently with surprise, a report that fifty thousand insurgents are under Northumberland and Scroop, whom he erroneously thinks are together ; but Warwick contradicts the rumour, knowing that the foe is not so numerous, and has no longer a chance against the king's forces.   He also reports the death of the brave Welsh chief Glendower, the last military leader among the malcontents who possessed any ability.   Henry is too weak, or too sad, to make any reply, except that he will follow Warwick's counsel, and postpone his journey to the Holy Land.   This project he seems to have steadily entertained since the death of Richard II., but the many troubles of his reign, and perhaps the opposition of his ministers, always prevented its accomplishment.

The next scene Shakespeare lays in Gloucestershire, at the house of a certain Justice Shallow, who, as his name indicates, is a silly, talkative boaster.   Another magistrate, Justice Silence, is with him, likewise described by his name, being a silent, and also a dull personage, but a patient listener to his chattering friend.   They now await Sir John Falstaff, and have chosen some luckless peasants as recruits for him, the fat old knight being again in the field against the king's enemies.   When joined by Falstaff and Bardolph, the two country justices call some of these recruits before them. They are five in number—Mouldy, Shadow, Bull-calf, Wart, and Feeble.   Shallow, after exhibiting them in turn to Falstaff, who is quite satisfied with them, amuses himself, but rather bores Sir John, by remembering or inventing several incidents when they were both young men and well acquainted, though probably they were never very intimate. When the recruits are left alone with Bardolph, Mouldy and Bull-calf try to bribe him to get them excused from military service.   On Falstaff's return with the justices, Bardolph secretly tells him of the bribe, which he at once accepts, and frees the two men.   Shallow is surprised at the best of the five recruits being rejected, knowing nothing of the bribe, but Sir John has no trouble in deceiving him.

SHALLOW.   Sir John, Sir John, do not yourself such wrong ; they are thy likeliest men, and I would have you served with the best.

FALSTAFF.   Will you tell me, Master Shallow, how to choose a man ?   Care I for the limb, the thews, the stature, bulk, and big assemblance of a man !   Give me the spirit, Master Shallow.— Here's Wart :—you see what a ragged appearance it is : he shall charge you, and discharge you, with the motion of a pewterer's hammer.   And this same half-faced fellow, Shadow—give me this man; he presents no mark to the enemy; the foeman may with as great aim level at the edge of a penknife: And, for a retreat—how swiftly will this Feeble, the woman's tailor, run off? O, give me the spare men, and spare me the great ones.—Act III.

Shallow and Falstaff are apparently about the same age, and most amusing contrasts, but the gay old London libertine finds the chattering, silly country justice a tiresome companion, and probably wishes himself again in the Boar's Head Tavern, amid more congenial society. It is difficult to understand how two such utter simpletons as Shallow and Silence could have administered justice, or exercised any authority, without getting themselves as well as others into constant trouble. They are even far inferior to many of their successors some two centuries later, whom Lord Macaulay, perhaps too unfavourably, describes.*

Shallow, who probably knows of Falstaff's intimacy with the prince, hopes he may some day go to court with his witty old acquaintance, and Sir John makes a civil reply, but in reality has no wish to see him in London or anywhere else.

FALSTAFF.   Fare you well, gentle gentlemen. [*Exeunt* SHALLOW *and* SILENCE.]   Lord, Lord, how subject we old men are to this vice of lying! This same starved justice hath done nothing but prate to me of the wildness of his youth, and the feats he hath done about Turnbull Street; and every third word a lie, duer paid to the hearer than the Turk's tribute. I do remember him at Clement's Inn, like a man made after supper of a cheese paring: when he was naked, he was, for all the world, like a forked radish, with a head fantastically carved upon it with a knife.

The shrewd knight, however, seldom offends people if he can help it, so, despite his licentiousness and constant falsehoods, he has scarcely an enemy except Chief Justice Gascoigne, who has both public and private reasons for dreading his future influence with the prince.

The fourth act introduces Archbishop Scroop, Lord Mowbray, and other insurgent leaders,. Mowbray is son and heir to King Henry's old enemy, the Duke of Norfolk, whom he had challenged in presence of Richard II. Both the prelate and he are much disappointed at hearing from their former ally Northumberland, in Scotland, that he cannot join them, though cordially wishing their complete success. While they

---

* Macaulay, when describing an English country squire of the seventeenth century, says:—" He was a magistrate, and as such administered gratuitously to those who dwelt around him a rude, patriarchal justice, which, in spite of innumerable blunders, and of occasional acts of tyranny, was yet better than no justice at all."—*History of England*, vol. i.

are depressed at this news, Lord Westmoreland comes from
the king's forces, now commanded by Prince John, to remonstrate with them—Scroop especially—for exciting insurrection.   The prelate defends his conduct, and he and
Westmoreland argue for some time together, when Mowbray,
apparently a bold, hot-headed young man, angrily answers
Westmoreland, who reminds him that Henry IV. has restored
to him all his late father's confiscated rights and property.
Mowbray, however, expresses no gratitude for this restitution,
declaring it was originally the king's doing, when known as
Bolingbroke, that his father had been despoiled and banished.
He rashly believes, or pretends to believe, that had his father
been allowed to fight Bolingbroke, he would certainly have
slain him, and thus saved England from his usurpation.

> MOWBRAY.   What thing, in honour, had my father lost,
> That need to be reviv'd and breathed in me?
> The king, that lov'd him, as the state stood then,
> Was force perforce compell'd to banish him :
> And then, that Harry Bolingbroke, and he,
> Being mounted, and both roused in their seats,
> Their neighing coursers daring of the spur,
> Their armed staves in charge, their beavers down,
> Their eyes of fire sparkling through sights of steel,
> And the loud trumpet blowing them together ;
> Then, then, when there was nothing could have staid
> My father from the breast of Bolingbroke—
> O, when the king did throw his warder down
> (His own life hung upon the staff he threw),
> Then threw he down himself; and all their lives,
> That, by indictment, and by dint of sword,
> Have since miscarried under Bolingbroke.—Act IV.

To this spirited speech Westmoreland truly replies that
Bolingbroke, or Hereford, as he was then often called, was
well known as "a most valiant gentleman," and quite as likely
to have slain Norfolk.   Mowbray, however, continues obstinate
and defiant ; but Scroop and Lord Hastings, probably men
of better judgment, are more anxious for peace, and, giving
Westmoreland a list of their alleged grievances, declare that,
if these are redressed, they will lay down their arms.   Westmoreland returns to Prince John with their statements,
and soon after the prince has a conference with them.
This fierce boy, though so young, already shows not only a
steady courage, firmness, and gravity, but also a deep dis-
crimination far beyond his years.   He civilly enough greets
both the archbishop and Mowbray, but reproves the former
for heading the insurgents with almost the dignity of a
superior prelate.

> PRINCE JOHN.   My lord of York, it better show'd with you,
> When that your flock, assembled by the bell,
> Encircled you, to hear with reverence
> Your exposition on the holy text,
> Than now to see you here an iron man,
> Cheering a rout of rebels with your drum,
> Turning the word to sword, and life to death.
> . . . . .   You have taken up,
> Under the counterfeited seal of God,
> The subjects of His substitute, my father ;
> And, both against the peace of heaven and him,
> Have here up-swarmed them.

The archbishop defends his conduct, while Mowbray and Hastings use bolder language, and John, after examining their proposals, declares he approves of them all, and will do what he can to have the alleged grievances redressed, provided that the rebel leaders discharge their followers, and surrender their arms. Scroop and Hastings gladly consent, while Mowbray is unwilling, but overruled. The insurgents then disarm and disband, when immediately their leaders are arrested by the treacherous prince, and sentenced to execution.*

The archbishop and Mowbray vainly remonstrate with the relentless youth, who, after scornfully ridiculing them, both for their rebellion and their credulity, orders them to be beheaded.

> MOWBRAY.   Is this proceeding just and honourable ?
> ARCHBISHOP.   Will you thus break your faith ?
> PRINCE JOHN.   I pawn'd thee none.
> I promised you redress of these same grievances
> Whereof you did complain ; which, by mine honour,
> I will perform with a most Christian care.
> But for you, rebels, look to taste the due
> Meet for rebellion, and such acts as yours.—Act IV.

In reality the archbishop's execution was so generally condemned that even Judge Gascoigne, despite his loyalty to the king, refused to sentence him ; but another judge, more compliant, was found, who passed the fatal sentence without any previous indictment or trial.†

---

* " Holinshed's account of the insurrection does not, perhaps, directly implicate Prince John in this unparalleled breach of faith and honour ; but it cannot be forgotten that the Earl Westmoreland [who presided at the executions] was acting under the orders of his general " [Prince John].—STAUNTON'S *Comments on Henry IV.*

† " This was the first instance in England of a capital punishment inflicted on a bishop, whence the clergy of that rank might learn that their crimes, more than those of laics, were not to pass with impunity."—HUME'S *History,* ch. xviii.

L

Although Gascoigne, in common doubtless with other learned and influential men, disapproved of Scroop's execution ; his fate did not apparently elicit either the express censure or remonstrance of the Pope. Probably, when a churchman abandoned his religious duties, and took the field as an armed rebel, or heading other armed rebels against an acknowledged king, he thereby forfeited the protection, if not the sympathy, of his spiritual chief and fellow-ecclesiastics. The arch-bishop, besides, had not joined this rebellion for any religious object. The execution of his brother, Lord Wiltshire, by Henry IV., was the chief cause of his desperate animosity towards him ; for the king, like most prudent or conscien-tious sovereigns, was always careful to be on good terms with the clergy.* Scroop's fate, therefore, though doubtless con-demned and lamented by many, yet excited less apparent pity or indignation than might have been expected.

Prince John, after ordering this prelate's execution, and those of Mowbray and Hastings, meets Falstaff, who has just captured a brave rebel leader—Sir John Colevile—without any trouble ; for this unlucky gentleman, knowing that all his fellow-insurgents are dispersed and disarmed, naturally despairs of further resistance. John reproaches, or rather scolds Falstaff, with the stern sharpness of his character, which is peculiarly disconcerting to the old knight, accustomed to such different language from the prince's wild, merry elder brother. Before this grave, determined boy, Falstaff is utterly confounded. He can neither defy, flatter, nor amuse him, and almost, for the first time in the play, seems at a loss what to say or how to answer.

> PRINCE JOHN.   Now, Falstaff, where have you been all
>   this while ?
> When everything is ended then you come :
> These tardy tricks of yours will, on my life,
> One time or other break some gallows' back.
> FALSTAFF.   I would be sorry, my lord, but it should be thus ; I
never knew yet but rebuke and check was the reward of valour.
Do you think me a swallow, an arrow, or a bullet ? have I, in my
poor and old motion, the expedition of thought ? I have speeded
hither with the very extremest inch of possibility : and here, travel-
tainted as I am, have, in my pure and immaculate valour, taken Sir
John Colevile of the dale, a most furious knight and valorous enemy :.
But what of that ? he saw me, and yielded ; that I may say, with
the hook-nosed fellow of Rome [Julius Cæsar], I came, saw, and
overcame.

* "Throughout Henry IV.'s career he is consistently devout, pure in life, temperate, and careful to avoid offence ; faithful to the church and clergy."— STUBBS's *Constitutional History*, vol. ii.

PRINCE JOHN.   It was more of his courtesy than your deserving.
—Act IV.

This relentless youth orders the luckless Colevile's execution, and, being re-joined by Westmoreland, one of the king's
new and chief adherents, bids a cold farewell to Falstaff,
whom he perhaps wishes to punish, but has not the power to
do so.   He probably dislikes Sir John all the more for
being his elder brother's evil genius and disreputable associate
in London, which he well knows has caused such grief to his
father, to whom he is enthusiastically and steadily dutiful.
Falstaff, though he would gladly please him if he could, is far
more discomfited by this stern boy than by the dignified
Chief Justice Gascoigne.   He slyly ridicules the latter under
a show of respect, but before young John of Lancaster all his
wit and effrontery alike fail him.   For the artful old man,
though shrewd and shameless as ever, is both checked and
puzzled by this grave youth, and perhaps seldom, if ever, felt
so disconcerted by any one or at any time before.

FALSTAFF.   My lord, I beseech you, give me leave to go
Through Gloucestershire : and when you come to court,
Stand my good lord, pray, in your good report.
PRINCE JOHN.   Fare you well, Falstaff : I, in my condition,
Shall better speak of you than you deserve.   [*Exit.*
FALSTAFF.   I would you had but the wit : 'twere better than your
dukedom.—Good faith, this same young sober-blooded boy doth not
love me : nor a man cannot make him laugh ; but that's no marvel,
he drinks no wine.   There's never any of these demure boys come
to any proof.—Act IV.

The next scene is in London, where the invalid king, constantly fretting about his wild heir apparent, blames his
son, Thomas of Clarence, for not being more with Prince
Henry which probably young Clarence could scarcely have
been, without associating with the inmates of the Boar's
Head.   The king hears with grief that his elder son is still
in some part of London, with Poins and other wild companions ; for directly the campaign was over, and the monarch
and his son were relieved of military duties, the former fell ill,
and the latter again returned to his dissipated way of life,
despite his previous promises and even signs of amendment.
While the invalid sovereign is still grieving about his troublesome son, news is brought him of the final defeat of the last
opponents to his authority.   These were the old Lord
Northumberland and Lord Bardolph, who, even after
Scroop's execution, had left Scotland, and made a desperate attempt at insurrection in the north of England.*

* "It was the effect either of Henry's vigilance or good fortune, or of the

In this engagement Northumberland was slain, but his death is not told to the king. Perhaps his ministers fear lest his feelings of triumph might be mingled with sadder emotions at hearing of the death, while in open rebellion, of his first zealous adherent. Henry is too weak to express exultation or even relief at the news of this victory, but it evidently agitates him, and he swoons. When he partially recovers, he is placed on a bed by his sorrowing younger son and the courtiers, and left alone, when Prince Henry enters the chamber as the others leave it, and sees the king lying insensible on the bed, the crown being on his pillow, placed there by his own express order. For the ensuing, most affecting scene, there may have been some historical foundation. It was well known that the king, especially during his last illness, often reproached the Prince for his wild conduct, and deplored the probable future state of England under his rule. These remonstrances, so long practically unheeded, at last prevailed, though no amendment was shown by young Henry till after his father's death, when he appeared a changed man. Shakespeare describes Prince Henry seated by his father's bedside, and addressing the insensible crown, wishing, indeed, to wear it as king, and longing, with the eagerness of his ardent nature, to accept all the cares, duties, and troubles of his future position, together with its attractions, pleasures, and glories. While exciting his mind with these thoughts, he really imagines that his unconscious father is dead ; for the king neither moves nor apparently breathes, and his look, while in sickly sleep or trance, has the appearance of death. The Prince, after vainly trying to rouse or wake him, places the coveted crown upon his own head, and leaves the room with it. His father awaking, first misses the crown, upon which his thoughts are also constantly dwelling, especially in his last illness. He calls his attendants, who tell him they left Prince Henry alone with him while he was asleep. He immediately suspects the truth, that the prince has taken away the crown, believing him already dead. He sends for his son instantly, and, on his entrance, orders every one to withdraw, and leave him alone with his heir.

Then ensues the grandest and most affecting scene in the whole play. The feeble king, knowing his end is near, rouses all the remaining force and energy of his powerful mind for a last exhortation to his dissolute, reckless, and hitherto disobedient son. He first reproaches him for taking the

narrow genius of his enemies, that no proper concert was ever formed among them. They rose in rebellion one after another, and thereby afforded him an opportunity of suppressing these insurrections, which, had they been united, might have proved fatal to his authority."—HUME's *History*, ch. xviii.

crown, and being apparently willing to believe in his death.
As he proceeds in his impassioned appeal, the awful importance of the moment both to his own conscience and to the
welfare of the kingdom inspire a new, irresistible eloquence.
For, as his noble father, John of Gaunt, had exclaimed at a
similar moment, "the words of dying men enforce attention
like deep harmony," so his illustrious son, when in his turn
about to pay the debt of nature, finally adjures, convinces,
and improves his hitherto incorrigible heir. Henry had often
before vainly appealed to the prince's pride of birth and
regard for his own dignity, as well as to his sense of public
and private duty.   Hitherto his remonstrances were naturally
mingled with feelings of anger and scorn ; they are now
accompanied by a very different emotion—that of actual
terror. The dying sovereign reasonably apprehends, like
most of his thoughtful subjects, the coming degradation and
perhaps ruin of his kingdom, as well as of his family. This
dreadful idea, supported, indeed, by every sign of probability,
he expresses in the powerful language natural to a noble yet
excited mind, at the last moment of earthly existence.

> King Henry.   For now a time is come to mock at form.
> Harry the Fifth is crown'd :—Up, vanity !
> Down, royal state ! all you sage counsellors, hence !
> And to the English court assemble now,
> From every region, apes of idleness !
> Now, neighbour confines, purge you of your scum :
> Have you a ruffian that will swear, drink, dance,
> Revel the night ; rob, murder, and commit
> The oldest sins the newest kind of ways ?
> Be happy, he will trouble you no more :
> England shall double gild his treble guilt :
> England shall give him office, honour, might :
> For the fifth Harry from curb'd licence plucks
> The muzzle of restraint, and the wild dog
> Shall flesh his tooth in every innocent.
> O, my poor kingdom, sick with civil blows !
> When that my care could not withhold thy riots,
> What wilt thou do when riot is thy care ?
> O, thou wilt be a wilderness again,
> Peopled with wolves, thy old inhabitants !—Act IV. Scene IV.

Prince Henry might have heard the sternest reproaches, the
most impassioned appeals, with comparative indifference ; but
the sight of his dying father, who had never feared the
bravest foes, showing actual terror about his future life and
conduct was a spectacle he had never before witnessed—
perhaps never thought possible—and it apparently had great
effect in producing that wonderful change in his character

which amazed and gratified all England. He answers his
father in the words and with the manner of perfect sincerity,
promising future amendment. The king, despite his weakness, perceives his sincerity, and believes him, and thus his
last moments are consoled.

After this final reconciliation, Prince John, the king's
favourite son, enters the room, and almost the last words of
his father are addressed to him with a pathos which probably
the young man never forgot.

> PRINCE JOHN.   Health, peace, and happiness to my royal
> father !
> KING HENRY.   Thou bring'st me happiness and peace, son
> John !
> But health, alas ! with youthful wings is flown
> From this bare, withered trunk : upon thy sight,
> My worldly business makes a period.—Act IV.

The king is then borne into another apartment, where his
eventful life ends in peace, though his death is not described.

Act V. is partly comic, partly serious. The first scene is
in Gloucestershire, where Justice Shallow is entertaining
Falstaff with his attendants, Bardolph and the Page. Shallow
is much hurried and flurried, between acting as host to Falstaff, whom he wants to please, and his magisterial business.
His name well expresses his weak, silly character, of which
his roguish servant Davy takes advantage by inducing him
to befriend a well-known rascal named Visor, in a coming
trial. Davy, with an impudent effrontery, like Falstaff on a
small scale, easily induces Shallow to promise favour towards
his friend.

> DAVY. I beseech you, sir, to countenance Visor of Wincot
> against Clement Perkes of the hill.
> SHALLOW. There are many complaints, Davy, against that
> Visor ; that Visor is an arrant knave, on my knowledge.
> DAVY. I grant your worship that he is a knave, sir : but yet,
> God forbid, sir, but a knave should have some countenance at his
> friend's request. An honest man, sir, is able to speak for himself,
> when a knave is not. I have served your worship truly, sir, this
> eight years ; and if I cannot once or twice in a quarter bear out a
> knave against an honest man, I have but very little credit with your
> worship. The knave is mine honest friend, sir ; therefore, I beseech
> your worship, let him be countenanced.
> SHALLOW. Go to ; I say, he shall have no wrong.—Act V.

Shakespeare, by this sketch, probably means to give an
amusing caricature of how the law was occasionally administered in country districts at this time.* While, however,

* "Justices of the Peace were first instituted in 1326. Their duties were

Shallow is trying to please Falstaff, the latter worthy is observing the justice's many follies, for the sake of ridiculing him to Prince Henry when he returns to town.

FALSTAFF.   I will devise matter enough out of this Shallow to keep Prince Henry in continual laughter.

He evidently believes his influence with the prince to be much greater than it ever was before, and has no idea that it is already over.

The next scene reverts to the palace in London, immediately after the king's death, where his younger sons, Judge Gascoigne, and other ministers are assembled.   They are all mournful and apprehensive about the future conduct of the new king, who has apparently concealed his real character and intentions from his own brothers as completely as if they had been utter strangers.   None of them seem to understand him more than another, which ignorance appears very improbable, considering their ages and positions.   His wild life hitherto has evidently inspired every one—relatives, courtiers, and ministers—with the same complete distrust ; yet the idea of his being disinherited is never hinted at by any of them. His younger brothers, Chief Justice Gascoigne, and the ministers, Westmoreland and Warwick, discuss their future prospects with deep dejection, expressing sincere grief at the king's death, and equally sincere apprehension about the conduct of their new sovereign.   The princes frankly sympathize with Gascoigne, openly fearing that he may now suffer for having formerly committed their brother to prison.   The judge is evidently prepared for the worst ; while the young Prince Thomas of Clarence even advises him to appease Falstaff if possible, whom they all think will soon have real power or influence in the kingdom.

GASCOIGNE.   Alas ! I fear all will be overturned.
PRINCE JOHN.   Though no man be assured what grace to find,
You stand in coldest expectation :
I am the sorrier ; would 'twere otherwise.
CLARENCE.   Well, you must now speak Sir John Falstaff fair.
JUDGE GASCOIGNE.   Sweet princes, what I did I did in honour,
Led by the impartial conduct of my soul ;
If truth and upright innocency fail me,
I'll to the king my master that is dead,
And tell him who hath sent me after him.

It is clear, from the words of the princes, that their elder

described in the most general terms.   They were 'assigned to keep the peace,' and empowered ' to take and arrest all those they may find by indictment or suspicion and put them in prison.' "—STEPHENS's *History of the English Criminal Law*, ch. vii.

brother was on very distant terms with them, while associating familiarly with Falstaff, Poins, &c. ; and that they are almost like strangers to him. When the youthful king joins this disconsolate assemblage, he immediately re-assures his brothers, saying he is an English, not a Turkish prince, and observes with surprise that they "look strangely" on him. He then pretends to rebuke the Chief Justice for having imprisoned him, and thus elicits a long and dignified defence from the judge, which is what the young monarch evidently wishes to hear, and at its conclusion completely satisfies the old man, praising his firmness, and declaring he will follow his father's policy, by surrounding himself with his most trusted ministers.

> KING HENRY V.   The tide of blood in me
> Hath proudly flow'd in vanity till now :
> Now doth it turn, and ebb back to the sea ;
> Where it shall mingle with the state of floods,
> And flow henceforth in formal majesty.
> Now call we our high court of parliament :
> And let us choose such limbs of noble counsel,
> That the great body of our state may go
> Inequal rank with the best govern'd nation.
>
>   .   .   .   .   .   .
>
> No prince, nor peer, shall have just cause to say,
> Heaven shorten Harry's happy life one day.

This important announcement, which has the effect of a proclamation, is heard by all present with admiring, thankful attention ; and the next scene is again in Justice Shallow's Gloucestershire abode. He and his friend Silence entertain Falstaff at one table, while Davy entertains Falstaff's servants, Bardolph and the Page, at another. All these country people know something of Falstaff's strange intimacy with Prince Henry, and Davy, like his master, hopes to see London, and be well received there by Bardolph. While the whole party are thus enjoying themselves—Silence singing, and Falstaff, the most honoured guest, listening graciously —the bravo Pistol arrives with London news. This man, though a swaggering, quarrelsome boaster, like Poins and Peto, always talks in a curious, fantastic style, rather like the Euphuists in Queen Elizabeth's reign. He has now ridden in hot haste from London, longing to be the first to announce the welcome news of Henry the Fifth's accession. Though he is overjoyed, expecting happy times of future dissipation and impunity, in common with the prince's former companions, he still, amid his delight, preserves his vague, fanciful way of talking, which provokes Falstaff's earnest request to tell his news "like a man of this world." Pistol then speaks plainly, and Falstaff immediately breaks forth into wild exultation.   He may, perhaps, by this time have drunk too freely of Justice Shallow's wine, otherwise the shrewd old knight would hardly have lost his self-control so completely in vehement rejoicing.   But the young king has practically deceived associates, friends, foes, and relatives alike, almost as thoroughly as the most artful hypocrite could have done. Falstaff and his party, accordingly, are as thoroughly mistaken in the young monarch as his brothers and ministers are.

Sir John, now nearly frantic with delight, hastens immediately to London, after making vague promises to Shallow, and wildly boasting of his own imaginary influence.

FALSTAFF.   What ! is the old king dead?

PISTOL.   As nail in door : the things I speak are just.

FALSTAFF.   Away, Bardolph ; saddle my horse.—Master Robert Shallow, choose what office thou wilt in the land, 'tis thine.—Pistol, I will double-charge thee with dignities.

BARDOLPH.   O joyful day !—

I would not take a knighthood for my fortune.

PISTOL.   What ! I do bring good news?

FALSTAFF.   Master Shallow, my Lord Shallow, be what thou wilt, I am fortune's steward.   Get on thy boots : we'll ride all night : —O, sweet Pistol !—Away, Bardolph. . . . . I know the young king is sick for me.   Let us take any man's horses ; the laws of England are at my commandment.   Happy are they which have been my friends, and woe unto my Lord Chief Justice !—Act V.

The next scene is very short, partly comic, partly painful, describing the two women, Mrs. Quickly and Dolly, roughly dragged to prison by some beadles, who then performed, probably with great harshness, the duties of modern policemen.* These hapless women, both probably drunk, abuse and revile their captors, who hint that there have been lives lost lately in the Boar's Head, and that Pistol was one of the homicides or murderers.   It is likely that Mrs. Quickly's establishment, in the absence of Prince Henry and Falstaff, became the scene of more dangerous revels than before, when the rank of the former, and the shrewd wit of the latter, were no longer there to inspire awe or preserve good humour.   Nothing, however, transpires about the alleged fray, and the women, longing for Falstaff to rescue them, are taken to jail, scolding and threatening the beadles, with much the same coarse, spiteful mockery still often displayed in police courts.

HOSTESS.   No, thou arrant knave ; I would I might die that I might have thee hanged : thou hast drawn my shoulder out of joint.

* " From the earliest times to our own days there were two bodies of police in England, namely, the parish and high constables, and the watchmen in cities and boroughs.   Nothing could exceed the inefficiency of the constables and watchmen."—STEPHENS'S *English Criminal Law*, ch. vii.

1st Beadle.   The constables have delivered her over to me:
and she shall have whipping-cheer enough, I warrant her. . . . . . .
Come, I charge you both go with me; for the man is dead that you
and Pistol beat among you.

Doll.   I will have you as soundly swinged for this, you blue-
bottled rogue! you filthy famished correctioner: if you be not
swinged, I'll forswear half-kirtles.   .

Beadle.   Come, come, you she knight-errant, come.

Hostess.   O, that right should thus overcome might!

Doll.   Come, you rogue, come; bring me to a justice.

Hostess.   Yes; come, you starved bloodhound.

Doll.   Come, you thin thing; come, you rascal.

Beadle.   Very well.—Act V.

The last scene returns to London, where Falstaff, Shallow,
Pistol, and Bardolph are assembled in a public place near
Westminster Abbey, which the king is about to pass in a
state procession. Falstaff feels sure that the young sovereign
will recognize and welcome him. He places Pistol behind
him, while Shallow is beside him, Bardolph and the Page
being near, when the king approaches, attended by many
courtiers, and also by Chief Justice Gascoigne. Falstaff instantly addresses his former young patron, and calls him
"My royal Hal." Pistol also greets him as "most royal
imp of fame!" The king first tells Gascoigne to answer,
but the judge is so shocked at Falstaff's freedom that he can
only ask him if he is in his senses, and knows what he says.
Falstaff takes no notice of him, but persists in addressing the
king, who then replies with stern gravity, bids him fall to
his prayers, and no longer to think him the same man he
was, for that he has turned away his former self, and also his
previous company. He even banishes Sir John from his
presence, forbidding him, on pain of death, to approach him
nearer than ten miles. Then, perhaps remembering Falstaff's
desperate circumstances, and that he will now lose all credit
after being thus cast off, and probably be ruined, he promises him an unearned "competence of life, ... that
lack of means enforce you not to evil," and directs Gascoigne
"to see performed the tenor of our word," though that judge
is probably the least likely of all people to recommend
liberality to Falstaff.

The king then passes on, and Shallow, who, with Falstaff's
other companions, is grievously disappointed at this reception, now asks the poor old knight to repay a thousand
pounds he had lent him. Falstaff, though doubtless amazed,
like the rest, at the king's words, has yet too much buoy-
ancy and self-confidence to believe himself really abandoned
to the mercies of Judge Gascoigne, and flatters himself that

Henry will send for him at night, having merely assumed this new manner towards him for some reasons of state. Shallow, however, despite his simplicity, is alarmed about his money, and begs for half of it, which Falstaff is apparently unable to pay. Sir John then asks both Shallow and Pistol to dine with him that evening, still persuading himself that he will yet be summoned at night to the palace, when enter his two chief enemies, old and young, Prince John and Judge Gascoigne, whom his wit could never amuse nor his effrontery deceive. Gascoigne immediately orders Falstaff and all his company to be conveyed to the Fleet Prison. Sir John attempts a remonstrance, but is removed a prisoner with his companions—an act for which there appears little or no reason at that moment.* For the prince could hardly have expected Falstaff's reformation, were such a thing ever possible, to commence precisely at the same time as his own. Prince John, however, intimates to Gascoigne that all the imprisoned party will be "provided for," but that "all are banished till their conversations appear more wise and modest to the world." Whether he means that Falstaff will be "provided for" in prison for the rest of his life, does not seem very clear; but probably his imprisonment was only meant to be a short one, to convince him and others that his influence with the king is over.†

Prince John and Gascoigne are now the men highest in the king's confidence, and in the last lines of this play John anticipates the war with France, which soon ensues. The play thus leaves Henry V. newly crowned, and surrounded by the late king's most trusted ministers. His former wild associates are either banished from his presence or imprisoned. The peaceful and respectable of his subjects are thus soon convinced of their young sovereign's thorough reformation, for he certainly behaved thenceforth as if the admonishing spirit of his illustrious father inspired all his thoughts and directed all his actions.

* Dr. Johnson thinks Falstaff's imprisonment an act of cruelty. Messrs. Dowden and Furnivall apparently think the young king was right. The former says :—"As no terms of half-acquaintance are possible with the fat knight, Henry must become to Falstaff an absolute stranger. Henry has been stern to his former self; therefore he can be stern to Falstaff." Mr. Furnivall writes :—"What other reception could Henry, in the midst of his new state, give in public to the debauched old sinner? . . . His end here is imprisonment for a time."

† As Shakespeare had no wish to represent the young monarch unfairly, it is evident that Henry only intended a slight punishment for Falstaff,—as Hume writes : "Henry V. called together his former companions, acquainted them with his intended reformation, exhorted them to imitate his example, but strictly inhibited them, till they had given proofs of their sincerity in this particular, from appearing any more in his presence, and he then dismissed them, with liberal presents."—*History of England*, ch. xix.

CHAPTER VIII.

KING HENRY V.

Sketch of Play.

THE king is induced, both by his own will and that of his subjects generally, to declare war against France. He is the more eager for a campaign as the late monarch had advised his turning the attention of his subjects to foreign war and conquest. Even the chief English prelates approve of a war with France, as that country being in great disorder, owing to the royal family disputing among themselves, the time seemed favourable for an English triumph. This whole play, therefore, is occupied with the French campaign, in which Henry V. greatly distinguishes himself. His bravery, generosity, and good sense endear him both to his soldiers and to his subjects at home. After the decisive victory of Agincourt, peace is concluded between France and England. Henry marries the French king's daughter, and at the time of his marriage the play ends.

THE first scene describes a political conversation between the Archbishop of Canterbury and the Bishop of Ely. These prelates, with the rest of the clergy, though delighted and thankful at the young monarch's change from being a dissipated youth to becoming a wise ruler, are yet alarmed at a proposal now made by parliament to seize the church revenues, and convert them to the use of the crown.* Hume and Shakespeare alike represent these prelates as trying to incline the king's mind from domestic plunder, as they thought, to foreign conquest. Henry V., the most popular of English kings, seems to have loved his subjects as much as they liked him.† He was by nature much more inclined to make war on foreigners than to offend any of his own countrymen, and he

---

* HUME's *History*, ch. xix.

† "Loved he certainly was throughout his life, as so intrepid, affable, and generous a temper well deserved, and this sentiment was heightened to admiration by successes still more rapid and dazzling than those of Edward III. During his reign, there scarcely appears any vestige of dissatisfaction in parliament."— HALLAM's *Middle Ages*, ch. viii.

succeeds in conciliating many adherents and descendants of his father's enemies. He restores to Hotspur's son the Percy fortune and honours, and treats his young rival, Lord March, with great kindness, though he does not appear to have completely liberated him.* He thus gratifies and reassures his English subjects, and, though one of the most warlike of his race, pacifies his fellow-countrymen among themselves by diverting them from domestic dissension to foreign conquest. He eagerly desires war with France, and this inclination is confirmed by a haughty message from the Dauphin, eldest son of the French king, evidently a prince more hostile to England than his father was, who seems to have been a weak monarch, both in body and mind. This French prince refuses Henry's demand to restore certain lands in France formerly conquered by England. He even insolently sends some tennis balls to the English king, as if to remind him that peaceful games are more in his line than warfare.† For the Dauphin has evidently little idea of Henry's really brave and martial character, probably thinking him still a dissipated, idle young man, revelling in London taverns. Henry, with the full consent of his subjects, now contemplates invading France. At first his object seems to have been the recovery of some lands formerly conquered by his ancestors, but the quarrels in the French royal family probably aroused ambitious hopes of conquering the whole country.

Act II. begins in Eastcheap, London, perhaps near the old Boar's Head Tavern. Here Bardolph, Falstaff's old attendant, meets Corporal Nym, a kindred spirit, and these worthies talk about their comrade Pistol, now married to Dame Quickly, his former favourite Dolly having vanished altogether as she never re-appears after being dragged to jail by the beadles. Pistol and his elderly bride soon join Nym and Bardolph, and they talk in their usual licentious manner, occasionally quarrelling and abusing each other, partly in jest, partly in earnest. Falstaff's former page-boy, a sharp-witted, precocious lad, showing, indeed, little sign of youthful innocence or simplicity, also joins the party, announcing poor old Falstaff's dangerous illness. The hostess exclaims, with probable truth, that the king "has killed his heart," and goes with the boy to see

---

* HUME's *History*, ch. xix.

† Shakespeare seems to invest this Dauphin Louis with the more warlike spirit of his younger brother Charles, who survived him, became Dauphin, and afterwards King Charles VII., surnamed the Victorious. The Dauphin Louis was more peaceful towards England, and wished his sister Catherine to marry Henry V., who, however, demanded more French territory than either King Charles VI. or his eldest son would then grant.—See *Student's History of France*.

him; while the others continue to jest and quarrel alternately for a short time. But Mrs. Pistol soon returns, and takes them all away with her to visit their invalid associate. Both Nym and Pistol declare, like the hostess, that the king's conduct has killed Falstaff's heart, and thereby ruined his health, which was perhaps the case. For an old drunken, extravagant profligate like Sir John would surely feel disappointment, humiliation, and surprise beyond expression at the young king's sudden change, and his open condemnation of him and his practices. These feelings in such a man would probably drive him to seek relief and forgetfulness in an excess of drinking far surpassing all previous instances. Moreover, his former acquaintances—doubtless including many creditors—would probably besiege him with claims which he might naturally have hoped to satisfy on the very occasion which had so unexpectedly abandoned him to hopeless poverty. No one in England is practically more deceived, or rather mistaken, in King Henry V. than his shrewd, witty old companion. His vanity and consequence, as well as his credit, are now alike at an end. Instead of his last hope being gratified—of a summons to the palace to amuse the king at night, though denied an audience in the daytime—he was sternly sent to jail, for no reason apparently, save that he had shared in the young prince's dissipated revels, whose sudden change both of habit and principle he was morally, if not physically, unable to follow, or, rather, to keep pace with. From this durance he seems to have been soon liberated, but only to survive a short time the combined effects of imprisonment, chagrin, and mortification preying upon a constitution doubtless weakened by a most intemperate life.

The next scene, in a great measure founded upon history, is at Southampton, whence the king is preparing to embark for France at the head of his army. Just before leaving, a dangerous plot against him is discovered, and the chief conspirators—the Earl of Cambridge, Lord Scroop, and Sir Thomas Grey—are now with the king, having no idea that their plot is detected; but Henry has the written proofs of it in his possession. He summons them, with many faithful ministers, together, and then shows the conspirators the evidence of their guilt. They, of course, can neither escape, nor in any way defend themselves, and are therefore executed, in accordance with the severe laws of that age against treasonable intentions as well as acts.* They were proved to

---

* "The conspirators, as soon as detected, acknowledged their guilt to the king, and Henry proceeded without delay to their trial and condemnation. The utmost that could be expected of the best king in those ages was that he would so far

have been allied with the French in their plot, and this circumstance, together with Henry's great and sudden popularity, prevented their obtaining any sympathy. Their object was to place the imprisoned Lord March on the throne. This prince, however, was kindly treated by Henry V., and on friendly terms with him. He was a youth of an unambitious nature, and it seems uncertain if he even knew of this plot in his behalf.*

The king, after sentencing the conspirators, embarks for France, and does not again appear in England during the play; but the following scene reverts to London, in Pistol's house, at Eastcheap, where the former hostess of the Boar's Head Tavern seems to be living with her husband. This strange couple, with Bardolph, Nym, and the boy now mention Falstaff's death, which has just occurred. Mrs. Pistol (late Quickly) records it, and, from her account, the poor old knight died " babbling about green fields," perhaps recalling his childhood, but he does not seem to have mentioned the king. As he latterly was so thoroughly disavowed and degraded, without any chance of his regaining influence, his former reckless associates—Bardolph, Nym, and Pistol—soon cease talking about him, and prepare to follow the king to France. The boy also accompanies them, while Mrs. Pistol remains in London, though it is not said if she still acts as landlady of the Boar's Head.

The next scene is in France. King Charles VI., with his son the Dauphin Louis, their retainers and ministers, are assembled together, preparing for defence against the English attack. The Dauphin seems defiant, calling King Henry a " vain, giddy, shallow, humorous youth," which was doubtless the reputation his former conduct had acquired, both in England and on the Continent. The Constable of France, however, and some other leading Frenchmen have heard more about Henry's real abilities, and are not so confident of success against him. Whilst these French leaders are debating, Lord Exeter is announced, bearing written proposals from Henry, which the French king finds demand his self-deposition and the surrender of his whole kingdom to the English. Charles is weak and irresolute; the Dauphin,

---

observe the essentials of justice as not to make an innocent person a victim to his severity."—HUME'S *History*, ch. xix.

* "The Earl of March was faithful [to the king], but he was childless, and his claim would pass, at his death, through a sister, who had wedded the Earl of Cambridge, to her son Richard, destined to play so great a part in the Wars of the Roses. It was to secure his boy's claims that the Earl of Cambridge seized on the king's departure to combine with Scroop and Grey to proclaim the Earl of March king. The plot, however, was discovered, and the plotters beheaded, before the king sailed."—GREEN'S *History of the English People*, ch. v.

angry and defiant.   War is now inevitable, and the following
act mentions the capture of Harfleur by the English, led by
the king in person, who exhorts his soldiers both by example
and precept rarely united, to carry all before them.

>   KING HENRY.   Once more unto the breach, dear friends, once
>   more ;
> Or close the wall up with our English dead !
> In peace, there's nothing so becomes a man
> As modest stillness and humility :
> But when the blast of war blows in our ears,
> Then imitate the action of the tiger :
> Stiffen the sinews, summon up the blood,
> Disguise fair nature with hard-favoured rage :
> Then lend the eye a terrible aspect.
>
>   .   .   .   .   .
>
> Now set the teeth, and stretch the nostril wide :
> Hold hard the breath, and bend up every spirit
> To his full height !—On, on, you noble English !—Act III.

After his spirited address to the troops, Henry marches on
with them, and in their rear follow Shakespeare's comic
characters, Bardolph, Nym, Pistol, and the boy, who is really
the most intelligent and sober of the party. These rogues are
evidently more inclined to plunder the dead and wounded
than to fight ; but a brave, talkative Welsh captain, Fluellen,
one of the few interesting characters in this play, drives them
on after the other soldiers, while the sharp-witted lad originally " given " by Prince Henry to Falstaff remains behind,
moralising and ridiculing his three elder companions, who are
as distasteful to him as the London thieves were to Oliver
Twist, and for somewhat similar reasons.

>   BOY.   As young as I am, I have observed these three swashers.
> . . . . . indeed, three such antics do not amount to a man. For
> Bardolph—he is white-livered, and red-faced ; by the means whereof
> 'a faces it out, but fights not.   For Pistol—he hath a killing tongue
> and a quiet sword ; by the means whereof 'a breaks words, and keeps
> whole weapons.   For Nym—he hath heard that men of few words
> are the best men ; and therefore he scorns to say his prayers, lest 'a
> should be thought a coward : but his few bad words are matched
> with as few good deeds ; for 'a never broke any man's head but his
> own, and that was against a post, when he was drunk.   They will
> steal anything, and call it purchase, and would have me as familiar
> with men's pockets as their gloves and their handkerchers : which
> makes much against my manhood. . . . . . I must leave them, and
> seek some better service : their villainy goes against my weak
> stomach, and therefore I must cast it up.—Act III.

Fluellen and another officer named Gower, with a Scottish

and an Irish captain, Jamy and-Macmorris, have a curious conversation. This is Shakespeare's only play, and the sole scene in it, where he introduces an Irish character, in Captain Macmorris, who threatens to kill Fluellen, apparently half in jest, half in earnest. He is a fiery, hot-headed, quarrelsome fellow, and a very unfair specimen of Irish officers—a class distinguished in every military service they enter—though a fair enough sample of a brawling, ignorant peasant.

MACMORRIS. What ish my nation? ish a villain, and a bastard, and a knave, and a rascal? What ish my nation? Who talks of my nation? . . . . I do not know you so good a man as myself: so Chrish save me, I will cut off your head.—Act III.

The Scottish officer Jamy is comparatively cool and quiet, but neither he nor Macmorris again appear, while the Welsh Fluellen is often introduced as a loyal, steady officer.

After the capture of Harfleur by the English, the next scene introduces the French princess and future English queen, Catherine, trying to learn some English words from her attendant, Lady Alice, who has been in England ; while her father, the French king, and her brother, the Dauphin, send more defiances to King Henry, whose army is so small, compared to that of the French, that the latter expect a certain and easy victory. But Henry has succeeded wonderfully in inspiring his few gallant followers with his own ardour, while the French, during this whole campaign, displayed neither that bravery nor skill for which they have been always distinguished. They apparently had no leaders of much talent or popularity at this time. The king was an invalid, and there were constant quarrels between his sons and their adherents. On the other hand the English were thoroughly united and firm, from the king to the private, except in such instances as Bardolph's, who, being detected in robbing a church, was sentenced to death, his friend Pistol vainly beseeching Fluellen's intercession to save him. Upon Fluellen's refusal, Pistol is in a fury, but the Welsh captain, who first thought him a brave soldier, now guesses his real character, which is certainly a strange one. He is evidently a man of some education for those times, but a reckless, cowardly, yet cunning boaster, unworthy of the least confidence.

There soon ensues an exchange of proud defiances between the French and English kings ; but Shakespeare introduces no interesting French characters, nor does he seem to know or care much about their national peculiarities. In Scene VII. he introduces the Dauphin and his courtiers, praising their horses and armour in a fantastic style, and calling the English

brave but "stupid mastiffs." They naturally enough think
the English invaders are quite in their power, being so few,
and almost surrounded by the French forces. But they
express no bitter hatred against their foes, nor does their
language display any of that brilliancy and intelligence for
which the French have been usually remarkable. Almost the
only interesting character in this play is King Henry, whose
marvellous energy, spirit, and eloquence are ably seconded
by his trusty follower Fluellen. His gallant brother, John of
Lancaster, is now styled Duke of Bedford, and enjoys his
full confidence. Henry is evidently the poet's special favourite
throughout. He describes him with reckless companions,
friends, foes, courtiers, relatives, private soldiers, and lastly
with his French bride. In conduct and language to all he
shows the same frank, open, courteous, yet fearless spirit.
He has an amusing conversation with two of his common
soldiers, Bates and Williams, who do not know him when
disguised. Williams, thinking him an insolent comrade,
offers him a challenge, which Henry accepts, taking the
man's glove, and promising to meet him on some future day.
This curious scene occurs just before the famous and decisive
battle of Agincourt, and the warlike king, when alone, implores the "God of battles" to grant him success. In this
prayer he mentions the late King Richard II., whose deposition and suspected murder always disturbed his father's peace
of mind, and at times affect his own.

> KING HENRY.   O God of battles ! steel my soldiers' hearts !
> Possess them not with fear ! take from them now
> The sense of reckoning, if the opposed numbers
> Pluck their hearts from them.   Not to-day, O Lord,
> O, not to-day, think not upon the fault
> My father made in compassing the crown !
> I Richard's body have interred new ;
> And on it have bestowed more contrite tears
> Than from it issued forced drops of blood.
> Five hundred poor I have in yearly pay,
> Who twice a day their wither'd hands hold up
> Toward heaven, to pardon blood ; and I have built
> Two chantries, where the sad and solemn priests
> Sing still for Richard's soul.—Act IV.

The English were now greatly outnumbered, and Henry,
whose heroic spirit rises higher and yet higher to meet the
danger, has the rare, inestimable gift of inspiring others with
his own courage.*

* "The king's courage rose with the peril. 'I would not have a single man
more,' he said. 'If God give us the victory, it will be plain we owe it to His

His feelings, indeed, were precisely those which Shakespeare ascribes to him, and his real sentiments, as recorded by historians, quite coincide with those expressed in the poet's splendid words. In the finest speech throughout the whole play, just before the battle, he reproves Westmoreland for naturally wishing for more English soldiers, who are at peace in their own country.

> KING HENRY. No, 'faith, my coz, wish not a man from
> England:
> God's peace! I would not lose so great an honour,
> As one man more, methinks, would share from me,
> For the best hope I have. O, do not wish one more!
>
> . . . . . .
> This day is called the Feast of Crispian:
> He that outlives this day, and sees old age,
> Will yearly on the vigil feast his friends,
> And say, "To-morrow is Saint Crispian:"
> Then will he strip his sleeve and show his scars;
> And say, "These wounds I had on Crispian's Day."
> . . . . . Then shall our names,
> Familiar in their mouths as household words,—
> Harry the King, Bedford and Exeter,
> Warwick and Talbot, Salisbury and Gloster,—
> Be in their flowing cups freshly remember'd.
> . . . . We few, we happy few, we band of brothers;
> For he to-day that sheds his blood with me
> Shall be my brother; be he ne'er so vile
> This day shall gentle his condition:
> And gentlemen of England, now a-bed,
> Shall think themselves accurs'd they were not here;
> And hold their manhood cheap, whiles any speak
> That fought with us upon Saint Crispian's Day.—Act IV.

These heroic words evidently produced their full effect upon his men. The English fought with that invincible courage and coolness for which they have been so famous in history. The French, probably too sanguine of success, and therefore careless, besides not being well commanded, were defeated, with terrible loss.* During this battle, the desperado Pistol, with Falstaff's boy, appear with a French soldier, evidently a prisoner. The French captive begs Pistol to spare his life, promising him a large sum of money; and Pistol, after some boasting, accepts the offer, and spares him, the boy acting as interpreter with his usual intelligence.

grace. If not, the fewer we are, the less loss for England.' The handful of men whom he led shared the spirit of their king."—GREEN's *History of the English People*, ch. v.

* "No battle was ever more fatal to France, from the number of princes and nobility slain or taken prisoners."—HUME's *History*, ch. xix. Hume and Green estimate the French loss at about ten thousand. The former first states the English

Boy.   He prays you to save his life : he is a gentleman of a good house ; and for his ransom he will give you two hundred crowns.

Pistol.   Tell him my fury shall abate,
    And I the crowns will take.   [*Exit with French prisoner.*

Boy.   Bardolph and Nym had ten times more valour than this roaring devil i' the old play ; and they are both hanged ; and so would this be, if he durst steal anything adventurously.   I must stay with the lackeys, with the luggage of our camp : the French might have a good prey of us, if he knew it ; for there is none to guard it but boys.—Act IV.

This poor lad well deserves pity, for he seems without friend or relative, yet is quite fearless, and, though placed by Prince Henry among Falstaff's set, gives signs of being far superior to any of them.   Bardolph and Nym have been both executed—the former for what was thought an act of sacrilegious robbery—and this luckless boy, after the Agincourt battle, is probably slain by the French peasants, who, it appears, killed all who were in charge of the English camp luggage.†   This butchery, as well as the fear of being attacked by these ferocious peasants, provoked Henry to order the execution of French prisoners, but he immediately recalled this mandate, for he was evidently a merciful as well as a gallant conqueror.   He rewards the brave soldier Williams, who, finding Fluellen with his glove, which he had previously given to the disguised king, challenges and strikes him, when Henry appears on the scene, and tells Williams that he himself was his challenged foe.

Williams.   My liege, this was my glove ; here is the fellow of it : and he that I gave it to in charge promised to wear it in his cap ; I promised to strike him, if he did : I met this man [Fluellen] with my glove in his cap, and I have been as good as my word.

King Henry.   Give me thy glove, soldier !   Look, here is the fellow of it.   'Twas I, indeed, thou promised'st to strike ; it was ourself thou didst abuse.

Williams.   Your majesty came not like yourself : you appeared to me but as a common man ; witness the night, your garments, your lowliness ; and what your highness suffered under that shape, I beseech you to take it for your own fault, and not mine : for had you been as I took you for, I made no offence ; therefore, I beseech your highness, pardon me.

King Henry.   Here, Uncle Exeter, fill this glove with crowns, and give it to this fellow.

slain were about *forty*, but reasonably adds that there were probably more not recorded.   Green does not mention the number, but the great slaughter of the French was evidently astonishing, in comparison, and can only be explained by their being badly officered and ill-armed.

  * Hume's *History*, ch. xix.
  † Hume's *History*, ch. xix.

FLUELLEN. Py this day and this light, the fellow hath mettle enough in his pelly:—Hold, there is twelve pence for you, and I pray you to serve Got, and keep you out of prawls.

WILLIAMS. I will none of your money.—Act IV.

The king's conduct in this affair quite accords with his frank, generous character, for he seems to have made himself immensely and deservedly popular with all classes. This fourth act ends with Henry's ordering a public thanksgiving for his glorious and decisive victory.

The last act describes the celebrated meeting between the French and English kings at Troyes, in Champagne, where they made a treaty, by which Henry agreed to marry the Princess Catherine, and accept some French provinces, including Normandy, during her father's life, but afterwards to inherit all France, he and his heir, to the utter exclusion of the Dauphin and his younger brother. Shakespeare amuses his readers, and perhaps himself, by inventing a long conversation between King Henry and the French princess, neither of whom quite understand the other's language, yet are evidently pleased with each other.

KING HENRY. Put off your maiden blushes; avouch the thoughts of your heart with the looks of an empress; take me by the hand, and say, "Harry of England, I am thine:" which word thou shalt no sooner bless mine ear withal, but I will tell thee aloud, "England is thine, Ireland is thine, France is thine, and Harry Plantagenet is thine:" who, though I speak it before his face, if he be not fellow with the best king, thou shalt find the best king of good fellows. Come, your answer in broken music: for thy voice is music, and thy English broken: therefore, queen of all, Catherine, break thy mind to me in broken English, Wilt thou have me?

CATHERINE. Dat is, as it sall please de *roy mon père*.

KING HENRY. Nay, it will please him well, Kate; it shall please him, Kate.

CATHERINE. Den it sall also content me.

KING HENRY. Upon that I kiss your hand, and call you my queen.—Act V.

The French king and his court are satisfied with this marriage, which brings peace between the two nations, and with this event the play ends. King Henry is attended by his brothers, Gloster and Bedford, and his ministers, Westmoreland and Warwick, who all appeared in the former play; but in this one they take very little part. Henry engrosses nearly all the interest; he is its only hero, and the whole play records his continued triumph, beginning with the suppression of the one plot against him, then describing his French victories, and ending with his happy marriage to the daughter of his defeated foe, Charles VI.*

The remaining two years of his life and reign Shakespeare does not notice. In the chief events of his glorious French campaign the poet apparently follows history with great exactness, except, indeed, when describing French characters, which are drawn without much animation or interest. It is probably this indifference of Shakespeare to his French personages which irritates the usually calm statesman and writer, M. Guizot, into declaring that, when narrating his own country's history with those of others, Shakespeare is no longer just, but thinks and judges "like John Bull."† This opinion is scarcely fair, however, for Shakespeare never reveals any prejudices against the French. He neither describes their heroes nor villains in this play. All he mentions are merely uninteresting personages, but he never rouses any English feelings against them. He seems only ignorant or indifferent about their national habits and peculiarities, but shows no dislike whatever towards them, which probably many English writers, before, during, and since his time, would have strongly expressed when writing dramatic plays concerning French warfare with their own country.

* "Henry V. had the talent of attaching his friends by affability, and of gaining his enemies by address and clemency. The English, dazzled by the lustre of his character still more than by that of his victories, were reconciled to the defects in his title. The French almost forgot that he was an enemy."—HUME'S *History*, ch. xix.

† After praising Shakespeare's genius in Hamlet, Othello and other fictitious plays, M. Guizot proceeds respecting the historical ones :—"Toute independance et toute impartialitè d'esprit l'abandonnent, en toutes choses et sur toutes les personnes il croit et juge absolument comme John Bull."—*Shakespeare and his Times.*

CHAPTER IX.

FIRST PART OF KING HENRY VI.

Sketch of Play.

DURING the minority of Henry VI. the French king died, and his second son, Prince Charles, who never sanctioned his father's peace with the English, is proclaimed king as Charles VII. The Duke of Bedford, formerly Prince John of Lancaster, being left Regent of France by his brother, Henry V., is soon at war with the new monarch, who, aided by the enthusiastic Joan of Arc, recovers the greater part of France from the English. The Duke of Burgundy is allied with England against Charles, and Joan is captured by him, and delivered over to the English, by whom, after a trial in which her own countrymen opposed her, she was condemned and burned for alleged witchcraft. England, during Henry VI.'s youth, was chiefly ruled by his uncle Gloster, styled "The Protector." He is vehemently opposed by Cardinal Beaufort, great uncle of the young king, and who has charge of his education. In this play, the young Duke of York, son of the executed Lord Cambridge, and nephew of the imprisoned Mortimer, Lord March, secretly aspires to the English crown, and his uncle's words, whom he sees in prison, confirm his resolution to overthrow the reigning dynasty on the first opportunity. He remains quiet, however, during this play, which ends with announcing the approaching marriage of Henry VI. to Margaret of Anjou. This match is chiefly arranged by Cardinal Beaufort of Winchester and William Poole, Earl of Suffolk, and is much opposed by the Protector, who, though deservedly esteemed and popular, gradually loses influence over his weak young sovereign. His gloomy anticipations of future troubles in England conclude this play.

THE first act mentions the funeral of Henry V., whose death is mourned by all his subjects, and especially by his brothers, Bedford and Gloster, the former being left Regent of France, and the latter Protector of England, by the late king's appointment. These princes are opposed by numerous and powerful enemies. Gloster's violent quarrels with Cardinal Beaufort, his illegitimate uncle, so distract England that the French, availing themselves of these English dissensions, and the absence of the energetic Bedford, proclaim Prince Charles their king, and re-take Paris, Rouen, and other towns from the English. This new French monarch is the younger brother of the vain, weak Dauphin Louis, described in the last play, and who, dying without heirs, is succeeded in his rights, or rather in his hopes of recovering them, by his braver and more powerful brother.* When this disas-trous news is told to the English princes, Bedford resolves to return to France immediately, where he and the brave Talbot now command the English forces. Gloster remains nomin-ally supreme in England, where his quarrels with Beaufort become daily more serious and dangerous to the kingdom. Bedford's arrival in France revives for a time the fortunes of the English. The French were defeated by him with great loss, and he showed a spirit and daring worthy of his heroic brother. At this moment of defeat and impending ruin to France, the young King Charles, interesting alike by his position and character, found an unexpected, and, what was then believed, a miraculous ally, in the poor country girl, Joan of Arc.† Shakespeare, in his account of this heroic woman, apparently follows Holinshed's narrative, who seems to have regarded her with superstitious horror as being allied with Satan ; and she was similarly suspected by many of her own countrymen. When she first appears, she declares to the astonished king that she has a divine mission to recover a part of France from the English, having seen the Virgin Mary in a vision, who has revealed her future duty.

> JOAN. Lo ! whilst I waited on my tender lambs,
> And to sun's parching heat display'd my cheeks,
> God's mother deigned to appear to me ;
> And, in a vision full of majesty,
> Will'd me to leave my base vocation,
> And free my country from calamity ;
> Her aid she promis'd and assur'd success :
> In complete glory she reveal'd herself ;

---

* " Sincere, generous, affable, he engaged from affection the services of his followers. . . . . Amidst all his irregularities, the goodness of his heart still shone forth, and, by exerting at intervals his courage and activity, he proved that his general remissness proceeded not from the want either of a just spirit, of ambition, or of personal valour."—HUME's *History*, ch. xx.

† " The girl was in her eighteenth year ; tall, finely formed, with all the vigour and activity of her peasant rearing; able to stay from dawn to nightfall on horseback without meat or drink."—GREEN's *History of the English People*, ch. vi.

> And, whereas I was black and swart before,
> With these clear rays which she infused on me,
> That beauty am I bless'd with which you see.—Act I.

Charles himself engages her in a mock combat, in which he is overcome, and then, believing her entirely, gives her a command in his army. For this supposed encounter between Charles and Joan, there seems no historical foundation ; and Shakespeare's whole account of her seems unworthy alike of his heart and understanding. It is, however, stated by able modern commentators that he only wrote a part of this play, and none of the odious description of Joan of Arc.* The writer, whoever he was, apparently shared—in common, indeed, with many superior men, even among the French—a vague idea that she was inspired by some evil spirit, and, though he cannot avoid describing her actions as heroic, he makes her speak in a boastful, cruel, extravagant manner, totally different from what many historians describe.† Even the profound writers, Hume, Hallam, and Green, make her far more interesting and noble in the pages of real history than the unknown poet inclines to do in a brilliant historical drama.‡ Joan was a heroine in every sense of the word, but, like many other victims of superstitious ignorance, she lived at a period when neither friends foes, strangers, nor countrymen could understand her. In the first scene, she obtains the king's confidence before that of his more suspicious courtiers, and prepares to drive the English from Orleans.

The next scene reverts to London, describing a violent quarrel between Cardinal Beaufort and the Protector Gloster, in the streets of the capital, which the peaceful Lord Mayor, shocked at such disputes among princes, pacifies with some trouble. These fierce dissensions between the two chief men in England during the king's youth greatly weaken the strength of the country. At Henry V.'s death, both England and France were comparatively quiet, but when his great spirit was gone, open war began in France, as well as danger-

---

* "The only part of it to be put down to Shakespeare is the Temple Garden scene. . . . . Traditional as the witch view of Joan of Arc was in Shakespeare's time, one is glad that Shakespeare did not set it forth to us."—FURNIVALL's *Notes to the Royal Shakspere.*

† "The Pucelle of this play is a parody on the Pucelle of history. In the actions and speeches attributed to her we have no indication whatever of that simplicity and meekness which, in strange combination with undaunted resolution and the most reckless personal bravery, so pre-eminently distinguished the heroic Maid of Orleans."—H. STAUNTON's *Notes to the Illustrated Shakespeare.*

‡ HUME's *History,* ch. xx. ; HALLAM's *Middle Ages,* vol. i. ; and GREEN's *History of the English People,* ch. vi.

ous dissensions in England. The play almost alternately describes these commotions, for the next scene returns to France, where the brave Joan of Arc, called La Pucelle, wins her first victory at the head of French troops, who at the beginning of her career admire and obey her, though perhaps always with some latent distrust. After the recovery of Orleans from the English, Joan declares, as she did in history, that she has now kept her word ; that King Charles, by her means, has regained her native city, and asks leave to retire again to her former way of life.* Charles VII. was, however, so .full of admiration and gratitude for her exploits that he could not bring himself to grant this request, but, praising her highly, persuaded her to continue in the French army as its good genius, and even declared that she should be canonised as a saint. The first act ends with a triumphant banquet given by Charles VII. in honour of his heroic subject. Joan is, indeed, the heroine of this play, despite the author's sharing the superstitious fancies of the period with regard to her. Had he taken the same view as recent historians have done, and which seems to accord with all that is known about her, Joan would, indeed, have equalled in interest and merit most of the fictitious, as well as the historical, heroines of Shakespeare.

Act II. describes the English generals, Bedford and Talbot, wondering at the power and success of Joan, whom they prepare to encounter in the field. Lord Talbot, one of the bravest English generals in France, is nearly captured by the French Countess of Auvergne, who treacherously receives him as a guest at her house, which he had secretly surrounded by his own soldiers previously, and thus captures it without resistance. He, however, makes a generous use of his victory, and feasts with the countess as if they were old friends. This singular incident does not seem historical, and is, perhaps, only introduced to show the clemency, as well as bravery, of Talbot, who was in many ways a fine specimen of the English character, yet unhappily imbued, like most other men at this period, with an absurd, superstitious horror of the supposed witch, Joan of Arc.

The next scene reverts to London, in the Temple Garden, and is of great importance, as it first describes the rising ambition of Richard Plantagenet, future Duke of York, who secretly aspires to the crown. Lords Somerset and Suffolk pluck red roses in the garden as emblems of the reigning House of

---

* " In the midst of her triumph, she remained the pure, tender-hearted peasant girl of the Vosges. Her first visit as she entered Orleans was to the great church, and there, as she knelt at mass, she wept in such a passion of devotion that all the people wept with her."—GREEN'S *History*, ch. vi.

Lancaster, while Richard and Lord Warwick gather white ones as emblems of the House of York.*

   PLANTAGENET.   Let him that is a true-born gentleman,
And stands upon the honour of his birth,
If he suppose that I have pleaded truth,
From off this briar pluck a white rose with me.
   SOMERSET.   Let him that is no coward, nor no flatterer,
But dare maintain the party of the truth,
Pluck a red rose from off this thorn with me.
   PLANTAGENET.   Hath not thy rose a canker, Somerset ?
   SOMERSET.   Hath not thy rose a thorn, Plantagenet ?
   PLANTAGENET.   Ay, sharp and piercing, to maintain his truth ;
Whiles thy consuming canker eats his falsehood.
   SOMERSET.   Well, I'll find friends to wear my bleeding roses,
That shall maintain what I have said is true,
Where false Plantagenet dare not be seen.—Act II.

Still, neither open rebellion nor civil war are declared, but the proud spirits of Richard, Somerset, and Suffolk cause a violent quarrel, during which Somerset taunts Richard about his father Lord Cambridge's death, who, he reminds him, was executed for high-treason against the father of the present king. Warwick, as brave and ambitious as any of them, but more cautious and far-seeing, promises aid to Richard in having him acknowledged Duke of York, but no mention is yet made of his claim to the crown. Somerset and Suffolk, after this quarrel, leave the garden, while Richard, Warwick, Vernon, and an unnamed lawyer remain, Warwick truly predicting that this ominous dispute will cause future civil war in England.

   PLANTAGENET.   How I am brav'd, and must perforce endure it !
   WARWICK.   This blot, that they object against your house,
Shall be wip'd out in the next parliament,
Called for the truce of Winchester and Gloster ;
And if thou be not then created York,
I will not live to be accounted Warwick.
Meantime, in signal of my love to thee,
Against proud Somerset, and William Poole,
Will I upon thy party wear this rose :
And here I prophesy,—this brawl to-day,
Grown to this faction, in the Temple garden,
Shall send, between the red rose and the white,
A thousand souls to death and deadly night.—Act. II.

* Mr. Courtenay, in his *Commentaries on Shakespeare's Historical Plays*, says he cannot find any foundation for this celebrated dispute in the Temple Garden, or any authority for using the roses as a popular symbol. He admits, however, that the Yorkist party considered the white rose among their heraldic devices, but finds no mention of the red rose of Lancaster.—Vol. ii.

The next scene, though one of the most interesting in the
play, has no certain historical foundation. It introduces the
aged Edmund Mortimer, Lord March, a prisoner in the
Tower, and in a dying state. He is described as bewailing his
long imprisonment, which he dates from before Henry V.'s
accession to the crown, declaring that previously he was
"great in arms."   There is apparent confusion here between
Lord March, Richard Plantagenet's uncle, who, though long a
prisoner, was much attached to Henry V., and his warlike
uncle, Edmund Mortimer, who must have been dead before
this time.*   Lord Mortimer, maternal uncle to Richard,
sends for his nephew, and, in an affecting scene, acquaints
him both with his own wrongs and with the royal rights of
their family.   His sentiments were doubtless those of many
adherents to the Mortimer family, and the expressed feelings
of young Richard are apparently confirmed by history, and
explain his future conduct.

> RICHARD.   For my father's sake,
> In honour of a true Plantagenet,
> And for alliance' sake, declare the cause
> My father, Earl of Cambridge, lost his head.
> MORTIMER.   That cause, fair nephew, that imprison'd me,
>
>   .   .   .   .
>
> Was cursed instrument of his decease.
>
>   .   .   .   .   .
>
> But, as the rest, so fell that noble earl,
> And was beheaded.   Thus the Mortimers,
> In whom the title rested, were suppress'd.
>
>   .   .   .   .   .   .
>
> Thou art my heir; the rest, I wish thee gather;
> But yet be wary in thy studious care.
> RICHARD.   Thy grave admonishments prevail with me :
> But yet, methinks, my father's execution
> Was nothing less than bloody tyranny.
> MORTIMER.   With silence, nephew, be thou politic;
> Strong-fixed is the House of Lancaster,
> And, like a mountain, not to be remov'd.
> But now thy uncle is removing hence.
>
>   .   .   .   .

---

* Hume states that Henry V., instead of continuing the restraints which his
father had imposed on Lord March, treated him with favour and courtesy, and
" so gained on his gentle, unambitious nature " that he remained ever after
sincerely attached to him.—Ch. xix. Again, in the same chapter, Hume says :—
"There remains in history few instances of such mutual trust." The dying Lord
Mortimer in the play is imbued, and inspires his nephew with the greatest hatred
to the House of Lancaster, so that historian and poet seem opposed in this indi-
vidual case. *See* HOWARD STAUNTON's remarks on this scene.—*Illustrated
Shakespeare.*

And so farewell ; and fair be all thy hopes ;
And prosperous be thy life, in peace and war !   [*Dies.*
   RICHARD.   And peace, no war, befall thy parting soul !
In prison hast thou spent a pilgrimage,
And like a hermit overpass'd thy days.
Well, I will lock his counsel in my breast ;

And therefore haste I to the parliament ;
Either to be restored to my blood,
Or make my ill the advantage of my good.—Act II.

This only interview between the aged prisoner, inspired
to the last by the high spirit of his race, and his ambitious
nephew, sharing the same feelings with all the energy of
ardent youth, is one of the most impressive scenes in this
play and, though historically incorrect respecting Mortimer,
it seems to express truly the sentiments of Richard and his
party.

Act III. describes a quarrel in the king's presence, at
Westminster, between Beaufort and Gloster.   Richard Plantagenet is also there, apparently the king's loyal subject, but
really watching his opportunity to take advantage of the
fierce dissensions now increasing in the English Court.   The
Lord Mayor, a most peaceful personage, again complains of
the savage tumults and affrays between the partisans of
Beaufort and Gloster in the streets of London.   King Henry
tries to make peace between these noblemen, and, with
Warwick's assistance, persuades them to make a show of
reconciliation, Gloster being sincere in his professions, and
steadily faithful to the king, while Beaufort is utterly selfish,
unscrupulous, and vindictive.   In this scene, the mild, unsuspicious monarch restores the title of Duke of York to
his ambitious kinsman, Richard, at the urgent request of
Warwick.   In return, Richard vows complete obedience to
Henry ; but the courtiers differ in opinion about the wisdom
of the king's proceeding.   Lord Exeter, one of his most
faithful ministers, truly foresees the coming misfortunes of
so weak a sovereign amid such resolute, aspiring spirits as
Beaufort, Warwick, and Richard, who have all their own
ambitious objects in view, and alike perceive the irresolution
of the king.

The next scene is in France, describing the capture of
Rouen by the French, led by Joan of Arc, who, with King
Charles, obtains this success over Talbot and the Duke of
Burgundy.   The Regent Bedford dies in this scene, displaying to the last the same calm courage which distinguished
him as John of Lancaster.   Joan is here supposed to abuse
and defy both him and Talbot from the walls of Rouen,

scoffing at the sick Regent, and being reviled in turn by Talbot.   Their language is alike unworthy of them and of Shakespeare.   There is certainly no historical foundation for it, and probably the great poet never wrote it.*

> PUCELLE.   What will you do, good grey-beard? break a lance,
> And run a-tilt at death within a chair?
> TALBOT.   Foul fiend of France, and hag of all despite,
> Encompass'd with thy lustful paramours !
> Becomes it thee to taunt his valiant age,
> And twit with cowardice a man half-dead?
> Damsel, I'll have a bout with you again,
> Or else let Talbot perish with this shame.
> PUCELLE.   Are ye so hot, sir?—Act III.

Bedford dies, generally regretted by his countrymen, Talbot declaring—

> A braver soldier never couched a lance,
> A gentler heart did never sway in court.

Thus the stern, grave youth whom Falstaff could neither amuse nor deceive became one of the most distinguished and popular members of the royal family.   He was alike faithful to father, brother, and nephew, and in advanced age acquired the fame of generosity as well as of sagacity and valour.†

The unexpected triumphs of the French seem, in the play, to hasten his death, as he well remembers the glorious victories of his martial brother in France before La Pucelle appeared.   Joan is often described exchanging insolent and abusive language with Talbot and other English generals, wholly unlike what is recorded of her in history, and which was probably not composed by Shakespeare.   Talbot, after Bedford's death, leads the English forces, but the Duke of York becomes commander-in-chief.   Talbot bravely defeats the French, but his ally, the Duke of Burgundy, won over by the entreaties and valour of Joan, forsakes him, and joins Charles VII. of France.   King Henry, with Gloster and other courtiers, arrive in Paris at the end of this act, and congratulate Talbot on his late success, which was not, however, of much importance.

The next act begins in Paris, where Henry and his nobles

---

* FURNIVALL'S *Notes to the Royal Shakspere.*

† " For genius for war, as in political capacity, John was hardly inferior to Henry V. himself."—GREEN'S *History of the English People*, ch. vi.   " A prince of great abilities and of many virtues, and whose memory, except from the barbarous execution of the Maid of Orleans, was unsullied by any considerable blemish."—HUME'S *History*, ch. xx.   In the play, Bedford dies before the capture of Joan, whereas, really, he was her chief enemy, and died in France some time after her execution.

hear the unwelcome news of their former ally, the Duke of Burgundy, having joined the French king.   Yet, during the dismay caused by the news, the unruly spirits of York and Somerset excite a quarrel among the English leaders, even in presence of the common foe.   Somerset and York challenge each other, but Henry and his uncle Gloster prevent more strife on this occasion, and they all prepare to encounter the French.   York, despite his secret ambition, which is evidently suspected by Somerset and others devoted to the king, was yet entrusted by Henry with the chief command of the English forces.   Unfortunately, however, his enemy, Somerset, also commanded some English troops, and he quarrels with York so violently that between them Talbot's expected reinforcements are never sent him, while each blames the other for not assisting this brave general.   He and his gallant son, therefore, are soon surrounded by the French, under Joan of Arc, and both are slain fighting valiantly.   In reality, Talbot was captured, but in the play he dies in battle beside the body of his slain son.   Another English general, Sir Henry Lucy, who had vainly entreated York to reinforce Talbot, now has an interview with the King of France and Joan.   The latter utters coarse, violent language, expressing a savage spirit, quite different from what history records of her, while Lucy buries the remains of the two brave Talbots.   This scene is imaginary, and, though powerfully written, gives a thoroughly false version of Joan's character and conduct, as if designed to prevent any sympathy for her approaching fate by imputing to her a spirit of insolent brutality in triumph.   On hearing Lucy's request to King Charles to bury the gallant Talbots, Joan is supposed to exclaim—

> Him that thou magnifiest with all these titles,
> Stinking and fly-blown, lies here at our feet.
>
>   .   .   .   .   .   .
>
> For God's sake, let him have them; to keep them here,
> They would but stink and putrefy the air.—Act IV.

Act V. begins in London, where Henry is consulting with his uncle and faithful minister, Gloster and Exeter, about his future bride.   This amiable but very weak sovereign is advised by his two best friends to marry the daughter of the Earl of Armagnac, and conclude peace with France.   In this matter, as in all others, Cardinal Beaufort and Suffolk oppose Gloster, but no decision is arrived at; and the next scene reverts to France, where Joan is defeated by York.   Upon this defeat, after so many victories, she was reported to have invoked certain evil spirits, who had formerly assisted her, and to have implored their continued favour.   This absurd story is here gravely related, and Joan vainly entreats help from these fiends, but they forsake her, and make no reply. She was soon after captured by York, who speaks both to and of her as if she were a hideous witch, whilst she furiously abuses him.

This short and repulsive scene is followed by the courteous capture of the young Princess Margaret, daughter of King René of Naples, by Suffolk, who asks his fair captive if she will consent to wed his master, Henry VI.   The princess leaves her answer to her father, who has a conference with Suffolk, and gives his consent.   Suffolk, while highly gratified, is yet captivated himself by Margaret's beauty, although a married man, and they are firm allies from this time.

The next scene is, indeed, the saddest, and, by falsifying history, the most discreditable part of this irregular play.   It describes the unfortunate Joan sentenced to death by York, after refusing to acknowledge an old shepherd as her father, who then vehemently urges her savage captors to burn her as a witch, as, indeed, they all desire.   Joan is supposed to declare herself with child, vainly hoping thus to escape, at least, immediate execution.   York and Warwick, however, sentence her to the stake, and she is dragged away, cursing her enemies in frantic desperation.

> YORK.   Damsel of France, I think I have you fast :
>
> .   .   .   .
>
> A goodly prize, fit for the devil's grace !
> See, how the ugly witch doth bend her brows.
> JOAN.   A plaguing mischief light on Charles, and thee !
> And may ye both be suddenly surpris'd,
> By bloody hands, in sleeping on your beds !

Then, when finally sentenced, she is made to exclaim,—

> Then lead me hence ;—with whom I leave my curse :
> May never glorious sun reflex his beams
> Upon the country where you make abode !
> But darkness and the gloomy shade of death
> Environ you ; till mischief, and despair,
> Drive you to break your necks, or hang yourselves !—Act V.

This frantic language is, indeed, a loathsome contrast to the last words of the real Joan, and equally so to any she was ever proved to have uttered.   In reality, her conduct, as well as fate, were not unworthy of a Christian martyr. She was captured by the Burgundians, who were again allied with the English, and by them sold to the Duke of Bedford.*   Her trial for witchcraft and sorcery was

* Hume states it was generally thought that the French officers, out of jealousy

then commenced, in which even ecclesiastics of her own nation were against her.*　She met, indeed, with almost as little pity from the French as from the English, though the guilt of her death must rest chiefly on the latter.†　In spite of her pure character and noble conduct, Joan thus fell a victim to the superstitions of her period, and was publicly burnt at Rouen, evincing to the last a totally different spirit from that ascribed to her in this play, though the ferocious bigotry of her executioners was almost beyond the power of imagination to exaggerate.‡　Yet it is consoling to all lovers of Shakespeare to believe, on good authority, that he never wrote the false and disgraceful description of Joan contained in this play.§　She was, indeed, in the opinions of grave, impartial historians, worthy to be ranked among the noblest heroines of the immortal poet's fancy. The wonders of reality, Bacon declares, exceed those conceivable by any human imagination, and likewise there have been historical personages whose heroism and virtues apparently equalled the noblest creations of human genius. Of these heroines, Joan of Arc was one of the most illustrious in European history. The sorrows, virtues, and sufferings of the imaginary characters, Cordelia, Juliet, and Desdemona, were not more terrible nor exalted than those of this noble victim of united French and English bigotry, and whose awful fate was long unpitied by both nations. The wild idea of her being leagued with evil spirits appears to have completely influenced even the wise and humane men of her ignorant period.‖　It was not as a victorious enemy to England, or as a cruel foe, that she suffered, but as the alleged

at Joan's victories, had wilfully exposed her to capture by the Burgundians, and adds—"The service of Te Deum was publicly celebrated on this fortunate event in Paris," then held by the English, and she evidently met with little sympathy at this time from her own countrymen.

* Hallam mentions the eagerness shown by the University of Paris in her prosecution, and also that it was "conducted before an inquisitor—a circumstance exceedingly remarkable in the ecclesiastical history of France."—*Middle Ages*, ch. i.

† "Charles VII. made not the slightest effort of intervention to save the life of one to whom he owed all his recent successes."—*Student's History of France*, ch. xi.　The same authority states that, twenty years after Joan's death, "an inquiry was instituted, the result of which completely established her fame and memory.　The sentence was publicly reversed and cancelled, and two solemn processions in her honour were ordained to take place annually at Rouen."

‡ *See* the detailed account of Joan's execution, written by Lord Mahon, and quoted in Staunton's edition of Shakespeare, from which it seems that both the French Bishop of Beauvais, with the English Cardinal Beaufort, as well as the Duke of Bedford, sentenced her to death.　They evidently believed that they were burning a person possessed by a devil, and were right in doing so.

§ FURNIVALL's *Notes to the Royal Shakspere.*

‖ "Such bigotry may be pleaded as an excuse, though a very miserable one, for the detestable murder of this heroine."—HALLAM's *Middle Ages*, ch. i.

ally of Satan, without a single crime being ever proved against her.*

This play ends with a contest in London between rival factions, about who is to be the future queen. Henry, though the person most interested, is completely ruled by Beaufort and Suffolk, who wish him to marry Margaret of Anjou, to the grief of the Protector Gloster, who, though nominally in power, is fast losing influence over the king, now chiefly guided by Beaufort and Suffolk. This ambitious pair, though they have no personal attachment to the monarch, hope to govern England in his name while striving to promote his marriage with the Princess Margaret. They evidently have some idea of the rare energy and courage which she possesses—qualities in which Henry, unlike all his family, was utterly deficient. Suffolk reveals his ambitious thoughts to himself in a few expressive words which conclude this play :—

> Thus Suffolk hath prevail'd ; . . . .
> Margaret shall now be queen, and rule the king ;
> But I will rule both her, the king, and realm.—Act V.

---

* Hume says that she never, in her military capacity, committed any act of treachery or cruelty. "She was unstained by any civil crime. . . . . even the virtues and the very decorum of her sex had ever been rigidly observed by her." —ch. xx. "In the midst of her enthusiasm, her good sense never left her. The people crowded round her as she rode along, praying her to work miracles, and bringing crosses and chaplets to be blessed by her touch. 'Touch them yourself,' she said to an old Dame Margaret ; 'your touch will be quite as good as mine.' . . . . On the charge of sorcery and diabolical possession, she still appealed firmly to God. 'I hold to my Judge,' she said, as her earthly judges gave sentence against her ; 'to the King of Heaven and Earth. God has always been my Lord in all that I have done. The devil has never had any power over me.'"— GREEN'S *History of the English People*, ch. vi.

CHAPTER X.

SECOND PART OF KING HENRY VI.

Sketch of Play.

AFTER the king's marriage with Margaret of Anjou, the dissensions in England increase, even among his most loyal subjects. Gloster is poisoned by Beaufort and Suffolk, while York, taking advantage of the general consternation at his death, raises a rebellion against the king. During this civil war, the Kentish men, headed by a certain Jack Cade, who had been a soldier, revolted, secretly encouraged by York, and march into London. They are defeated, and their leader is afterwards slain. The quelling of this singular revolt, however, does not hinder the progress of York's insurrection. This prince had governed Ireland in the king's name, but, perceiving the discontented state of England after Gloster's death, he declares war against Henry and proclaims himself lawful king. Warwick and many other influential nobles join him, while Queen Margaret supports her weak husband's cause with the utmost zeal and energy. This play, after recording the alternate triumphs and defeats of the York and Lancaster factions, ends by announcing the success of the former, who, however, have not yet secured their final triumph, so that the rival Houses are still contending at its conclusion.

IN the opinions of the latest writers on Shakespeare,* the Second and Third Parts of Henry VI. contain more of the poet's own writing than the First Part does ; but there seems some uncertainty on this point. The first act of the Second Part describes the grief and shame of Gloster at the king's giving up part of his French dominions to his father-in-law. He addresses the assembled English nobles, after the king and queen have left the apartment, in a spirited speech, reminding them of their former glorious conquests in France, but his counsels are now quite overruled in Henry's court.

* Messrs. Howard Staunton, Furnivall, and Dowden.

> GLOSTER.   Brave peers of England, pillars of the state,
> To you Duke Humphrey must unload his grief.
>
> Shall Henry's conquest, Bedford's vigilance,
> Your deeds of war, and all our counsel die?
> O peers of England, shameful is this league!
> Fatal this marriage! cancelling your fame;
> Blotting your names from books of memory;
> Razing the characters of your renown;
> Defacing monuments of conquer'd France;
> Undoing all, as all had never been!—Act I.

Cardinal Beaufort, Suffolk, and Somerset are allied with Queen Margaret against him, and their united animosity is deep and dangerous. York, while admiring Gloster, will not take his part, as he wishes to increase the present dissensions, and well knows that Humphrey is the king's best friend and chief support. Warwick is more in York's confidence than any one, but as yet there is no mention of civil war. While Gloster is in authority, Henry is safe, but, unluckily for the king, his queen and many of his loyal ministers combine against their best friend, without apparently suspecting that York, Warwick, and others are only waiting for Gloster's death or degradation to declare open war against the House of Lancaster; yet, despite York's caution, there are already rumours of his dangerous ambition throughout England.

An armourer, named Horner, is accused, by his apprentice, Peter, of having declared, while they were "scouring" York's armour, that York had the real right to the crown. Peter, probably hoping for reward, acquainted Suffolk, a well-known zealous supporter of the king, with his employer's words. Horner and Peter were then arrested, and brought before the king, the former vehemently denying, the latter as firmly reiterating, the charge. Henry, by Gloster's advice, and according, perhaps, to the custom of the times, fixes a day for the accuser and accused to fight in single combat before him. Horner boldly agrees to fight, while his apprentice is nervous and frightened, but forced to support his statements with his staff, on pain of death. York himself blames Horner for naming his rights at all, not being yet prepared to assert them, and wishing to lull all suspicion till the dissensions at court afford him a favourable opportunity for declaring himself. He has therefore hitherto successfully concealed his plans, though surrounded by suspicious foes, of whom Somerset and Suffolk are the most formidable, though the queen eventually becomes his worst enemy. As yet she does not apparently suspect him, being fully occupied

in opposing Gloster's influence, and strengthening that of her
first English friend, Suffolk. York, however, reveals his
ambitious thoughts in safe soliloquy, at the end of this scene,
in words which, if generally known, would have probably cost
him his life.

> YORK.   Then, York, be still awhile, till time do serve:
> Watch thou, and wake, when others be asleep,
> To pry into the secrets of the state;
> Till Henry, surfeiting in joys of love,
> With his new bride, and England's dear-bought queen,
> And Humphrey with the peers be fall'n at jars:
> Then will I raise aloft the milk-white rose,
> With whose sweet smell the air shall be perfumed;
> And in my standard bear the arms of York,
> To grapple with the House of Lancaster;
> And, force perforce, I'll make him yield the crown,
> Whose bookish rule hath pull'd fair England down!—Act I.

Margaret appears from the first to have made both warm
friends and bitter enemies among her new subjects. She
was evidently a woman of rare talents, and her energetic
character could not endure Gloster's influence over her weak
husband, probably not believing that he was really the king's
best friend.*   Her pride, however, could not bear that even
a friend and relative should have much authority over the
king; while Somerset, Suffolk, Beaufort, and others increased
and shared her jealousy of the Protector Gloster, who was
now beset with enemies. As if to increase his misfortunes,
his wife, who was apparently a strange compound of ambition, vanity, and superstitious folly, was openly accused of
witchcraft, and of conspiring against the king. In the play,
she tells her dreams to her husband—that she herself was
crowned at Westminster, vaguely hinting, and evidently
hoping, that they may become king and queen. Gloster,
with his usual good sense and right feeling, urges her to
banish all such ideas, but the duchess, who hates Margaret,
and is hated by her, still nourishes these wild, ambitious
fancies. After Gloster leaves her, she decides to meet a certain alleged witch named Margery Jourdain, a conjuror named
Bolingbroke, and some other people, who are to tell her fortunes. These wretched impostors make secret arrangements
before their foolish dupe appears. They accordingly meet

* "This princess seemed to possess those qualities which would equally qualify
her to acquire the ascendant over Henry, and to supply all his defects and weaknesses."—HUME'S *History*, ch. xx. Hume admits her "masculine, courageous
spirit, and enterprising temper," saying that she allied herself with Somerset and
Suffolk, "who, fortified by her powerful patronage, resolved on the final ruin of
the Duke of Gloster."

by appointment in Gloster's garden, unknown to him, and there, with the duchess at a convenient distance, they summon a supposed spirit, ask it questions, and hear its answers.

BOLINGBROKE.   Mother Jourdain, be thou prostrate, and grovel
on the earth :—John Southwell, read you ; and let us to our work.
 .   .   .   First, of the king.   What shall of him become ?
     SPIRIT.   The duke yet lives that Henry shall depose ;
But him outlive, and die a violent death.

The spirit then foretells terrible misfortunes to Somerset and Suffolk.   In the midst of this folly, they are arrested by York, with a guard of soldiers, who seize the whole party, doubtless including the poor spirit, and also some papers supposed to be treasonable, and bear them all off to prison.

Previous to this extraordinary arrest, there had occurred a violent quarrel before the peaceful king, in which Margaret, Suffolk, Beaufort, and even York reproach or abuse the luckless Protector.   This scene is the more distressing to read, as in its leading features it is supported by historical facts.   A weak monarch, with a proud, ambitious wife, surrounded by fierce' and violent noblemen, patiently hears his best friend—his own uncle, the most respected man in England, and trusted by the late king with supreme authority—now insulted, accused, and reviled with shameless effrontery. Henry still loves and believes him, yet is afraid to defend him ; while the Duchess Eleanor of Gloster, hearing her husband slandered on all sides, instead of imitating his firm self-control, quarrels with the haughty queen, who hates both the Glosters.   Margaret so far forgets her dignity as to strike her, and the duchess is evidently ready to return the compliment, when Henry, a willing peace-maker between women as well as men, interferes and prevents an actual combat between the angry ladies in his royal presence.

QUEEN MARGARET.   Give me my fan : what, minion ! can you
     not ?.   [Gives the DUCHESS a box on the ear.
I cry you mercy, madam ; was it you ?
     DUCHESS.   Was't I ? yea, I it was, proud Frenchwoman :
Could I come near your beauty with my nails,
I'd set my ten commandments in your face.
     KING HENRY.   Sweet aunt, be quiet ; 'twas against her will.
     DUCHESS.   *Against her will !*   Good king, look to 't in time ;
She'll hamper thee, and dandle thee like a baby.
She shall not strike Dame Eleanor unrevenged.   [*Exit.*]—Act I.

After this scene, the enraged duchess hurries off to keep her appointment with Dame Jourdain and her associates.

In reality, the duchess and some accomplices were accused of certain strange practices very similar to those described in the play.*   Hume apparently thinks her falsely accused, but she was condemned to imprisonment for life, after doing public penance by walking barefoot in white garments through the streets of London.

The first act ends with her arrest, and that of her confederates, and the second begins with describing a royal hawking party at St. Albans.   Here king, queen, Protector, cardinal, Suffolk, and others are present.   During the sport, however, Beaufort and Gloster have another vehement dispute, which ends by their challenging each other to a duel with swords—a proceeding unlikely in men of their age and position, and which is merely invented by the writer, who may not have been Shakespeare.   During, or soon after, the hawking party, the royal group are met by the Mayor of St. Albans and his attendants, with a blind cripple called Simpcox, and his wife.   They declare that he has just received his sight, but remains a cripple.   Gloster, who suspects he is an impostor, well able both to see and run, has him struck with a whip, at which the lame man regains immediate use of his legs, and makes off at full speed, to the amusement of all, except the detected rogues and the melancholy, gentle king, who is shocked at their deceit.   Henry VI., indeed, apparently had very little pleasure in life.   He is kind, sincere, and religious, but so intensely timid and irresolute that he is awed by both friends and foes.   Among his many quarrelling nobles, ambitious relatives, and artful subjects of all kinds, this simple-minded monarch is completely puzzled how to act, and the sketch of him in the play thoroughly coincides with the statements of history.   Gloster, in every way qualified to advise and guide Henry, as the late king well knew, is grieved to hear from the unfriendly Duke of Buckingham of his wife's conduct and arrest.   At this news, Beaufort and Margaret immediately taunt the Protector, while Henry, though pitying his uncle, does not defend him nor insist on respectful treatment for him, even in his own presence.   The faction now combined against Gloster consist of the queen, Beaufort, Somerset, Suffolk,

* "She had been accused of witchcraft, and it was pretended that there was found in her possession a waxen figure of the king, which she and her associates—Sir Roger Bolingbroke and one Margery Jordan—melted in a magical manner before a slow fire, with an intention of making Henry's force and vigour waste away by like insensible degrees."—HUME'S *History*, ch. xx.   "It appears that these parties were solemnly tried for sorcery before the Archbishop of Canterbury.   The woman Jordan was burnt, and Bolingbroke hanged ; another impostor received a pardon, and the duchess was condemned to perpetual imprisonment in the Isle of Man."—STAUNTON'S *Notes to the Illustrated Shakespeare.*

and Buckingham ; while the designing York, with his adherents, Salisbury and Warwick, craftily await the result of these suicidal quarrels in the Lancastrian party.

In the next scene, York confers with Salisbury and Warwick about his royal rights and his chances of obtaining them. He gives a long account of his own family descent, and finally asks his hearers if he is not entitled by birth to the crown in place of the present king. They agree that he certainly is, though probably they knew all about his pedigree long before, and, kneeling, acknowledge him their sovereign. York thanks them, saying he must await the approaching death or degradation of Gloster before venturing on a contest with the king ; for he and his friends well know that Duke Humphrey's high character and great popularity confirm Henry's power, but that, when he is removed by death or disgrace from the royal counsels, the English nation will be thoroughly discontented, and, therefore, more inclined to favour York's contemplated insurrection.

The next scene describes the Duchess of Gloster and the luckless impostors—Dame Jourdain, the conjuror Bolingbroke, and two accomplices—receiving their dreadful sentences from Henry VI. This naturally mild monarch, enforcing the cruel laws of the time, condemns the duchess to perpetual imprisonment, Dame Jourdain to be burnt, and the rest hanged, with less emotion than a modern judge would sentence the most atrocious murderer to penal servitude. Gloster, though deeply grieved at his wife's disgrace, cannot defend her, and is now told by his master, at the instigation of Margaret, to resign his staff of office, and cease to be Lord Protector. He accordingly resigns, to the delight of the queen and Suffolk, and to the secret exultation of York, who dreads Gloster's influence more than that of any among Henry's loyal subjects.

After Duke Humphrey has left the king's presence, the accused armourer, Horner, and his apprentice come before the sovereign and court, ready for their appointed combat. Horner's neighbours, probably tradesmen, drink to his success, while some apprentices drink to Peter, and try to encourage him.

PRENTICE. Be merry, Peter, and fear not thy master : fight for credit of the prentices.

PETER. I thank you all : drink, and pray for me, I pray you ; for I think I have taken my last draught in this world.—Here, Robin, an if I die I give thee my apron ; and here, Will, thou shalt have my hammer ; and here, Tom, take all the money I have. O Lord, bless me, I pray God ! for I am never able to deal with my master, he hath learnt so much fence already.

LORD SALISBURY.   What's thy name?

PETER.   Peter.

SALISBURY.   Peter—what more?

PETER.   Thump.

SALISBURY.   *Thump!* then see thou thump thy master well.

HORNER.   Masters, I am come hither, as it were, upon my man's instigation, to prove him a knave and myself an honest man; and therefore, Peter, have at thee with a downright blow!

_[*They fight, and* PETER *strikes down his master.*

HORNER.   Hold, Peter, hold! I confess, I confess treason.

[*Dies.*

KING HENRY.   Come, fellow, follow us for thy reward.—Act II.

The apprentice thus departs triumphant, and with a promised reward; but nothing has transpired to implicate York in the revealed treason of his partisan. This story of Horner and Peter seems the poet's invention, whereas the strange doings and wretched fate of Dame Jourdain are founded on history. The reason for introducing this curious episode is probably to show that York's claims are beginning to be discussed among the people, and are suspected by the court.

The next scene presents another instance of Gloster's many griefs and trials; indeed, the first half of this play is chiefly composed of the insults, sorrows, and humiliations to which this great and good man was subjected. He meets his disgraced wife doing penance by walking barefoot through London, holding a torch, while papers fastened to her dress proclaim what her offence has been. She is, of course, followed and surrounded by large crowds, and guarded by soldiers, during her melancholy walk. In an affecting speech to her husband, she foretells his ruin, being beset, as she knows, by powerful enemies, while his loyalty to the king prevents his alliance with York's faction, which would then have befriended him. She goes to prison, while Gloster returns to the court. The last three acts of this play are now devoted to three great events, and adhere closely to historical record. The first is the arrest and imprisonment of Gloster, on the absurd charge of treason, by the reluctant king, at the instigation of his imperious wife, Beaufort, Somerset, Buckingham, and Suffolk. Henry "thus throws away his crutch," as Gloster prophetically exclaims, when led off guarded to prison; for he well knows his nephew's danger, surrounded by ambitious, unscrupulous intriguers, who will soon make his rule hateful to the nation, and thus incline it to favour York's pretensions. In a noble speech to the king, Gloster vainly exposes in turn the vindictiveness of his many foes, all of whom he knows well. Henry remains silent and irresolute, while his uncle and true friend is removed a prisoner from his sight, and he never again sees him alive.

> GLOSTER.   Ah, gracious lord, these days are dangerous.
> Virtue is chok'd with foul ambition,
> And charity chas'd hence by rancour's hand;
>
> .   .   .   .   .   .
>
> Beaufort's red, sparkling eyes blab his heart's malice,
> And Suffolk's cloudy brow his stormy hate;
> Sharp Buckingham unburdens with his tongue
> The envious load that lies upon his heart;
> And dogged York, that reaches at the moon,
> Whose overweening arm I have pluck'd back,
> By false accuse doth level at my life;
> And you, my sovereign lady, with the rest,
> Causeless have laid disgraces on my head;
> And, with your best endeavour, have stirr'd up
> My liefest liege to be mine enemy:
> Ay, all of you have laid your heads together;
> And all to make away my guiltless life.—Act III.

Immediately after Gloster's imprisonment, York is entrusted with the government of Ireland, and goes there, after uttering a remarkable soliloquy, in which he reveals his hopes and designs.

> YORK.   Now, York, or never, steel thy fearful thoughts,
> And change misdoubt to resolution:
> Let pale-fac'd fear keep with the mean-born man,
> And find no harbour in a royal heart.
> Faster than spring-time showers comes thought on thought;
> And not a thought but thinks on dignity.
> I have seduc'd a head-strong Kentishman,
> John Cade of Ashford,
> To make commotion, as full well he can,
> Under the title of John Mortimer.
> In Ireland have I seen this stubborn Cade
> Oppose himself against a troop of kerns;
> And fought so long, till that his thighs with darts
> Were almost like a sharp-quill'd porcupine.
>
> .   .   .   .   .   .
>
> Full often, like a shag-hair'd, crafty kern,
> Hath he conversèd with the enemy;
> And, undiscover'd, come to me again,
> And given me notice of their villanies.
> This devil here shall be my substitute;
> For that John Mortimer, which now is dead,
> In face, in gait, in speech, he doth resemble:
> By this I shall perceive the commons' mind,
> How they affect the house and claim of York.

Say, he be taken, rack'd, and tortur'd,
I know no pain they can inflict upon him
Will make him say I mov'd him to those arms.
Say, that he thrive (as 'tis great like he will),
Why, then from Ireland come I with my strength,
And reap the harvest which that rascal sow'd :
For, Humphrey being dead, as he shall be,
And Henry put apart, the rest for me.—Act III.

He naturally foresees both Gloster's murder and the popular hatred to the present ministers, with whose characters he is well acquainted. The connection between him and Cade, though probable, is not absolutely confirmed by history.*

Shortly before Cade's revolt, Gloster was found dead in bed, and his murder by his two worst enemies, Beaufort and Suffolk, was generally suspected. Queen Margaret tries to vindicate them both before the king and Warwick, when the latter bitterly replies :—

Who finds the heifer dead and bleeding fresh,
And sees fast by a butcher with an axe,
But will suspect 'twas he that made the slaughter ?
Who finds the partridge in the puttock's† nest,
But may imagine how the bird was dead,
Although the kite soars with unbloodied beak ?
Even so suspicious is this tragedy.
    MARGARET.   Are you the butcher, Suffolk ? where's your knife ?
Is Beaufort term'd a kite ? where are his talons ?
    SUFFOLK.   I wear no knife to slaughter sleeping men ;
But here's a vengeful sword, rusted with ease,
That shall be scoured in his rancorous heart
That slanders me with murder's crimson badge :
Say, if thou dar'st, proud lord of Warwickshire,
That I am faulty in Duke Humphrey's death.—Act. III.

The king is grieved and shocked, while Warwick, a man of high spirit and resolution, boldly denounces Suffolk as the murderer. The public indignation against the latter became so general that he escaped from London, by the advice of Queen Margaret, with whom he was a special favourite, intending to go to France. His parting from Margaret would be most affecting, being described in beautiful language, had their characters and positions been different. Their words are, indeed, more worthy of innocent and

* " It was imagined at the court that York had secretly instigated Cade."— HUME's *History*, ch. xxi. Hume describes York as "a man of valour and abilities, of a prudent conduct, and mild disposition," but, though brave and sagacious, by no means so energetic as the play represents.
† The common Kite.—YARRELL's *British Birds*.

unfortunate lovers than of a proud queen who is both a
wife and fond mother, and a crafty unscrupulous statesman.

> QUEEN MARGARET. . . . . Give me thy hand,
> That I may dew it with my mournful tears ;
> Nor let the rain of heaven wet this place,
> To wash away my woful monuments.
>
> I will repeal thee, or, be well assured,
> Adventure to be banished myself :
> And banished I am, if but from thee.
> Go ; speak not to me : even now be gone.—
>
> Yet now farewell ; and farewell life with thee !
>   SUFFOLK.   Thus is poor Suffolk ten times banished ;
> Once by the king, and three times thrice by thee. ·
> 'Tis not the land I care for, wert thou thence ;
> A wilderness is populous enough,
> So Suffolk had thy heavenly company :
> For where thou art, there is the world itself,
> With every several pleasure in the world,
> And where thou art not, desolation.
> I can no more :—live thou to joy thy life ;
> Myself no joy in nought but that thou liv'st.—Act III.

Beaufort, Suffolk's supposed accomplice in Gloster's murder,
died a few weeks after that event, and was said to have
evinced great remorse, and vaguely confessed his guilt.*   In
the play, he dies in the king's presence, whom he does not
recognise, intimating, while in a distracted state, having
poisoned Gloster, for it was generally thought he and Suffolk
had committed this crime.

> KING HENRY.   How fares my lord ? speak, Beaufort, to thy
>   sovereign.
> CARDINAL.   If thou be'st death, I'll give thee England's treasure,
> Enough to purchase such another island,
> So thou wilt let me live, and feel no pain.
>   WARWICK.   Beaufort, it is thy sovereign speaks to thee.
>   CARDINAL.   Bring me unto my trial when you will.
> Died he not in his bed ? where should he die ?
> Can I make men live, whe'r they will or no ?—
> O ! torture me no more, I will confess.—
> Alive again ? then show me where he is ;

* "The cardinal died six weeks after Gloster, whose murder was universally
ascribed to him, as well as to Lord Suffolk, and which, it is said, gave him more
remorse in his last moments than could naturally be expected from a man hardened,
during the course of a long life, in falsehood and politics.   What share the queen
had in this guilt is uncertain."—HUME's *History,* ch. xx.

I'll give a thousand pounds to look upon him.—
Comb down his hair ; look ! look ! it stands upright,
Like lime-twigs set to catch my wingèd soul !—
Give me some drink ; and bid the apothecary
Bring the strong poison that I bought of him.
   KING HENRY.   Lord Cardinal, if thou think'st on heaven's bliss,
Hold up thy hand, make signal of thy hope.—
He dies, and makes no sign ; O God, forgive him !—Act III.

The following act describes the fugitive Suffolk's capture at sea, either by a pirate vessel, or, more likely, by men employed to execute justice upon him secretly ; for the captain reproaches him with Gloster's murder, and then has him executed.* The play adheres closely to history in this affair.

   CAPTAIN.   Convey him hence, and on our long-boat's side
Strike off his head.
   SUFFOLK.   Thou dar'st not for thy own.
   CAPTAIN.   Now will I dam up this thy yawning mouth,
For swallowing the treasure of the realm :
Thy lips, that kiss'd the queen, shall sweep the ground :
And thou, that smil'dst at good Duke Humphrey's death,
Against the senseless winds shalt grin in vain.

     .   .   .   .   .   .

The commons here in Kent are up in arms :
And, to conclude, reproach and beggary
Is crept into the palace of our king,
And all by thee :—Away ! convey him hence.—Act IV.

These terrible events hasten Jack Cade's revolt, who, declaring himself one of the Mortimer family, is joined by a number of people. He defeats the king's forces in some slight engagements, and marches in triumph to London, neither proclaiming York king, nor a republic, but declaring, like most revolutionists, that he is in arms to redress popular grievances.† In the play, however, the sketch of Cade is evidently a caricature, and is scarcely consistent with itself. For even the proud York admits that Cade strongly resembles a member of the noble House of Mortimer, and is a man of extraordinary bravery and calm courage, amounting to heroism. Yet he is represented speaking like an insolent and very ignorant boaster, and is ridiculed by some of his own followers.

---

   * "A captain of a vessel was employed by his enemies to intercept him in his passage to France. He was seized near Dover, his head struck off on the side of a long-boat, and his body thrown into the sea." —HUME's *History*, ch. xxi.
   † HUME's *History*, ch. xxi.

Enter JACK CADE, DICK *the Butcher*, SMITH *the Weaver*, &c.

CADE.   We, John Cade, so termed of our supposed father,—

DICK (*aside*).   Or rather, of stealing a cade of herrings.

CADE.   My father was a Mortimer,—

DICK (*aside*).   He was an honest man, and a good bricklayer.

CADE.   My mother was a Plantagenet,—

DICK (*aside*).   I knew her well, she was a midwife.

CADE.   Therefore am I of an honourable house.

DICK (*aside*).   Ay, by my faith, the field is honourable; and there was he born, under a hedge.

CADE.   I am able to endure much.

SMITH (*aside*).   No question of that; for I have seen him whipped three market-days together.

CADE.   I fear neither sword nor fire.

DICK (*aside*).   But methinks he should stand in fear of fire, being burnt i' the hand for stealing of sheep.

CADE.   Be brave, then; for your captain is brave.   There shall be, in England, seven halfpenny loaves sold for a penny: the three-hooped pot shall have ten hoops; and I will make it felony to drink small beer: all the realm shall be in common, and in Cheapside shall my palfrey go to grass.   And, when I am king, as king I will be——

ALL.   God save your majesty!

CADE.   I thank you, good people:—there shall be no money; all shall eat and drink on my score.

DICK.   The first thing we do, let's kill all the lawyers.

CADE.   Nay, that I mean to do.   Is not this a lamentable thing, that of the skin of an innocent lamb should be made parchment? that parchment, being scribbled o'er, should undo a man?   Some say the bee stings: but I say 'tis the bee's wax, for I did but seal once to a thing, and I was never mine own man since.—Act IV.

He is thus described talking nonsense, and leading a disorderly rabble, while he was really a soldier who had seen much service, and, therefore, unlikely to speak in such a style. He was, moreover, joined in his revolt at first by many influential people, and even by some clergymen.*   King Henry never met Cade, but the latter defeated Sir Henry Stafford and Lord Say successively, who head the royal troops against him.   His interview with Stafford, though amusing, evidently misrepresents Cade, describing him as a mere ignorant boor, whereas, having been a soldier in France as well as in Ireland, he probably knew something of the French language.†

* "The insurgents were joined by more than a hundred squires and gentlemen, and the Abbot of Battle and the Prior of Lewes openly favoured their cause. John Cade, a soldier of some experience in the French wars, placed himself at their head."—GREEN's *History of the English People*, ch. vi.

† Mr. Courtenay observes that this view of Cade and his schemes is very consistent with the political notions of Shakespeare.—*Commentaries on Shakespeare's Historical Plays*, vol. i.

CADE.   Tell the king from me, that I am content he shall reign ;
but I'll be protector over him.

DICK.   And, furthermore, we'll have the Lord Say's head, for
selling the dukedom of Maine.

CADE.   And more than that, he can speak French, and therefore
he's a traitor.

STAFFORD.   O gross and miserable ignorance !

CADE.   Nay, answer me, if you can : the Frenchmen are our
enemies : go to, then.   I ask but this—can he that speaks with the
tongue of an enemy be a good counsellor, or no ?

ALL.   No, no ; and therefore we'll have his head.

Stafford is slain in battle soon after this parley, but Lord
Say is captured, and brought before Cade, who, after a
ridiculous conversation with him, has him executed.

CADE.   Ah ! thou say, thou serge, nay, thou buckram lord !
Thou hast most traitorously corrupted the youth of this realm, in
erecting a grammar-school.   It will be proved to thy face that thou
hast men about thee that usually talk of a noun and a verb ; and
such abominable words as no Christian ear can endure to hear.

LORD SAY.   Large gifts have I bestow'd on learned clerks,
    Because my books preferr'd me to the king,
    And seeing ignorance is the curse of God,
    Knowledge the wing wherewith we fly to heaven,
    Unless you be possess'd with devilish spirits,
    You cannot but forbear to murder me.

DICK.   Why dost thou quiver, man ?

SAY.   The palsy, and not fear, provokes me.

CADE.   I'll see if his head will stand steadier on a pole, or no.
Take him away, and behead him.—Act IV.

Soon after this atrocity Cade was defeated, and his followers, becoming discouraged, abandoned their leader ; but
the real Cade tried to restrain their violence, while the play
represents him as bad as the worst of them.*   When utterly
deserted by the mob, whom he had hitherto led to victory,
he exclaims in suspicious desperation :—

Was ever feather so lightly blown to and fro as this multitude?
The name of Henry the Fifth hales them to an hundred
mischiefs, and makes them leave me desolate.   I see them
lay their heads together to surprise me : my sword make way
for me, for here is no staying.   In despite of the devils and
hell, have through the very middest of you ! and heavens and

* " Cade maintained, during some time, great order and discipline among his
followers, and published severe edicts against plunder or violence of every kind."
—HUME's *History*, ch. xxi.   Hume adds that Cade was forced by his followers
to execute Lord Say, and that after this crime he could no longer control them,
and all his orders were neglected.

honour be witness, that no want of resolution in me, but only my followers' base and ignominious treasons, makes me betake me to my heels. [*Exit.*]—Act. IV.

After the suppression of this strange revolt, Henry hoped to enjoy peace and quiet, but these blessings he never had during his distracted reign. He, with his queen, Somerset, Buckingham, and Clifford, are congratulating each other over Cade's defeat, whose followers are all pardoned, when news comes of York's approach, heading an army from Ireland, and declaring he is in arms to make the king dismiss Somerset, who, since the deaths of Beaufort and Suffolk, has chief power in the Government,* and was formerly one of Gloster's mortal enemies. Henry, always anxious for peace, sends Buckingham to treat with the advancing York if possible, who is now a formidable foe. Meantime Cade, universally abandoned, finds his way, when half-starved, into the garden of a Kentish gentleman named Iden, who, meeting him there, slays him, probably without much trouble, and takes his head to London, where he sees the king, and is both thanked and rewarded. Cade's last words when falling by Iden's sword are worthy of that invincible courage which he really possessed,—

CADE.   Iden, farewell, and be proud of thy victory. Tell Kent from me she hath lost her best man; and exhort all the world to be cowards; for I, that never feared any, am vanquished by famine, not by valour.—Act IV.

Act V. describes an interview between York and Buckingham, the latter sent by Henry to inquire what he demands or intends. York immediately declares that his sole object is to remove Somerset from power, and Buckingham replies that this minister has already been disgraced, and confined in the Tower.

YORK.   Upon thine honour, is he prisoner?
BUCKINGHAM.   Upon mine honour, he is prisoner.
YORK.   Then, Buckingham, I do dismiss my powers.
And let my sovereign, virtuous Henry,
Command my eldest son—nay, all my sons,
As pledges of my fealty and love,
I'll send them all as willing as I live;
Lands, goods, horses, armour, anything I have
Is his to use, so Somerset may die.—Act V.

York, on this news, is about to disband his forces, when both

* HUME'S *History*, ch. xxi.

the king and queen appear on the scene, the latter accompanying her husband, and attended by Somerset, who is apparently as high in her favour as Suffolk had been.*

> QUEEN MARGARET.　For thousand Yorks he shall not hide
> 　　his head,
> But boldly stand, and front him to his face.
> 　YORK.　How now !　Is Somerset at liberty ?
> Then, York, unloose thy long-imprison'd thoughts,
> And let thy tongue be equal with thy heart.
> Shall I endure the sight of Somerset ?—
> False king ! why hast thou broken faith with me,
> Knowing how hardly I can brook abuse ?
> King did I call thee ? no, thou art not king ;
> Not fit to govern and rule multitudes,
> Which dar'st not, no, nor canst not rule a traitor.—Act V.

York then summons his two sons, Edward and Richard, and also Clifford, to his assistance, by giving bail for him, but Clifford adheres to Henry ; while Warwick and his aged father, Lord Salisbury, appear on York's behalf.　A violent quarrel now ensues between the adherents of the rival kings, in which Margaret and young Richard, son of York, are the most earnest and vehement.

> QUEEN MARGARET.　He is arrested, but will not obey ;
> His sons, he says, shall give their words for him.
> 　YORK.　Will not you, sons ?
> 　EDWARD.　Ay, noble father, if our words will serve.
> 　RICHARD.　And if words will not, then our weapons shall.
> 　CLIFFORD.　Why, what a brood of traitors have we here !
> 　YORK.　Look in a glass, and call thy image so.
>
> 　　　·　　　·　　　·　　　·　　　·　　　·
>
> Bid Salisbury and Warwick come to me.
> 　KING HENRY.　Why, Warwick, hath thy knee forgot to bow ?
> Old Salisbury—shame to thy silver hair,
> Thou mad misleader of thy brain-sick son !
>
> 　　　·　　　·　　　·　　　·　　　·　　　·
>
> O, where is faith ? O, where is loyalty ?
> If it be banish'd from the frosty head,
>
> 　　　·　　　·　　　·　　　·
>
> For shame ! in duty bend thy knee to me.

* " Somerset succeeded to Suffolk's power in the ministry and credit with the queen. . . . . York insisted upon the removal of Somerset, and submitting to a trial in parliament.　The court pretended to comply with his demand, and that nobleman was put in arrest.　York was then persuaded to pay his respects to the king in his tent, and, on repeating his charge against Somerset, he was surprised to see that minister step from behind the curtain, and offer to maintain his innocence.　York now found that he had been betrayed.　No violence, however, was attempted against him.　He had many friends in Henry's camp, and he retired to his seat on the border of Wales."—HUME's *History*, ch. xxi.

> SALISBURY.   My lord, I have consider'd with myself
> The title of this most renowned duke ;
> And in my conscience do repute his grace
> The rightful heir to England's royal seat.
>   KING HENRY.   Call Buckingham, and bid him arm himself.
>   YORK.   Call Buckingham, and all the friends thou hast,
> I am resolv'd for death or dignity.—Act V.

The two factions soon resolve on immediate battle, but in reality some time elapsed after York's return from Ireland before actual warfare took place. He was, however, really enraged at finding his old foe, Somerset, at liberty and in power, instead of in prison, and from this time he probably contemplated civil war. His sons—the youngest, Richard, especially—urged him to open warfare, and the first battle between the two parties was at St. Alban's. In this engagement Henry was defeated, and Somerset, the nominal cause of the war, was slain, as were also Clifford and some other Lancastrian leaders. This last act ends with old Salisbury's exulting congratulations to York and the brave princes, Edward and Richard, and also to his own valiant son, Warwick. The young Prince Richard, on this occasion of his first battle, shows signs of that fierce spirit and savage temper afterwards so fearfully developed when king of England ; for, on slaying Somerset, he exclaims,—

> So lie thou there ;—
> Sword, hold thy temper : heart, be wrathful still :
> Priests pray for enemies, but princes kill.

In the play, he three times rescues Salisbury, who, despite his age, ventures into the midst of the battle, being one of York's most devoted adherents.

> YORK.   Of Salisbury, who can report of him ?—
> That winter lion, who in rage forgets
> Aged contusions and all brush of time.
> .   .   .   .   . This happy day
> Is not itself, nor have we won one foot,
> If Salisbury be lost.
>   RICHARD.   My noble father,
> Three times to-day I holp him to his horse,
> Three times bestrid him, thrice I led him off.
>
>   .   .   .   .
> But, noble as he is, look where he comes.
>   SALISBURY.   Now, by my sword, well hast thou fought to-day ;
> By the mass, so did we all.—I thank you, Richard.
>   WARWICK.   Now, by my hand, lords, 'twas a glorious day :
> St. Alban's battle, won by famous York.

Shall be eternized in all age to come.
Sound, drum and trumpets :—and to London all :
And more such days as these to us befall !—Act V.

But the civil War of the Roses is only beginning, and
its first battle ends this play, leaving the York party in
triumph, nearly five thousand of their foes being slain,
while their own loss was comparatively slight.* Somerset,
Northumberland, Stafford and Clifford—all Lancastrians
—fell in this encounter; while the White Rose party lost
no leaders of distinction. The two future kings—Edward IV.
and Richard III.—in this battle first displayed that valour
and energy which distinguished them throughout their eventful and sanguinary reigns.

* " This was the first blood spilt in that fatal quarrel, which was not finished
in less than a course of thirty years, which opened scenes of extraordinary violence
and cruelty, and almost entirely annihilated the ancient nobility of England. Yet
affairs did not immediately proceed to the last extremities ; the nation was kept
some time in suspense ; the vigour and spirit of Queen Margaret, supporting her
small power, still proved a balance to the great authority of Richard of York,
which was checked by his irresolute temper."—HUME's *History*, ch. xxi.

CHAPTER XI.

THIRD PART OF KING HENRY VI.

Sketch of Play.

THIS play throughout records the terrible strife between the Houses of York and Lancaster. The Duke of York, at first victorious, was really killed in battle, but in the play he is stabbed when a prisoner. His claims devolve on his eldest son, Edward, who, with his brothers, Clarence and Richard, Duke of Gloster, head the York faction; while Henry's party is chiefly represented, both in counsel and on the field, by his brave queen. After the defeat of the Lancastrians, Margaret and her son, Edward, go to France, to seek assistance; while Henry is a prisoner in England, and Prince Edward, York's son, reigns under the title of Edward IV. Warwick, however, quarrels with him, and joins the Lancastrians. War is resumed, and Edward captured. In a short time, the York party regain their ground, Warwick being slain in battle, and Margaret and her son taken prisoner. The latter is stabbed by the princes of the House of York, and his mother banished from England. King Henry is murdered in prison, Edward IV. reigns undisturbed, and thus the play ends with the complete triumph of the York faction.

THE first act describes the triumph of the Yorkists in Parliament after their first victory.* Prince Richard shows and throws down Somerset's head, amid general rejoicing, and, indeed, these English princes and noblemen, when excited after the battle, talk more like North American Indians than Christian or civilized men.

PRINCE EDWARD. Lord Stafford's father, Duke of Buckingham,
Is either slain or wounded dangerous:

* The Second and Third Parts of *Henry VI.*, Bishop Wordsworth says, should be "regarded and read as one play;" adding that they consist of retributive justice "tracking the House of Lancaster for its usurpation."—*Notes to Shakespeare's Historical Plays.*

I cleft his beaver with a downright blow;
That this is true, father, behold his blood.
> [*Showing his bloody sword.*
PRINCE RICHARD.   Speak thou for me, and tell them what I did.
> [*Throwing down* SOMERSET'S *head.*
YORK.   Richard hath best deserv'd of all my sons.
But is your grace dead, my Lord of Somerset?
PRINCE RICHARD.   Thus do I hope to shake King Henry's head.
LORD WARWICK.   And so do I.—Act I.

This savage spirit shown by both parties alternately appears
through the whole of this terrible drama, which describes
more slaughter in battle and in executions than any of
the historical plays.*   Warwick and others persuade York
to assume the royal title immediately, and he then seats
himself on the throne, when Henry, with his adherents,
also enter the House of Parliament, and the rival kings
confront each other.   A fierce argument soon ensues between the leaders of the two factions, in which the Princes
Edward and Richard are perhaps the most vehement.
Henry, weak, nervous, and shocked at all the violence around
him, is supported chiefly by Exeter and Clifford; but Warwick, the boldest of York's adherents, summons a party of
soldiers to his support.   Henry, always irresolute, vaguely
hints that, if allowed to reign for the rest of his life,
York shall succeed him, to the exclusion of his own son.
York and his party instantly agree to this proposal, while
the more spirited Lancastrians—Clifford, Northumberland,
&c.—bitterly reproach Henry for his weakness in making
such an agreement, which they tell the queen.   Exeter alone
supports his unfortunate master in all he does; while York
and his friends, well satisfied, leave the assembly.   This
extraordinary scene between the rival kings is imaginary;
but there really was some strange temporising between
the two parties a short time before the civil war again
broke out.†   Henry becomes alarmed and depressed at his
own concession, and more so when his proud queen, with her
son, approach.   The king and Exeter both try to escape,
but Margaret angrily stops them, not only reproaching her

---

* Hallam states that the Second and Third Parts of this play were in great part
written by Marlowe, a poet of genius, but of dissolute character; and adds—
"These plays claim certainly a very low rank among those of Shakespeare."—
Literary History, ch. vi.

† "An outward reconciliation only was procured, and in order to ratify this
accord to the whole people, a solemn procession to St. Paul's was appointed,
where the Duke of York led Queen Margaret, and a leader of one party marched
hand in hand with the leaders of the other.   The less real cordiality prevailed,
the more were the exterior demonstrations of amity redoubled."—HUME'S
History, ch. xxi.

husband with cowardice, but boldly declaring she will not submit to her son's rights being denied, and that, in the prince's name, she will urge the Lancastrians to continue the war, and utterly ignore Henry's acts and promises.   .

   EXETER.   Here comes the queen, whose looks betray her anger.
I'll steal away.
   KING HENRY.   Exeter, so will I.
   QUEEN MARGARET.   Nay, go not from me, I will follow thee.
   KING HENRY.   Be patient, gentle queen, and I will stay.
   QUEEN MARGARET.   Who can be patient in such extremes?
I shame to hear thee speak.   Ah, timorous wretch !
Thou hast undone thyself, thy son, and me :
And given unto the House of York such head,
As thou shalt reign but by their sufferance.
Had I been there, which am a silly woman,
The soldiers should have toss'd me on their pikes
Before I would have granted to that act.
The northern lords, that have forsworn thy colours,
Will follow mine, if once they see them spread :
And spread they shall be ; to thy foul disgrace,
And utter ruin of the House of York.
Thus do I leave thee : come, son, let's away ;
Our army's ready ; come, we'll after them.
   KING HENRY.   Gentle son Edward, thou wilt stay with me ?
   QUEEN MARGARET.   Ay, to be murder'd by his enemies.
   PRINCE.   When I return with victory from the field,
I'll see your grace : till then I'll follow her.—Act I.

Margaret and her son thus leave Henry in scornful anger. The prince, who admires and resembles his courageous mother more than his timid father, accompanies her, leaving Henry and Exeter to condole with each other.

The next scene describes York and his warlike sons— all more violent and stern than he is—hearing that Margaret and her son, disregarding Henry's peaceful wishes, are again in the field.   Margaret, from the very first, threw herself heart and soul into the contest for her husband's rights, which she supported by her energy in counsel and by her presence on the battle-field.*   Yet no admiration for her courage is ever expressed by the York party, who, indeed, had reason to dread her cruelty ; for throughout the dreadful contest now commencing in these scenes there seems a total want of generosity on either side.   Revenge, malice, and cruelty apparently actuated not only each party, but almost

* "Her affability, insinuation, and address—qualities in which she excelled— her caresses, her promises, wrought a powerful effect on every one who approached her.   The admiration of her great qualities was succeeded by compassion towards her helpless condition."—HUME'S *History*, ch. xxi.

every member of them, and in this respect the dramatic representation is fully confirmed by history.*

The next battle, at Wakefield, was a Lancastrian triumph, disgraced by the cruelty of the victors, which, however, was fully equalled during the war by the Yorkists.   Among the victims deliberately murdered was York's son, the Earl of Rutland, a mere youth, stabbed by Clifford, in revenge for his father's death in the battle of St. Alban's.   But this was no palliation for Clifford's crime, who was evidently a savage, cruel man, as his father was killed in the battle-field, while Rutland was slain when a helpless prisoner.   In the battle of Wakefield, York himself was killed, his head struck off, and placed on the gates of York, covered with a paper crown, by Margaret's order, in mockery of his regal pretensions.†   In the play he is captured, and after exchanging bitter re-proaches with Margaret, is stabbed to death by her and Clifford.   Their supposed language was certainly not used by either of them, and probably it was never written by Shake-speare.‡

> Queen Margaret.   Brave warriors, Clifford and Northumber-
>   land,
> Come, make him stand upon this molehill here:
>
> .   .   .   .   .   .
>
> What! was't you that would be England's king?
> Was't you that revell'd in our parliament,
> And made a preachment of your high descent?
> Where are your mess of sons, to back you now?
> The wanton Edward, and the lusty George?
> And where's that valiant crook-back prodigy,
> Dicky your boy, that, with his grumbling voice,
> Was wont to cheer his dad in mutinies?
> Or, with the rest, where is your darling Rutland?
> Look, York; I stain'd this napkin with the blood
> That valiant Clifford, with his rapier's point,
> Made issue from the bosom of the boy.
>
> .   .   .   .   .   .
>
> York cannot speak unless he wears a crown.
> A crown for York;—and, lords, bow low to him.
> Hold you his hands, whilst I do set it on.
> Ay, marry, sir, now looks he like a king!

---

* "There is no part of English history since the Conquest so obscure, so un-certain, so little authentic or consistent, as that of the wars between the two roses.   All we can distinguish with certainty through the deep cloud which covers that period is a scene of horror and bloodshed, savage manners, arbitrary execu-tions, and treacherous, dishonourable conduct in all parties."—Hume's *History*, ch. xxii.

† Hume's *History*, ch. xxi.

‡ *See* Hallam's *Literary History*, ch. vi.

YORK.   She-wolf of France, but worse than wolves of France,
Whose tongue more poisons than the adder's tooth !
How ill-beseeming is it in thy sex,
To triumph, like an Amazonian trull,
Upon their woes whom fortune captivates !

See, ruthless queen, a hapless father's tears.

There, take the crown, and with the crown my curse.
                    [*Throwing off the paper crown.*
And in thy need such comfort come to thee
As now I reap at thy too cruel hand !
Hard-hearted Clifford, take me from the world;
My soul to heaven, my blood upon your heads !
        CLIFFORD.   Here's for my oath, here's for my father's death.
                              [*Stabbing him.*
        QUEEN MARGARET.   And here's to right our gentle-hearted king.
                              [*Stabbing him.*
Off with his head, and set it on York gates;
So York may overlook the gates of York.—Act I.

That Margaret would have been capable of this act seems
not improbable, from her violent temper and the terrible
excitement of her present position, but, as York was slain in
battle, this revolting scene never occurred.   The old Lord
Salisbury, who had so eagerly joined the Yorkists at their first
rising, was captured and executed after this battle.   Neither
age nor youth were spared, though apparently no women on
either side were slain or executed.   Margaret, after the
victory at Wakefield, prepares to meet the Yorkist princes,
Edward and Richard, who, with Warwick, head a large army
against the Lancastrians.   The cruelty of the latter party
apparently roused general indignation through England after
the battle of Wakefield.*   But the Yorkists were eager to
follow their example, and emulate them in their savage
cruelty, which, by giving no quarter in battle, and executing prisoners, destroyed the greater part of England's
nobility.†
The princes and Warwick accordingly hear of the executions of their relatives with grief, rage, and threats of vengeance, but before another battle the two parties meet

---

* " The fierce spirit of Margaret began a system of extermination, by acts of
attainder and executions of prisoners, that created abhorrence, though it did not
prevent imitation.   And the barbarities of her northern army, whom she led
towards London after the battle of Wakefield, lost the Lancastrian cause its
former friends, and might justly convince reflecting men that it was better to risk
the chance of a new dynasty than trust the kingdom to an exasperated faction."
—HALLAM's *Middle Ages*, ch. viii.
† HUME's *History*, ch. xxi.

near York.   Here Margaret and the Yorkist princes, with their respective adherents, fiercely defy each other; while Henry, vainly hoping to make peace, tries to speak, but cannot get a hearing.   The York party are now strongly reinforced; while the three princes, the elder styled Edward IV. by his party, and his brothers, George and Richard, with Warwick, are in chief command.   Prince Edward, though severe and vindictive, was at first much respected, owing to his father's high character, to whom, in some qualities he was inferior.*   He, with his brothers, George and Richard, exchange bitter reproaches with Margaret, and they soon prepare for battle.   Their next encounter was the terrible battle of Towton, in which the Lancastrians were utterly defeated.   While this conflict is raging, Henry, instead of heading his army, which apparently he never did, is represented seating himself on a hill near the battle-field, in a concealed place, and utters long, dreary reflections on the woes of men, especially of kings.   These sentiments seem consistent with his mild, thoughtful, timid character, which was, indeed, a complete contrast to his own family, as well as to nearly all his adherents and opponents.

> KING HENRY.   Here on this molehill will I sit me down.
> To whom God will, there be the victory!
> For Margaret my queen, and Clifford too,
> Have chid me from the battle; swearing both
> They prosper best of all when I am thence.
> O God! methinks it were a happy life,
> To be no better than a homely swain:
> To sit upon a hill, as I do now,
> To carve out dials quaintly, point by point,
> Thereby to see the minutes how they run.
>
> .   .   .   .   .   .
>
> Gives not the hawthorn bush a sweeter shade
> To shepherds, looking on their silly sheep,
> Than doth a rich embroider'd canopy
> To kings, that fear their subjects' treachery?—Act II.

While thus musing alone, the sad monarch sees and hears a son bewailing his father, slain by him, and then a father mourning over the body of his son, whom he has likewise

* "This prince in the bloom of youth, remarkable for the beauty of his person, for his bravery, his activity, his affability, and every popular quality, determined to assume the name and dignity of king. . . . . He was bold, active, enterprising, and his hardness of heart and severity of character rendered him impregnable to all those movements of compassion which might relax his vigour in the prosecution of the most bloody revenges upon his enemies."—HUME'S *History*, ch. xxi., xxii.

killed, without knowing him, in the murderous civil war which is now desolating England.

> Son.   Ill blows the wind that profits nobody.
> This man, whom hand to hand I slew in fight,
> May be possessèd with some store of crowns.
>
> Who's this?—O God! it is my father's face,
> Whom in this conflict I unawares have kill'd.
> O heavy times, begetting such events!
> From London by the king was I press'd forth;
> My father, being the Earl of Warwick's man,
> Came on the part of York, press'd by his master;
> And I, who at his hands receiv'd my life,
> Have by my hands of life bereaved him.
> Pardon me, God, I knew not what I did!
> > *Enter* FATHER *who has slain his son.*
> FATHER.   Thou that so stoutly hast resisted me,
> Give me thy gold, if thou hast any gold.
> But let me see:—is this our foeman's face?
> Ah, no no, no, it is mine only son!
>
> O, pity, God, this miserable age!
> What stratagems, how fell, how butcherly,
> This deadly quarrel daily doth beget!
> KING HENRY.   O pity, pity, gentle Heaven, pity!
> The red rose and the white are on his face,
> The fatal colours of our striving houses:
> The one his purple blood right well resembles;
> The other, his pale cheeks, methinks, presenteth.
> Son.   I'll bear thee hence, where I may weep my fill.
> > [*Exit with his father's body.*
> FATHER.   These arms of mine shall be thy winding-sheet;
> My heart, sweet boy, thy sepulchre.
> KING HENRY.   Sad-hearted men, much overgone with care,
> Here sits a king more woeful than you are.—Act II.

Neither of his unhappy subjects, however, see him, and, after their departure, Henry is rejoined by his wife and son, who, announcing their defeat, escape with him to Scotland, leaving England in possession of the triumphant Edward IV. This prince gave no quarter in the battle, and above 3,500 men were reported slain, among them Clifford, Westmoreland, Northumberland, and many other Lancastrian chiefs. Warwick, surnamed "the king-maker," is now in his glory, and assumes control over the three victorious young princes, to which they good-humouredly submit, but only for a short time.*

* "Warwick's undesigning frankness and openness of character rendered his

This officious earl, after ordering Clifford's head to be set on one of the gates at York, in place of the late Duke of York's,* proposes that the princes and he should repair to London. He also intends going to France, to negotiate a marriage between Lady Bona, the French king's sister, and Edward. The latter hears these plans and proposals favourably, and creates his brothers, George and Richard, Dukes of Clarence and Gloster. Warwick addresses the young men with almost the authority of a parent or guardian, quite approves these arrangements, and all set off to London in high spirits.

> WARWICK.   And now to London with triumphant march,
> There to be crownèd England's royal king.
> From whence shall Warwick cut the sea to France,
> And ask the Lady Bona for thy queen.
>   EDWARD.   Even as thou wilt, sweet Warwick, let it be:
> For in thy shoulder do I build my seat;
> And never will I undertake the thing
> Wherein thy counsel and consent is wanting.
> Richard, I will create thee Duke of Gloster;
> And George, of Clarence; Warwick, as ourself,
> Shall do, and undo, as him pleaseth best.
>   RICHARD.   Let me be Duke of Clarence; George, of Gloster;
> For Gloster's dukedom is too ominous.
>   WARWICK.   Tut, that's a foolish observation;
> Richard, be Duke of Gloster.   Now to London,
> To see these honours in possession.—Act II.

The three princes apparently submit to Warwick's directions at first, owing their success so much to his valour, ability, and influence; but his power over them was not fated to continue.

Meantime, Margaret and her son succeed in escaping to France, but the unfortunate Henry was captured in an English wood by two keepers, and imprisoned. This play never mentions the historical incident of Margaret and her son, who, when captured by robbers in a forest, revealed their names, and were protected by these outlaws, through whose assistance they escaped to France.† This highly romantic episode, which Shakespeare could have described so admirably, is ignored; while the treachery of the keepers to Henry seems an invention, though he was

conquests over men's affections the more certain and infallible. No less than thirty thousand persons are said to have daily lived at his board in the different manors and castles which he possessed in England. . . . . . His numerous retainers were more devoted to his will than to the prince or to the laws, and he was the greatest, as well as the last, of those mighty barons who formerly overawed the crown."—HUME'S *History*, ch. xxi.

  * HUME'S *History*.   † *Ibid.* ch. xxii.

certainly arrested in Lancashire, after a year's concealment there, and sent a prisoner to the Tower, where he was apparently well treated.*

Edward IV., now in complete triumph at London, fell in love with a Lady Grey, whose husband was slain in battle, fighting on the Lancastrian side. His estates being therefore confiscated, the widow, in a remarkable scene founded on history,† implores their restitution from Edward IV., in presence of his two brothers, Clarence and Gloster, and is astonished to find her amorous young sovereign wishing to make her his mistress, and, on her firm refusal, offering to marry her.

KING EDWARD. Say that King Edward take thee for his queen?
LADY GREY. 'Tis better said than done, my gracious lord:
I am a subject fit to jest withal,
But far unfit to be a sovereign.

. . . . . .

I know I am too mean to be your queen:
And yet too good to be your concubine.
KING EDWARD. You cavil, widow; I did mean my queen.
LADY GREY. 'Twill grieve your grace my sons should call you father.
KING EDWARD. No more than when my daughters call thee mother.
Answer no more, for thou shalt be my queen.
GLOSTER (*aside to* CLARENCE). The ghostly father now hath done his shrift.
KING EDWARD. Brothers, you muse what chat we two have had.
GLOSTER. The widow likes it not, for she looks very sad.
KING EDWARD. You'd think it strange if I should marry her.
CLARENCE. To whom, my lord?
KING EDWARD. Why, Clarence, to myself.
GLOSTER. That would be ten days' wonder, at the least.
CLARENCE. That's a day longer than a wonder lasts.
GLOSTER. By so much is the wonder in extremes.
KING EDWARD. Well, jest on, brothers: I can tell you both
Her suit is granted for her husband's lands.

. . . . . .

Widow, go you along :—Lords, use her honourably.—Act III.

To this proposal she consents, and her late husband's property was restored.‡

* "The safety of his person was less owing to the generosity of his enemies than to the contempt which they entertained of his courage and his understanding."
—HUME's *History*, ch. xxii.
† HUME's *History*, ch. xxii.
‡ "The cruel and unrelenting spirit of Edward, though inured to the ferocity of the civil war, was at the same time extremely devoted to the softer passions, which, without mitigating his severe temper, maintained a great influence over

During this scene, the two princes, though present in the play, were probably not so in reality; but their comments during Edward's love-making well indicate the thoughtless nature of Clarence and the deep envy of Gloster, who already perceives how much more admired and popular his brothers are than he is. For among a remarkably handsome family he stood alone, repulsive and deformed in appearance, though gifted with average bodily strength and far more than common powers of mind. He has and desires no confidant to his most secret thoughts, which he reveals in soliloquy directly after Edward's successful courtship to the Lady Grey. In this extraordinary speech to himself, which no one hears, he avows his desperate resolve to become King of England, despite all possible dangers he may incur, and all crimes he may have to commit in accomplishing his purpose. In the moment of his family's triumph, he finds no lasting joy—no real pleasure; his handsome, attractive brothers are admired and honoured everywhere, while he, utterly unlike them both in mind and body, meets certainly with respect, but with neither admiration nor love from men and women, and attributes their disgust to his bodily deformity.

> GLOSTER.   Then, since this earth affords no joy to me
> But to command, to check, to o'erbear such
> As are of better person than myself,
> I'll make my heaven to dream upon the crown;
> And, whiles I live, to account this world but hell,
> Until my misshap'd trunk, that bears this head,,
> Be round impalèd with a glorious crown.
> And yet I know not how to get the crown,
> For many lives stand between me and home;
> And I—like one lost in a thorny wood,
>
>   .   .   .   .   .
>
> Not knowing how to find the open air,
> But toiling desperately to find it out—
> Torment myself to catch the English crown:
> And from that torment I will free myself,
> Or hew my way out with a bloody axe.
> Why, I can smile, and murder while I smile;
> And cry, content, to that which grieves my heart;
> And wet my cheeks with artificial tears;
> And frame my face to all occasions.

him. During the present interval of peace, he lived in the most familiar and sociable manner with his subjects. . . . . The young widow [Lady Grey] entreated him to take pity on her impoverished and distressed children. The sight of so much beauty in affliction strongly affected the amorous Edward; love stole insensibly into the heart, under the guise of compassion."—HUME'S *History*, ch. xxii.

I'll play the orator as well as Nestor;
Deceive more slily than Ulysses could ;
And set the murd'rous Machiavel to school.
Can I do this, and cannot get a crown ?
Tut ! were it further off, I'll pluck it down.—Act III.*

Richard's fierce, restless spirit frets and chafes at his singular
position, but the renewed civil war again tempts him to draw
his sword in his brother's cause. Yet his secret and unscrupulous ambition remains the same, though no one apparently
suspects it. He seems really to have been one of the most
successful dissemblers in English history, and would have
well merited the compliments of Machiavelli himself. King
Edward has no idea, therefore, that in his triumphant court,
and even in his joyous family circle, there lurked his most
dangerous foe, whose plots, though now postponed, were
destined to avenge the ruin of the House of Lancaster.
Edward resolves to marry Lady Grey, apparently forgetting
Warwick's mission to France, or probably thinking himself
so strongly established in England that he might disregard
that powerful subject's influence. Meantime, however, Warwick, knowing nothing of Edward's love for Lady Grey,
arrives in Paris, where he is received by King Louis XI., with
whom he finds Margaret, she and her son having found a
welcome in France. The slight sketch of Louis in this play
gives no idea whatever of his real character, so ably described
by the French historian, De Comines, and also by Scott
in "Quentin Durward," and which, from its rare combination of talent, superstition, cunning, and hypocrisy, was
admirably suited to Shakespeare's descriptive genius. The
poet, as in *Henry V.*, apparently takes no interest in any
French characters, and he makes Louis say only a few formal
words, consenting to Lady Bona's marriage with Edward,

---

* That Gloster liked literature, and wished foreign books sold in England
without hindrance, by retail or otherwise, is certain (GREEN's *History of the
English People*) ; but he could not have read Macbiavelli's works, as the latter
was a mere youth of fourteen, born in 1469, when Gloster was killed at Bosworth
field in 1485. But Shakespeare probably knew Machiavelli's writings, and may
have remembered his words when alluding to him ; for Gloster's daring usurpation was apparently founded on Machiavelli's advice and principles :—"I conclude that the usurper of a state should commit all the cruelties which his
safety renders necessary at once, that he may never have cause to repeat them.
If, from bad counsel or timidity, he takes another course, he must ever have a
poniard in his hand. . . . . As a prince must learn how to act the part of a
beast sometimes, he should make the fox and the lion his patterns. . . . a prudent
prince cannot and ought not to keep his word, except when he can do it without
injury to himself."—*The Prince*. Shakespeare's sketch of Gloster's conduct,
both as prince and king, agrees with these ideas, and the real Gloster appears,
from many, though not from all historians, to have greatly resembled the poet's
description.

when news comes to both Margaret and Warwick of the king's unexpected marriage with his subject, Lady Grey. Margaret is delighted at the news, while Warwick, overwhelmed with rage and confusion, almost immediately renounces allegiance to Edward IV., transferring it, heart and soul, to Margaret's son, Edward. He also agrees with the queen that his daughter should marry her son, who is to be his future king.* Louis, who was always friendly to Margaret, is much gratified at this sudden change in political designs. Warwick consequently prepares to return to England, and upraise the fallen standard of Lancaster, while Margaret and her son intend to follow him.

The next scene describes the anger of Clarence, Gloster, and many noblemen, at Edward's singular marriage, as they all dread the coming influence of the new queen's relatives. Clarence, deeply offended, actually joins the Lancastrians, under Warwick, whose daughter he had married, while Gloster remains faithful to his brother, Edward IV. Richard is as yet understood by none. Though he has done so much in counsel and in the field for the House of York, and hates the Lancastrians with peculiar bitterness, he has no real attachment to any one, but only studies his private interests, or rather wishes. Clarence, being much influenced by his father-in-law, Warwick, for a short time actually joins the party which had slain both his father and brother. His marriage with Warwick's daughter thus for the present allies him closely with the Lancastrians, but his impetuous and wayward temper made him distrusted by all parties. Warwick and Clarence, now united, are joined by powerful adherents on all sides, and Edward is surprised and captured in his tent by Warwick, who declares he will replace the crown on the head of the imprisoned Henry VI. In reality, however, Edward was not captured, but fled to the Continent, in his turn, leaving Warwick for a short time virtual master of England.† A parliament was then summoned, and Clarence declared heir to the throne, in default of Prince Edward of Lancaster dying without issue, while, during the latter's minority, Warwick and Clarence were to be joint-regents, and Henry acknowledged as nominal sovereign.‡

Margaret and her son come to England soon after this arrangement, and in the play Edward escapes from prison by the help of his brother Gloster, though in reality he was in Holland, preparing to return to England, and assisted with

* "This reconciliation was not effected easily, as Shakespeare has it. Many days elapsed before Warwick's excuses and Louis's persuasions brought the high-spirited queen to agree to the connection."—COURTENAY'S *Commentaries*, vol. ii.

† HUME'S *History*, ch. xxii.　　　　　　　　　　　‡ *Ibid.*

money by the Duke of Burgundy, who, hating Louis XI., also detested the Lancastrians as being favoured by him.* Henry is released from the Tower during his rival's absence, and restored to his throne with every demonstration of respect, though despised for his weakness by all parties. In the play, the scene of his liberation is made very interesting, by his supposed meeting with the young Earl of Richmond, afterwards Henry VII., now a mere youth, in charge of Lord Somerset. The mild, thoughtful monarch predicts, in the lad's presence, that he will be the future king. This is the only time Richmond is introduced in the play.

> KING HENRY.   Come hither, England's hope : If secret powers
> [*Lays his hand on his head.*
> Suggest but truth to my divining thoughts,
> This pretty lad will prove our country's bliss.
> His looks are full of peaceful majesty,
> His head by nature fram'd to wear a crown,
> His hand to wield a sceptre ; and himself
> Likely, in time, to bless a regal throne.
> Make much of him, my lords ; for this is he
> Must help you more than you are hurt by me.—Act IV.

This notice of young Richmond by Henry seems to have been a historical fact, but the lad makes no reply in the play.† The Lords Somerset and Oxford, however, both earnest Lancastrians, fear that Richmond will not be safe in England when they hear of Edward's advance ; for that prince, whose hatred to the Lancastrians was deep and implacable, had always forbidden his soldiers to allow quarter to their defeated fellow-countrymen.‡ Richmond was therefore sent to Brittany, but he apparently did not arrive there till after the final defeat of the Lancastrians at Tewkesbury. King Edward, with his brother Gloster, are described both in the play and Hume's History as making triumphant progress through England after their return from the Continent. Clarence, either from some quarrel with Warwick, or motives of policy, deserted the Lancastrians, rejoining his former partisans in Yorkshire, and this unexpected desertion caused Warwick's defeat and death at the battle of Barnet.

Before these two battles Edward had entered London, where he was always popular, without opposition,§ recapturing

---

* HUME's *History*, ch. xxii.

†. " One day, when King Henry VI., whose innocency gave him holiness, was washing his hands at a great feast, and cast his eyes upon Henry VII., then a young youth, he said—'This is the lad that shall possess quietly that we now strive for.'"—LORD BACON's *History of Henry VII.*

‡ HUME's *History*.   § *Ibid.* ch. xxii.

e luckless Henry VI., who thus, after a short interval of
lerty, was again committed a prisoner to the Tower. War-
ck had fully reckoned on Clarence's assistance, who so
ddenly deserts to his brother: in the play, he plucks the
l rose from his cap, and flings it at his father-in-law,
arwick, declaring that he thus abandons the Lancastrian
use. This announcement he makes to Warwick before
th his brothers, King Edward and Gloster, when all are
ading their respective forces.

CLARENCE.   Look here, I throw my infamy at thee:
/ill not ruinate my father's house,
10 gave his blood to lime the stones together,
d set up Lancaster.   Why, trow'st thou, Warwick,
at Clarence is so harsh, so blunt, unnatural,
 bend the fatal instruments of war
ainst his brother and his lawful king?
d so, proud-hearted Warwick, I defy thee,
d to my brother turn my blushing cheeks.
rdon me, Edward, I will make amends ;
d, Richard, do not frown upon my faults,
r I will henceforth be no more inconstant.
KING EDWARD.   Now welcome more, and ten times more belov'd,
an if thou never hadst deserv'd our hate.
GLOSTER.   Welcome, good Clarence ; this is brother-like.—Act V.

arwick, thus abandoned by an ally whom he had im-
idently trusted, and not yet joined by Margaret, was out-
mbered, and, after a brave resistance, slain on the battle-
d. In the play, Edward brings in Warwick, mortally
unded, and, throwing him down, leaves him, when the latter
ers a noble speech to himself.

KING EDWARD.   So, lie thou there: die thou, and die our fear ;
: Warwick was a bug* that fear'd us all.
WARWICK.   Ah, who is nigh? come to me friend or foe,
d tell me who is victor, York or Warwick ?
y ask I that? my mangled body shows,
 blood, my want of strength, my sick heart shows,
it I must yield my body to the earth,
d, by my fall, the conquest to my foe.
is yields the cedar to the axe's edge,
ose arms gave shelter to the princely eagle,
der whose shade the ramping lion slept.
  .   .   .   .   .
ese eyes, that now are dimm'd with death's black veil,
ve been as piercing as the mid-day sun
search the secret treasons of the world.

* " Bug is a bugbear, a terrific being."—JOHNSON's *Notes to Henry VI.*

Lo, now my glory smear'd in dust and blood !
My parks, my walks, my manors that I had,
Even now forsake me ; and of all my lands
Is nothing left me, but my body's length !—Act V.*

The decisive battle of Tewksbury, both in history and in
the play, soon follows the encounter at Barnet, completing the
ruin of the Lancastrian party, Margaret and her son being
captured, and their forces utterly routed. A dreadful scene
now took place, in which historians and poet agree, to the
disgrace of a nominally Christian land. The captured
mother and son were brought before King Edward and his
two brothers, and the captive prince, though a mere boy,
with a heroism worthy of his grandfather, Henry V., boldly
asserts his rights before his triumphant relatives, and reproaches them all.

> PRINCE EDWARD. I know my duty, you are all undutiful :
> Lascivious Edward, and thou perjur'd George,
> And thou misshapen Dick, I tell ye all,
> I am your better, traitors as ye are ;
> And thou usurp'st my father's rights and mine.

But he was a helpless prisoner, and, with his mother, was now
in the power of three fierce young men, who well remembered their own slain father, whose head had been set on a
gate at York, covered with a paper crown, in savage derision
of his royal claims. King Edward, enraged at his young captive's spirit, instead of admiring it, basely struck him, and he
was then dragged away, and slain by the Princes Clarence
and Gloster.†

In the play, he is killed before his mother, who was imprisoned, and then banished.‡

Gloster, after this murder, starts alone for London, omin-
ously hinting that he is going to the imprisoned king in the
Tower.

> GLOSTER. Clarence, excuse me to the king my brother ;
> I'll hence to London on a serious matter :
> Ere ye come there, be sure to hear some news.

* "In outer seeming, Warwick was the very type of a feudal baron. He could
raise armies at his own call from his own earldoms. Six hundred liveried retainers followed him to parliament. But few men were really further from the
feudal ideal. Active and ruthless warrior as he was, his enemies denied to
Warwick the gift of personal daring. A Burgundian chronicler who knew him
well describes him as the craftiest man living."—GREEN'S *History of the English
People*, book v.

† HUME'S *History*, ch. xxii.

‡ "The presence of Margaret at her son's examination and death is a dramatic
incident, as is Gloster's attempt to murder her. She was taken, kept prisoner
for five years, and then ransomed by Louis XI. of France."—COURTENAY'S
Commentaries on Shakespeare's Historical Plays, vol. ii.

CLARENCE.   What ? what ?
GLOSTER.   The Tower ! the Tower ! [*Exit.*]
KING EDWARD.   Where's Richard gone ?
CLARENCE.   To London, all in post ; and, as I guess,
To make a bloody supper in the Tower.
KING EDWARD.   He's sudden, if anything comes in his head.—
Act V.

After Margaret is removed a prisoner from Edward's presence, he says a few words to Clarence, proposing a return to London, as their triumph is now complete, and no enemy is in the field—the imprisoned Henry alone representing the House of Lancaster—for as yet Richmond's claims were never publicly mentioned. The next scene, in the Tower, may, indeed, be true, as King Henry's death is considered mysterious by comparatively old and recent historians.*

The king is reading a book, the Lieutenant of the Tower being with him, when Gloster enters, and dismisses the latter. Richard's expression and manner at once alarm Henry, for he apparently expects the worst. Gloster says little, while the king, with his usual melancholy talkativeness, something like that of Richard II., begins a long and useless complaint, feebly reproaching Gloster with his son Edward's murder, of which he has been told. Gloster admits the crime, upon which the grieved father, with desperate courage, foretells Gloster's destructive career of wickedness in bitter words, which only hasten his own death, for Richard stabs him during his prediction.

KING HENRY.   And thus I prophesy—that many a thousand,
Which now mistrust no parcel of my fear ;
And many an old man's sigh, and many a widow's,
And many an orphan's water-standing eye—
Men for their sons', wives for their husbands',
And orphans for their parents' timeless death—
Shall rue the hour that ever thou wast born.
The owl shriek'd at thy birth, an evil sign ;
The night-crow cried, aboding luckless time ;
Dogs howl'd, and hideous tempests shook down trees.

.   .   .   .   .   .

Teeth hadst thou in thy head when thou wast born,

* Hume and Green.   " King Henry expired in the Tower a few days after the battle of Tewksbury.   It was generally believed that the Duke of Gloster killed him with his own hands, but the universal odium which that prince has incurred inclined perhaps the notion to aggravate his crimes without sufficient authority."—HUME'S *History*, ch. xxii.   Mr. Staunton (*Notes to the Illustrated Shakespeare*) states that the Yorkist party maintained that Henry died of a broken heart in the Tower ; but mentions the current report, that was generally believed, of Gloster having " stykked him with a dagger."

> To signify thou com'st to bite the world :
> And, if the rest be true which I have heard,
> Thou cam'st ——
>   GLOSTER.   I'll hear no more :—Die, prophet, in thy speech :
>   [*Stabs him.*]
>
> What, will the aspiring blood of Lancaster
> Sink in the ground ?   .   .. .   .   .
> O, may such purple tears be always shed
> From those that wish the downfall of our house !—Act V.

Although a man of Gloster's courage must have despised Henry's timidity, he was evidently both irritated and impressed by his words. Henry was the oldest member of the royal family, and imbued with the superstitious feelings of the times, from which Gloster himself was not entirely free. He therefore recalls other strange circumstances or stories connected with his own birth, besides those of which Henry had reminded him, which probably King Edward and Clarence never knew, or would not wish revealed. Thus Henry's last words certainly affect Gloster strangely. They, indeed, arouse neither remorse, pity, nor shame in such a breast, yet they evidently increase that hatred of mankind to which Richard yields more and more, till finally this feeling acquires complete mastery over all his thoughts and actions.

> GLOSTER.   Indeed, 'tis true that Henry told me of ;
> The midwife wonder'd : and the women cried,
> " *O, Jesus bless us, he is born with teeth !*"
> And so I was ; which plainly signified
> That I should snarl, and bite, and play the dog.
> Then, since the heavens have shap'd my body so,
> Let hell make crook'd my mind to answer it.
> I have no brother, I am like no brother :
> And this word *love*, which greybeards call divine,
> Be resident in men like one another,
> And not in me ; I am myself alone.
>
> King Henry and the prince his son are gone :
> Clarence, thy turn is next, and then the rest.—Act V.

This is the second time in this play where Gloster reveals in soliloquy those dangerous ideas and designs that were so fully developed, and so successfully accomplished, both in reality and in the play which bears his name. While any Lancastrian foes remain in the field, his most ardent energies are directed against them, but with Henry's death disappears, as he thinks, all opponents to his ambition, except his own family. They now, by the removal of their common foe, become the sole obstacles to his ambition, and he secretly contemplates their destruction, not from any anger or personal dislike, but simply because, by English law, they are interposed between him and the crown. When slaying Henry, he indeed wished the same fate to all desiring the downfall of his House ; but at the moment he uttered these awful words, he was himself its most fatal enemy. How far he really nourished ambitious or murderous designs during his brother's reign seems uncertain from history, but his subsequent career of murder and usurpation apparently inspired reasonable suspicions of his guilt in cases where it was never actually proved.

The next and last scene of this play is in London, where Edward, his queen Elizabeth, and their little son, with the Princes Gloster and Clarence, are all assembled in peaceful exultation after the late sanguinary campaign.*   Edward IV., now thinking his power secure, liberates and banishes Margaret to France, receiving a large ransom from the French king, and, believing that there remains nothing but peace and happiness before him, announces festive entertainments, with public rejoicings, celebrating the triumph of the House of York.

> KING EDWARD.   Once more we sit in England's royal throne,
> Re-purchas'd with the blood of enemies.
> What valiant foemen, like to autumn's corn,
> Have we mow'd down, in tops of all their pride !
> Two Cliffords, as the father and the son ;
> And two Northumberlands : two braver men
> Ne'er spurr'd their coursers at the trumpet's sound :
> With them the two brave bears, Warwick and Montague,
> That in their chains fetter'd the kingly lion,
> And made the forest tremble when they roar'd.
> Thus have we swept suspicion from our seat,
> And made our footstool of security.
> Come hither, Bess, and let me kiss my boy :
> Young Ned, for thee, thine uncles and myself
> Have in our armours watch'd the winter's night ;
> Went all afoot in summer's scalding heat,
> That thou might'st re-possess the crown in peace ;
> And of our labours thou shalt reap the gain.
>   GLOSTER. (*aside*)   I'll blast his harvest if your head were laid :
> For yet I am not look'd on in the world.

---

* "Though all classes of men, and in all parts of England, were divided into factions by this unhappy contest, yet the strength of the Yorkists lay in London and the neighbouring counties, and generally among the middle and lower ranks of people. And this is what might naturally be expected ; for notions of hereditary right take easy hold of the populace, who feel an honest sympathy for those whom they consider as injured, while men of noble blood and high station have a keener sense of personal duty to the sovereign, and of the baseness of deserting their allegiance."—HALLAM'S *Middle Ages*, ch. viii.

> KING EDWARD.   Clarence and Gloster, love my lovely queen
> And kiss your princely nephew, brothers both.
>   CLARENCE.   The duty that I owe unto your majesty
> I seal upon the lips of this sweet babe.
>   KING EDWARD.   Thanks, noble Clarence : worthy brother,
>   thanks.
>   GLOSTER.   And, that I love the tree from whence thou sprang'st,
> Witness the loving kiss I give the fruit :
>   (*Aside*) To say the truth, so Judas kiss'd his master ;
> And cried, " *All hail !*" whereas he meant—all harm.
>   KING EDWARD.   Now am I seated as my soul delights,
> Having my country's peace, and brothers' loves.
>
> And now what rests, but that we spend the time
> With stately triumphs, mirthful comic shows,
> Such as befit the pleasure of the court ?
> Sound drums and trumpets, banish sour annoy
> For here, I hope, begins our lasting joy.—Act V.

Thus ended for a time this terrible civil war, in which, despite the generosity usually attributed to the English character, and notwithstanding the nominal prevalence of Christianity, there was an amount of deliberate cruelty committed by the rival parties, which makes the recital, both in history and the play, a most melancholy study.*   No recognition of personal merit, no respect for honour or virtue in a political foe, appears in this dreadful contest between fellow-countrymen, who were often also near relatives.†   The one mild and truthful character of Henry VI. appears amid cruel, unscrupulous friends and foes, a complete contrast to both ; but, unfortunately, in his case, irresolution and timidity destroyed his influence, so that his many good qualities were practically useless to himself and his subjects. A ruler like his father and grandfather, who, though firm and even severe occasionally, yet detested useless cruelty,

---

* "The law relating to treason was unaltered during the fifteenth century, though throughout the Wars of the Roses, in Hall's words, 'every new revolution occasioned the attainder by Parliament of the most considerable of the adverse party.' This period has, however, left one singular mark upon the Statute Book in the shape of the statute in the reign of Henry VII., which provides in substance that obedience to a king *de facto*, but not *de jure*, shall not expose his adherents to the punishment of treason when the rightful king re-establishes himself. The words of the Act are very remarkable, and if the history of the Wars of the Roses were unknown would be unintelligible."—STEPHENS'S *English Criminal Law*, ch. xxiii.

† Yet, according to MACAULAY, England generally suffered far less than might have been expected during this long and terrible contest. "The national wealth consisted chiefly in flocks and herds, in the harvest of the year, and in the simple buildings inhabited by the people. The calamities of civil war were confined to the slaughter on the battle-field, and to a few subsequent executions and confisca-

and spared all foes when they could do so with safety to themselves, would have been well suited for this contest.* Edward IV., who carried his "party spirit" to the extent of ferocity, repeatedly ordered his victorious troops to grant no quarter ;† while Margaret, who really represented her weak husband in heading the Lancastrians, was equally relentless, though she may not have showed such a spirit of savage mockery as this play represents. At the close of this eventful tragedy, she is its most mournful and most romantic figure. She returns to France, widowed, childless, and dethroned. Almost every mental grief and disappointment sustainable by a human mind seems to have been destined for her. The play represents her as soon liberated and banished, after the war, by the triumphant Edward ; but in reality she was ransomed, after a long imprisonment in England, by the King of France, for 50,000 crowns.‡ Walter Scott's description, during her last days in France,§ is perhaps too favourable, for the chivalrous novelist certainly invests her with more nobleness and generosity than are allowed by either poet or historian.‖ The Wars of the Roses, indeed, offered little attraction to Scott's romantic mind, though he was so learned and interested in the study of history, and he never introduces them in his works.¶   But

tions. In a week the peasant was driving his team and the esquire flying his hawks over the field of Towton or Bosworth as if no extraordinary event had interrupted the regular course of human life. . . . Even while the wars of the Roses were actually raging, our country appears to have been in a happier condition than the neighbouring realms [France and Belgium] during years of profound peace."—*History of England*, c. i.

* "From no period in our annals do we turn with such weariness and disgust. Their savage battles, their ruthless executions, their shameless treasons, seem all the more terrible from the pure selfishness of the ends for which men fought ; the utter want of all nobleness and chivalry in the contest itself—of all great result in its close."—GREEN's *History of the English People*, book v.

† HUME's *History*, ch. xxii.

‡ HUME's *History*, ch. xxii.

§ *Anne of Geierstein.*

‖ "An admirable princess, but more illustrious by her undaunted spirit in adversity than by her moderation in prosperity. She seems neither to have enjoyed the virtues, nor been subject to the weaknesses, of her sex, and was as much tainted with the ferocity, as endowed with the courage, of that barbarous age in which she lived."—HUME's *History*, ch. xxii. Hume adds that she spent the rest of her life in privacy. Her presence in England during the reign of Richard III. is evidently Shakespeare's invention.

. ¶ Scott mentions having seen "our immortal Siddons" personate Queen Margaret—probably Shakespeare's fancy sketch of her in Richard III. Perhaps with the remembrance of the great poet in his mind, Scott indulgently writes of Margaret :—" If she occasionally abused victory by cruelty and revenge, she had made some atonement by the indomitable resolution with which she had supported the fiercest storms of adversity."—*Anne of Geierstein.* Yet this atonement was not likely to benefit her prisoners, whom she appears to have deliberately executed without mercy. Her insulting the Duke of York's memory by covering his head, after death, with a paper crown, proves how thoroughly this princess shared the savage spirit of her times.

the earlier crusades, and the subsequent civil wars in
England and Scotland, where with great crimes were
mingled many instances of religious devotion and chivalrous generosity, interested his mind and attracted his
fancy. Yet the cruel Wars of the Roses, repulsive alike
to the novelist and philanthropist, the poet narrates, with
wonderful force, genius, and truth, in this noble series
of "dramatic chronicles;"* while practical hisorians have,
in the main points and chief characteristics, confirmed the
grand, pictorial description which Shakespeare's genius has
bequeathed to posterity.†

* HALLAM's *Literary History*, vol. ii.
† "Shakespeare is the privileged inheritance of Englishmen of all ages and of
all times. . . . . I have learned to feel, though yet far from fully, the inexpres-
sible value of Shakespeare as an interpreter and a guide, not for his time only,
but for the present ; not only as the great seer of those sons of Anak in the six-
teenth and seventeenth centuries, but for the men of the nineteenth century."—
BREWER's *English Studies*, Essay vi.   "Of these three plays I think the second
the best."—JOHNSON's *Notes to Henry VI.*

CHAPTER XII.

KING RICHARD III.

Sketch of Play.

EDWARD IV., in the height of power and prosperity, falls dangerously ill. He distrusts and imprisons his brother Clarence, while Gloster increases his dislike to him. Soon after imprisonment, Clarence is assassinated by order of Gloster. The King dies soon after his brother's murder, and Gloster then plots against the widowed queen. He marries the Lady Anne, Prince Edward's widow, and daughter-in-law of Henry VI. Being left Regent, Gloster has supreme authority, and wins over Buckingham and Hastings, with other nobles, to his side, and imprisons his two nephews, Edward V. and the Duke of York, in the Tower, where they are secretly murdered. Lord Hastings and other noblemen were previously executed by him, while Buckingham, his most zealous adherent, will not sanction the murder of the two princes, and knowing he has mortally offended Gloster by this refusal, joins in a general rebellion. Gloster is now proclaimed King Richard III.; he captures and executes Buckingham, but the insurrection, headed by the young Earl of Richmond, becomes more and more formidable. Richard, though deserted by many adherents, encounters him at the battle of Bosworth, where he is slain, fighting desperately, and Richmond is proclaimed King by the title of Henry VII.

THIS play, throughout, is one of the most spirited of all Shakespeare's works, and, unlike *Henry VI.*, seems to have been written entirely by himself.* King Edward IV., as he had intended, is now having public rejoicings in London. All England enjoys peace under his rule, the Lancastrians are completely crushed, and not even Rich-

---

* "The first lines of this play lift you out of the mist and confusion of the *Henry VI.* plays into the sunshine of Shakepeare's genius."—FURNIVALL'S *Notes to the Royal Shakspere.*

mond's name as an aspirant to the throne is publicly mentioned.*   As in the former play, Gloster finds no pleasure in
his family's triumph, though he had been so active in promoting it.   He expresses, in still more resolute language, the
same designs he had twice previously intimated when the
renewed war with the Lancastrians had diverted his dangerous thoughts from moody reflections to martial duties.   Now
these have terminated in triumphant security, and again the
ambitious, deformed prince remains solitary and apart from
the general rejoicing.   Yet he has many reasons also for
exultation.   He enjoys the king's full confidence, and is
generally respected and admired for his bravery; but the
sight of his two handsome brothers, and the brilliant, lively
court around him, inspire his restless mind with envious
dejection, which in a man so fierce and determined, soon
suggests fatal designs.†   He does not reveal his state of mind
to any confidant, but again speaks to himself in words full of
power, energy, and thought, expressing both deep vexation at
his bodily deformity, and sole relief in political ambition.

> GLOSTER.   Now is the winter of our discontent
> Made glorious summer by this sun of York ;
> And all the clouds that lower'd upon our house
> In the deep bosom of the ocean buried.
> Now are our brows bound with victorious wreaths ;
> Our bruised arms hung up for monuments ;
> Our stern alarums chang'd to merry meetings ;
> Our dreadful marches to delightful measures.
> Grim-visag'd war hath smooth'd his wrinkled front ;
> And now, instead of mounting barbed steeds,
> To fright the souls of fearful adversaries,
> He capers nimbly in a lady's chamber,
> To the lascivious pleasing of a lute.
> But I, that am not shap'd for sportive tricks,
> Nor made to court an amorous looking-glass,
> Cheated of feature by dissembling nature,
> Deform'd, unfinished, sent before my time,
> Into this breathing world, scarce half made up,
> And that so lamely and unfashionable

* "Edward IV.'s love of pleasure, his affability, his courage and beauty, gave
him credit with his subjects which he had no real virtue to challenge.   The latter
years of his reign were passed in repose at home, after scenes of unparalleled
convulsions, and in peace abroad, after more than a century of expensive warfare."—HALLAM'S *Middle Ages*, ch. viii.

† "He was close and secret, a deep dissembler, lowly of countenance, arro-
gant óf heart, outwardly companionable where he inwardly hated, not letting to
kiss whom he thought to kill; despiteful and cruel not for evil will always but
often for ambition, and either for the surety or increase of his estate.   He spared
no man's death whose life withstood his purpose."—SIR T. MORE'S *Life of
Richard III.*

That dogs bark at me as I halt by them ;—
Why, I, in this weak, piping time of peace,
Have no delight to pass away the time,
Unless to see my shadow in the sun,
And descant on mine own deformity.
And therefore, since I cannot prove a lover
To entertain these fair, well-spoken days,
I am determined to prove a villain,
And hate the idle pleasures of these days.
Plots have I laid, inductions dangerous,
By drunken prophecies, libels, and dreams,
To set my brother Clarence and the king
In deadly hate the one against the other.—Act I.

He perceives how superior his brothers and their courtiers
are to himself in every external gift, and yet how inferior
they all are to him in mental power, energy, and knowledge
of character. The first blow he strikes at his own family is
by increasing the king's distrust of Clarence, who is soon
imprisoned in the Tower. Richard finds no trouble in caus-
ing his arrest, for Edward had long suspected Clarence,
more in reality even than is represented in the play.* The
brothers King Edward and Clarence dislike one another,
while each admires and trusts Gloster, who on his part desires
the destruction of both. These facts described by Shakespeare, and confirmed by history, show the first signs of
Richard's marvellous dissimulation, in which he was perhaps
unrivalled in mediæval history, save by Cæsar Borgia, and
was probably not much inferior to Tiberius Cæsar. He succeeded in deceiving his elder brothers, who knew him from
childhood, as thoroughly as if they had been comparative
strangers, which was a sure proof of his extraordinary power
of deception.

The first scene describes Gloster meeting the luckless
Clarence on his way to the Tower as a state prisoner.
Richard, the chief, but not the only, cause of his disgrace,
professes much sympathy, which his brother fully believes in,
still thinking him his sincere friend.

GLOSTER. But what's the matter, Clarence ? may I know ?
CLARENCE. Yea, Richard, when I know ; for I protest
As yet I do not
GLOSTER. Why, this it is when men are ruled by women ;
'Tis not the king that sends you to the Tower ;

* "Clarence, by all his services in deserting Warwick, had never been able to
regain the king's friendship. . . . . He was still regarded at court as a man of
dangerous and fickle character, and the imprudent openness and violence of his
temper tended extremely to multiply his enemies and to incense them against
him."—HUME'S *History*, ch. xxii.

My Lady Grey, his wife, Clarence, 'tis she
That tempers him to this extremity.
We are not safe, Clarence, we are not safe
   CLARENCE. By Heaven, I think there is no man secure
But the queen's kindred.
   GLOSTER. We are the queen's abjects, and must obey.
Brother, farewell : I will unto the king ;
And whatsoe'er you will employ me in,
I will perform, to enfranchise you.
Meantime, this deep disgrace in brotherhood
Touches me deeper than you can imagine.
   CLARENCE. I know it pleases neither of us well.
   GLOSTER. Well, your imprisonment shall not be long.
Meantime, have patience.   [*Exeunt* CLARENCE *and guard.*
   GLOSTER. Go, tread the path that thou shalt ne'er return,
Simple, plain Clarence ! I do love thee so,
That I will shortly send thy soul to heaven,
If heaven will take the present at our hands.—Act. I.

In reality, Clarence was imprisoned owing to the combined
malevolence of the queen and Gloster, who, though hating
each other, were allied against him ;* but Shakespeare makes
Richard admit having set the king against Clarence, whilst
he is also plotting against the queen and her relatives. Clarence declares he is imprisoned because his name is George,
and that the king fears a prophecy he has heard that his sons
should be slain or disinherited by a man whose name began
with the letter G. It apparently never occurred to Edward
that Gloster's title furnished the same cause for distrust.
This absurd story may have had some historical foundation.†
But Richard's skill, and address, as well as the extraordinary confidence in himself with which he managed to inspire
both his brothers, completely shielded him from the least
suspicion of being the dangerous enemy so obscurely indicated in the prophecy. He easily convinces Clarence, therefore, that it is solely owing to the influence of the queen's faction that he is now imprisoned. Clarence, believing all he
says, goes sadly to the Tower, and Richard next meets Lord
Hastings, who is just freed from prison, and greatly disliked
by the court. Though a brave, intelligent man, he is quite
misled by Richard, who tells him that the queen's party
alone have imprisoned both him and Clarence. Hastings
mentions the king's increasing illness, to whom he is going to

* HUME'S *History.*
  † Hume, after mentioning this strange fear of the king's, says that it was not
impossible that in those ignorant times such a silly reason might have had some
influence in the arrest and prosecution of Clarence, but that it was more likely
the story was a subsequent invention, and founded on the murder of Edward's
children by Gloster.—Ch. xxii.

pay his respects.   Richard, telling him to go before, remains behind, and, when alone, reveals, as usual, his plans
and hopes in a few expressive words which no one hears.

HASTINGS.   The king is sickly, weak, and melancholy,
And his physicians fear him mightily.
   GLOSTER   Go you before, and I will follow you. [*Exit* HASTINGS.
   GLOSTER.   He cannot live, I hope ; and must not die
Till George be pack'd with post-horse up to heaven.
I'll in, to urge his hatred more to Clarence,
With lies well steel'd with weighty arguments :
And, if I fail not in my deep intent,
Clarence hath not another day to live :
Which done, God take King Edward to his mercy,
And leave the world for me to bustle in !
For then I'll marry Warwick's youngest daughter.
What though I killed her husband and her father,
The readiest way to make the wench amends
Is to become her husband and her father.

   .   .   .   .   .   .

But yet I run before my horse to market :
Clarence still breathes ; Edward still lives and reigns ;
When they are gone then must I count my gains.   [*Exit.*

The next person he meets is the Lady Anne, widow of
Prince Edward, attending her father-in-law, Henry VI.'s
funeral, whose remains were removed to Chertsey from St.
Paul's.*   The interview between Richard and the young
widow is strange and unnatural, apparently introduced
merely to illustrate, with all Shakespeare's power, Gloster's
marvellous power of winning over and influencing even those
persons whom he had most injured and infuriated.   He orders
the procession to stop, and Lady Anne, with something of her
father Warwick's spirit, at first boldly reproaches him for
having caused all her misery.   Had Richard made a stern or
brutal answer, Anne, in her state of indignant excitement,
might have defied him ; but, on the contrary, he humbly
flatters her, declaring he has been long in love with her, and
that his passion has urged him on to crime.   Anne, on hearing this, becomes scornful, incredulous, yet less angry.   He
instantly perceives the change, and perseveres in flattery till
she is quite puzzled, and doubtful whether to believe him or
not.   He finally offers her his sword, and, falling on his knees,
bids her slay him on the spot if she wishes.

* " Shakespeare's character of Queen Anne is imaginary, and not well imagined."
—COURTENAY'S *Commentaries.*   Hallam (*Literary History*) says that in Richard
III. Shakespeare introduces no imaginary personages, and there may have been
some resemblance between the real Lady Anne and Shakespeare's portrait, though
the scene between her and Richard is evidently an invention and scarcely possible.

GLOSTER.   If thy revengeful heart cannot forgive,
Lo ! here I lend thee this sharp-pointed sword ;
Which if thou please to hide in this true breast,
And let the soul forth that adoreth thee,
I lay it naked to thy deadly stroke,
And humbly beg the death upon my knee.   [*Lays his breast open.*
Nay, do not pause ; 'twas I did kill King Henry,—
　　　　　　　　　　　[*She offers at it with his sword.*
But 'twas thy beauty that provoked me.
Nay, now despatch ; 'twas I that kill'd King Henry.
　　　　　　　　　　　[*She again offers at his breast.*
But 'twas thy heavenly face that set me on.   [*She lets fall the sword.*
Take up the sword again, or take up me.
　ANNE.   Arise, dissembler : though I wish thy death,
I will not be thy executioner.—Act I.

At this sight, her anger, which gradually diminishes during
his flattery, disappears ; she bids him put up his sword, and,
accepting his ring, agrees to meet him again.*   After she is
gone, Gloster, when alone, exultingly rejoices at his success
with her, his faith in his power of deceit being confirmed,
and his sardonic spirit highly amused at such a complete
triumph over this vain and foolish princess.

　　GLOSTER.   Was ever woman in this humour woo'd?
Was ever woman in this humour won?
I'll have her, but I will not keep her long.
What ! I, that kill'd her husband and his father,
To take her in her heart's extremest hate ;
With curses in her mouth, tears in her eyes ;

　　．　　　．　　　．　　　．　　　．

And I nothing to back my suit withal,
But the plain devil, and dissembling looks,
And yet to win her—all the world to nothing   Ha !
Hath she forgot already that brave prince,
Edward, her lord, whom I, some three months since,
Stabb'd in my angry mood at Tewksbury?

　　．　　　．　　　．　　　．　　　．　　　．

Upon my life, she finds, although I cannot,
Myself to be a marvellous proper man.
I'll be at charges for a looking-glass ;
And entertain some score or two of tailors
To study fashions to adorn my body :

　　．　　　．　　　．

* "Richard, with his distorted and withered body—his arm shrunk like ‘a
blasted sapling’—is yet a sublime figure, by virtue of his energy of will and tremendous power of intellect.   All obstacles give way before him—the courage of
men and the bitter animosity of women."—DOWDEN'S *Shakespeare's Mind and
Art.*

Shine out, fair sun, till I have bought a glass,
That I may see my shadow as I pass.—Act I.

The next scene introduces Queen Elizabeth, with her brother and friend, Lords Rivers and Grey. These men, with her son Dorset and others, form a strong faction about the king, but cannot shake his confidence in Gloster, though they dislike Clarence equally, and, with Richard's assistance, have had him imprisoned ; but, though Gloster and this party are allied against Clarence, they detest each other. The queen, her son, and some courtiers now compose one faction, while the nobles, Buckingham, Hastings, and others jealous of the queen's relatives, allow themselves to be directed by Gloster, who uses both parties as tools for his own ambitious designs. These, as yet, he has not revealed. The queen now foresees her husband's approaching death, and dreads the future, for, when he is gone, Gloster will be the most powerful man in the kingdom during the minority of her two sons, the Princes Edward and Richard, and she knows Gloster's hatred to all her family, as well as his great influence over the king.

QUEEN ELIZABETH. If he were dead, what would betide of me?
LORD GREY. No other harm but loss of such a lord.
QUEEN ELIZABETH. The loss of such a lord includes all harm.
GREY. The heavens have bless'd you with a goodly son,
To be your comforter when he is gone.
QUEEN ELIZABETH. Ah, he is young ; and his minority
Is put into the trust of Richard Gloster,
A man that loves not me, nor none of you.
RIVERS. Is it concluded he shall be protector?
QUEEN ELIZABETH. It is determined, not concluded yet ;
But so it must be if the king miscarry.—Act I.

Buckingham, who, though friendly to Gloster, is not completely his tool, now informs the queen that Edward longs to make peace between her party and his brother Gloster, and requests them all to come into his presence. Elizabeth, nervous and anxious, foresees that as soon as the king is dead her troubles will begin, when Gloster, Hastings, and Dorset enter. Richard, with the air of injured innocence, reproaches both the queen and her friends for their hostility, complaining that they misrepresent him to the king. The queen and Rivers try to defend themselves, but are no match for the keen-witted Gloster, whose royal rank, united to his extraordinary talents, give him a decided advantage over every opponent.

GLOSTER.   They do me wrong, and I will not endure it :
Who are they that complain unto the king,
That I, forsooth, am stern and love them not?
By holy Paul, they love his grace but lightly
That fill his ears with such dissentious rumours.
Because I cannot flatter, and speak fair,

   .   .   .   .   .   .

I must be held a rancorous enemy.
Cannot a plain man live, and think no harm,
But thus his simple truth must be abus'd
By silken, sly, insinuating Jacks ?
    GREY.   To whom in all this presence speaks your grace ?
    GLOSTER.   To thee, that hast nor honesty nor grace.
When have I injur'd thee ? when done thee wrong ?—
Or thee ?—or thee ?—or any of your faction ?
A plague upon you all !   His royal grace—
Whom God preserve better than you would wish !—
Cannot be quiet scarce a breathing-while,
But you must trouble him with lewd complaints.
    QUEEN ELIZABETH.   Come, come, we know your meaning,
       brother Gloster ;
You envy my advancement, and my friends' ;
God grant we never may have need of you !
    GLOSTER.   Meantime, God grants that we have need of you :
Our brother is imprison'd by your means,
Myself disgrac'd, and the nobility
Held in contempt. . . . . .
    QUEEN ELIZABETH.   By Him that rais'd me to this careful
       height,
I never did incense his majesty
Against the Duke of Clarence, but have been
An earnest advocate to plead for him.
    GLOSTER.   You may deny that you were not the cause
Of my Lord Hastings' late imprisonment.
    RIVERS.   She may, my lord ; for——
    GLOSTER.   She may, Lord Rivers ?—why, who knows not so ?
She may do more, sir, than denying that :
She may help you to many fair preferments ;
And then deny her aiding hand therein,
And lay those honours on your high deserts.
    QUEEN ELIZABETH.   My Lord of Gloster, I have too long
       borne
Your blunt upbraidings and your bitter scoffs :
By Heaven, I will acquaint his majesty
With those gross taunts I often have endur'd.—Act I.

In the midst of this dispute, their common foe, Queen
Margaret, appears on the scene, grimly rejoicing at these
quarrels among the York party, and reproaching them alike
with furious bitterness.   Gloster himself is less able to despise

ier reproaches than those of others, for Margaret, amid her
ierce indignation, constantly ridicules his bodily deformity,
vhich he cannot deny nor remember without intense vexa-
ion and even grief.   Margaret's appearance at this time in
he palace is imaginary, for she never returned to England
.fter her banishment, and, even if she had, would surely not
iave obtained access to the palace of her enemies, like a
irivileged person belonging to the court.*   Her sex alone
iad saved her life, for none of the executed Lancastrians
iad shown more cruelty to the Yorkists than she ; yet this
trange scene describes a violent interchange of reproaches,
n which Margaret certainly gets the "last word," denounc-
ng Gloster with peculiar bitterness, and warning his ally,
3uckingham, against him, as she perceives Buckingham's
.ttachment to Gloster, and, though no longer caring to win
iim over to her side, having no party to lead or advocate, she
.pprehends that his devotion to the crafty, murderous prince
vill surely cause his destruction.

> QUEEN MARGARET.   O Buckingham, take heed of yonder dog ;
> Look, when he fawns, he bites ; and, when he bites,
> His venom tooth will rankle to the death :
> Have not to do with him, beware of him;
> Sin, death, and hell have set their marks on him ;
> And all their ministers attend on him.
> > GLOSTER.   What doth she say, my Lord of Buckingham ?
> > BUCKINGHAM.   Nothing that I respect, my gracious lord.
> > QUEEN MARGARET.   What, dost thou scorn me for my gentle
> > counsel,
> And soothe the devil that I warn thee from ?
> O, but remember this another day,
> When he shall split thy very heart with sorrow ;
> And say, poor Margaret was a prophetess.
> Live each of you the subjects to his hate,
> And he to yours, and all of you to God's ! [*Exit.*]—Act I.

;he leaves them silenced and even appalled by her vehe-
nent denunciations, as well as by her evident knowledge of
heir characters and designs.   When she is gone, Gloster,
vith consummate duplicity, pretends to regret having ever
njured her, and reminds Queen Elizabeth that she is now
njoying "all the vantage of her wrong."   She and her friends
.re utterly unable to answer or repel his charges, as he
raftily lays all the blame of Clarence's imprisonment on
hem, whereas he himself is really his brother's worst enemy.

* Mr. Courtenay notices the absurdity of introducing Margaret here, "who
ad at no time been at large in Edward's court, and was now in France."—*Com-
ientaries on Shakespeare's Historical Plays.*

A crafty lawyer—Sir William Catesby, afterwards the most obedient of all Gloster's adherents—now summons the whole party to the king's presence, but Richard remains alone. He reveals, in a short soliloquy, how successfully he has imputed Clarence's misfortunes to the enmity of the queen's faction, thus deceiving Buckingham, Hastings, and others who are attached both to Clarence and himself, but who hate the queen's party.

> GLOSTER. I do the wrong, and first begin to brawl.
> The secret mischiefs that I set abroach
> I lay unto the grievous charge of others.
> Clarence—whom I, indeed, have cast in darkness—
> I do beweep to many simple gulls ;
> Namely, to Stanley, Hastings, Buckingham ;
> And say, it is the queen and her allies
> That stir the king against the duke my brother.
> Now they believe it : and withal whet me
> To be reveng'd on Rivers, Dorset, Grey :
> But then I sigh, and, with a piece of scripture,
> Tell them that God bids us do good for evil.—Act I.

Gloster then receives two hired murderers, whom he employs to slay his imprisoned brother. These ruffians demand a warrant of admission to the Tower, which he at once gives them.

> GLOSTER. But, sirs, be sudden in the execution,
> Withal obdurate, do not hear him plead :
> For Clarence is well spoken, and, perhaps,
> May move your hearts to pity, if you mark him.
> 1ST MURDERER. Tut, tut, my lord, we will not stand to prate ;
> Talkers are no good doers ; be assur'd
> We go to use our hands, and not our tongues.
> GLOSTER. Your eyes drop millstones, when fools' eyes drop tears :
> I like you, lads ;—about your business ;
> Go, go, despatch.—Act I.

Clarence is now under sentence of death, for alleged treason, which Edward in the play recalls, but he never did so in reality.* Gloster encourages his two satellites in much the same spirit as Macbeth, but in a different style, and sends them on their dreadful errand to the Tower.† This scene

---

* "The Act of Attainder of the Duke of Clarence, passed in 1477, is very long and oratorical, and after setting out at length the offences imputed to Clarence, enacts, 'that the said George, Duke of Clarence, be convicted and atteynted of high treason.' The act is followed by the appointment of the Duke of Buckingham as Lord High Steward for that occasion to do execution."—STEPHENS's *English Criminal Law*, ch. v.

† Hume states that Clarence was condemned to death by the House of Peers ; that the king appeared personally as chief accuser ; and that, after sentence of

between Gloster and the murderers is imaginary, for, though the former proved himself hardened and unscrupulous enough for any crime, he apparently had nothing to do with Clarence's death, who was executed, by the king's will, for treason, after a public trial and sentence.* The next scene describes the imprisoned Clarence talking to Brakenbury, Lieutenant of the Tower. The former, though he does not mention the fatal sentence passed on him, probably expects the worst, and has fearful dreams of being drowned· in the sea, and afterwards seeing the ghosts of his enemies.

> CLARENCE. Methought I saw a thousand fearful wracks :
> Ten thousand men that fishes gnawed upon :
> Wedges of gold, great anchors, heaps of pearl,
> Inestimable stones, unvalued jewels,
> All scatter'd in the bottom of the sea.
> Some lay in dead men's skulls ; and in those holes,
> Where eyes did once inhabit, there were crept
> (As 'twere in scorn of eyes) reflecting gems,
> Which woo'd the slimy bottom of the deep,
> And mock'd the dead bones that lay scattered by.
>
> I pass'd, methought, the melancholy flood,
> Unto the kingdom of perpetual night.
> The first that there did greet my stranger soul,
> Was my great father-in-law, renowned Warwick ;
> Who cried aloud, " What scourge for perjury·
> Can this dark monarchy afford false Clarence ? "
> And so he vanish'd : then came wandering by
> A shadow like an angel, with bright hair
> Dabbled in blood ; and he shrieked out aloud,
> " Clarence is come—false, fleeting, perjur'd Clarence—
> That stabb'd me in the field by Tewksbury ;—
> Seize on him, furies, take him to your torments."
> I trembling wak'd, and, for a season after,
> Could not believe but that I was in hell ;
> Such terrible impression made my dream.—Act I.

His agitated mind thus recalls his past career—first an ardent Yorkist, then deserting that party, and joining Warwick with the Lancastrians, and again returning to the York

death was passed upon him as a traitor, "the only favour which the king granted his brother was to leave him the choice of his death, and he was privately drowned in a butt of malmsy wine in the Tower—a whimsical choice—which implies that he had an extraordinary passion for that liquor."—Ch. xxii. Howard Staunton, however, disbelieves this strange story (*Notes to 'the Illustrated Shakespeare*), and adds that Clarence's disgrace was chiefly effected by the queen's relatives. Gloster was certainly not his murderer, though he was his enemy, and doubtless desired his death, as Clarence was among the many obstacles to his ambition.

* HUME'S *History*.

faction, of whom he became one of the fiercest champions, as he was said to have joined his brothers in slaying their brave young captive, Prince Edward, after Tewksbury. This cruel, wanton, and indefensible act can only be explained, though not palliated, by their recollections of the insults offered to their father by the prince's mother, whom, though she was then their captive, they were deterred, by the usages of war, from putting to death, owing to her sex alone. Clarence, evidently a man of fickle, wayward character, not, perhaps, deliberately cruel, but capable of any atrocity when excited, now in the gloomy solitude of a prison, recalls the stirring scenes, grand characters, and terrible events which he had known and witnessed. In sleep, these recollections return with the terrific force of reality, mingled with wild fancies, and his scared senses, when awake, urge and perhaps force him, while trembling from their agitation, to tell his dreams to the astonished Brakenbury. The scenes of the late civil war, with its attendant horrors'; Warwick's grand figure, whose powerful mind had once so completely ruled him ; and the heroic form of the captive prince whom he had so basely stabbed, again appear in dreamy visions, animated by the same passions of wrath and defiance which he remembered when he last saw them in active life. But he no longer defies them in return— no longer triumphs, or rejoices at their defeat ; for he is now imprisoned, and condemned by that very prince—his own brother—for whose cause he has risked his life and committed both perjury and cruelty.

> CLARENCE. O, Brakenbury, I have done those things—
> Which now bear evidence against my soul—
> For Edward's sake ; and see how he requites me !
> I pray thee, gentle keeper, stay by me ;
> My soul is heavy, and I fain would sleep.—Act I.

Thus, overcome by recollections of the past, and oppressed alike by the gloom of the present and the peril of the future, Clarence entreats the Lieutenant to stay with him, and again falls asleep. While he is sleeping, the two murderers enter, show their warrant to Brakenbury, who reads that he is ordered to deliver Clarence to them, and departs in horrified apprehension to the king. The assassins, when alone with their sleeping victim, have a strange talk together—the one reluctant to commit the crime for which he is hired, the other mentioning his promised reward, and urging him to keep his engagement, and despise his conscience, which, however, rather troubles his comrade.

2ND MURDERER.   I'll not meddle with it, it is a dangerous thing,
it makes a man a coward : a man cannot steal but it accuseth him ;
'tis a blushing shamefaced spirit that mutinies in a man's bosom; it
fills one full of obstacles : it made me once restore a purse of gold
that by chance I found ; it beggars any man that keeps it : it is turned
out of towns and cities as a dangerous thing ; and every man that
means to live well endeavours to trust to himself, and live without it.
—Act I.

After these curious remarks on the disadvantages of conscience to gentlemen of their profession, these wretches agree
to strike their victim on the head, and throw him into a butt
of malmsey wine in the next room.   As they decide on this
"excellent device," Clarence wakes, asking his keeper for
some wine, when he perceives his two savage-looking visitors,
whose harsh voices startle him.   He at once guesses their purpose, and pleads for his life, being unarmed, and not contemplating resistance, as some might have attempted even in his
case.   During this scene, Clarence again shows that implicit
confidence in Gloster which both King Edward and he
always reposed in their treacherous brother.

CLARENCE.   If you are hir'd for meed, go back again,
And I will send you to my brother Gloster ;
Who shall reward you better for my life
Than Edward will for tidings of my death.
  2ND MURDERER.   You are deceiv'd, your brother Gloster hates
    you.
  CLARENCE.   O, no ; he loves me, and he holds me dear ;
Go you to him from me.
  BOTH MURDERERS.   Ay, so we will.
  CLARENCE.   Tell him, when that our princely father York
Bless'd his three sons with his victorious arms,
And charg'd us from his soul to love each other,
He little thought of this divided friendship ;
Bid Gloster think on this, and he will weep.
  1ST MURDERER.   Ay, millstones, as he lesson'd us to weep.
  CLARENCE.   O, do not slander him, for he is kind.
  1ST MURDERER.   Right, as snow in harvest.—Come, you de-
    ceive yourself :
'Tis he that sends us to destroy you here.
  CLARENCE.   It cannot be, for he bewept my fortunes ;
And hugg'd me in his arms, and swore, with sobs,
That he would labour my delivery.—Act I.

The murderers, who already understand Gloster better than
his brothers do, though they knew him from infancy, grimly
ridicule Clarence's extraordinary confidence in the arch-
deceiver, and finally reveal to his incredulous mind that his

trusted brother is his murderer. They also reproach the luckless duke with previous treachery to the Lancastrians, and with slaying Prince Edward. These taunts seem hardly natural in such villains, unless, by recalling Clarence's crimes, they strive to harden themselves against him. The latter, trying to excuse himself, again pleads for his life, and apparently cannot believe that Gloster is his enemy, when the assassins, becoming impatient for their reward, stab him to death. The one whose peculiar ideas about conscience have not quite extinguished it even in his breast, repents his crime, and, bidding his associate take his fee with his own, leaves him in disgust. The other, who is utterly hardened, then takes Clarence's body away, meaning to conceal it till he hears more from Gloster ; and this atrocious crime ends the first act.

The second introduces the invalid king, with his wife and her relatives, Dorset and Rivers, together with Buckingham, Hastings, and other courtiers. Edward, who feels he has only a short time to live, earnestly wishes to guard his wife and sons from future dangers, but he has no more idea than Clarence had of Gloster's enmity, and, on the contrary, believes him to be his most valuable friend. The king is so anxious to prevent all danger to his heir's future authority that he vainly tries by every means to obtain the custody of the young Earl of Richmond, the last hope of the subdued Lancastrians.* But that future king now remains safe in Brittany, and never visits England during the reign of the jealous monarch.

Edward now imagines, and fondly hopes, that if he can publicly reconcile his queen's unpopular relatives with his brother Gloster, Buckingham, Hastings, and the chief nobles in his court, he will thus enable his sons to enjoy their respective hereditary rights, and that he will then die in peace. Probably his earnest command and even entreaty, when almost in a dying state, induces these haughty nobles to gratify their departing sovereign by consenting to at least an outward form of reconciliation.† Buckingham and Hastings accordingly declare their allegiance to the queen, and their friendship with her brother and son, Rivers and Dorset.

KING EDWARD. You have been factious one against the other.

---

* HUME's *History*.

† "Edward took care in his last illness to summon together several of the leaders on both sides. . . . . He recommended to them peace and unanimity during the tender years of his son, and engaged them to embrace each other with all the appearance of the most cordial reconciliation. But this temporary or feigned agreement lasted no longer than the king's life, after whose death each party, by separate messages, sought the Duke of Gloster's favour."—HUME's *History*, ch. xxiii.

Wife, love Lord Hastings, let him kiss your hand ;
And what you do, do it unfeignedly.
  QUEEN ELIZABETH.   There Hastings ; I will never more
      remember
Our former hatred, so thrive I and mine !
  KING EDWARD.   Dorset, embrace him ;—Hastings, love lord
      marquis.
  DORSET.   This interchange of love, I here protest,
Upon my part shall be inviolable.
  HASTINGS.   And so swear I.   [*They embrace.*
  KING EDWARD.   Now, princely Buckingham, seal thou this
      league
With thy embracements to my wife's allies,
And make me happy in your unity.
  BUCKINGHAM.   Whenever Buckingham doth turn his hate
On you or yours [*to the* QUEEN], but with all duteous love
Doth cherish you and yours, God punish me
With hate in those where I expect most love!
When I have most need to employ a friend,
And most assured that he is a friend,
Deep, hollow, treacherous, and full of guile,
Be he unto me !—This do I beg of heaven,
When I am cold in zeal to you or yours.
                          [*Embracing* RIVERS, *&c.*
  KING EDWARD.   A pleasing cordial, princely Buckingham,
Is this thy vow unto my sickly heart.—Act II.

Edward is cheered by this sight, when Gloster enters, and
makes the same promises of friendship to the queen and her
party, though in more eloquent language, of which he is
always a master.

          GLOSTER.   Among this princely heap, if any here
      By false intelligence, or wrong surmise,
      Hold me a foe ;
      If I unwittingly, or in my rage,
      Have aught committed that is hardly borne
      By any in this presence, I desire
      To reconcile me to his friendly peace :
      'Tis death to me to be at enmity ;
      I hate it, and desire all good men's love.
      First, madam, I entreat true peace of you,
      Which I will purchase with my duteous service ;
      Of you, my noble cousin Buckingham,
      If ever any grudge were lodg'd between us ;
      Of you, Lord Rivers, and Lord Grey, of you,
      That all without desert have frown'd on me ;
      Dukes, earls, lords, gentlemen ; indeed, of all.
      I do not know that Englishman alive

> With whom my soul is any jot at odds
> More than the infant that is born to-night.
> I thank my God for my humility.—Act II.

The queen expresses grateful thanks, when Gloster announces Clarence's death, which surprises the whole assembly. Edward declares that his previous sentence on his brother "was reversed," but Gloster replies that the reprieve came too late, and the whole assembled company, lately in peaceful reconciliation, are astonished and horrified. At this moment Stanley enters, entreating the king, according to the custom of those times, to pardon his servant, who has slain a man in a quarrel. The sick and melancholy king, while granting the request, sadly observes that no one had pleaded for the imprisoned and doomed Clarence, and he deeply regrets his own unreasonable distrust of his unfortunate brother, who, though once his enemy, had since served his cause at the risk of his life.

> KING EDWARD. Have I a tongue to doom my brother's death,
> And shall that tongue give pardon to a slave?
> My brother slew no man, his fault was thought,
> And yet his punishment was cruel death.
> Who sued to me for him? who, in my wrath,
> Kneel'd at my feet, and bade me be advis'd?
> Who spoke of brotherhood? who spoke of love?
> Who told me, how the poor soul did forsake
> The mighty Warwick, and did fight for me?
> Who told me in the field at Tewksbury,
> When Oxford had me down, he rescu'd me,
> And said, "*Dear brother, live, and be a king?*"
> All this from my remembrance brutish wrath
> Sinfully pluck'd, and not a man of you
> Had so much grace to put it in my mind.
> But when your carters, or your waiting-vassals,
> Have done a drunken slaughter, and defac'd
> The image of our dear Redeemer,
> You straight are on your knees for pardon, pardon;
> And I, unjustly too, must grant it you :—
> But for my brother not a man would speak.
> O God! I fear thy justice will take hold
> On me, and you, and mine, and yours, for this.
> Come, Hastings, help me to my closet. Ah! poor Clarence!—
> Act II.

The saddened, invalid king then retires with Hastings, and never re-appears in the play.

The next scene describes the king's mother, the old Duchess of York, with Clarence's son and daughter, her grandchildren.

She probably knows of their father's death, yet vaguely denies the report to the children, and again apparently believes it. She deplores the king's illness, and deeply suspects Gloster, whom she evidently and naturally knows better than any of his other relatives, and even hints to the children that he is a cunning dissembler, when Queen Elizabeth, with Lords Rivers and Dorset, enter in great terror, announcing the king's death. The whole party now, from the aged duchess to Clarence's little children, lament the loss of their relatives, when Gloster, attended by Buckingham and Hastings, join them. Buckingham says that Gloster and he are now going to Ludlow, to escort the late king's eldest son to London, where he will be crowned as Edward V., Gloster being appointed Regent during the prince's minority by 'Edward IV.'s will. With assumed courtesy, Gloster asks both his mother and sister-in-law to assist him in receiving the young king, and both agree to do so. All the party then leave the room, and Gloster and Buckingham are, for the first time in the play, alone together.· Buckingham is devoted to Gloster, and, detesting the queen's faction, wishes to place the king in the Regent's power, without apparently suspecting that the latter aims at being king himself, but believing he will be satisfied with almost absolute power as Regent. Gloster calls Buckingham his "other self," his "oracle," &c., declaring he will be guided like a child by his advice. This language, he evidently knows, both pleases and deceives Buckingham, whose friendly assistance he requires for some time before he can be safely dispensed with; for, proud and obstinate as Buckingham is in some respects, he is yet a man of great influence. All Gloster's enemies are also his own, which fact forms a strong bond of union between them. The next scene introduces some London citizens talking over the news, lamenting the king's death, regretting the extreme youth of the new monarch, and utterly distrusting the Regent Gloster. The latter, though so accomplished a dissembler, apparently never deceived the lower orders as successfully as he did the nobility. With the former, indeed, he was never popular, partly, perhaps, owing to his deformed appearance, or to his seldom trying to propitiate them. The nobility, and even his own relatives, he evidently deceived, ruled, and destroyed, with wonderful success, but these citizens believe and call him "full of danger," and separate with sad forebodings about the future state of England under such a Regent.

The last scene of the first act describes the old Duchess of York, with the widowed queen and her clever second son, together with the Archbishop of York. The young prince,

evidently a child of rare intelligence, wit, and vivacity, eagerly
talks to his fond grandmother about his uncle Gloster, whom
he dislikes and suspects with a keen penetration beyond his
years.

> YORK.   Grandam, one night, as we did sit at supper,
> My uncle Rivers talk'd how I did grow
> More than my brother; "*Ay*," quoth my uncle Gloster,
> "*Small herbs have grace, great weeds do grow apace :* "
> And since, methinks, I would not grow so fast,
> Because sweet flowers are slow, and weeds make haste.
>   DUCHESS.   Good faith, good faith, the saying did not hold
> In him that did object the same to thee :
> He was the wretched'st thing, when he was young,
> So long a-growing, and so leisurely,
> That, if this were a rule, he should be gracious.
>   YORK.   Now, by my troth, if I had been remember'd,
> I could have given my uncle's grace a flout,
> That should have nearer touched his growth than he did mine.
>   DUCHESS. How, my pretty York? I prithee, let me hear it.
>   YORK.   Marry, they say, my uncle grew so fast,
> That he could gnaw a crust at two hours old ;
> 'Twas full two years ere I could get a tooth.
> Grandam, this would have been a biting jest.—Act II.

While they are conversing, Dorset enters with the alarming
news that the queen's brother, Rivers, with his friends,
Lord Grey and Sir Thomas Vaughan, have been sent prisoners to the Tower, by the Regent's orders. The queen
and the duchess both foresee coming dangers, as they alike
abhor and dread their terrible son and brother-in-law.

> QUEEN ELIZABETH.   Ah me, I see the downfall of my house !
> The tiger now hath seiz'd the gentle hind.
> Welcome destruction, blood, and massacre !
> I see, as in a map, the end of all.
>   DUCHESS.   Accursed and unquiet wrangling days,
> How many of you have mine eyes beheld !
>   QUEEN ELIZABETH.   Come, come, my boy, we will to sanctuary.
>   DUCHESS.   Stay, I will go with you.
>   QUEEN ELIZABETH.   You have no cause.
>   ARCHBISHOP.   My gracious lady, go,
> And thither bear your treasure and your goods.
> For my part, I'll resign unto your grace
> The seal I keep : and so betide to me
> As well I tender you, and all of yours !
> Go, I'll conduct you to the sanctuary.—Act II.

The queen, dreading lest her little son York should next be

imprisoned by his uncle Gloster, takes him with her to a
sanctuary.   Her mother-in-law, the Duchess of York, accompanies her, while the archbishop advises them to take their
treasures there, and declares that he will protect the endangered
prince with all his clerical influence.

Act III. describes the young king's entrance into London,
where he is welcomed by his uncle Gloster and his adherent,
Buckingham. The prince, grieved at the arrest of Rivers,
says, in reply to Gloster, that he wishes he had more uncles
to welcome him.   His vexation at the arrests of his relatives
on this occasion is confirmed by history.* Gloster vainly
declares to his incredulous mind that his mother's relations
are hostile to him, but the prince, from the first, distrusts
Gloster, and longs to see his brother York.   Hastings, however, instead of bringing the latter with him, as expected, now
announces his detention in the sanctuary by the apprehensive
queen.   Upon this news, Buckingham asks Cardinal Bourchier and Hastings to prevail, either by persuasion or force,
on the queen to send York to meet his brother.   They agree,
and return to the sanctuary for this purpose. In their absence,
the young king first shows, in questions and remarks about
the Tower, his remarkable spirit and intelligence.   Although
annoyed when told he is to spend the night there, he convinces his two companions, Gloster and Buckingham, by his
language, of his rare, precocious ability, which, unhappily,
makes his uncle Gloster all the more anxious to destroy him.
During the prince's intelligent inquiries and shrewd remarks,
Gloster, who remains near him, like a dark shadow, observes
him closely.   His crafty mind easily perceives the youth's
talent, and, being not free from superstition, despite his practical nature, he predicts his nephew's untimely death, owing
to his precocity.

PRINCE.   I do not like the Tower, of any place:—
Did Julius Cæsar build that place, my lord?
GLOSTER.   He did, my gracious lord, begin that place;
Which, since, succeeding ages have re-edified.
PRINCE.   Is't upon record, or else reported
Successively from age to age, he built it?
BUCKINGHAM.   Upon record, my gracious lord.
PRINCE.   But say, my lord, it were not registered;
Methinks, the truth should live from age to age,
As 'twere retail'd to all posterity,
Even to the general all-ending day.
GLOSTER (*aside*).   So wise, so young, they say, do ne'er live long.
PRINCE.   That Julius Cæsar was a famous man:
With what his valour did enrich his wit,

* HUME'S *History*, ch. xxiii.

His wit set down to make his valour live ;
Death makes no conquest of this conqueror ;
For now he lives in fame, though not in life.
I'll tell you what, my cousin Buckingham,—
   BUCKINGHAM.   What, my gracious lord ?
   PRINCE.   An if I live to be a man,
I'll win our ancient rights in France again,
Or die a soldier, as I lived a king.
   GLOSTER (*aside*).   Short summers lightly have a forward spring.—
Act III.

The little Duke of York now appears with Hastings and
the cardinal, who have almost forcibly brought him from the
sanctuary against his mother's will, she naturally fearing the
worst when told that her sons are to be placed henceforth
under the care of their uncle.   Shakespeare does not describe
the scene where York is taken from his mother, but even in
the grave pages of history it is sufficiently pathetic.*   Apparently, however, the boy is not fully aware of his danger, for he
cheerfully greets his elder brother, and has a curious conversation with Gloster.   York is evidently more fearless and
ready-witted than his thoughtful, studious elder brother.
His keen intelligence, as well as his mother's fears, warn
him that Gloster is an enemy, while the bold spirit of his
race fully animates him even at his early age.   Accordingly,
he questions and answers his crafty uncle with mingled wit,
sarcasm, and playfulness, which inspires even the hostile
Buckingham with admiring wonder.

   YORK.   I pray you, uncle, give me this dagger.
   GLOSTER.   My dagger, little cousin ? with all my heart.
   PRINCE.   A beggar, brother ?
   YORK.   Of my kind uncle, that I know will give ;
And, being a toy, which is no grief to give.
   GLOSTER.   A greater gift than that I'll give my cousin.
   YORK.   A greater gift ?   O, that's the sword to it.
   GLOSTER.   Ay, gentle cousin, were it light enough.
   YORK.   O then, I see, you'll part but with light gifts ;
In weightier things you'll say a beggar, nay.
   GLOSTER.   What, would you have my weapon, little lord ?

---

* Hume says that Cardinal Bourchier and the Archbishop of York, both men
of integrity and honour, were completely deceived by Gloster when they prevailed on the queen to surrender her son to his charge.   " She long continued
obstinate, and insisted that the Duke of York, by living in the sanctuary, was
not only secure himself, but gave security to the king ; but, finding that force, in
case of refusal, was threatened by the council, she at last complied, and produced
her son to the two prelates.   She was here, on a sudden, struck with a kind of
presage of his future fate ; she tenderly embraced him ; she bedewed him with
tears, and, bidding him an eternal adieu, delivered him, with many expressions
of regret and reluctance, into their custody."—*History of England*, ch. xxiii.

YORK.   I would, that I might thank you as you call me.
GLOSTER.   How?
YORK.   *Little.*
PRINCE EDWARD.   My Lord of York will still be cross in talk;
Uncle your grace knows how to bear with him.
YORK.   You mean, to bear me, not to bear with me:
Uncle, my brother mocks both you and me;
Because that I am little, like an ape,
He thinks that you should bear me on your shoulders.
BUCKINGHAM (*aside*).   With what a sharp-provided wit he rea-
    sons!
To mitigate the scorn he gives his uncle,
He prettily and aptly taunts himself:
So cunning, and so young, is wonderful.—Act III.

The doomed princes then depart for the Tower, the elder
calm, thoughtful, and impressively saying that he fears no
dead uncles, in reply to his brother's remark that he shall not
sleep well in the Tower, for fear of their uncle Clarence's
ghost.

After the princes leave the scene, Gloster and Buckingham
remain behind, and hold another of their private conferences,
which are becoming more and more frequent, for these dangerous men are now resolved not only to execute Rivers,
Grey, and others of the queen's party, but also to slay their
own ally, Hastings, should he refuse to join them in proclaiming Richard king.   What Buckingham wishes done with
the princes does not seem clear.   He is evidently eager for
their exclusion from the throne, and probably hopes they
may be peacefully set aside, and allowed to live in banishment
or captivity.   In history, he seems to have aided Gloster
throughout, or at least till after their assassination; but his
share in that crime, though suspected, was never proved.*
He is now inspired more by hatred to the queen's party than
enmity to the princes; yet increases Gloster's wrath against
them by asking if " this little prating York was not incensed
by his subtle mother " to taunt him.   To this question Gloster replies eagerly, while admitting the rare intelligence of
this child,—

> No doubt, no doubt: O, 'tis a parlous boy;
> Bold, quick, ingenious, forward, capable;
> He's all the mother's, from the top to toe.

Buckingham unsuspiciously answers,—

> Well, let them rest.

* HUME'S *History*, ch. xxiii, xxiv.

Then Gloster and he receive their accomplice Catesby, who, of all Richard's adherents throughout, was apparently the most devoted to him. They now send him to "sound" Hastings—who, they know, rejoices at the approaching executions of their common foes, Rivers, Grey, &c.—about the exclusion of the princes from the throne; for as yet their deaths, though probably resolved on in Gloster's mind, have not been suggested to any one. Gloster, eager to win over Hastings by every available means, instructs the lawyer Catesby to tempt him not only by gratifying his enmity in announcing the coming executions of his foes, but also by friendly and merry allusion to the late king's mistress, Jane Shore, now apparently living under Hastings' protection.

> GLOSTER.   Tell him, Catesby,
> His ancient knot of dangerous adversaries
> To-morrow are let blood at Pomfret Castle;
> And bid my lord, for joy at this good news,
> Give Mistress Shore one gentle kiss the more.
> BUCKINGHAM.   Good Catesby, go, effect this business soundly.
> CATESBY.   My good lords both, with all the heed I may.
> GLOSTER.   Shall we hear from you, Catesby, ere we sleep?
> CATESBY.   You shall, my lord.—Act III.

Gloster thus, through Catesby, tempts Hastings by gratifying his hatred and playfully rallying him about his lady-love at the same time, being most anxious to win over a man of his importance, and resolved to destroy him if he refuses co-operation; for he thinks Hastings too powerful to be allowed either life or liberty, except as an obedient subject of his own will. Catesby, always a willing, artful, unscrupulous intriguer, much more suited to Gloster's service than the proud, influential men whom he first employs, accepts the mission, and goes to Hastings, leaving Gloster and Buckingham again alone. Then the latter—ambitious, plotting, and eager—asks what is to be done should Hastings refuse to join them. Richard immediately answers, "Chop off his head, man," and then adds "Somewhat we will do," as if thinking Buckingham unwilling to slay a scrupulous friend as coolly as if he were an enemy. Gloster, however, soon completes his conquest of Buckingham's selfish nature by promising him the earldom of Hereford, with some property which belonged to the late king. Buckingham, delighted at this promise, says no more about Hastings, but eagerly exclaims that he will claim this gift, to which his tempter rejoins that it shall be "yielded with all kindness," and they go to supper together, cordially united.

The next scene is in Hastings' house. This nobleman has

hitherto placed the greatest confidence in both Gloster and
Buckingham, but mortally detests the queen's relatives.   He
is evidently a thorough Yorkist, holding King Edward's
memory in great respect, and anxious to see his will obeyed,
which had appointed Gloster Regent during the young king's
minority.   He therefore wishes to aid Gloster and Buckingham in all their plans, except in excluding the late monarch's
lawful heirs.   His friend, Stanley, has similar political views,
but is more suspicious of Gloster.   He hints his suspicions,
which are confirmed by a dream, through a messenger, to
Hastings, who disbelieves them, sending back the man to
Stanley, assuring him that "the boar," meaning Gloster, will
use them both kindly, and asking for his company that day
to the Tower, to meet Gloster and Buckingham.   After the
servant has gone, the tempter Catesby enters, and, with great
address, quietly hints that there will be no peace in England
till Gloster is king.*   Hastings resents this insinuation instantly, for he admires Gloster as the champion, not as the
usurper, of the House of York's rights, and indignantly
scorns the idea of excluding the lawful heirs of the late king.
With consummate art, Catesby, by Gloster's suggestion, when
perceiving Hastings' indignation, instantly soothes him by
announcing the executions of his foes at Pomfret that very
day, by Gloster's orders, mentioning this event as an additional reason for his joining the usurper.   Hastings, though
malignantly pleased at this news, is still firmly opposed to
Gloster's meditated treason.   Catesby, who knows him well,
attempts no more persuasion, but secretly considers him a
condemned man from that moment.

> CATESBY.   It is a reeling world, indeed, my lord ;
> And I believe will never stand upright,
> Till Richard wear the garland of the realm.
> HASTINGS.   How! *wear the garland!* dost thou mean the
> crown ?
> CATESBY.   Ay, my good lord.
> HASTINGS.   I'll have this crown of mine cut from my shoulders
> Ere I will see the crown so foul misplac'd.
> But canst thou guess that he doth aim at it ?
> CATESBY.   Ay, on my life ; and hopes to find you forward
> Upon his party, for the gain thereof :
> And, thereupon he sends you this good news—
> That, this same very day, your enemies,
> The kindred of the queen, must die at Pomfret.

* Hume states that Catesby was a lawyer, and "lived in great intimacy with
Hastings."   He was, therefore, doubtless selected to ascertain the real feelings of
Hastings about Gloster's intended usurpation, and Catesby evidently devoted his
knowledge of that unfortunate nobleman's character entirely to Gloster's service.
—*History of England*, ch. xxiii,

HASTINGS.   Indeed, I am no mourner for that news,
Because they have been still my enemies :
But, that I'll give my voice on Richard's side,
To bar my master's heirs in true descent,
God knows, I will not do it, to the death.

Catesby, however, listens with a calm hypocrisy worthy of
his master, Gloster, whom he probably imitates, hoping that
Hastings will always be in the same mind, yet significantly
observing, in reply to the latter's exultation at the ruin of his
enemies, that death is peculiarly terrible to those who are
unprepared for it, and believe themselves secure.

CATESBY.   'Tis a vile thing to die, my gracious lord,
When men are unprepar'd and look not for it.
    HASTINGS.   O monstrous, monstrous ! and so falls it out
With Rivers, Vaughan, Grey : and so 'twill do
With some men else, who think themselves as safe
As thou and I ; who, as thou know'st, are dear
To princely Richard and to Buckingham.
    CATESBY.   The princes both make high account of you—
(*Aside*) For they account his head upon the bridge.—Act III.

Hastings assents, while uttering vague threats against other
political opponents, apparently hoping that he will soon be
able to influence Gloster, and thus reward and punish his own
friends and enemies by his authority. Catesby listens attentively, and makes only short answers, when Stanley arrives.
This nobleman suspects Gloster for holding separate councils
with Buckingham, and shrewdly apprehends that neither he
nor Hastings know the prince's ultimate designs.

HASTINGS.   Where is your boar-spear, man ?
Fear you the boar, and go so unprovided?
    STANLEY.   My lord, good morrow ; good morrow, Catesby :—
You may jest on, but, by the holy rood,
I do not like these several councils, I.
    HASTINGS.   My lord,
I hold my life as dear as you do yours ;

Think you, but that I know our state secure,
I would be so triumphant as I am ?
    STANLEY.   The lords at Pomfret, when they rode from London,
Were jocund, and supposed their states were sure.
But yet, you see, how soon the day o'ercast.
This sudden stab of rancour I misdoubt ;
Pray God, I say, I prove a needless coward !
But come, my lord, shall we to the Tower ?

HASTINGS.   I go ; but stay :—hear you not the news ?
This day those men you talk of are beheaded.
    STANLEY.   They, for their truth, might better wear their heads,
Than some that have accus'd them wear their hats.—Act III.

The sudden arrest and condemnation of Rivers, Grey, &c.,
have much alarmed Stanley, who naturally fears that at any
moment he or Hastings may be similarly treated ; but the
latter has no suspicion, and, with inveterate enmity, exults at
the executions of his foes.   Stanley almost hints that these
men were falsely accused, though politically opposed to them,
and departs for the Tower with Catesby, who, during the
conversation of these two friends, never spoke, but doubtless
listened to every word.   Hastings, when alone, receives a
priest, whom he promises to see again the following Sunday ;
and then Buckingham visits him, sarcastically observing that
Hastings' "friends"—meaning his condemned foes at Pomfret—now need the priest to confess them more than he does.
Buckingham, however, secretly consents to Hastings' death if
he refuses to aid Gloster's usurpation, and they go together
to the Tower.

The next scene is short and pathetic, describing the last
moments of the unfortunate statesmen, Rivers, Grey, and
Vaughan, now executed at Pomfret, under the immediate
direction of Sir Richard Ratcliff, who, like Catesby, is a
devoted follower of Gloster, though neither are as much
in his confidence as they were afterwards, when his more
powerful and less obedient supporters were destroyed.

The next and last scene of this act is the most important
in it, and appears historically true in almost every respect.*
It is in the Tower, where are assembled Buckingham, Stanley,
Hastings, the Bishop of Ely, Catesby, &c.   In the play, they
meet to consult about the young king's coronation.   In
reality† this eventful meeting was a council held by Gloster,
following the advice of Hastings, who little suspected its fatal
termination to himself.   Of the assembled party, Buckingham,
Catesby, and perhaps Lord Lovel, are alone in Gloster's
secret.   While the Bishop of Ely and others ask Buckingham
about Gloster's wishes, the latter pretends ignorance, when
the Regent enters.   He apparently distrusts the bishop, asking him to send for some strawberries which he had seen
before in his garden at Holborn.   The unsuspicious prelate
gladly goes for them, and, when he is away, Gloster tells
Buckingham that Hastings refuses to join in their plot.
This news he has evidently just heard from Catesby, in a
private interview with that worthy.   Gloster and Bucking-

* HUME's *History*, ch. xxiii.   † *Ibid*.

R

ham then leave the room together, and the bishop returns, having sent for the strawberries. Hastings notices Gloster's cheerful, lively expression this morning, believing that his pleasant manner proves him friendly towards all present; but Stanley, more nervous or suspicious, evidently distrusts him, without daring to say so. Gloster and Buckingham then re-enter, and the former's manner is changed. He asks all present, in excited words, to say what punishment people deserve who, by plots or witchcraft, either conspire against his life, or, by their evil charms, have deformed his body. Hastings, frank and eager, still believing that Gloster's foes and his own are the same persons, instantly exclaims that all such people deserve death. Gloster then shows them his distorted arm and misshapen shoulder, angrily declaring that the queen herself, together with Jane Shore and others, have thus marked him by their witchcraft. It seems strange that he should thus couple the widowed queen and her rival together in this absurd charge, but his doing so is an historical fact.* Hastings, utterly astounded, begins a reply, but Gloster interrupts, charging him with protecting Jane Shore, and calling him a traitor to his face, upon which he is immediately arrested by the Regent's adherents. Gloster then promptly orders his immediate execution, saying he will not dine till after it.

> GLOSTER. Thou art a traitor :—
> Off with his head :—now, by Saint Paul I swear,
> I will not dine until I see the same.
> . . . . . Some see it done.
> The rest that love me, rise, and follow me.— Act III.

Gloster then leaves the room, followed by all his adherents, except Catesby and Lovel, who remain to witness the execution of the unfortunate Hastings, as their associate, Ratcliff, had witnessed the similar executions of the queen's relatives at Pomfret. This unscrupulous trio—Catesby, Lovel, and Ratcliff—are becoming gradually more trusted by Gloster than men of greater influence, and seem all of one mind, for, like the three favourites of Richard II.—Bushy, Bagot, and Green—they are generally hated, and must stand or fall with their patron.†

* HUME'S *History*, ch. xxiii.

† Upon these three favourites the following lines were written by one Colingbourne :—

> "The Cat, the Rat, and Lovel, that dog,
> Rule all England under the Hog."

Colingbourne was executed owing to this unlucky composition, though nominally for joining Buckingham's rebellion. "Richard was often compared to a boar, because he had the boar's head on his coat of arms."—HUME'S *History*, ch. xxiii.

Hastings, when left for immediate execution, makes an affecting speech, which Catesby and Lovel insist on shortening, being eager for the destruction of every living obstacle to Gloster's designs.

> HASTINGS.   Woe, woe, for England ! not a whit for me ;
> For I, too fond, might have prevented this :
> Stanley did dream the boar did rase his helm ;
> But I disdain'd it, and did scorn to fly.
> Three times to-day my foot-cloth horse did stumble,
> And started when he looked upon the Tower,
> As loath to bear me to the slaughter-house.*
> O, now I need the priest that spake to me.
>
> .   .   .   .   .   .
>
> CATESBY.   Despatch, my lord, the duke would be at dinner ;
> Make a short shrift, he longs to see your head.
>   HASTINGS.   O momentary grace of mortal men,
> Which we more hunt for than the grace of God !
> Who builds his hope in air of your fair looks,
> Lives like a drunken sailor on a mast ;
> Ready, with every nod, to tumble down
> Into the fatal bowels of the deep.
>   LOVEL.   Come, come, despatch ; 'tis bootless to exclaim.
>   HASTINGS.   O, bloody Richard !—miserable England !
> I prophesy the fearfullest time to thee
> That ever wretched age hath looked upon.
> Come, lead me to the block, bear him my head ;
> They smile at me who shortly shall be dead.—Act III.

After the arrest of Hastings, Gloster and Buckingham, attired in old rusty armour, appear on the Tower walls. Their object now is to justify to the Lord Mayor and others the execution of Hastings, by alleging that he had conspired to murder them that very day, and they had therefore put on old shabby armour, in a great hurry, to protect themselves from immediate assassination.   They are met by the Lord Mayor and Catesby, who probably brings the former to them, when they are duly prepared, like actors rehearsing a part, to seem alarmed and desperate, like men in danger of their lives.†   Their previous conversation proves, like Hamlet's directions to the players, how admirably Shakespeare knew the art of impressing hearers or spectators by appro-

---

* " Certain is it also that in the riding toward the Tower the same morning on which he was beheaded, his horse twice or thrice stumbled with him almost to the falling."—MORE's *Life of Richard III.*

† Gloster and Buckingham appearing in old rusty armour, "marvellously ill-favoured," on this occasion, is a historical fact, according to Mr. Staunton (*Notes to the Illustrated Shakespeare*), who quotes a passage from the old chronicler, Hall, which Shakespeare's account follows.

priate tone, look, and gesture, as well as by accompanying language.

> GLOSTER.   Come, cousin, canst thou quake and change thy
>   colour,
> Murder thy breath in middle of a word,
> 'And then again begin, and stop again,
> As if thou wert distraught and mad with terror?
>   BUCKINGHAM.   Tut, I can counterfeit the deep tragedian;
> Speak, and look back, and pry on every side,
> Tremble and start at wagging of a straw,
> Intending deep suspicion: ghastly looks
> Are at my service, like enforced smiles;
> And both are ready in their offices to grace my stratagems.—
>   Act III.

While, by apparently watching on the Tower walls, as if expecting armed enemies, they completely deceive the astonished Mayor, Gloster's two satellites, Ratcliffe and Lovel, appear on the scene, bearing the head of the victim, Hastings. Gloster immediately pretends to regret his death, while insinuating that he was not only treacherous but dangerous to him ever since his intimacy with Jane Shore. Buckingham warmly confirms his words, declaring besides that on this very day Hastings had conspired to kill both Gloster and himself. The Mayor is therefore soon convinced that Hastings deserved his fate; for both he and his brother, the Rev. Dr. Shaw, favour Gloster, and he departs, eagerly declaring that he will use all his influence with the London citizens to persuade them that Hastings, as a traitor, deserved death. Gloster sends Buckingham after him, charging the duke to insinuate and circulate reports that the young princes are illegitimate; to exaggerate and comment on the late king's profligacy; and, lastly, to arouse suspicions that Edward IV. was not the late Duke of York's son. This idea was often mentioned by the Lancastrians,* but even Gloster feels doubtful about spreading it, and, in rather hesitating words, tells Buckingham to "touch" this subject "sparingly," as his mother is still living.

Buckingham goes eagerly to the Guildhall, where he expects to meet the Mayor and many influential London citizens, Gloster bidding him to rejoin him at Baynard's Castle, where he intends to surround himself "with reverend fathers and well learned bishops." For, being now Protector, as well as a royal prince, Gloster can doubtless summon all English dignitaries—lay and clerical—to his presence when he pleases.

* *See* SCOTT's *Anne of Geierstein.*

The implicit confidence which the late king thus placed in him greatly increases his authority over all classes, especially in London, where Edward IV. was always very popular. After Buckingham departs, Gloster bids Lovel go to Dr. Shaw, and Catesby to a certain Friar Penker, but does not say for what purpose.* Both these churchmen, however, were devoted to him—the former especially, who was now ably assisting his brother, the Lord Mayor, in Gloster's behalf; for this stupid, or perhaps crafty, divine was about this time actually preaching a political sermon in St. Paul's Cathedral, trying to persuade his hearers that neither the late king nor the young princes were legitimate, and that the Duke of Gloster was everything that was good and great.† This strange discourse is not mentioned in the play, nor is Dr. Shaw again named, but the historical account of his extraordinary sermon throws some additional light on Gloster's conspiracy.

Richard having sent his ally, Buckingham, and his agents, Catesby and Lovel, in different directions, now says to himself that he will imprison his late brother Clarence's two children, and also forbid any access to the princes in the Tower; for these nephews are still obstacles to his ambition, and on their exclusion from the throne, by death or otherwise, he is fully resolved. When Buckingham re-joins him, at Baynard's Castle, he has rather disappointing news to tell his patron. The London citizens were not so easily deceived or pleased as the two plotters had hoped, and even expected; for among the lower classes Gloster was apparently never popular. Buckingham had vainly reminded his audience at

---

* "Of these two the one had a sermon in praise of the Protector before the coronation, the other after, both so full of tedious flattery that no man's ears could abide them. Penker in his sermon so lost his voice that he was fain to leave off and come down in the middle. Dr. Shaw by his sermon lost his honesty, and soon after his life, for very shame of the world into which he durst never after come abroad."—MORE's *Life of Richard III.*

† "Dr. Shaw chose for his text, 'Bastard slips shall not thrive.' He enlarged on all the topics which could discredit the birth of Edward IV., the Duke of Clarence, and of all their children. He then broke out in a panegyric on Gloster, exclaiming, 'Behold this excellent prince, the express image of his noble father; the genuine descendant of the House of York; bearing no less in the virtues of his mind than in the features of his countenance the character of the gallant Richard, once your hero and favourite;—he alone is entitled to your allegiance,' &c. It was previously concerted that as the doctor should pronounce these words, Gloster should enter the church, and it was expected the audience would cry out, 'God save King Richard!' which would immediately have been laid hold of as a popular consent, and interpreted to be the voice of the nation; but, by a ridiculous mistake, worthy of the whole scene, Gloster did not appear till after this exclamation was already recited by the preacher. The doctor was therefore obliged to repeat his rhetorical figure out of its proper place. The audience, less from the absurd conduct of the discourse than from their detestation of these proceedings, kept a profound silence."—HUME's *History*, ch. xxiii.

the Guildhall of Gloster's courage and bravery, and had also
hinted at the illegitimacy of the imprisoned princes.*   The
Lord Mayor Shaw was with him, but neither could induce
the people to cheer for King Richard, except a few adherents
of Buckingham who did so, and the latter, pretending that
they expressed the feelings of the meeting, thanked them,
and returned to Gloster.   The latter, though vexed at the
coldness of the citizens, is not daunted, and prepares to
receive the Mayor, who, with a party of aldermen and others,
wait upon him to pray his acceptance of the crown.   By the
advice of Buckingham, Gloster resolves to have two bishops
beside him, between whom he intends to appear, as a sign of
his pious inclinations ; while Buckingham means to introduce
the Mayor and aldermen.

BUCKINGHAM.   The Mayor is here at hand ; pretend some fear ;
Be not you spoke with but by mighty suit :
And look you, get a prayer-book in your hand,
And stand between two churchmen, good my lord ;
For on that ground I'll make a holy descant :
And be not easily won to our requests ;
Play the maid's part, still answer " Nay," and take it.—Act III.

Gloster then goes to another part of the castle, leaving
Buckingham to see the Mayor first, who enters with his
companions, and Buckingham receives them, observing that
he fears Gloster is too much engaged to grant an interview.
Catesby, who is fully in the plot, now comes with a message
from Gloster, begging the Mayor to call next day, being too
much occupied in prayer or religious study and conversation
with the bishops to speak on any worldly business.   The
Mayor and his party say nothing, and Buckingham instantly

* "Still the audience kept a profound silence.   'This is wonderful obstinacy,'
cried Buckingham ; 'express your meaning, my friends, one way or the other.
When we apply to you on this occasion, it is merely from the regard which we
bear to you.   The Lords and Commons have sufficient authority, without your
consent, to appoint a king ; but I require you here to declare, in plain terms,
whether or not you will have the Duke of Gloster for your sovereign.'   After all
these efforts, some of the meanest apprentices, incited by the Protector's and
Buckingham's servants, raised a feeble 'God save King Richard !'   The sentiments of the nation were now sufficiently declared, the voice of the people was
the voice of God, and Buckingham, with the Mayor, hastened to Baynard's
Castle, where the Protector then resided, that they might offer him the crown.
When Richard was told that a great multitude was in the court, he refused to
appear to them.   At last he was persuaded to step forth.   He was told that the
people had determined to have another prince, and if he rejected their unanimous voice, they must look out for one who would be more compliant.   This
argument was too powerful to be resisted, he was prevailed on to accept the
crown, and he thenceforth acted as legitimate and rightful sovereign.   This ridiculous farce was soon followed by a scene truly tragical—the murder of the young
princes."—HUME'S *History*, ch. xxiii.

ends Catesby back, entreating Gloster to see them on most
.nportant State affairs, and, after his departure, he praises
Richard to the Mayor for his piety, and greatly fears he will
ot be induced to accept the crown.   After a little more delay,
Gloster himself appears, and, as before agreed, between two
ishops.   Buckingham and the Lord Mayor then entreat him,
1 the name of the English nation, to become their king.
Gloster refuses, and Buckingham, after making two long
peeches, persuades him to take the crown.

MAYOR.   See where his grace stands between two clergymen !
BUCKINGHAM.   Two props of virtue for a Christian prince,
To stay him from the fall of vanity.

Know, then, it is your fault, that you resign
The supreme seat, the throne majestical,
The scepter'd office of your ancestors,
The lineal glory of your royal house,
To the corruption of a blemish'd stock :
The noble isle doth want her proper limbs ;
Her face defac'd with scars of infamy,
Her royal stock graft with ignoble plants ;
Which to secure we heartily solicit
Your gracious self to take on you the charge
And kingly government of this your land : .
Not as protector, steward, substitute,
Or lowly factor for another's gain ;
But as successively, from blood to blood,
Your rights of birth, your empery, your own.
For this, consorted with the citizens,
Your very worshipful and loving friends,
And by their vehement instigation,
In this just cause come I to move your grace.
MAYOR.   Do, good my lord ; your citizens entreat you.
BUCKINGHAM.   Refuse not, mighty lord, their proffered love.
CATESBY.   O make them joyful, grant their lawful suit.
GLOSTER.   Alas, why would you heap these cares on me?
I cannot, nor I will not, yield to you.
BUCKINGHAM.   Yet know, whe'r you accept our suit or no,
Your brother's son shall never reign our king :
But we will plant some other in the throne,
To the disgrace and downfall of your house.
And in this resolution here we leave you :—
Come, citizens, we will entreat no more.
                    [*Exeunt* BUCKINGHAM *and Citizens.*
CATESBY.   Call them again, sweet prince, accept their suit ;
If you deny them, all the world will rue it.
GLOSTER.   Will you enforce me to a world of cares ?
Call them again ; I am not made of stone.

Re-enter BUCKINGHAM *and the rest.*

Cousin of Buckingham, and sage, grave men,
Since you will buckle fortune on my back,
To bear her burden, whe'r I will or no,
I must have patience to endure the load.
   BUCKINGHAM.   Then I salute you with this royal title—
Long live King Richard, England's worthy king !
   ALL   Amen.
   BUCKINGHAM.   To-morrow may it please you to be crown'd ?
   GLOSTER.   Even when you please, since you will have it so.
   BUCKINGHAM.   To-morrow, then, we will attend your grace;
And so most joyfully do we take our leave.
   GLOSTER (*to the Bishops*).   Come, let us to our holy work
      again :—
Farewell, my cousin ;—farewell, gentle friends.—Act III.

Buckingham's speeches were probably partly composed by
Gloster, and taught to the former, as, in art, craft, and eloquence, they surpass what was apparently Buckingham's
ability ; for Gloster, like a first-rate actor, knew the parts of his
fellow-players as well as his own in this extraordinary farce
which he and Buckingham, aided by Catesby, Ratcliff, and
Lovel, now perform so successfully before the astonished, but
hitherto passive, English nation.*

The fourth act introduces Queen Elizabeth, her son Dorset,
the old Duchess of York, and the Lady Anne, now
Gloster's wife, assembled before the Tower. They wish to
see the imprisoned princes, but are denied access by the
Lieutenant Brakenbury, when Stanley appears, summoning
Anne to be crowned at Westminster as Richard's queen.
The three ladies—mother, wife, and sister-in-law—all vehe-
mently express their dread and horror of Richard. The
duchess and Elizabeth advise Dorset, who, they fear, will be
Richard's next victim, to escape to France ; while Anne, terri-
fied at Gloster, whom she has been induced or forced to marry,
expects the worst, knowing his hatred to all her family.
This disconsolate party then separate, and go different ways—
Dorset to the Earl of Richmond in France, Anne to the
Duke of Gloster, and Elizabeth to the sanctuary ; while the
duchess, deeply grieved at being the mother of such a murderous son, is yet in comparative safety from him. Before

---

* M. Guizot remarks that Richard deceives men for the pleasure of despising
them. "Il trompe les hommes pour se donner le plaisir de les mepriser."—
Shakespeare and his Times. This was probably one of his motives, yet he used
his vast powers of dissimulation for much more practical purposes than the mere
gratification of scorn or pride.

ley disperse, Elizabeth takes a last look at the fatal Tower,
where her little sons are now hidden from her sight.

> QUEEN ELIZABETH.   Stay; yet look back, with me, unto the
> Tower.
> Pity, you ancient stones, those tender babes,
> Whom envy hath immur'd within your walls!
> Rough cradle for such little pretty ones!
> Rude, ragged nurse! old, sullen playfellow
> For tender princes, use my babies well!
> So foolish sorrow bids your stones farewell."—Act IV.

She doubtless anticipates their fate, not, however, mentioning her worst fears, and, without again attempting to see
them, she and the rest leave the place.

The next scene describes Richard crowned in the palace,
with Buckingham and Catesby beside him, and surrounded
by courtiers and pages. He bids all "stand apart," except
Buckingham, and, in guarded language, asks his consent to
the assassination of the princes. Buckingham hesitates, and,
requesting time to consider, leaves the king for a short while.

> KING RICHARD.   O, Buckingham, now do I play the touch,
> To try if thou be current gold, indeed:—
> Young Edward lives:—Think now what I would say.
> BUCKINGHAM.   Say on, my loving liege.
> KING RICHARD.   Why, Buckingham, I say I would be king.
> BUCKINGHAM.   Why, so you are, my thrice-renowned liege.
> KING RICHARD.   Ha! am I king? 'Tis so: but Edward lives.
> BUCKINGHAM.   True, noble prince.
> KING RICHARD.   O bitter consequence,
> That Edward still should live!—*true, noble prince!*
> Cousin, thou wast not wont to be so dull:
> Shall I be plain? I wish the bastards dead;
> And I would have it suddenly perform'd.
> What say'st thou now? speak suddenly, be brief.
> BUCKINGHAM.   Your grace may do your pleasure.
> KING RICHARD.   Tut, tut, thou art all ice; thy kindness freezeth:
> Say, have I thy consent that they shall die?
> BUCKINGHAM.   Give me some breath, some little pause, my lord,
> Before I positively speak in this:
> I will resolve your grace immediately.   [*Exit* BUCKINGHAM.
> CATESBY (*aside*).   The king is angry; see, he bites his lip.*
> KING RICHARD.   I will converse with iron-witted fools [*Descends
> from his throne*],

---

* Even Richard's habit of biting his lip, which the shrewd lawyer Catesby
notices, is founded on history. "And while he did muse upon anything standing, he would bite his under-lip continually, whereby a man might perceive his
cruel nature within his wretched body; also the dagger which he bore about him,
he would always be chopping of it in and out."—MORE's *Life of Richard III.*

And unrespective boys : none are for me
That look into me with considerate eyes.
High-reaching Buckingham grows circumspect.
     Boy !
  PAGE. My lord.
  KING RICHARD. Know'st thou not any whom corrupting gold
Would tempt unto a close exploit of death ?
  PAGE. I know a discontented gentleman,
Whose humble means match not his haughty mind :
Gold were as good as twenty orators,
And will, no doubt, tempt him to anything.
  KING RICHARD. What is his name ?
  PAGE.   His name, my lord, is Tyrrel.
  KING RICHARD. I partly know the man :' Go, call him hither,
     boy.   [*Exit* PAGE.
The deep-revolving, witty Buckingham
No more shall be the neighbour to my counsel :
Hath he so long held out with me untired,
And stops he now for breath ?—well, be it so.—Act IV.

Catesby, ever watchful, though he cannot hear what has
passed, rightly guesses from Richard's expression that he is
angry ; for the king had reasonably expected to have Buckingham's ready consent, considering all that he had previously
sanctioned. Why, indeed, Buckingham now hesitates is
rather surprising, when his past conduct is remembered ; for
he had cordially assisted in the deliberate murder of his old,
trustful friend, Lord Hastings. He had also done all in his
power to exclude the princes from their rights by alleging
their illegitimacy, and, having thus proved himself cruel,
treacherous, and deceitful, Richard naturally expected he
would complete the policy he had so zealously aided, by
removing all remaining obstacles to their united designs.
Perhaps at this moment of temptation, Buckingham may
have suddenly recollected his oath before King Edward to be
true to his children, though he had previously violated it
when asserting their illegitimacy to the London citizens.
Buckingham's whole behaviour in this scene, though natural
for a grateful courtier in his position, is strangely inconsistent
with his previous conduct, and there seems to be no historical
foundation for it. On the contrary, he appears to have either
sanctioned, or at least not opposed, the murder of the princes,
for his quarrel with Richard occurred some time after that
crime, and apparently had no connection with it.*

---

* "It was impossible that friendship could long remain inviolate between two
such corrupt minds as Richard and Buckingham. Historians ascribe their first
rupture to the king's refusal of making restitution of the Hereford estate ; but it

This important and striking scene admirably represents Richard's character, tempting and provoking his ally while closely observing the latter's first signs of reluctance to obey his will, and instantly resolving to destroy him, with the prompt decision of his relentless nature. All who are not willing to obey him thoroughly he now considers enemies. Buckingham's high rank, which had made him a valuable ally, would also render him a dangerous foe ; while his previous devotion to the usurper had doubtless alienated all his friends, save those who supported Richard. The duke, therefore, could hardly now abandon politics and retire into private life ; he must either join Richard thoroughly, like Catesby and Ratcliff, or conciliate the usurper's foes by close alliance with them, and thus repudiate his former policy. Richard well knew Buckingham's dangerous position, and directly the latter hesitates to obey his wishes, without absolutely refusing, he summons an intelligent young page, asking him to name any of his acquaintance who would take life for money. The youth instantly mentions a needy desperado—Sir James Tyrrel—whom Richard then sends for, as he knew something of him before.* He tells him, in brief, expressive words, about the crime he wishes committed, and to which Tyrrel makes no objection.

KING RICHARD. Dar'st thou resolve to kill a friend of mine ?
TYRREL. Please you, but I had rather kill two enemies.
KING RICHARD. Why, then thou hast it ; two deep enemies,
Foes to my rest, and my sweet sleep's disturbers,
Are they that I would have thee deal upon :
Tyrrel, I mean those bastards in the Tower.

is certain, from records, that he passed a grant for that purpose. . . . . Perhaps Richard was soon sensible of the danger which might ensue from conferring such an immense property on a man of so turbulent a disposition, and afterwards raised difficulties about the execution of his own grant ; perhaps he refused some other demands of Buckingham, whom he found it impossible to gratify for his past services ; perhaps he resolved, according to the usual maxims of politicians, to seize the first opportunity of ruining this powerful subject, who had been the principal instrument of his own elevation ; and the discovery of this intention begat the first discontent in the Duke of Buckingham. However this may be, it is certain that the duke, soon after Richard's accession, began to form a conspiracy against the Government, and attempted to overthrow that usurpation, which he himself had so zealously contributed to establish."—HUME's *History*, ch. xxiii.

* "Sir," quoth his page, "there lyeth one on your pallet without that I dare well say, to do your grace pleasure, the thing were right hard that he would refuse,"—meaning by this Sir James Tyrrel. "The man had an high heart, and sore longed upward, not rising yet so fast as he had hoped, being hindered and kept under by Sir Richard Ratcliff and Sir William Catesby, who, longing for no more partners of the prince's favour, kept him by secret drift out of all secret trust. Which thing this page well had marked and known."—MORE's *Life of Richard III.*

TYRREL.   Let me have some means to come to them,
And soon I'll rid you from the fear of them.
   KING RICHARD.   Thou sing'st sweet music. Come hither, Tyrrel.
Go, by this token :—Rise, and lend thine ear :
(*Whispers*) There is no more but so :—say it is done,
And I will love thee, and prefer thee too.
   TYRREL.   'Tis done, my gracious lord.—Act IV.

After giving these directions, and while awaiting Buckingham's return, Richard hears that Dorset, the queen's son,
has gone to Brittany, to join Richmond, upon which he bids
Catesby report that his wife, Anne, is ill, and likely to die ;
for he has now a vague idea of marrying his own niece, King
Edward's daughter, to whom he knows the Lancastrian party
wish to betroth their young champion, Richmond. This
scheme he certainly then contemplated but abandoned it,*
for many dangers are now thickening around him, and even
his energetic mind, though never daunted, becomes perplexed.
The artful Catesby, perhaps surprised at Richard's agitation,
assumes a dull, listless manner, thus forcing his dangerous
master to repeat his orders before undertaking the risk of
obeying them.

   KING RICHARD.   Rumour it abroad
That Anne, my wife, is sick and like to die ;
I will take order for her keeping close.
Inquire me out some mean-born gentleman,
Whom I will marry straight to Clarence' daughter—
The boy is foolish, and I fear not him.—
Look, how thou dream'st ?—I say again, give out
That Anne, my wife, is sick, and like to die :
About it ; for it stands me much upon,
To stop all hopes whose growth may damage mine. [*Exit* CATESBY.
I must be married to my brother's daughter,
Or else my kingdom stands on brittle glass !
Murder her brothers, and then marry her !
Uncertain way of gain ! But I am in
So far in blood, that sin will pluck on sin.
Tear-falling pity dwells not in this eye.—Act IV.

Whilst Richard is in anxious thought, Buckingham re-
enters, and the usurper quietly checks his further allusion to
the princes. Buckingham now thinks it time to remind him
of his promise to grant him the earldom of Hereford, with
some other gifts in moveable property. Richard pretends
not to hear, in reality thus revenging himself on Buckingham
for his sudden reluctance to obey him, which has evidently

* HUME'S *History*.

both irritated and disappointed him. He therefore hears Buckingham's eager requests with assumed indifference, talking aloud to himself, instead of answering, till Buckingham, alarmed and astonished, becomes more and more anxious, to the sardonic delight of the other, who asks him "what's o'clock?" and remains silent as it strikes; while Buckingham's eagerness becomes uncontrollable, and he finally entreats for a decided answer. This Richard will not give, but scornfully leaves him, saying he is troublesome, and that he himself is not in the humour to make presents.

BUCKINGHAM. My lord, I have considered in my mind
The late request that you did sound me in.
KING RICHARD. Well, let that rest. Dorset is fled to Richmond.
BUCKINGHAM. I hear the news, my lord.
KING RICHARD. Stanley, he is your wife's son :—well, look to it.
BUCKINGHAM. My lord, I claim the gift, my due by promise,
For which your honour and your faith is pawned ;
The earldom of Hereford, and the moveables,
The which you promised I should possess.
KING RICHARD. Stanley, look to your wife ; if she convey
Letters to Richmond, you shall answer it.
BUCKINGHAM. What says your highness to my just demand ?
KING RICHARD. As I do remember, Henry the Sixth
Did prophesy that Richmond should be king,
When Richmond was a little peevish boy. ·
A king !—perhaps—perhaps——
BUCKINGHAM. My lord.
KING RICHARD. How chance the prophet could not at that time
Have told me, I being by, that I should kill him ?
BUCKINGHAM. My lord, your promise for the earldom——
KING RICHARD. Richmond !—When I was last at Exeter,
The mayor in courtesy showed me the castle,
And call'd it Rougemont ; at which name I started,
Because a bard of Ireland told me once
I should not live long after I saw Richmond.
BUCKINGHAM. My lord——
KING RICHARD. Ay, what's o'clock ?
BUCKINGHAM. I am thus bold to put your grace in mind
Of what you promised me.
KING RICHARD. Well, but what's o'clock ?
BUCKINGHAM. Upon the stroke of ten.
KING RICHARD. Well, let it strike.
BUCKINGHAM. Why, let t strike ?
KING RICHARD. Because that, like a jack, thou keep'st the stroke
Betwixt thy begging and my meditation.
I am not in the giving vein to-day.
BUCKINGHAM. Why, then resolve me whe'r you will or no.

King Richard.   Tut, tut, thou troublest me. I am not in the vein.
                    [*Exeunt* King Richard *and train.*
Buckingham.   Is it even so? repays he my true service
With such contempt? made I him king for this?
O, let me think on Hastings; and be gone
To Brecknock, while my fearful head is on. [*Exit.*]—Act IV.

Buckingham, when alone, not only abandons hope of reward, but trembles for his life. Something in Richard's manner or expression, besides his contemptuous words, has evidently convinced him of immediate danger, for, without seeking another interview, and apparently dreading sudden arrest, he leaves London, resolved to join Richmond, who is now the hope and the chief of Richard's enemies.

The next scene introduces Sir James Tyrrel, after he has committed the crime for which he has been hired. The speech he makes to himself about it, however, besides being Shakespeare's invention, seems inconsistent—even unnatural —in such a man. He not only feels deep remorse, but mentions the two subordinate murderers, Dighton and Forrest, whom he has employed to slay the princes when asleep, as being equally remorseful after their crime, and talking about it more like imaginative poets than the low ruffians which they are even by his own description.

> Tyrrel.   The tyrannous and bloody deed is done;
> The most arch act of piteous massacre
> That ever yet this land was guilty of.
> Dighton and Forrest, whom I did suborn
> To do this ruthless piece of butchery,
> Albeit they were flesh'd villains, bloody dogs,
> Melting with tenderness and mild compassion,
> Wept like two children, in their death's sad story.
> "*Lo, thus,*" quoth Dighton, "*lay those tender babes,*"—
> "*Thus, thus,*" quoth Forrest, "*girdling one another*
> *Within their innocent alabaster arms:*
> *Their lips like four red roses on a stalk,*
> *Which, in their summer beauty, kiss'd each other.*
> *A book of prayers on their pillow lay:*
> *Which once,*" quoth Forrest, "*almost changed my mind;*
> *But, oh! the devil!*"—there the villain stopped;
> When Dighton thus told on—"*We smothered*
> *The most replenished sweet work of nature,*
> *That, from the prime creation, e'er she framed.*"
> Hence both are gone with conscience and remorse;
> They could not speak.—Act IV.

He terms them both thoroughly hardened villains, as they surely were, before undertaking to commit such a crime, and yet declares that they were quite affected by the innocent looks of the victims—their " alabaster arms," " lips like roses," &c.* It is most unlikely, if not impossible, that such ruffians could either have used such language or felt such emotions as are ascribed to them. They also "wept," "melting with tenderness and mild compassion," when describing the sleeping children, though, had they retained such feelings, it would probably have been less trying to destroy them while unconscious than if they had been pleading for their lives. In reality these wretches were never known to have repented, and were probably incapable of repentance. They lived for some time afterwards, and were never punished by Henry VII.† Tyrrel, after making this strange, remorseful confession to himself, then announces the deed to the gratified king, with half-suppressed disgust, which the latter does not notice, but dismisses him, with a promise of great reward, and then avows his intention of marrying his niece, the Princess Elizabeth, as his wife, Anne, is now dead. This unfortunate woman really died about this time, and it was generally suspected that Richard poisoned her ; but Hume, while mentioning this suspicion, doubts the king's guilt in her case.‡ While thinking of the Princess Elizabeth, Richard is joined by Catesby, who says that the Bishop of Ely has joined Richmond's forces, and that Buckingham, with some Welsh followers, are now in the field, and have also declared for Richmond. The king instantly resolves to attack his old associate, and quell his rebellion before he has time actually to join the invader, whose landing in England, though anxiously expected, has not yet taken place. The idea of war again inspirits Richard, as it always had done, and he prepares for the coming struggle with all the fiery ardour of his nature.

The next scene, for the second and last time, introduces

* Mr. Staunton thinks that Shakespeare borrowed this pretty description from an old ballad—" The most Cruel Murder of Edward V."—*Notes to the Illustrated Shakespeare.*

† " Tyrrell, choosing three associates, Slater [not mentioned by Shakespeare], Dighton, and Forrest, came in the night-time to the doors of the chambers where the young princes were lodged, and, sending in the assassins, he bade them execute their commission, while he himself stood without. They found the young princes in bed, and fallen into a profound sleep. After suffocating them with the bolster and the pillows, they showed their bodies to Tyrrell, who ordered them to be buried at the foot of the stairs, under a heap of stones. These circumstances were all confessed by the actors in the following reign, and they were never punished for the crime, perhaps because Henry [VII.], whose maxims of government were extremely arbitrary, desired to establish it as a principle that the commands of the reigning sovereign ought to justify every enormity in those who paid obedience to them."—HUME's *History*, ch. xxiii. "This account," says the *Student's Hume* (published 1870), "has been questioned by Walpole in his *Historic Doubts,* and subsequently by other writers ; but, on the whole, the balance of probability greatly preponderates in its favour."—Ch. xiii.

‡ Ch. xxiii.

Queen Margaret, in the palace, with the Queen Elizabeth and the old Duchess of York. They all lament their slain relatives, Margaret finding morbid consolation for her past woes in beholding the misfortunes of the York family. This scene is fanciful, unnatural, and quite opposed to history. None of the chroniclers whom Shakespeare and Hume follow—Holinshed, Hall, Sir T. More, &c.—mention Margaret being in the English court at this time, which would, indeed, have been a political impossibility. The sentiments Shakespeare ascribes to her, however, seem consistent enough with her character, but could only have been uttered either in her English prison or in France, after being ransomed thither by Louis XI. In the play, after dwelling with vindictive joy on the sorrows of the Duchess of York and Queen Elizabeth, she goes to France, as if free to leave when she pleased, and, after her departure, Richard himself appears, and is passionately reproached by his mother and sister-in-law.

DUCHESS. Art thou my son?
KING RICHARD. Ay; I thank God, my father, and yourself.
DUCHESS. Then patiently hear my impatience.
KING RICHARD. Madam, I have a touch of your condition,
Which cannot brook the accent of reproof.
DUCHESS. I will be mild and gentle in my language.
KING RICHARD. And brief, good mother; for I am in haste.
DUCHESS. Art thou so hasty? I have stayed for thee,
God knows, in anguish, pain, and agony.
KING RICHARD. And came I not at last to comfort you?
DUCHESS. No, by the holy rood, thou know'st it well,
Thou cam'st on earth to make the earth my hell.
A grievous burden was thy birth to me;
Tetchy and wayward was thy infancy;
Thy school-days frightful, desperate, wild, and furious;
Thy prime of manhood daring, bold, and venturous;
Thy age confirmed, proud, subtle, bloody, treacherous:
What comfortable hour canst thou name,
That ever grac'd me in thy company?
KING RICHARD. Faith, none but Humphrey Hour, that called
   your grace
To breakfast once, forth of my company.
If I be so disgracious in your sight,
Let me march on, and not offend you, madam.
Strike up the drum.
DUCHESS. O let me speak,
For I shall never see thee more.
KING RICHARD. Come, come, you are too bitter.
DUCHESS. Either thou wilt die, by God's just ordinance,
Ere from this war thou turn a conqueror,

Or I with grief and extreme age shall perish,
And never look upon thy face again.
Therefore, take with thee my most heavy curse ;
Which, in the day of battle, tire thee more
Than all the complete armour that thou wear'st !
My prayers on the adverse party fight :
And there the little souls of Edward's children
Whisper the spirits of thy enemies,
And promise them success and victory.—Act IV.

To his mother Richard is quiet, sarcastic, and indifferent ;
but, when she is gone, he detains Elizabeth, and has a long
conversation about her daughter, whom at this time he has
vague thoughts of marrying, to prevent her probable union
with his rival, Richmond. His sister-in-law at first hears
and answers him with horror, but, after a long talk, he contrives either to deceive or frighten her, for she consents to
tell his offer to her daughter, and let him know the result.
This extraordinary scene is apparently founded, at least
partly, on fact, for Elizabeth did not oppose him, and
was either so cajoled or terrified by Richard that she wrote
to her friends, and to her son Dorset advising them to forsake
Richmond ;* but her weak conduct had little influence, for
the general indignation against Richard was now so great
that Richmond left France for England, being promised
support by a vast number of the English of all ranks.
Richard hears this unwelcome news from his trusty followers,
Catesby and Ratcliffe, and sends the former to the Duke of
Norfolk, summoning him to his aid. This nobleman seems
hitherto to have taken no part in the government, and to be
more faithful to the king than any of the English nobility
were, either from hereditary loyalty to the House of York, now
alone represented by Richard, or from some personal enmity
to the king's foes. Richard in this scene is evidently perplexed, though undaunted, by all his sudden dangers, when
Stanley enters, saying that Richmond is certainly at sea, and
approaching England. The king suspects Stanley's loyalty,
yet is not sure of his treason, and allows him to leave London, and "muster men" for his defence, bidding him leave
behind his son George as a hostage for his own fidelity,
sternly warning him that if he wavers in his loyalty,
the young man's life will be forfeited.

STANLEY.   Pleaseth your majesty to give me leave,
I'll muster up my friends, and meet your grace
Where, and what time, your majesty shall please.

* HUME'S *History*, ch. xxiii.

S

KING RICHARD.   Ay, thou wouldst be gone to join with
    Richmond :
But I'll not trust thee.
    STANLEY.   Most mighty sovereign,
You have no cause to hold my friendship doubtful ;
I never was, nor never will be, false.
    KING RICHARD.   Go, then, and muster men. But leave
    behind
Your son, George Stanley ; look your heart be firm,
Or else his head's assurance is but frail.
    STANLEY.   So deal with him as I prove true to you.—Act IV.

Stanley, protesting his loyalty, then leaves Richard's
dangerous presence.   This nobleman, though married to
Richmond's mother, and probably always on his step-son's
side, was yet for a long time trusted by Richard with important military commands, which seems very singular, considering his connection with Richmond.*   Richard now remains
with Ratcliffe, while three messengers come in succession, announcing the general rebellion throughout England.
In impatient anger, Richard strikes the second messenger,
who, however, after the blow, announces the dispersion of
Buckingham's forces by sudden storms and floods, upon
hearing which the king pays him, to make amends, and
orders a reward to be offered to any one who captures his old
ally, his "other self," his "oracle," his "prophet," but now
"the traitor."   The next messenger announces the dispersion of Richmond's fleet by a tempest, but that Dorset and
Sir T. Lovel are heading the rebellion in Yorkshire.
Richard instantly orders a forward march to crush these
scattered insurgents, who, he fears, may effect a junction,
when Catesby returns, announcing Buckingham's capture as
the best news, but also that Richmond has succeeded in
landing, with a large force, at Milford.   Richard orders an
immediate march to Salisbury, directing that Buckingham
should be brought there, but saying nothing about his fate.
It is, however, in this scene that Richard was supposed to
exclaim, "Off with his head ! So much for Buckingham ! "
but these words, as well as " Richard's himself again !" were
not written by Shakespeare, yet have been often introduced
on the stage, though not in the more recent representations
of this play.
    In a very short scene, the perplexed Lord Stanley sends a
friend with letters to his step-son, Richmond (erroneously

* " Stanley had become obnoxious by his marrying the Countess of Richmond,
but, sensible of the necessity of submitting to the present government, he feigned
such zeal for Richard's service that he was entrusted with the most important
commands by that politic and jealous tyrant."—HUME'S *History*, ch. xxiii.

termed his son-in-law), saying he wishes and means to join him, but must be cautious, as his son George is in "The Boar's" power; also that Queen Elizabeth joyfully consents to her daughter's marriage with him, thereby uniting the rival families of York and Lancaster.

Act V. describes the execution of the guilty, unfortunate Buckingham at Salisbury. Before kneeling at the block, he pathetically regrets his past services to the murderous usurper. He invokes some of his victims whom he had known in happier days, and then vividly remembers his solemn oath of fidelity to King Edward's sons, whose destruction he has hastened, at least indirectly, through his devotion to their uncle.*　He also repeats Margaret's warning that Richard would one day "split his heart with sorrow," and, owning that he deserves death for having assisted the usurper, he submits, and is beheaded.

> BUCKINGHAM.　Will not King Richard let me speak with him?
> SHERIFF.　No, my good lord: therefore be patient.
> BUCKINGHAM.　Hastings, and Edward's children, Rivers, Grey,
> Holy King Henry, and thy fair son Edward,
> Vaughan, and all that have miscarried
> By underhand, corrupted, foul injustice!
> If that your moody, discontented souls
> Do through the clouds behold this present hour,
> Even for revenge mock my destruction!
>
> .　　.　　.　　.　　.　　.
>
> Now Margaret's curse falls heavy on my neck—
> "*When he,*" quoth she, "*shall split thy very heart with sorrow,*
> *Remember Margaret was a prophetess.*"—
> Come, sirs, convey me to the block of shame;
> Wrong hath but wrong, and blame the due of blame.—Act V.†

Meanwhile, though Buckingham's insurrection is suppressed, the rising in England becomes more general. Richmond addresses his followers near Somerset, saying that his step-father, Stanley, is secretly on his side, and will join him whenever he can do so safely. His army, increased in number and animated by the general hatred to Richard, approaches Bosworth field, where the king now pitches his tent, and resolves to give battle. Norfolk and Surrey are with

---

* "One idea pervades all this play—the just punishment of those crimes which stained with blood the quarrels between the Houses of York and Lancaster."—GUIZOT's *Shakespeare and his Times.*

† It seems from the subsequent play of *Henry VIII.*, that, had Richard consented to see Buckingham on this occasion, the latter meant to stab him—so, at least, his son was said to have declared, though it is unlikely that a state prisoner would have been allowed to retain any weapon about his person. Buckingham was really executed at Salisbury, by Richard's orders, but none of his last words are recorded.—*See* HUME's *History*, ch. xxiii.

him, besides Catesby and Ratcliffe, but Lord Lovel is not mentioned again. Richard distrusts Surrey, who looks sad, and probably cares little for the king's cause ; but Norfolk obeys him to the last. Richard, summoning all his wonted resolution, now tries to encourage the loyal, and detect the disaffected, but, for the first time in his eventful life, he betrays signs of mental depression. This last act presents alternate scenes between the tents of the rival princes, Richmond and Richard—the former cheerful and hopeful, encouraged by his adherents, and confident of success ; the latter moody, suspicious, with bodily or mental fatigue gradually weakening his former energy. He enters his tent for the night, with Norfolk, Catesby, and Ratcliffe, asks for wine and a watch, orders a favourite horse to be saddled next day for the battle, and then asks Ratcliffe about Lord Northumberland, another adherent, whose " melancholy " looks apparently betray his dislike to the royal cause. Richard then, after briefly admitting his sudden depression, asks for ink and paper, dismissing his attendant, while remaining alone in his tent.

> KING RICHARD (*to* CATESBY).   Fill me a bowl of wine.—Give me
>   a watch !
> Saddle white Surrey for the field to-morrow.
> Look that my staves be sound, and not too heavy.
> Ratcliff !
>   RATCLIFFE.   My lord?
>   KING RICHARD.   Saw'st thou the melancholy Lord Northumber-
>   land ?
>   RATCLIFFE.   Thomas the Earl of Surrey, and himself,
> Much about cock-shut time, from troop to troop,
> Went through the army cheering up the soldiers.
>   KING RICHARD.   So, I am satisfied.   Give me a bowl of wine :
> I have not that alacrity of spirit,
> Nor cheer of mind, that I was wont to have.
> Set it down.—Is ink and paper ready ?
>   RATCLIFFE.   It is, my lord.
>   KING RICHARD.   Bid my guard watch ; leave me.
> Ratcliffe, about the mid of night, come to my tent,
> And help to arm me.—Leave me, I say.—Act V.

Stanley now secretly visits Richmond, saying he dares not openly join him, lest his son George, a hostage in Richard's power, should be executed in consequence. But he assures Richmond of his devotion to his cause and promises to join him, with all his followers, in the next day's expected battle. He then leaves Richmond, who, when alone, utters a beautiful prayer for victory, and sleeps in peace.

RICHMOND.   O Thou, whose captain I account myself,
Look on my forces with a gracious eye ;
Put in their hands Thy bruising irons of wrath,
That they may crush down with a heavy fall
The usurping helmets of our adversaries !
Make us Thy ministers of chastisement,
That we may praise Thee in this victory !
To Thee I do commend my watchful soul,
Ere I let fall the windows of mine eyes ;
Sleeping and waking, O, defend me still !   [*Sleeps.*]—Act V.

Meanwhile, Richard, when asleep, is tormented by the
ghosts of his victims, who, in fancy, rise successively before
him, denouncing and threatening him ; and then, turning to
Richmond, they promise him success and victory.

The GHOST *of* PRINCE EDWARD, *son to* HENRY VI., *rises between the
tents.*
GHOST (*to* KING RICHARD). Let me sit heavy on thy soul
      to-morrow !
Think, how thou stabb'dst me in my prime of youth
At Tewkesbury : despair, therefore, and die.
(*To* RICHMOND).   Be cheerful, Richmond ; for the wrongèd souls
Of butcher'd princes fight in thy behalf :
King Henry's issue, Richmond, comforts thee.
            GHOST *of* HENRY VI. *appears.*
GHOST (*to* KING RICHARD).   When I was mortal, my anointed
      body
By thee was punched full of deadly holes :
Think on the Tower and me : despair, and die ;
Henry the Sixth bids thee despair, and die !
(*To* RICHMOND).   Virtuous and holy, be thou conqueror !
Harry, that prophesied thou shouldst be king,
Doth comfort thee in thy sleep : live and flourish.
            GHOSTS *of the young* PRINCES *rise.*
GHOSTS (*to* KING RICHARD).   Dream on thy cousins smothered
      in the Tower,
Let us be lead within thy bosom, Richard,
And weigh thee down to ruin, shame, and death !
Thy nephews' souls bid thee despair, and die !
(*To* RICHMOND). Sleep, Richmond, sleep in peace, and wake in joy ;
Good angels guard thee from the boar's annoy !
Live, and beget a happy race of kings !
Edward's unhappy sons do bid thee flourish !
            GHOST *of* BUCKINGHAM *rises.*
GHOST (*to* KING RICHARD).   The first was I that helped thee
      to the crown ;
The last was I that felt thy tyranny :
O, in the battle think on Buckingham,
And die in terror of thy guiltiness!

Dream on, dream on, of bloody deeds and death !
Fainting, despair ; despairing, yield thy breath !
(*To* RICHMOND).   I died for hope, ere I could lend thee aid :
But cheer thy heart, and be thou not dismay'd :
God and good angels fight on Richmond's side ;
And Richard fall in height of all his pride !

When the ghosts vanish, Richard wakes, and, starting up,
calls for his war horse ; then, instantly recollecting he is alone,
he utters his last and grandest soliloquy.

> KING RICHARD. Give me another horse, bind up my wounds !
> Have mercy, Jesu !—Soft ; I did but dream.
> O coward conscience, how dost thou afflict me !
> The lights burn blue. —It is now dead midnight.*
> Cold, fearful drops stand on my trembling flesh.
> What, do I fear myself ? there's none else by :
> Richard loves Richard ; that is, I am I.
> Is there a murderer here ? No ;—Yes ; I am :
> Then fly—What, from myself ? great reason : why ?
> Lest I revenge.   What, myself upon myself ?
> O, no : alas, I rather hate myself,
> For hateful deeds committed by myself.
> I am a villain : yet I lie, I am not.
> Fool, of thyself speak well :—fool, do not flatter.
> My conscience hath a thousand several tongues,
> And every tongue brings in a several tale,
> And every tale condemns me for a villain.
> Perjury, perjury, in the highest degree ;
> Murder, stern murder, in the dir'st degree ;
> All several sins, all us'd in each degree,
> Throng to the bar, crying all, " Guilty, guilty ! "
> I shall despair.—There is no creature loves me ;
> And if I die, no soul will pity me :—
> Nay, wherefore should they ? since that I myself
> Find in myself no pity to myself.
> Methought, the souls of all that I had murdered
> Came to my tent : and every one did threat
> To-morrow's vengeance on the head of Richard.—Act V.

It is, indeed, a wonderful revelation of his mental power,
vivid fancy, and deep remorse, without real penitence, seeming to arise more from dreamy recollections of his many
victims, and vague terror at their menaces, than from any
sense of personal responsibility to a higher power.   Ratcliff
enters the king's tent, and Richard partly reveals his dream,

* " This is extremely fine.   The speaker had entirely got the better of his conscience, and banished it from his *waking* thoughts.   But it takes advantage of his
sleep and frights him in his dream."—JOHNSON's *Notes to Richard III.*

while the other, apparently a man of more spirit, though perhaps less artful than Catesby, urges him not to fear such
fancies.   Richard seems to rouse himself at his words, and
to gradually dispel his terrors as daylight approaches.   He
bids Ratcliffe accompany him secretly about his soldiers'
tents, and detect, if possible, any contemplated treason among
them, which he apprehends, and with reason.

Meanwhile, Richmond wakes, refreshed by sleep, attended
by pleasing dreams, and, addressing his followers, again
urges them to stand bravely by him, and crush the hateful
tyrant whom they are about to encounter.   Richard, though
he has dispelled vague terrors, is yet depressed, apprehensive,
and even rather superstitious.   He notices uneasily that the
morning sun will not shine upon him, and wishes the " dewy
tears " were off the ground, when Norfolk tells him the foe is
in the field, ready for action.   Then Richard, for the last
time, rouses the undaunted spirit of his race, adjuring his
followers to be faithful, when Norfolk shows him a strange
scroll which he found in his tent :—

> Jockey of Norfolk, be not too bold,
> For Dickon thy master is bought and sold.

Richard instantly exclaims that this missive is "a thing
devised by the enemy " to induce desertion, and is thus an
additional proof of the efforts made to corrupt his followers.
He then hears that Stanley refuses to obey him, and fiercely
orders young George Stanley to be instantly executed.   Norfolk, however, probably from pity for the prisoner, suggests
that after the coming battle would be the best time for his
execution.   At any other moment Richard would probably
have insisted on George's immediate death, and perhaps
arrested or suspected Norfolk for apparent sympathy for the
hostage ; but now he only thinks of immediate conflict with
his advancing foe, and the fatal battle begins.

In the next scene, Catesby entreats Norfolk to rescue
the king, whose horse is slain, and who is fighting desperately on foot, having already killed some of Richmond's
adherents, who, being attired in similar armour to that worn
by Richmond, were thus mistaken for him.*   Richard himself

---

* The last scenes of this popular tragedy, so nobly represented by Garrick,
Macready, Edmund Kean, and Henry Irving, have apparently been often vulgar-
ised.   Mr. Dickens, himself an excellent comic actor, amusingly describes what
he evidently saw.   " The bustle of the fourth act can't be dear at ten shillings
more, that's only £1 10s. including the ' off with his head ! ' which is sure to
bring down the applause, and it is very easy to do.   ' Orf with his ed ' (very
quick and loud, then slow and sneeringly) ' So much for Bu-u-u-uckingham ! '
lay the emphasis on the ' uck,' get yourself gradually into a corner, and work
with your right hand, while you're saying it, as if you were feeling your way, and

then appears, calling eagerly for a horse, to enable him to renew the fight. Catesby promises to get one, while Richard, apparently maddened with excitement, and perfectly desperate, seems hardly to recognize him. He fiercely declares that he has slain "five Richmonds" already, but not the real one, and his last words frantically entreat his followers to bring him a horse.

> KING RICHARD.   A horse! a horse! my kingdom for a horse!
> CATESBY.   Withdraw, my lord, I'll help you to a horse.
> KING RICHARD.   Slave, I have set my life upon a cast,
> And I will stand the hazard of the die!
> I think there be six Richmonds in the field;
> Five have I slain to-day, instead of him:
> A horse! a horse! my kingdom for a horse! [*Exeunt.*]—Act V.

He apparently imagines that his kingdom will surely be recovered if he can only kill his rival, whose troops would then either disperse or acknowledge him.

The last scene mentions, without describing, a hand-to-hand encounter between Richard and Richmond, in which the former is slain; but in reality he was killed by Sir William Stanley, brother to Lord Stanley, and his followers; for several foes had apparently the honour of slaying this desperate king, whose rare courage was, indeed, his only noble quality.*   Sir William Stanley placed a small, battered crown, plucked from Richard's helmet, on Richmond's head

---

it's sure to do.   The tent scene is confessedly worth half-a-sovereign, and so you have the fight in gratis, and everybody knows what an effect may be produced by a good combat.   One-two-three-four-over; then one-two-three-four-under; then thrust; then dodge and slide about; then fall down on one knee; then fight upon it: and then get up again and stagger.   You may keep on doing this as long as it seems to take—say ten minutes—and then fall down (backwards, if you can manage it without hurting yourself) and die game—nothing like it for producing an effect."—*Sketches by "Boz"—Private Theatres.*

* "The intrepid tyrant, sensible of his desperate situation, cast his eyes around the field, and descrying his rival at no great distance, he drove against him with fury, in hopes that either Henry's death or his own would decide the victory between them.   He killed with his own hands Sir William Brandon, standard-bearer to the earl; he dismounted Sir John Cheyny; he was now within reach of Richmond himself, who declined not the combat, when Sir William Stanley, breaking in with his troops, surrounded Richard, who, fighting to the last moment, was overwhelmed by numbers, and perished by a fate too mild and honourable for his multiplied and detestable enormities. . . . . This prince was of small stature, hump-backed, and had a harsh, disagreeable countenance, so that his body was in many particulars no less deformed than his mind."—HUME'S *History*, ch. xxiii.   The old Countess of Desmond, however, who lived to a great age, and was killed by a fall, had danced with King Richard, and probably found him very agreeable, for she persisted in declaring he was "a very handsome man."—*See* MARKHAM'S *History of England.*   His personal appearance, therefore, has found vindicators as well as his character; though Bacon, Hume, Shakespeare, and Hallam apparently formed much the same estimate of him.

while on the battle-field.* Richmond, after hearing of young Stanley's safety, then asks what " men of note" were slain on both sides. Among the personages in this play, Norfolk, Brakenbury the Lieutenant of the Tower, and Ratcliffe were killed in this battle, fighting on Richard's side, while the lawyer, Catesby, " a great instrument of Richard's crimes,"† was captured during it, and afterwards executed at Leicester ; but the fate of this satellite is not mentioned by Shakespeare. The play ends with Richmond's speech, announcing a general amnesty, and his own approaching marriage with the Princess Elizabeth.‡ Richmond's real character, however, is not shown in this play ; nor in any part of it are his peculiar qualities described or even indicated. He merely appears as the successful avenger of Richard's victims and the deliverer of England from that tyrant's yoke, but his own character is never described.

Richard's death Shakespeare describes, or rather mentions, as it is recorded in history ; while his character, though portrayed in fanciful, poetical language, closely resembles the statements of the chroniclers, Holinshed, Sir Thomas More, and Hall, re-produced by Hume. His successful usurpation certainly proved his great abilities, knowledge of character, and dauntless courage, as well as his unscrupulous and unsparing cruelty. But, though his amazing energy and determination obtained supreme power, he never showed the peculiar talents essential to confirm it. His fall was as terrible and complete as his success was rapid and unexpected.§ He apparently never conciliated determined enemies, but induced eager adherents to commit crime after crime in his service, and immediately destroyed them upon their showing the least hesitation to fulfil his wishes. He never made himself popular with the lower classes, and was always detested by them. Unlike the deceitful tyrants, Tiberius Cæsar

---

* " Sir William Stanley, after some acclamations of the soldiers in the field, put a crown of ornament, which Richard wore in the battle, and was found among the spoils, upon Henry's head."—LORD BACON'S *Life of Henry VII.*

† HUME'S *History.*

‡ " Henry, immediately after the victory, as one that had been bred by a devout mother, and was in his nature a great observer of religious forms, caused a ' Te Deum laudamus ' to be solemnly sung in the presence of the whole army. The body of Richard, after many indignities and reproaches, was obscurely buried, ... no one thinking any ignominy or contumely unworthy of him that had been the executioner of Henry VI., that innocent prince, with his own hands ; the contriver of the death of the Duke of Clarence, his brother ; the murderer of his two nephews, one of them his lawful king ; and vehemently suspected to have been the impoisoner of his wife."—BACON'S *Henry VII.*

§ " The ascent to greatness, however steep and dangerous, may entertain an active spirit with the consciousness and exercise of its own powers ; but the possession of a throne could never yet afford lasting satisfaction to an ambitious mind."—GIBBON'S *Decline and Fall*, ch. vi.

and Louis XI. of France, Richard III. seems not to have much
dissembled after he became king, though previously he had
completely deceived almost every one he knew. When once
monarch of England, he only used his vast powers of deception for some immediate object, and then displayed, or
was unable to conceal, all his natural ferocity. The Roman
Emperor and French King, on the contrary, though equally
remorseless and wicked in every sense, showed, when in
power, far more self-control, always making their vindictive
feelings subsérvient to their political interests.* They thus
had long and successful reigns, being even more feared than
detested by all who knew them. But Richard made mortal
foes among his early adherents and others, without reconcil-
ing any enemies, till at last he roused the greater part of the
nation against him. His extraordinary usurpation seemed,
indeed, more like an ambitious dream than a political fact.
He was at one time the most honoured and powerful subject
in England—Protector of the realm, guardian of the young
king, implicitly trusted by both his brothers, Edward IV.
and the Duke of Clarence. His great bravery was proved,
and generally praised and respected; his family had tri-
umphed greatly owing to his exertions over all foes ; and his
own position at the English court, during Edward IV.'s last
year and immediately after his death, was legally and actually
supreme. Yet, for the sake of becoming an absolute
monarch, he destroyed all his near relatives, alienated his
chief adherents, forcing them to join his foes, and thus
increasing his enemies on all sides, he at last seized the crown,
only to forfeit it with his life, owing to the general hatred
which his impolitic as well as criminal acts inevitably
incurred.† As a plotting usurper, he was, indeed, thoroughly
successful, and apparently possessed all the qualities required
to make him so ; but as a sovereign he seems to have shown
far less ability. He never had so many enemies as when
he became king, while his last adherents were no longer
men like Buckingham and Hastings, his first allies, who
could influence powerful relations and extensive connections
in his favour.‡ His most trusted followers, Catesby and

---

* *See Annals of Tacitus*, and DE COMINES's *Memoirs of Louis XI.*

† " The crimes of Richard were so horrid and so shocking to humanity that
the natural sentiments of men, without any political or public views, were suffi-
cent to render his government unstable, and every person of probity and honour
was earnest to prevent the sceptre from being any longer polluted by that bloody
and faithless hand which held it."—HUME's *History*, ch. xxiii.

‡ " Scarce any nobleman of distinction was sincerely attached to Richard's
cause, except the Duke of Norfolk, and all those who feigned the most loyalty
were only watching for an opportunity to desert him."—HUME's *History*,
ch. xxiii. Norfolk's rare fidelity to Richard is thus explained by a later historian :—
" He had received from Richard III. the old dignities of the House of Mowbray,

latcliffe, were neither ministers nor influential adherents, ut merely clever satellites, little better than actual slaves ɔ his will. That such men could have ever ruled the ːnglish nobility, or the nation at large, was surely impossi- le, yet Richard apparently hoped to become a despot by heir unscrupulous assistance. But his talent and energy, ῥhich had so wonderfully acquired supreme power, were tterly unable to retain it over a brave, firm nation gradually ɔused from confiding loyalty in the House of York to revolt gainst its last king, whose extraordinary career had proved im alike its champion and destroyer.

The play ends with a noble speech of the triumphant ᴌichmond in eloquent language, which that shrewd, avaricious ῥrince would have been unlikely to use. He alludes to his ῥpproaching marriage with the Princess Elizabeth, daughter ιf the Duke of Clarence.

> RICHMOND. We will unite the white rose with the red.—
> Smile, Heaven, upon this fair conjunction,
> That long hath frown'd upon their enmity!
> What traitor hears me and says not—Amen?
> England hath long been mad and scar'd herself;
> The brother blindly shed the brother's blood;
> The father rashly slaughter'd his own son;
> The son compell'd been butcher to the sire:
> All this divided York and Lancaster
> Divided in their dire division.
> O, now let Richmond ånd Elizabeth,
> The true succeeders of each royal house,
> By God's fair ordinance conjoin together!
> And let their heirs (God, if Thy will be so)
> Enrich the time to come with smooth-fac'd peace,
> With smiling plenty, and fair, prosperous days!
> Abate the edge of traitors, gracious Lord,
> That would reduce these bloody days again,
> And make poor England weep in streams of blood!
> Let them not live to taste this land's increase,
> That would with treason wound this fair land's peace!
> Now civil wounds are stopp'd, peace lives again,
> That she may long live here, God, say Amen!—Act V.

he office of Earl Marshal, and the dukedom of Norfolk. But he had hardly isen to greatness when he fell, fighting by Richard's side, at Bosworth field."— ᴳREEN'S *History of the English People*, book v.

CHAPTER XIII.

KING HENRY VIII.

Sketch of Play.

THIS play begins .with describing the discontent of many English noblemen at the power of Cardinal Wolsey, who completely influences the king.   One of these malcontents, the Duke of Buckingham, son of Richard III.'s confidant and victim, is arrested, and tried for high treason, Queen Catherine of Aragon vainly pleading for him, and is executed as a traitor.   Henry VIII., after this event, endeavours to obtain a divorce from Catherine.   Wolsey eagerly assists him, and offends the queen in consequence ; but he is disappointed at finding that Henry wishes to marry the Lady Anne Boleyn.   Catherine, separated, though not legally divorced, retires to Kimbolton, and Henry marries Anne Boleyn. Wolsey, who has offended both queens, and also irritated his jealous king by amassing great wealth and by his ambition, is disgraced, expelled from the court, and dies broken-hearted. Soon afterwards, Catherine expires in her retirement at Kimbolton.   The king has an only daughter—the future Queen Elizabeth—by Anne Boleyn, with whose christening the play ends.   Thus about thirteen years of Henry VIII.'s reign are described.

THE first act describes the nobles, Buckingham, Norfolk, and others, sons and relatives of those who had fought on opposite sides at Bosworth field, now amicably, in the palace, discussing the late splendid meeting between the French king, Francis I., and their sovereign, Henry VIII., at Arde, in France.   Norfolk beautifully describes this magnificent, scene, which he witnessed, to Buckingham, who had remained in England.

NORFOLK.   Each following day
Became the next day's master, till the last
Made former wonders its : to-day, the French,

All clinquant, all in gold, like heathen gods,
Shone down the English ; and, to-morrow, they
Made Britain, India : every man that stood
Show'd like a mine.   Their dwarfish pages were
As cherubims, all gilt : the madams too,
Not us'd to toil, did almost sweat to bear
The pride upon·them, that their very labour
Was to them as a painting : now this masque
Was cried incomparable ; and the ensuing night
Made it a fool and beggar.   The two kings,
Equal in lustre, were now best, now worst,
As presence did present them ; him in eye
Still him in praise : and, being present both,
'Twas said they saw but one ; and no discerner
Durst wag his tongue in censure.   .   .   .
All this was order'd by the good discretion
Of the right reverend Cardinal of York.
    BUCKINGHAM.   The devil speed him ! no man's pie is freed
From his ambitious finger.   What had he
To do in these fierce vanities ?   .   .   .
    NORFOLK.   Surely, sir,
There's in him stuff that puts him to these ends :
For, being not propp'd by ancestry, whose grace
Chalks successors their way ; nor call'd upon
For high feats done to the crown ; neither allied
To eminent assistants ; but, spider-like,
Out of his self-drawing web, he gives us note.—
The force of his own merit makes his way
A gift that heaven gives for him, which buys
A place next to the king.—Act I.

This grand assemblage of the two kings with their courtiers
had been attended with all kinds of gay festivities, and the
whole affair was in great measure arranged by the energetic
Wolsey, now in high favour with Henry, much respected on
the Continent, but detested by the English nobility, and
unpopular with the English people.*   Of all the nobles, however, Buckingham was his chief enemy, and the cardinal
detested him cordially in return.   This duke was the son of
Richard III.'s victim ; he had been reinstated in all his
family possessions by Henry VII. ; and was somewhat like
his father—ambitious, proud, and turbulent.   Being related

* "So quick a rise stirred envy in the men about him, and his rivals noticed
bitterly the songs, dances, and carousals which had won, as they believed, the
favour of the king.   But sensuous and worldly as was Wolsey's temper, his power
lifted him high above the level of a court favourite.   His noble bearing, his varied
ability, his enormous capacity for toil, the natural breadth and grandeur of his
mind, marked him naturally out as the minister of a king who showed throughout his reign a keen eye for greatness in the men about him."—GREEN'S *History
of the English People*, vol. iv.

to the royal family, he was weak enough to mention his pretensions to the crown, failing the king without direct heirs, and was encouraged in ambitious hopes by a certain Nicholas Hopkins, a Carthusian friar.* Buckingham was suspected alike by the king and the cardinal, and Norfolk warns him in this scene to beware of Wolsey's special hostility, and while saying this the cardinal appears. He and Buckingham behold each other without speaking, but Wolsey asks one of his numerous attendants if the duke's surveyor is ready with evidence against Buckingham, and, calmly remarking that the latter will change his haughty looks when the accusation against him is known, walks away. Buckingham, deeply irritated, is about to follow him to the king's presence, when he is restrained by Norfolk, who dreads lest his rashness should endanger his safety. While remonstrating with him, Brandon, the Sergeant-at-Arms, arrives with an escort of soldiers, and arrests both Buckingham and Lord Abergavenny, conducting them to the Tower as State prisoners. Brandon then states that John de la Car, Buckingham's confessor, together with the monk Hopkins, are also prisoners, charged with treason, and Buckingham instantly guesses that a man employed as his surveyor has been bribed to betray him by Wolsey, whom he considers his chief enemy. He bids farewell to Norfolk, and is taken a prisoner to the Tower, anticipating speedy execution.

The next scene introduces Henry VIII., thanking Wolsey for his loyal devotion and skill in detecting Buckingham's treason. He orders the duke's surveyor to be summoned, and seats himself with Wolsey near him, as the Dukes of Norfolk and Suffolk enter, escorting Queen Catherine, whom Henry seats beside him. Catherine earnestly entreats the king to remit certain taxations which he had authorised, and which she thinks Wolsey had been the means of imposing on the nation without Henry's full knowledge.† The king is

* "By those writers who are accustomed to attribute to the counsels of the cardinal every event which occurred under his administration, it has been supposed that resentment induced Wolsey to bring the duke, by false accusations, to the scaffold. But more authentic documents refer the cause of his ruin to the vanity and imprudence of Buckingham himself, who indulged a notion that he should one day ascend the throne. Buckingham had the misfortune to become acquainted with Hopkins, Prior of the Charter House at Henton, who pretended to the gift of prophecy, and employed that gift to flatter the vanity of his benefactor. How far the unfortunate nobleman allowed his ambition to be deluded by these predictions may be uncertain, but enough had transpired to awaken the suspicion of Henry, who for two years carefully watched his conduct."—LINGARD'S *English History*, vol. iv.

† "The demands made by Henry VIII. on parliament were considerable, both in frequency and amount. . . . . Commissioners were appointed in 1525, with instructions to demand the sixth part of every man's substance, payable in money, plate or jewels, according to the last valuation. This demand Wolsey made in

surprised, and promises her he will inquire into the matter, and directs the cardinal to stop the alleged taxation till there is a further examination.*

> KING HENRY. Have you a precedent
> Of this commission? I believe, not any.
> We must not rend our subjects from our laws,
> And stick them in our will. To every county
> Where this is questioned, send our letters, with
> Free pardon for each man that has denied
> The force of this commission : pray, look to 't ;
> I put it to your care.
> WOLSEY. A word with you.
> (*To the Secretary.*) Let there be letters writ to every shire,
> Of the king's grace and pardon. The grieved commons
> Hardly conceive of me ; let it be nois'd,
> That through our intercession this revokement
> And pardon comes.—Act I.

Whether Wolsey would have stooped to such meanness as this may be doubted, yet even his admirers own that, with many good and great qualities, he was extremely artful ; while his enemies charged him with almost every vice.†

The Duke of Buckingham's surveyor is now examined. Catherine pities and pleads for the duke, but this man's declaration of Buckingham's threats against the king, which he states positively that he heard, and which seem to have had some foundation, convinces Henry that Buckingham is

person to the mayor and chief citizens of London. They attempted to remonstrate, but were warned to beware, lest 'it might fortune to cost some their heads.' "—HALLAM'S *Constitutional History*, vol. i. Evidently Hallam believes that for this taxation Henry was fully as accountable as Wolsey, upon whom Shakespeare lays the chief responsibility. There is no mention by Lingard, Hume, Hallam, or Green of Catherine's intercession on this subject, though her doing so is consistent with her noble and charitable disposition, admitted even by historians of such opposite views as Froude, Hume, and Lingard.

* "Henry VIII. encountered no opposition when he wished to send Buckingham, Surrey, Anne Boleyn, and Lady Salisbury to the scaffold. But when without the consent of Parliament he demanded of his subjects a contribution amounting to one-sixth of their goods, he soon found it necessary to retract. The cry of hundreds of thousands was that they were English and not French, free men and not slaves. In Kent the royal commissioners fled for their lives. In Suffolk four thousand men appeared in arms. Those who did not join in the insurrection declared that they would not fight against their brethren in such a quarrel. Henry, proud and self-willed as he was, shrank, not without reason, from a conflict with the roused spirit of the nation. He not only cancelled his illegal commissions, he not only granted a general pardon to all the malcontents, but he publicly and solemnly apologized for his infraction of the laws."—LORD MACAULAY'S *History of England*, vol. i.

† "We may pronounce him greedy of wealth and power and glory ; anxious to exalt the throne on which his own greatness was built, and the church of which he was so distinguished a member ; but capable, in the pursuit of these different objects, of stooping to expedients which sincerity and justice would disavow."— LINGARD'S *History*, vol. iv.

dangerous, though no proof of actual conspiracy is brought against him.

> KING HENRY.   There's mischief in this man : canst thou say further?
> SURVEYOR.   I can, my liege.
> KING HENRY.   Proceed.
> SURVEYOR.   Being at Greenwich,
> After your highness had reprov'd the duke
> About Sir William Blomer—
> KING HENRY.   I remember
> Of such a time—he being my sworn servant,
> The duke retain'd him his.——But on ; what hence ?
> SURVEYOR.   "*If*," quoth he, "*I for this had been committed,*
> *As, to the Tower, I thought—I would have play'd*
> *The part my father meant to act upon*
> *The usurper Richard ; who, being at Salisbury,*
> *Made suit to come in's presence ; which if granted,*
> *As he made semblance of his duty, would*
> *Have put his knife into him.*
> KING HENRY.   A giant traitor !
> WOLSEY.   Now, madam, may his highness live in freedom,
> And this man out of prison ?
> QUEEN CATHERINE.   God mend all !
> KING HENRY.   There's something more would out of thee ;
>   what say'st ?
> SURVEYOR.   After—"*the duke his father*"—with "*the knife*"—
> He stretch'd him, and, with one hand on his dagger,
> Another spread on 's breast, mounting his eyes,
> He did discharge a horrible oath ; whose tenor
> Was—were he evil used, he would outgo
> His father, by as much as a performance
> Does an irresolute purpose.
> KING HENRY.   There's his period,
> To sheathe his knife in us.   He is attach'd ;
> Call him to present trial : if he may
> Find mercy in the law, 'tis his ; if none,
> Let him not seek 't of us ; by day and night,
> He's traitor to the height.—Act I.

The king, however, really believes him a murderous traitor, and orders him to be tried immediately.

The next scene merely introduces some noblemen and courtiers talking over the late royal visit to France, and the great liking for French manners and customs that had since arisen among the young English nobility.

> LORD CHAMBERLAIN.   What news, Sir Thomas Lovel ?
> LOVEL.   Faith, my lord,
> I hear of none, but the new proclamation
> That's clapp'd upon the court-gate.

LORD CHAMBERLAIN.   What is't for?
LOVEL.   The reformation of our travell'd gallants,
That fill the court with quarrels, talk, and tailors.
    LORD CHAMBERLAIN.   I am glad 'tis there; now I would pray
                our monsieurs
To think an English courtier may be wise,
And never see the Louvre.—Act I.

Amid this light talk, they cannot refrain from mentioning
the all-powerful cardinal, whom they both dread and dislike.
In reality, much of the odium he incurred was more due to his
singular and friendless position in a court full of ambitious
noblemen and their friends than to any other cause; for
his influence in some respects benefited the country, though
it was not so acknowledged till after his fall.*   Although
an ecclesiastic as well as an active statesman, he lived in all
the luxury of a wealthy nobleman, but even his splendid
assemblies and receptions had their own political as well as
pleasurable objects and purposes.   At one of these gorgeous
entertainments, the king, in disguise, which he soon lays aside,
falls in love with Ann Boleyn, which the cardinal perceives,
but is unable to prevent.   In reality, Henry probably knew
her before this occasion, but in the play they first meet at
Wolsey's house.   The king dances with her, and the cardinal
watches them with anxiety.   The latter is now in a difficult
position, having offended Catherine and her friends by wishing to promote Henry's desired divorce, and he is yet
thoroughly opposed to the king's marrying the Protestant
Anne Boleyn, whom he knows is influenced by persons
hostile to his church.†
    At this time, Wolsey was perhaps even more powerful, or
at least more respected, abroad than in England.   His mind

* "His office of Chancellor afforded him the opportunity of displaying the
versatility and superiority of his talents. He always decided according to the
dictates of his own judgment, and the equity of his decrees was universally admitted and applauded."—LINGARD'S *History of England*, vol. iv. Hallam,
while blaming Wolsey's rapacity as well as profuseness, admits that "the latter
years of Henry VIII.'s reign were far more tyrannical than when he listened to
the counsels of Wolsey, and it is but equitable to allow some praise to a minister
for the mischief which he may be presumed to have averted."—*Constitutional
History*, vol. i. Mr. Green says:—"The Court of Chancery, indeed, became
so crowded, through the character for expedition and justice which it gained under
his rule, that subordinate courts had to be created for its relief."—*History of the
English People*, book v.

† "The royal wish for a divorce from Catherine was no sooner communicated
to Wolsey than he offered his aid, and ventured to promise complete success.
His views, however, were very different from those of his sovereign. Either un-
apprised of Henry's intentions in favour of Anne, or believing that the present
amour would terminate like so many others, he looked forward to the political
consequences of the divorce, and, that he might perpetuate the alliance between
England and France, had already selected for the successor of Catherine a daughter
of the late French King, Louis XII."--LINGARD'S *History*, vol. iv.

T

was much engrossed by foreign politics, and speculations ;
but he was an English subject all the time, and, as such,
at the mercy of a capricious and absolute king.* During his
brilliant midnight reception, therefore, Wolsey was perhaps
the most discontented of all the assemblage, when perceiving
Henry admiring and complimenting Anne Boleyn, whose
friendship he never possessed. The first act ends with this
important meeting, so joyous, gay, and light-hearted at first,
yet fraught with such fatal future consequences.

> KING HENRY (*to* ANNE BOLEYN). The fairest hand I ever
>   touched ! O, beauty,
> Till now I never knew thee !
>
> .   .   .   .   .
>
> You hold a fair assembly ; you do well, lord :
> You are a churchman, or I'll tell you, cardinal,
> I should judge now unhappily.
>   WOLSEY.   I am glad
> Your grace is grown so pleasant.
>
> .   .   .   .   .   .
>
>   Your grace,
> I fear, with dancing is a little heated.
>   KING HENRY.   I fear, too much.
>   WOLSEY.   There's fresher air, my lord,
> In the next chamber.
>   KING HENRY.   Lead in your ladies, every one.—Sweet partner,
> I must not yet forsake you.—Let's be merry ;—
> Good my lord cardinal, I have half a dozen healths
> To drink to these fair ladies, and a measure
> To lead them once again ; and then let's dream
> Who's best in favour.—Let the music knock it.—Act I.

The next act describes Buckingham's execution. This
nobleman, "the mirror of courtesy,"† was very popular, and
much regretted. Though he may have used hasty, vehement
words, few people apparently believed that he ever contemplated violence against the king.‡ Yet it seems likely that
Henry was as anxious to be rid of him as Wolsey, for both
distrusted him. His last speech, in Shakespeare's noble

---

* "Wolsey's mind was European rather than English ; it dwelt little on home
affairs, but turned almost exclusively to the general politics of the European
Powers, and of England as one of them."—GREEN'S *History of the English
People*, book v.

† LINGARD'S *History*.

‡ "He drew on himself the jealousy of the king, and the resentment of Wolsey.
The evidence on his trial for high treason was almost entirely confined to idle and
vaunting language held with servants, who betrayed his confidence. . . . It seems
manifest that Buckingham was innocent of any real conspiracy. In fact, the condemnation of this great noble was owing to Wolsey's resentment acting on the
savage temper of Henry."—HALLAM'S *Constitutional History*, vol. i.

words, when leaving prison for the scaffold, probably expressed the feelings of the real man, though in language which only the poet could command.

BUCKINGHAM. All good people,
You that thus far have come to pity me,
Hear what I say, and then go home and lose me.
I have this day received a traitor's judgment,
And by that name must die: yet, heaven bear witness,
And if I have a conscience let it sink me,
Even as the axe falls, if I be not faithful!
The law I bear no malice for my death,
It has done, upon the premises, but justice:
But those that sought it I could wish more Christians:
Be what they will, I heartily forgive them:
Yet let them look they glory not in mischief,
Nor build their evils on the graves of great men;
For then my guiltless blood must cry against them.
For further life in this world I ne'er hope,
Nor will I sue, although the king have mercies
More than I dare make faults. Ye few that lov'd me,
And dare be bold to weep for Buckingham,
His noble friends and fellows, whom to leave
Is only bitter to him, only dying,
Go with me, like good angels, to my end;
And, as the long divorce of steel falls on me,
Make of your prayers one sweet sacrifice,
And lift my soul to heaven.—Lead on, o' God's name.—Act II.

It is evident, from the spectators' language in this scene, that Wolsey bore all the blame of Buckingham's execution, and probably also in the victim's own mind; but it seems doubtful if the king himself was not the more responsible.*

The next scene is in the palace, where the Lord Chamberlain and other courtiers are talking about the cardinal, whose power over the king and unpopularity with the nobles are now at their height. Even the Chamberlain's new and handsome horses, "of the best breed in the north," are claimed by the imperious cardinal, who, like Falstaff, apparently believes that the laws of England are at his commandment, and that he can "take any man's horses."

LORD CHAMBERLAIN (*reading a letter*).—"When they were ready to set out for London, a man of my lord cardinal's, by commission and main force, took 'em from me; with this reason—His master would be served before a subject, if not before the king; which stopped our mouths, sir."
I fear, he will, indeed:—well, let him have them:
He will have all, I think.—Act II.

* HUME's and LINGARD's *Histories*.

This strange case is not again mentioned, and is perhaps introduced to show the great power of Wolsey at this time, whose influence over Henry, though opposed by Catherine, was generally known and regretted; and the cardinal was therefore often blamed for the king's acts, as if he were more completely under his guidance than he probably ever was in reality. But the king's fancy for Anne Boleyn now hastens his determination to be separated, by legal divorce or otherwise, from his queen, that he might marry his new favourite. Catherine was generally respected; although older than Henry, and his elder brother Prince Arthur's widow, she had lived many years with him, and had at one time considerable influence over the king, but was never very friendly with the cardinal. As Henry himself earnestly desired a divorce, Wolsey may have incurred more than his fair share of blame for too zealously trying to promote the king's wishes. He was now accused by Catherine, her friends, and the public generally, of setting Henry against her; but from much that is known of the king's character, had Wolsey never existed, his wish to be divorced from Catherine would have been equally strong. Shakespeare makes the noblemen at the court all blame Wolsey for the approaching separation, but historians of very opposite views * infer that Henry himself was quite resolved to banish Catherine, and to marry some one else, though he chose a bride most unacceptable to Wolsey.† Although Shakespeare, however, makes these intriguing noblemen blame Wolsey, as doubtless they did in reality, he does not thereby state his own views on the subject.

SUFFOLK.   How is the king employ'd?
LORD CHAMBERLAIN.   I left him private,
Full of sad thoughts and troubles.
    NORFOLK.   What's the cause?
LORD CHAMBERLAIN. It seems the marriage with his brother's
        wife
Has crept too near his conscience.
    SUFFOLK.   No, his conscience
Has crept too near another lady.
    NORFOLK.   'Tis so:
This is the cardinal's doing, the king-cardinal:
That blind priest, like the eldest son of fortune,
Turns what he list.   The king will know him one day.

---

* Froude and Lingard.

† " Anne Boleyn was not his friend. Her relatives and advisers were his rivals and enemies, and he knew that they only waited for the expected marriage to effect his downfall, with the aid of her influence over the mind of the king."— LINGARD'S *History of England*, vol. iv.

SUFFOLK.   Pray God he do ! he'll never know himself else.
NORFOLK.   He dives into the king's soul; and there scatters
Dangers, doubts, wringing of the conscience,
Fears, and despairs, and all these for his marriage :
And out of all these to restore the king,
He counsels a divorce : a loss of her
That, like a jewel, has hung twenty years
About his neck, yet never lost her lustre :
Of her that loves him with that excellence
That angels love good men with ; even of her
That when the greatest stroke of fortune falls
Will bless the king.—Act II.

At this time, the king was really anxious and uneasy, as described in the play. He and his friends often declared that he could never regard his marriage, contracted when very young, with his sister-in-law, as likely to be fortunate.* In this scene, Shakespeare, who, though too partial to Henry, yet describes his feelings in accordance with history, represents him as being sad and perplexed. He summons the two cardinals, Wolsey and Campeius, the latter sent specially from Rome to hear and advise about the approaching divorce. Henry, when asked by Wolsey for a private conference, instantly sends off Norfolk and Suffolk, both angry at being dismissed from the royal presence, and the more so as they suspect that important State business may be transacted in their absence. They therefore leave the chamber vexed and discontented, but obliged to conceal their feelings for the moment. The king courteously welcomes Campeius, while Wolsey, in flattering terms, lauds the king's good sense in having a public trial, by which the informality of his marriage may be proved, and the queen be termed the Princess Dowager as Prince Arthur's widow, thus virtually annulling her marriage with Henry.

WOLSEY.   Your grace has given a precedent of wisdom
Above all princes, in committing freely

---

* " Even if the marriage itself had never been questioned, he might justly have desired the dissolution of it, and when he considered the circumstances under which it was contracted—the hesitation of the council, the reluctance of the Pope, the alarms and vacillations of his father—we may readily perceive how scruples of conscience must have arisen in a soil well prepared to receive them ; how the loss of his children must have appeared as a judicial sentence on a violation of the divine law. The design presented itself to him as a moral obligation, when national advantage combined with superstition to encourage what he secretly desired."—FROUDE'S *Reign of Henry VIII.*, ch. ii. Hume writes rather similarly on the subject :—" Though Queen Catherine had borne him several children, they all died in early infancy, except one daughter, and Henry was the more struck with this misfortune because the curse of being childless is the very threatening contained in the Mosaical law against those who espouse their brother's widow."—Ch. xxx.

Your scruple to the voice of Christendom :
Who can be angry now ? what envy reach you ?
The Spaniard, tied by blood and favour to her,
Must now confess, if they have any goodness,
The trial just and noble.   All the clerks,
I mean the learned ones, in Christian kingdoms,
Have their free voices—Rome, the nurse of judgment,
Invited by yourself, hath sent
One general tongue unto us, this good man,
This just and honest priest, Cardinal Campeius,
Whom, once more, I present unto your highness.

    KING HENRY. And, once more, in mine arms I bid him welcome,
And thank the holy conclave for their loves ;
They have sent me such a man I could have wished for.

    CAMPEIUS.   Your grace must needs deserve all strangers' loves,
You are so noble.   To your highness' hand
I tender my commission; by whose virtue
(The court of Rome commanding) you, my lord
Cardinal of York, are joined with me their servant,
In the impartial judgment of this business.

    KING HENRY. Two equal men. The queen shall be acquainted,
Forthwith, for what you come.—Act II.

For Wolsey and Campeius are now to be the chief authorities
at this extraordinary trial, but both are puzzled how to act.
Wolsey, though always anxious to please Henry, would
gladly see him married to a foreign Catholic princess, but the
king's sudden fancy for Anne Boleyn alarms him, and he
secretly wishes to delay the divorce trial while he consults
with his friends abroad about the best course to take with
his imperious sovereign. Henry asks to see his new secretary,
Gardiner, Bishop of Winchester, a friend of Wolsey's, and
one who professes grateful devotion to the cardinal ; but all
these ecclesiastics have a difficult part to play between a
violent king, hostile nobles, and an offended, high-spirited
queen. Campeius warns Wolsey that he has many foes, but
the latter is now so proud and confident of Henry's favour
that he disregards the warning ; while the king sends a note
to Catherine, whom he seems to have really loved and respected, though, for many reasons, he now wishes his marriage dissolved.

    KING HENRY.   The most convenient place that I can think of,
For such receipt of learning, is Black Friars ;
There ye shall meet about this weighty business :
My Wolsey, see it furnish'd.   O, my lord,
Would it not grieve an able man to leave
So sweet a bedfellow ?   But, conscience, conscience—
O, 'tis a tender place, and I must leave her.—Act II.

The next scene introduces Anne Boleyn, with an old lady, talking over the expected separation between the king and queen, which was doubtless the general topic of interest in England. Anne, who evidently is aware how the king admires her, declares to her incredulous, shrewd old friend, who probably knows her disposition, that she has no wish to become a queen.

ANNE.   By my troth and maidenhead,
I would not be a queen.
   OLD LADY.   Beshrew me, I would, ... and
      so would you,
For all this spice of your hypocrisy.
   . . . . . You would not be a queen?
   ANNE.   No, not for all the riches under heaven.
   OLD LADY.   'Tis strange: a threepence bowed* would hire me,
Old as I am, to queen it : but, I pray you,
What think you of a duchess? have you limbs
To bear that load of title ?
   ANNE.   No, in truth.
   OLD LADY.   Then you are weakly made : pluck off a little ;
I would not be a young count in your way,
For more than blushing comes to.
   ANNE.   How you do talk!
I swear again, I would not be a queen
For all the world.
   OLD LADY.   In faith, for little England
You'd venture an emballing† : I myself
Would for Carnarvonshire, although there 'longed
No more to the crown but that.—Act II.

The old court lady rallies her playfully, and while they are talking the Lord Chamberlain enters, with a message from Henry that he creates Anne Marchioness of Pembroke, and bestows on her a thousand pounds a year. Anne sends her grateful thanks, and the Chamberlain retires, praising her to himself, and anticipates that she will soon be queen, although both she and her companion are now merely ladies attached to Catherine's court.

When Anne and the old lady are again alone, the latter, while highly pleased, cannot help envying her young friend's early success in life compared to her own ; for she had long lived about the court, and is evidently a worldly, vain woman, and perhaps more artful than attractive.

   OLD LADY.   Why, this it is: see, see !
I have been begging sixteen years in court
(Am yet a courtier beggarly) nor could

   * Bent.
   † You would venture to be distinguished by the *ball*, the ensign of royalty."—
JOHNSON'S *Notes to Henry VIII.*

Come pat betwixt too early and too late,
For any suit of pounds : and you, O fate
A very fresh-fish here—fie, fie, fie upon
This compell'd fortune !—have your mouth fill'd up
Before you open it.
   ANNE.   This is strange to me.
   OLD LADY. How tastes it ? is it bitter. . .
    .   .   . The Marchioness of Pembroke !

    .   .   .   By this time,
I know, your back will bear a duchess ;—say,
Are you not stronger than you were ?
   ANNE.   Good lady,
Make yourself mirth with your particular fancy,
And leave me out on't.   Would I had no being,
If this salute my blood a jot ; it faints me
To think what follows.
The queen is comfortless, and we forgetful
In our long absence : pray, do not deliver
What here you have heard to her.
   OLD LADY.   What do you think me ?—Act II.

She is surprised, or pretends to be, that Anne does not
show more pleasure ; but the latter is beset by many anxious
thoughts, as she vaguely foresees the dangers, risks, and
enemies that will probably thicken around her if she is destined
to openly supplant the popular queen.   She therefore cannot
quite share in her companion's almost triumphant rejoicings
until she has seen her own relatives, who, it is said, were very
anxious for the marriage, which she seems to have wished also,
though it was believed that she had some attachment to young
Lord Percy, who is never mentioned in this play.   The next
scene, ending the second act, is in the Hall at Black Friars,
the place Henry had fixed for the trial.   He is here with the
queen, the two cardinals, and all the chief dignitaries of the
realm, lay and clerical.   On this occasion, Catherine besought
Henry, if not in Shakespeare's noble words, yet in affecting
and dignified terms, to do her justice, and allow her to consult her friends in Spain about what course to adopt in trying
to prove their marriage lawful.

      QUEEN CATHERINE.   Please you, sir,
The king, your father, was reputed for
A prince most prudent, of an excellent
And unmatch'd wit and judgment : Ferdinand,
My father, king of Spain, was reckon'd one
The wisest prince that there had reign'd by many
A year before : it is not to be question'd
That they had gather'd a wise council to them

Of every realm, that did debate this business,
Who deem'd our marriage lawful : wherefore I humbly
Beseech you, sir, to spare me, till I may
'Be by my friends in Spain advis'd ; whose counsel
I will implore : if not, i' the name of God,
Your pleasure be fulfill'd !—Act II.

She then boldly charges Wolsey with having set Henry
against her, which he denies, but she openly rejects him as a
judge or authority in her case, and surprises the whole
assembly by declaring she will appeal to the Pope (Clement
VII.), and then leaves the court. Wolsey requests the king
to publicly free him from the odious and perhaps rather hasty
imputation thrown on him by the indignant queen, who, apparently afraid of offending Henry, turns her angry reproaches
against his minister. The king, whose many faults did not
include hypocrisy, immediately clears Wolsey from the
charge of having incited him to his present course, and even
declares that the cardinal rather wished that the question of
divorce had never been raised.

CARDINAL WOLSEY. In humblest manner I require your highness,
That it shall please you to declare, in hearing
Of all these ears (for where I am robb'd and bound,
There must I be unloos'd ; although not there
At once and fully satisfied), whether ever I
Did broach this business to your highness ; or
Laid any scruple in your way, which might
Induce you to the question on't ? or ever
Have to you—but with thanks to God for such
A royal lady—spake one the least word that might
Be to the prejudice of her present state,
Or touch of her good person ?
    KING HENRY.   My lord cardinal,
I do excuse you ; yea, upon mine honour,
I free you from 't.   You are not to be taught
That you have many enemies, that know not
Why they are so, but, like to village curs,
Bark when their fellows do : by some of these
The queen is put in anger.   You are excus'd :
But will you be more justified ? you ever
Have wish'd the sleeping of this business ; never
Desired it to be stirr'd ; but oft have hinder'd, oft,
The passages made toward it :—on my honour,
I speak my good lord cardinal to this point,
And thus far clear him.—Act II.

Henry then makes a long speech to both cardinals about
his own duties and wishes in this matter. After he has

finished, the Italian cardinal, Campeius, or Campeggio, acting on instructions from Rome, somewhat suddenly adjourns the case. The king, in great anger at this delay, summons Bishop Cranmer to his counsels, and, for the first time, begins to distrust Wolsey. The latter had now, unfortunately for himself, incurred the displeasure of all parties. Catherine and her friends blamed him for having first " blown this coal" between her and the king, whereas he really seems to have only, though to a blamable extent, tried to please Henry in this matter, hoping he might marry a Catholic princess, and have an heir male to the crown. Anne Boleyn's party were, if possible, yet more angry with him for his evident dislike to her marriage with Henry; while he himself had secretly set his heart on becoming the next Pope, in which aspiration he had been encouraged by Henry.* But the sudden adjournment of this trial so enraged the king that he began to admit not only Cranmer, but other advisers hostile to Wolsey, into his confidence, and resolves to marry Anne Boleyn without consulting the Pope about the validity of his previous marriage with Catherine.†

In this important act, and, indeed, during the whole play, the three chief characters are Henry, Catherine, and Wolsey. The others—even Bishops Gardiner and Cranmer—though destined to take such an important part in history, are only briefly sketched, for the play ends before they have distinguished themselves. This grand second act displays the three strongest characters curiously contrasted with each other, and though their noble language is, of course, Shakespeare's, he evidently attributes carefully to each the precise sentiments which, according to history, actuated their conduct. The king, impatient and angry at the postponement of the trial, breaks up the court, he and Catherine being alike dissatisfied with it, though for very different reasons. It appears, however, that from this time Henry's character changed greatly for the worse, by the admission of most impartial historians.‡ He is now surrounded by artful advisers, availing themselves of his violent temper to set him against both Catherine and the cardinal, who were, in their turn, hopelessly opposed to each other. Wolsey, despite his pride and

* Hume and Lingard.

† " Anne Boleyn had imputed to Wolsey the failure of her hopes [in having Henry's previous marriage dissolved], and, as she was newly returned to court, whence she had been removed from a regard to decency during the trial before the legates, she had naturally acquired an additional influence over Henry, and she served much to fortify his prejudices against the cardinal. Even the queen and her partisans, judging of Wolsey by the part he had openly acted, had expressed great animosity against him, and the most opposite factions seemed now to combine in the ruin of this haughty minister."—HUME'S *History*, ch. xxx.

‡ HALLAM'S *Constitutional History*.

arrogance, was, indeed, in many ways superior, both in education, knowledge, and prudence, to most, if not all, of his opponents among the nobles at the court. For a long time they had endeavoured to effect his downfall, and at length succeeded, chiefly owing to the aid of Anne Boleyn and her friends.*

The third act introduces Catherine in retirement, receiving an unwelcome visit from Wolsey and Campeius. They both advise her yielding to Henry's wish about the divorce, without further opposition. Catherine distrusts both, and, alike in the play and in history, refuses, and insists on maintaining her position as lawful queen.†

> CATHERINE. Ye turn me into nothing : woe upon ye,
> And all such false professors ! Would you have me
> Put my sick cause into his hands that hates me ?
>
> My lord, I dare not make myself so guilty,
> To give up willingly that noble title
> Your master wed me to : nothing but death
> Shall e'er divorce my dignities.—Act III.

The next scene is in the palace, introducing the nobles Norfolk, Surrey, Suffolk, and the Lord Chamberlain, talking about Wolsey, whose downfall they now expect and desire. Anne Boleyn and her friends are at present high in the king's favour, while the cardinal has few friends in England. He enters the chamber where these noblemen are, followed by his faithful secretary, Thomas Cromwell, a man who, like Gardiner and Cranmer, was destined to be well known in English history, but who, like them, is in a very subordinate position throughout this play. Wolsey is thoughtful, depressed, and apprehensive. The assembled courtiers rejoice at seeing his perturbed expression, as they all dislike and dread him ; while, after hearing from Cromwell that he gave a certain packet of letters to Henry, he bids the secre-

---

* "It was a struggle for pre-eminence between two factions—that of the nobles, headed by Norfolk, backed up by the Emperor Charles [of Germany], and supported by Anne Boleyn ; and that of the cardinal—a head without followers."—BREWER'S *English Studies*, Essay vii.

† In réality, she made a somewhat similar answer to the royal commissioners sent by Henry to the reply Shakespeare describes her giving to the cardinals. "I stick not so for vain glory, but because I know myself the king's true wife. . . . . If he take me not for his wife, I came not into this realm as merchandise, ... nor do I continue in the same but as his lawful wife, and not as subject to him, under his dominion otherwise. I have always demeaned myself well and truly towards the king. . . . . I have done England little good, and I should be sorry to do it any harm. But if I should agree to your motions and persuasions, I should slander myself, and confess to have been the king's harlot for twenty-four years."—FROUDE'S *Reign of Henry VIII.*, vol. i. "*Extract from State Papers.*"

tary leave him, and, when alone with the courtiers, who vainly try to guess his thoughts, he reveals his feelings in a remarkable soliloquy, the nobles eagerly observing his evident, yet mysterious, uneasiness.

> WOLSEY.   It shall be to the Duchess of Alençon,
> The French king's sister : he shall marry her.—
> Anne Boleyn ! No : I'll no Anne Boleyns for him :
> There's more in't than fair visage.—Boleyn !
> No, we'll no Boleyns.—Speedily I wish
> To hear from Rome—The Marchioness of Pembroke !
>   NORFOLK.   He's discontented.
>   SUFFOLK.   Maybe he hears the king
> Does whet his anger at him.
>   SURREY.   Sharp enough,
> Lord, for thy justice.
>   WOLSEY.   The late queen's gentlewoman ; a knight's daughter,
> To be her mistress's mistress ! the queen's queen !—
> This candle burns not clear ; 'tis I must snuff it ;
> Then, out it goes.—What though I know her virtuous
> And well-deserving ; yet I know her for
> A spleeny Lutheran ; and not wholesome to
> Our cause, that she should lie i' the bosom of
> Our hard-rul'd king.   Again, there is sprung up
> A heretic, an arch one, Cranmer ; one
> Hath crawl'd into the favour of the king,
> And is his oracle.—Act III.

While Wolsey is thus absorbed in thought, Henry enters, reading some papers about the cardinal's great wealth, splendid furniture, &c., which, by mistake, had been given him, together with Wolsey's letter to the Pope.   This scene, though so ably described, seems without much historical foundation.*   Henry had long known about the cardinal's wealth, which could never have been concealed from him, while previous to this scene he had wished his powerful subject to become Pope.   In reality, his anger with Wolsey was by no means so sudden as Shakespeare describes ; but the gradual effect of the intrigues at the palace, with Anne Boleyn's hostile influence, added to Henry's disappointment at the postponement of the divorce, for which he blamed Wolsey.   Yet in this grand scene, the characters of Henry and Wolsey seem truly and admirably represented.   The king at first shows that self-control, while deeply offended, which he could usually command whenever he chose, speaking in sarcastic yet dignified language.†

* *See* Hume's, Froude's, Lingard's, and Hallam's *Histories.*
† Mr. Froude states that Henry, when he liked, could display a much more ' calm and rational " spirit than some historians have represented. In describing

WOLSEY.   Ever God bless your highness !
   KING HENRY.   Good my lord,
You are full of heavenly stuff, and bear the inventory
Of your best graces in your mind ; the which
You were now running o'er ; you have scarce time
To steal from spiritual leisure a brief span
To keep your earthly audit : sure, in that
 deem you an ill husband : and am glad
To have you therein my companion.
   CARDINAL WOLSEY.   Sire,
For holy offices I have a time ; a time
To think upon the part of business, which
 bear i' the state ; and nature does require
Her times of preservation, which perforce
, her frail son, among my brethren mortal,
Must give my tendance to.
   KING HENRY.   You have said well.
   CARDINAL WOLSEY.   And ever may your highness yoke together,
As I will give you cause, my doing well
With my well-saying.
   KING HENRV.   'Tis well said again ;
And 'tis a kind of good deed to say well :
And yet words are no deeds.   My father lov'd you :
He said he did ; and with his deed did crown
His word upon you.   Since I had my office,
 have kept you next my heart ; have not alone
Employ'd you where high profits might come home,
But par'd my present havings, to bestow
My bounties upon you.
   WOLSEY (aside).   What should this mean ?
   SURREY (aside to the others).   The Lord increase this business.
   KING HENRY.   Have I not made you
The prime man of the state ?   I pray you, tell me,
If what I now pronounce you have found true :
And, if you may confess it, say withal,
If you are bound to us or no.   What say you ?
   WOLSEY.   My sovereign, I confess your royal graces,
Shower'd on me daily, have been more than could
My studied purposes requite. . . . .
Though all the world should crack their duty to you,
And throw it from their soul ; though perils did
Abound as thick as thought could make them, and
Appear in forms more horrid ; yet my duty,

is letters to the Pope about the divorce, Henry, according to Froude, must have
nown a similar coolness and self-control which he manifests in this scene. "He
isplayed a most efficient mastery over himself, although he did not conclude
ithout touching the pith of the matter with telling clearness."—*Reign of Henry
VIII.*, ch. ii.   It was apparently Shakespeare's wish to describe both king and
ardinal truly, on the whole, while occasionally placing them in imaginary
tuations.

As doth the rock against the chiding flood,
Should the approach of this wild river break,
And stand unshaken yours.
   KING HENRY.   'Tis nobly spoken :
Take notice, lords, he has a loyal breast,
For you have seen him open 't.—Read o'er this [*giving him papers*] ;
And, after, this : and then to breakfast, with
What appetite you have. [*Exit, frowning upon the cardinal ; the
    nobles throng after him, smiling and whispering.*
   WOLSEY.   What should this mean ?
What sudden anger's this ? how have I reap'd it ?
He parted frowning from me, as if ruin
Leap'd from his eyes : so looks the chafed lion
Upon the daring huntsman that has gall'd him ;
Then makes him nothing. I must read this paper :
I fear, the story of his anger.—'Tis so :
This paper has undone me : 'tis the account
Of all that world of wealth I have drawn together
For mine own ends. . . .   O negligence,
Fit for a fool to fall by ! What cross devil
Made me put this main secret in the packet
I sent the king ? . . . . . What's this—" *To the Pope* " ?
The letter, as I live, with all the business
I writ to 's holiness. Nay then, farewell !
I have touch'd the highest point of all my greatness :
And, from that full meridian of my glory,
I haste now to my setting. I shall fall
Like a bright exhalation in the evening,
And no man see me more.—Act III.

Throughout this interview, Henry has apparently put a
strong constraint upon himself, and at last, but only for a
moment, reveals his anger, although in a way sufficiently un-
mistakable to terrify Wolsey to the utmost. The cardinal also
in this scene displays many qualities attributed to him by
history. He is calm, courteous, and dignified, yet submissive ;
his answers are, indeed, well fitted to turn aside wrath and
soothe irritation ; but Henry is now so completely set against
him, being entirely under hostile influences, that Wolsey
despairs of regaining favour. While alarmed, and astonished
at his king's reproaches, he is assailed by the bitter insults of
the nobles and courtiers, formerly on their best behaviour
towards him, but who are now authorised by Henry to
demand his resignation of the great seal, and to consider
him a prisoner till the king's will is known. Wolsey tries
to repel their taunts with dignity and self-command ; but,
when alone with his faithful follower, Cromwell, he yields to
remorse, entreating his adherent to be warned by his example
never to set his heart upon objects of worldly ambition.

Probably at this trying moment, the political cardinal recalls his early days, when his ardent spirit had chosen theology for a profession, little thinking, while a youth, that his vigorous mind would ever be so completely diverted from a holy life to the dangerous career of an ambitious statesman.   Yet, though repentant for some unscrupulous acts, thoughts, and designs, Wolsey's conscience, when fully awakened, never accuses him of ingratitude to the king, whom he had certainly served faithfully, on the whole, though he was unable to keep pace with all the sudden, capricious, changes in his imperious master's mind and inclinations.   His last well-known words in this scene, wishing he had served his God as well as he had served his king, were not said to Cromwell, but to the Constable of the Tower of London, by whom, long after his disgrace, he was arrested on a vague charge of treason, but died before his trial.   Shakespeare never again introduces him after this scene, at the close of which Cromwell leads him away disgraced, friendless, and ruined : but in reality he lived in comfortable retirement for some time after his dismissal from the court, though his numerous foes were constantly intriguing against him.   In the play, he hears from Cromwell of Sir Thomas More's being appointed Lord Chancellor in his place.   This great man's abilities Wolsey knows and appreciates, and, in his present grief and depression, utters an expressive and pathetic blessing on him, alluding to More's future guardianship of helpless orphans, in his high legal position.

> WOLSEY.   He's a learned man.   May he continue
> Long in his highness' favour, and do justice
> For truth's sake, and his conscience ; that his bones,
> When he has run his course, and sleeps in blessings,
> May have a tomb of orphans' tears wept on them.—Act III.

When hearing of his rival Cranmer's being made Archbishop of Canterbury, he, with brief emphasis, exclaims, "That's news indeed!" but feelings of wonder, apprehension, and foreboding are doubtless comprised in this short sentence.   Lastly, he hears of Anne Boleyn's coronation, and the certainty of her having been married for some time previously to the king.   In her he recognises his chief enemy, but expresses no resentment towards any one.

> WOLSEY. There was the weight that pull'd me down. O Cromwell,
> The king has gone beyond me ; all my glories
> In that one woman I have lost for ever.
>
> Cromwell, I charge thee, fling away ambition.

. . . . . .   Be just and fear not :
Let all the ends thou aim'st at be thy country's,
Thy God's, and truth's; then, if thou fall'st, O Cromwell,
Thou fall'st a blessed martyr.   Serve the king ;
And—prithee, lead me in :
There take an inventory of all I have,
To the last penny ; 'tis the king's : my robe,
And my integrity to heaven, is all
I dare now call mine own.   O Cromwell, Cromwell,
Had I but serv'd my God with half the zeal
I serv'd my king, He would not in mine age
Have left me naked to mine enemies.—Act III.*

Wolsey is now perhaps more like himself when, in early youth, he had chosen the church as his profession, the ambitious dream of his later years having so suddenly vanished.   In many respects, he was evidently a man far in advance of his times.   Among comparatively ignorant, proud nobles, and in the power of a jealous, passionate, and unscrupulous king, his powers of intrigue and dissimulation, as well as his arrogance and vanity, had all been intensified, and devoted to political purposes.   But his rare abilities, and his noble wish to encourage learning throughout the nation, were neither appreciated nor perhaps understood by his impetuous master or by the jealous, worldly statesmen who rejoiced at his downfall, and who, indeed, had more reason to fear his political ambition than to admire his intellectual tastes or acquirements.†

Act IV. opens cheerfully, describing the London citizens watching the splendid ceremony of Anne Boleyn's coronation in Westminster Abbey, and the state procession through the capital ; while a fortunate spectator describes, in beautiful language, to his friends what he saw in the Abbey :—

                              The rich stream
        Of lords and ladies having brought the queen
        To a prepar'd place in the choir, fell off
        A distance from her : while her grace sat down

* Wolsey's last words, addressed shortly before his death to Sir William Kingston, Constable of the Tower, though they resemble this speech to Cromwell, show less devotion to Henry :—" I do assure you that I have often kneeled before him, sometimes three hours together, to persuade him from his will and appetite, but could not prevail.   Had I but served my God as diligently as I have served the king, He would not have given me over in my grey hairs."—Hume's *History*, ch. xxx.

† "Literature found in the cardinal a constant and bountiful patron.   On native scholars he heaped preferment, and the most eminent foreigners were invited by him to teach in the universities. . . . . Oxford chiefly experienced his munificence in the endowment of seven lectureships, and the foundation of Christchurch, which, though he lived not to complete it, still exists a splendid monument to his memory."—Lingard's *History*.

To rest awhile, some half an hour or so,
In a rich chair of state, opposing freely
The beauty of her person to the people.
Believe me, sir, she is the goodliest woman
That ever lay by man : which when the people
Had the full view of, such a noise arose
As the shrouds make at sea in a stiff tempest,
As loud, and to as many tunes : hats, cloaks
(Doublets, I think), flew up : and had their faces
Been loose, this day they had been lost.   Such joy
I never saw before. . . . . . .
At length her grace rose, and with modest paces
Came to the altar : where she kneel'd, and, saint-like,
Cast her fair eyes to heaven, and prayed devoutly.
Then rose again, and bow'd her to the people :
When by the Archbishop of Canterbury
She had all the royal makings of a queen ;
As holy oil, Edward Confessor's crown,
The rod, and bird of peace, and all such emblems,
Laid nobly on her ; which perform'd, the choir,
With all the choicest music of the kingdom,
Together sung *Te Deum.*—Act IV.

Although Catherine, now practically divorced, and living in strict retirement, was generally pitied and respected, yet Anne Boleyn and her friends soon became popular, though but for a short time. Her youth and beauty attracted much interest and admiration, while Henry, even in his political acts, and in the choice of his ministers, was greatly under her influence. Anne's real character, however, is not described by Shakespeare at all ; she merely appears as a pretty, interesting young bride, and is then withdrawn.

The next scene is a remarkable, affecting contrast, introducing Catherine in her last illness, at Kimbolton ; but she really died at a later period than the poet describes, though her conduct, language, and sentiments in the play seem founded in a great measure on historical record.* She is attended by a gentleman named Griffith, a man evidently of discernment, ability, and good feeling, truly attached, like her female attendant, to their unfortunate mistress. He now announces the death of her former enemy, as she believes, Cardinal Wolsey, somewhat suddenly, after being arrested, by the king's orders, to be tried for treason. While under the escort of Kingston, the Constable of the Tower, he stopped at Leicester Abbey, exhausted both in body and mind, and there died. He was apparently suspected and

* "This scene is above any other part of Shakespeare's tragedies, and perhaps above any scene of any other poet, tender and pathetic."—JOHNSON'S *Notes to Henry VIII.*

arrested most unjustly, at the instigation of some personal enemies about the court, yet even the wilful, violent king showed sorrow at hearing of his death.*   His fate is now told to Catherine by Griffith, and her noble nature, incapable of vindictiveness, freely forgives all real or imaginary wrong he may have done her in assisting Henry about the divorce. At first, however, she gently censures Wolsey's pride, arrogance, and craft, when Griffith reminds her of his many high qualities—his generosity, munificence, and the efforts he had made to promote learning in England.

> GRIFFITH.   This cardinal,
> Though from an humble stock, undoubtedly
> Was fashion'd to much honour from his cradle.
> He was a scholar, and a ripe and good one ;
> Exceeding wise, fair-spoken, and persuading :
> Lofty and sour to them that lov'd him not ;
> But to those men who sought him sweet as summer.
> And though he were unsatisfied in getting,
> Which was a sin, yet in bestowing, Madam,
> He was most princely : ever witness for him
> Those twins of learning that he rais'd in you,
> Ipswich and Oxford ! one of which fell with him,
> Unwilling to outlive the good he did it ;
> The other, though unfinish'd, yet so famous,
> So excellent in art, and still so rising,
> That Christendom shall ever speak his virtue.
> His overthrow heap'd happiness upon him ;
> For then, and not till then, he felt himself,
> And found the blessedness of being little :
> And, to add greater honours to his age
> Than man could give him, he died fearing God.
>   CATHERINE.   Whom I most hated living, thou hast made
>   me,
> With thy religious truth and modesty,
> Now in his ashes honour : peace be with him !—Act IV.

Catherine listens calmly, and praises him for thus defending Wolsey, for, though still believing herself injured by him, she is incapable of malice towards any one.   She then falls asleep, and a beautiful vision is described of angels bringing garlands, and consoling her saddened and departing spirit. They vanish, and she awakes, asking her attendants if they saw them, which they had not, but they perceive and remark to each other that her end is fast approaching.   An ambas-

---

* "Henry much regretted Wolsey's death when informed of it, and always spoke favourably of his memory—a proof that humour, more than reason, or any discovery of treachery, had occasioned the last persecutions against him."— HUME'S *History*, ch. xxx.

sador named Capucius, her near relative, now arrives from
court, whom she immediately recognises, and he brings a
kind message and inquiries from Henry.

   QUEEN CATHERINE.   What is your pleasure with me ?
   CAPUCIUS.   Noble lady,
First, mine own service to your grace ; the next,
The king's request that I would visit you ;
Who grieves much for your weakness, and by me
Sends you his princely commendation,
And heartily entreats you take good comfort.
   QUEEN CATHERINE.   O my good lord, that comfort comes too
       late ;
Tis like a pardon after execution :
That gentle physic, given in time, had cur'd me ;
But now I am past all comforts here but prayers.
How does his highness ?
   CAPUCIUS.   Madam, in good health.
   QUEEN CATHERINE.   So may he ever do, and ever flourish.—
                                    Act IV.

At mention of Henry's name, her spirits for a moment
apparently revive, and, summoning all her strength of mind,
she gives Capucius a last letter to the king, with a verbal
message of farewell, and two last entreaties in behalf of her
daughter, the Princess Mary, and her faithful servants, both
men and women, whom she fears may be exposed to poverty
and neglect after her death. Capucius solemnly promises to
deliver her letter and message to Henry, and Catherine then
bids adieu to her attendants, and soon after expires in peace
and charity with all.

   CATHERINE.   Remember me
In all humility unto his highness :
Say, his long trouble now is passing
Out of this world : tell him, in death I bless'd him,
For so I will.—Act IV.

In reality, the queen was treated more harshly than appears
from the play, being forbidden to again see her daughter,
which she greatly desired.* Yet, when Henry heard of her
death, he wept, and showed real sorrow, by the accounts of
many historians.† He thus evidently felt grief at the loss
of both Catherine and Wolsey, those illustrious victims of
his wayward temper, as apparently both their deaths were
hastened, if not chiefly caused, by the effects of his conduct
towards them ; yet neither they, their friends, nor, indeed,
any of Henry's subjects, whether injured by him or not, ever

    * LINGARD'S *History*.   † Hume, Lingard, and Froude.

showed that resentment against him which might have been expected.* Despite his tyrannical conduct, he was apparently always one of the most popular of the English kings. Even his subjects who were either executed or ill-used by him usually attributed their misfortunes to their own faults or to the king's ministers and advisers, when really his worst counsellors were apparently his own unresisted passions.†

The fifth and last act of this eventful play is entirely in London, at first relating a vehement dispute between Bishop Gardiner and the future Archbishop Cranmer, in which the king favours the latter, Cranmer being much esteemed both by himself and the new queen, Anne Boleyn. Yet neither of these ecclesiastics, so distinguished at a later period, are made very interesting in the play, for their abilities were not much displayed during the time it comprises. The end of this serious, if not melancholy, play is, however, brilliant and joyful, celebrating the birth and christening of the Princess Elizabeth, amid the rejoicings of the London populace. Her birth is announced to the king by a chattering old lady, perhaps Anne Boleyn's former companion, and this little scene, though probably imaginary, is lively and amusing.

OLD LADY.   Now, good angels
Fly o'er thy royal head, and shade thy person
Under their blessed wings.
KING HENRY.   Now, by thy looks
I guess thy message.   Is the queen deliver'd?
Say, *Ay ; and of a boy.*
OLD LADY.   Ay, ay, my liege ;
And of a lovely boy : the God of heaven
Both now and ever bless her—'tis a girl,
Promises boys hereafter.   Sir, your queen
Desires your visitation, and to be
Acquainted with this stranger ; 'tis as like you
As cherry is to cherry.
KING HENRY.   Give her an hundred marks.   I'll to the queen.
OLD LADY.   An hundred marks !   By this light, I'll ha' more.

* There were in all nine acts in the time of Henry VIII. which created new treasons.   Such laws were beyond all question of terrible severity.   No doubt the recollection of the Wars of the Roses, and the result of a disputed succession, must have been present to all minds, and have exercised a powerful influence both on the king and on his counsellors.   Much also must be ascribed to haughty self-will, and something to mere passion, though Henry's character was not that of a sensualist. . . . As soon as Henry VIII. was dead his legislation on the subject of treason was repealed."—STEPHENS's *History of the English Criminal Law*, ch. xxiii.

† "It may seem a little extraordinary that, notwithstanding his cruelty, his extortion, his violence, his arbitrary administration, Henry not only acquired the regard of his subjects, but never was the object of their hatred ; he seems even in some degree to have possessed to the last their love and affection."—HUME's *History*, ch. xxxiii.

An ordinary groom is for such payment.
I will have more, or scold it out of him.
Said I for this the girl was like to him ?
I will have more, or else unsay' t ; and now,
While it is hot, I'll put it to the issue.—Act V.

Henry, though deeply disappointed at not having a son,
was pleased at the birth of this child, and soon after gave her
the title of Princess of Wales.*

The christening of the princess, a brilliant ceremony,
attended with great joy and festivity, ends the play, the
London people crowding round and into the palace yard, to
the annoyance, yet perhaps rather to the gratification, of
the gate-porter and his assistants. Such noisy demonstrations of loyalty evidently surprise the Lord Chamberlain as
well as the lower officials.

Scene III.—The Palace Yard.   Noise and tumult without; enter
PORTER *and his* MAN.

PORTER.   You'll leave your noise anon, ye rascals: ye rude slaves,
leave your gaping.
CROWD *without*.   Good master porter, I belong to the larder.
PORTER.   Belong to the gallows, and be hanged, you rogue : Is
this a place to roar in ?   You must be seeing christenings.   Do you
look for ale and cakes here, you rude rascals ? .   .   .   How got
they in, and be hanged ?
MAN.   Alas, I know not ; how gets the tide in ?
As much as one sound cudgel of four foot
(You see the poor remainder) could distribute,
I made no spare, sir.
PORTER.   You did nothing, sir.
MAN.   I am not Samson, nor Sir Guy, nor Colbrand,
To mow 'em down before me. .   .   .   .
They fell on ; I made good my place ; at length they came to the
broomstaff to me ; I defied them still ; when suddenly a file of
boys behind 'em delivered such a shower of pebbles, loose shot,
that I was fain to draw mine honour in, and let them win the work :
The devil was amongst 'em, I think, surely.
PORTER.   These are the youths that thunder at a play-house, and
fight for bitten apples.

Enter LORD CHAMBERLAIN.

CHAMBERLAIN.   Mercy on me, what a multitude are here !
They grow still too, from all parts they are coming,
As if we kept a fair here ! Where are these porters,
These lazy knaves ? Ye have made a fine hand, fellows.
There's a trim rabble let in : are all these

* HUME's *History*.

Your faithful friends of the suburbs?   We shall have
Great store of room, no doubt, left for the ladies,
When they pass back from the christening.
    PORTER.   An't please your honour,
We are but men ; and what so many may do,
Not being torn a-pieces, we have done :
An army cannot rule 'em.
    CHAMBERLAIN.   As I live,
If the king blame me for 't, I'll lay ye all
By the heels, and suddenly ; and on your heads
Clap round fines, for neglect.   .   .   .   .
    PORTER.   Make way there for the princess.
    MAN.   You great fellow,
Stand close up, or I'll make your head ache.
    PORTER.   You i' the camblet, get up o' the rail ;
I'll pick you o'er the pales else.—Act V.

In English history, such general delight had not for a long
period been exhibited.   The quarrels caused for many years
by the Wars of the Roses had so divided popular sympathy
that neither royal marriages nor christenings could be celebrated without arousing opposite feelings of triumph or
depression among the people.   But now the rejoicings were
almost unanimous, for Henry's tyranny was as yet but little
known ; while to the last he was surprisingly popular with
all those of his subjects who were not personally afraid of his
anger.

The play ends with a beautiful speech of Cranmer before
the king at the christening of the future queen.

    CRANMER.   This royal infant (heaven still move above her !),
Though in her cradle, yet now promises
Upon this land a thousand thousand blessings,
Which time shall bring to ripeness : she shall be
A pattern to all princes living with her,
And all that shall succeed ;   .   .   .   .
In her days every man shall eat in safety,
Under his own vine, what he plants ; and sing
The merry songs of peace to all his neighbours :
She shall be, to the happiness of England,
An aged princess ; many days shall see her,
And yet no day without a deed to crown it.
Would I had known no more ! but she must die,
She must, the saints must have her ; yet a virgin,
A most unspotted lily, shall she pass
To the ground, and all the world shall mourn her.—Act V.

Of all Shakespeare's works, the historical plays may surely
be considered the most instructive, and to many the most
interesting.   While occasionally placing real persons in ima-

ginary situations, and inspiring them with his own language, he usually adheres, with surprising accuracy, to the accounts given of them by historical records.* His noble language and grand ideas are, of course, his own, but if these plays are compared with the best English histories, even the recent ones, possessing all the advantages of modern education and research, they will be found to give a remarkably correct version, on the whole, of the chief characters and events they describe. He probably ascribes too much personal importance to the English kings, attributing to them alone many thoughts, designs, and motives which might have been more justly ascribed to their ministers and statesmen, who sometimes really governed the nation under their sovereign's nominal authority. It has been said of Shakespeare that "he wrote not for an age, but for all time," and if the historians, literary men, and commentators in former times are compared to those of this nineteenth century, it will be found that the latter have been far more decided and even enthusiastic in his praise than their literary predecessors were. Ben Jonson, Hume, Dryden, Pope, Warburton, Hanmer, and even Dr. Johnson praise him less warmly than do the comparatively modern writers, Hallam, Macaulay, Walter Scott, M. Guizot, Schlegel, Coleridge, H. Staunton, Furnivall, Dowden, &c. During this century—a period unequalled in history for the extension of knowledge, the progress of education, and the increasing multitudes of books and readers— Shakespeare has been more generally appreciated than ever, both in England and on the Continent. Notwithstanding the enormous increase of reading, and the unprecedented number of authors in this century, his peculiar genius has never been equalled, and very slightly resembled, by any other writer, English or foreign. The vast changes in the social, moral, literary, and political world since his time, have never diminished the interest inspired by his works. On the contrary, they still command and elicit the admiration of successive generations, whose educational advantages only arouse the higher appreciation of a superiority independent of them. Thus the present position of

* "The historical plays have had a great effect on Shakespeare's popularity. . . . . And these dramatic chronicles borrowed surprising liveliness and probability from the national character and form of government. . . . . What he invented is as truly English, as truly historical in the large sense of moral history, as what he read."—HALLAM's *Literary History*, ch. vi. "At the present day, it can hardly be necessary to vindicate Shakespeare from the charge of having falsified history in those of his performances which are founded on historical subjects. The marvel, indeed, is how he has contrived to combine the highest dramatic effect with so close an adherence to historic truth."—H. STAUNTON's *Preface to the Illustrated Shakespeare*. Published 1858.

Shakespeare's works in the estimation and history of civilized men fully justifies the noble words of Dr. Johnson, that "the stream of Time, which is continually washing the dissoluble fabrics of other poets, passes, without injury, by the adamant of Shakespeare."*

* *Preface to Shakespeare.*

THE END.

Woodfall and Kinder, Printers, Milford Lane, Strand, London, W.C.

www.ingramcontent.com/pod-product-compliance
Lightning Source LLC
Chambersburg PA
CBHW020938120726

47905CB00008B/2576